W9-BUQ-390

MEET YOUR MAKER

MEET YOUR MAKER

MATTHEW MATHER

BLACK STONE PUBLISHING

Copyright © 2020 by Matthew Mather
Published in 2020 by Blackstone Publishing
Cover and book design by K. Jones

All rights reserved. This book or any portion
thereof may not be reproduced or used in any manner
whatsoever without the express written permission
of the publisher except for the use of brief quotations
in a book review.

The characters and events in this book are fictitious.
Any similarity to real persons, living or dead, is coincidental
and not intended by the author.

Printed in the United States of America

First edition: 2020
ISBN 978-1-5385-8944-1
Fiction / Mystery & Detective / General

1 3 5 7 9 10 8 6 4 2

CIP data for this book is available
from the Library of Congress

Blackstone Publishing
31 Mistletoe Rd.
Ashland, OR 97520

www.BlackstonePublishing.com

For David

1

Vasily hated it when rats got into the system. He couldn't blame them—they were as hungry as he was, he imagined. But it was his job to root them out. A messy, bloody job.

And always thankless.

"What is this?" his manager asked. The man held aloft a stringy bit of flesh, draped over a pencil.

Vasily looked closer. A chicken gizzard? Not unless someone had brought it in here. Which wasn't impossible, though it wasn't something they served on the polished inlaid tables of the Persian Palace, Kiev's aching-to-be-most-famous hotel.

His manager's round Slavic face radiated disgust, his low brow furrowed. "Take care of it," he said in Russian.

Again, the not-so-subtle reminder of pecking order. This Russian thought of himself as superior to Ukrainians—even to the Finns, Balts, Poles, and Scandinavians. Yes, a firm belief that the Finns were Nazis, with that same broad Cyrillic brushstroke applied across Ukrainians and Germans. How could he imagine he was better? This Russian was as Slavic as Vasily.

"What room?" Vasily asked in Ukrainian.

"Ten-oh-four."

The manager gave a deferential grin to two customers who advanced up the dark wood hallway. From the casual perfection of their teeth, and the man's buttoned-down blue shirt, they had to be Americans. The manager indicated a side table adorned with a hookah. Vasily grinned, too, but not because he was trying to be polite. He imagined the day when they could finally rid his city of the Russian pretenders lording it over his people.

At least the Americans were honest. He had a sister in New York.

"Just take care of it," the manager repeated under his breath. He dropped the pencil with the scrap of raw meat into the garbage can under the bar and turned to greet the newcomers.

The tenth floor. That was the executive level, renovated last year. Like a fortress up there.

Vasily slid past the American couple now chatting with the manager, down the hallway, and across the cherrywood lobby to the polished brass elevators. Just beyond them was a new addition, a small hallway with the security elevator to the tenth.

The Persian Palace was built at the start of the twentieth century but tried to give the impression it had been built two centuries earlier, in a more regal era. The overall impression, if Vasily bothered trying to verbalize it, was of wanting to be something more. An overhaul in the eighties had pasted on a layer of glitzy plastic that had by now acquired a faded patina.

The place was almost empty. Aside from that conference two weeks ago, February had been a grim month in Kiev.

Vasily inserted his security card into the elevator control panel, then stood in front of the new display, as he'd been instructed, for the camera to scan his retina. He was surprised this machine could do anything with his rheumy eighty-year-old eyes. He could barely see through them himself.

His identity accepted, the keypad appeared, and he entered today's code. The lift accelerated smoothly upward.

Could it be the rats?

According to the manager, the cleaning staff had mentioned that the air in the room stank, that it didn't seem to be venting properly. Rodents inhabited the crawl spaces between the lower floors, but the ninth and tenth had been sealed off. Military-grade security systems for important guests. Filtered air. Electronically isolated, the young men who did the work said.

Vasily strode down the plush-carpeted hallway to 1004.

An American had disrupted the manager's orderly little world last week when he skipped out on a bill for this same room. An art dealer, Vasily had heard in the lunchroom, who stayed a week and then disappeared.

At the door, he inserted his security card and submitted again to a retinal scan. This time, he was connected to the front desk, who had to verbally accept his voice scan and unlock the door. It hissed open.

The room could be sealed from the inside. Totally isolated if the occupant so chose. The exterior windows were triple-layered polycarbonate, bulletproof, designed to deflect anything up to a rocket-propelled grenade. Maybe they could survive even that, if it came to it. Possible forms of attack this floor could withstand had been the topic of many a lunchtime rumination by the staff. The decade-long conflict in Ukraine had made a certain set of high-profile business travelers nervous—with good reason.

The Persian Palace aimed to accommodate.

Ten-oh-four was the Czar's Suite. Twelve-foot ceilings. Thick ivory wall-to-wall carpet, adorned with winter garden embroidery, bone-colored furniture bordered in gold leaf. Vasily made his way into the bedroom and opened his tool kit, selected a multi-tool screwdriver. He shifted the attending chair by the window to the opposite wall, stepped onto it, and got up on his tiptoes to unscrew the vent cover.

Except that it was already undone, the screws nowhere to be seen.

Was it the cleaning crew? Maybe they opened it. They were the ones who found the chunk of flesh hanging from the outflow vent and described the lingering smell.

This near the vent, Vasily did pick up the scent of dead rat—probably more than one.

He slid the casing out, got down off the chair, and deposited the cover on the floor. Then he pushed the chair aside and maneuvered the vanity table into position to get more height. One foot on the bed, the other on the table, and his eyes were almost at the vent. He explored the metal shaft with the tip of the screwdriver. It dug into something soft.

"*Derʹmo,*" he muttered.

The only rat he should be cleaning out of this hotel was that manager downstairs. He didn't understand how the politicians could allow Russians to stay after all the mess they'd been causing. The current president, Yulya Voloshyn, seemed more intent on forgetting and forgiving than protecting. Every fifty years for the past thousand, regular as some fatalistic clockwork, either the Russians or the Germans would storm over their borders to attack the other, destroying our *kraina* each time in the process.

And they think we're *the Nazis?*

He dislodged a hunk and flicked it from the vent. It tumbled onto the carpet. He didn't look down, for fear of losing balance. Cursing again, he gave up on the screwdriver and reached in with his bare hand.

In his eighty years, he'd done worse things than grab a rotting rodent. Or maybe he classified those people he did these things to as less than rodents.

His fingers searched around. It didn't feel like a rat. That was not fur. It felt like . . .

He gripped and pulled. Whatever it was, it had really jammed itself in there. He yanked and looked up. What was he holding?

Someone's hand.

Vasily held a lump of gray-fleshed human fingers in his grip. As if they were greeting him with a handshake.

One of the fingers unstuck from the meat lump and fell onto his face. He lurched back and tried to bat it away with his other arm, but the only thing he had a grip on was the misshapen hand. He pulled as he fell into open space, and out came a decapitated torso, and innards that coiled out around him onto the gold-brocaded bedspread.

2

A high-pitched alarm assaulted Delta Devlin's ears. She awoke with a start and almost fell from her chair. Strobing lights flashed against the white walls of the Fourth Precinct's fifth floor. Outside the floor-to-ceiling windows, a column of red taillights snaked into the distance along Veterans Memorial Highway—rush-hour traffic out of the city and into Long Island. Only 7:00 p.m., but in New York, night came early in February.

"Can we turn that off?"

She had to yell over the noise.

"Sorry, Detective, no can do," the young officer replied.

Clean-cut, rosy cheeks. Were the new recruits getting younger? Delta answered her own question. No, she was getting older.

"Devlin," Delta said, and held out her hand. She hadn't met this kid before.

"Smollin." The young man shook hands.

Strong grip. Good kid, even if he looked as if he should still be in high school.

The alarm warbled and whined. Delta winced. Just the two of them, alone, half crouched by her metal desk at the edge of the half-height cubicle warren that occupied most of this floor.

"Smollin, what can you tell me?"

"They caught him down in the evidence locker."

"Caught him?"

"It was between shifts. The day and night managers were changing. We set up a perimeter outside, so he's somewhere in the building."

"What does he look like?"

"Caucasian, maybe eighteen, nineteen. Tight cornrows and tats—you know the type. Baggy white sweatshirt."

"How long?"

"Ten minutes."

"That he's been lost?"

Delta watched his face carefully—an ingrained habit impossible to turn off. She didn't watch his eyes, but more the area around them. They didn't change shade in her unique vision. He was being truthful, but then, what would he lie about? She couldn't help it, the reaction automatic. His forehead glowed from sustained stress.

"Can we turn the alarm off?" she asked again. "Unless we're trying to deafen him into submission?"

"Following protocol," Smollin said. "You keep watch here, and I'll head down."

Delta grabbed the recruit's shirtsleeve as he started to leave. "Is he armed?"

"Evidence locker had lot of weapons."

"Did they see what's missing?"

"No time to do inventory, but my guess is drugs. A pound of coke and amphetamines from a bust a few weeks ago was still in there."

These days, you couldn't assume that anyone wasn't armed. She swore and unclipped her Glock and checked the side. The loaded indicator nub confirmed one in the chamber.

The evidence locker was in the basement.

Six floors down.

She was the only person in here this late on a Saturday in Suffolk County Police Department headquarters, the new seven-story, glass-walled edifice that was the pride of Commissioner Basilone. Everyone fell upward to the level of their incompetence, as the saying went, and

Delta had fallen upward here to be mired in departmental management paperwork. Her own fault—a reward for her good work.

She had come in on her day off to host a tour of the precinct for a local school's career day. Orders came in from the top, tipping the hat to her for reasons unknown. She didn't mind. She enjoyed the kids, and it gave her a chance to catch up on paperwork.

In the past hour, she hadn't heard anything or seen any movement, but she had been wearing her earbuds. Old-school jazz made paperwork easier to bear. She would have noticed the elevator pinging, or someone opening the stairway door—wouldn't she?

Better to be safe.

She unholstered her Glock and unconsciously gripped it in a weak-hand-thumb-past-the-straight-strong-thumb position, with the weapon out in front of her. The siren blared. With Smollin gone, she felt exposed. She retreated to the wall and opened the double doors going into the stairwell, checked the corners and edges, and glanced down a few flights. Smollin's head bobbed on its way down two floors below. She crept back through the doors and scanned the desktops.

Was she nervous?

She always asked herself the question when she got her gun out. Her father drilled it into her head every time she went home for dinner, each Tuesday at their family home in Brooklyn. Every cop had better take stock of themselves when they reached for their weapon, he said. Too many civilian lives had paid the price for undertrained and overstressed officers twitchy on the trigger.

The first door by the stairs was the technical services bureau. With her gun down and away in her right hand, she unlatched the door with her left and swung it open. She checked the edges and ducked her head in for a second before retreating and reaching around the corner to flick on the lights. With her right foot, she pushed the door fully open as it swung back.

The fluorescent tubes in the ceiling panels popped on.

Three half-height cubicles down the right side of the thirty-foot room. An equipment bench down the left, next to the windows, the tables scattered with electronic devices half dismantled.

Anything digital forensics related, from all six Suffolk precincts, that needed evaluating ended up here. In fact, anything from upstate and even Albany. Most of it involved extricating data from disk drives and reconstructing erased digital images. At the end of the room was a squat box with rounded corners, two feet high and three wide—the new 3-D printer, the pride of Lucius, their resident tech guru. It was surrounded by plastic odds and ends it had spat out.

Nothing seemed out of place.

Not that Del would be able to notice if anything had been disturbed. The place was a mess. Still smelled of sardines. Lucius loved the damn things. It was why the rest of the squad on this floor made sure the door stayed shut.

The alarm screeched.

She flicked the light switch off. The 3-D printer at the end of the room glowed orange through its plastic housing. The thing was busy at work. Lucius often left it on at night to complete his projects. He made sure to tell everyone not to touch it.

No problem. Nobody even wanted to go in there. It wasn't just the lingering smell of the tech's lunch choices, but also the desire not to disturb stuff the average cop didn't understand and didn't *want* to understand. Life was complicated enough.

The next door over, thirty feet to the right, was the sergeant's office. Lights off. Door locked. Brake lights of cars winding down the highway winked through the blinds pulled down over the windows on the far wall.

Lights were off in the vice pit as well.

Del had her hand on the doorknob just as the alarm went silent. Her ears rang with an audio afterimage, a piercing whine that died away slowly. Her shoulders relaxed an inch from their hunch against the siren's assault.

They must have got the guy.

Her shoulders relaxed another inch. It was late. Time to go home.

An almost imperceptible creaking noise behind her. A door hinge.

She turned and said, "Smollin, so you caught the—"

Windmilling arms flailed over baggy jeans as the kid tried to keep his balance sprinting out the tech services doorway. Sneakers squeaked against the linoleum floor.

"*Damn it,*" Del muttered under her breath. Then: "Stop! Stop right there!"

She swung her weapon up, then lowered it. The building was full of cops, and she didn't even know whether this was the perp Smollin came up about—but a half second of mental processing confirmed the description: close-shaved head, white sweater, jeans almost falling off his ass. Had to be Smollin's guy.

Del sprinted to her desk and rifled through the top drawer to find her walkie-talkie but had to settle for her cell phone. The kid had fled to the stairwell, the door already closing behind him. His footsteps echoed. The heavy clumping sounded as though he was going up.

He wouldn't go down, would he?

She tried to search for the phone number of the desk downstairs. Glanced up to make sure the kid hadn't backtracked. Cursing again, she gave up and pocketed the phone and ran to the stairwell's double doors. She was about to scream out a warning for any officers below when the alarm wailed to life again.

"What the hell . . . ?"

She swung the door back with her left hand, weapon raised. She edged forward and tried to scream over the alarm. Reaching the stairs, she swung her weapon up and checked corners and edges for any movement.

Should she go up?

The next floor up was the mechanical room. Heating and ventilation. Then a set of stairs onto the roof. The structure was like a half pyramid. If he got onto the roof, he could jump down one level to the next and exit onto the parking lot. Smollin said they had a perimeter.

But could the perp be up to something else?

Her Glock out ahead of her and aimed upward, she worked her way up the stairs. Impossible to hear anything over the piercing shriek. One level up was the door to the mechanical. Metal railings. Polished concrete floor. Still smelled of fresh paint.

She jogged up the steps to the doorway and clicked the handle, crouched, and swung it open. Pitch black beyond. Not quite black. Her eyes picked up a faint red glow to one side.

"Put your hands up." Del pivoted and raised the Glock.

The red smudge levitated, and a light clicked on. A cell phone light. The kid ran up another set of stairs and banged the door's exit bar.

"Stop, or I'll . . ."

Del's command trailed off as she sprinted forward and found the stairs to the rooftop. He hadn't turned, hadn't stopped. Probably couldn't hear her over the siren—but he'd seen her. She had announced herself. She could have fired.

But she didn't.

Was he armed? Not sure, but he didn't shoot at her. He was probably just one more drugged-up teenager, either a tweaker or a victim of the opioid epidemic. Long Island ranked depressingly high in the sad statistics nationwide.

Still, she had to be careful. Just because he hadn't fired at her didn't mean he wasn't armed. At the door, she paused before edging out onto the rooftop, leading with her weapon, scanning back and forth.

The door swung shut behind her, mercifully muting the siren's racket.

"Hey," she shouted as she scanned right, toward the terraced rooftops. "This doesn't have to end with you getting hurt. The building is surrounded."

A sleeting rain had started. Cars hissed by on the freeway. She wiped her eyes with the back of her left forearm. Her eyes adjusted to the dim glow from the streetlights twenty feet below. The second she stepped out on the roof, the wet cold assaulted her. Forgot to grab her coat.

"I can't go to jail," said a quavering voice.

The sound wasn't to her right. She swung around left, gun up.

"Put your arms up," Del said.

A dim ghost appeared in the direction of the voice. The kid must have been crouching by an exhaust vent. In her enhanced vision, his hands and face glowed in the dark. His two hands, red blots in her eyes, went skyward.

Del said, "Get on your knees," and advanced toward him.

The kid backed up. "It's not my fault."

"*What* isn't your fault?"

"They said I wouldn't get caught."

Her eyes had adjusted better now. She could make out his face, the sneakers, the whites of his eyes. His hands up, palms out. He stood at the far corner of the rooftop.

"Get on your knees," Del repeated. "And then flat on your stomach. Hands out."

She advanced ten feet toward him. As she neared the edge of the building, the glow of a streetlamp flashed in her eyes, illuminating her and the kid. If Smollin looked as though he should still be in high school, the young man before her now surely couldn't have graduated from middle school yet. He still didn't get down though. Still had his hands up.

"Come on," she said. "Please, get on your—"

"You're Detective Devlin, right?"

She stopped in her tracks. "How do you know my name?" Her weapon lowered an inch.

The kid reached into his pocket.

"Don't do it," Del yelled as she crouched, the Glock aimed at center mass.

He pointed something at her. Her finger moved from trigger guard to trigger, but she hesitated. She gritted her teeth, half-expecting a muzzle flash and the thudding impact of a bullet.

The kid stumbled, his arm still out, and toppled backward over the parapet.

Del sprinted forward and skidded to a stop on the tar-and-gravel roof. One of the kid's arms was hooked over the low wall—the only thing keeping him from falling. His fingers and knuckles blanched. She holstered her gun, grabbed his arm, and tried to haul him in. She took a wide stance and pinned her quads against the three-foot wall.

He slipped an inch, then another, away from her.

As she tried to get a better grip, his sweater pulled up, exposing a pale, emaciated torso. He dangled in open space over the four-story drop to the grassy slope in front of the building. His chest heaved in and out, rib cage stretching his pallid skin, each breath puffing out a white cloud of dissipating vapor. Glowing taillights swam past the periphery of Del's blurry, water-fogged vision.

His left hand still held on to whatever he had pulled from his pocket. Was it a gun?

"Drop it," Del said through gritted teeth. She leaned farther over the parapet, into space, and tried to get a hand under his armpit, all the while keeping an eye on that left hand. What was that? It looked like a—

"Don't let go," the kid shrieked. His arm slipped farther through the sweater in her grip.

His weight pulled Del forward, her feet scrabbling against the gravel. Her left hand gripped his right triceps, her right under his left armpit. He flailed and scratched at her face, grasping for something, anything. His feet bicycled frantically against the glass wall.

"Stop . . ." Del grunted.

The kid was stick thin but six feet tall—had to weigh at least 150. She dug her nails into his exposed skin, clenched her teeth, and hauled back with everything she had. The young man moved up a foot, his right hand thrashing to find a grip.

Del's feet slid away in the sleet-and-gravel slurry. She slumped forward, her nails peeling back the kid's skin. He squealed and grabbed her hair. She felt herself off balance, losing the battle. She had to let go.

No. I can do this.

In a quick motion, she repositioned her left hand under his chin. She tensed her midsection and tried to straddle the parapet.

But it was too late.

She spun forward in a wrenching cartwheel and sailed headfirst into the darkness.

3

"Do you know why you're here?"

The woman asking stared straight at Del, her gaze unwavering.

She sat across a conference table, its gray melamine surface bordered in chipped wood laminate. The walls of the ten-by-ten room were unadorned, featureless eggshell, the carpet the same institutional worn-out gray that Del had seen in countless other government buildings. White acoustic panels sagged overhead, one of them stained in concentric brown rings by some long-ago leak, all of it lit by the blue-white glow of six exposed neon tubes.

Not what she had imagined of the Interpol Washington offices.

One wall was mirrored glass.

This felt more like an interrogation than an interview. After she'd waited an hour in the attending room, a young man had escorted her in and presented Director Dartmouth, but both the man and the woman inside had shaken her hand in turn without introducing themselves.

Del replied after a pause: "Sorry, ma'am, I don't understand the question."

"What didn't you understand?"

The woman's skin was topaz brown with a scattering of freckles over the nose and cheeks. Tight dark curls cut short, with the left side shaved in a flare just above the ear. Black hoop earrings and a tailored business suit matched with low-heeled pumps.

The man beside the woman remained silent. He looked off to one side. Didn't fidget. Remained absolutely still. Navy tie and jacket, square jaw and goatee, a carelessly coiffed wave of thick black hair over blue eyes. Was he the director? Or was she?

"Please answer the question," the woman said.

Del sat up straight and brushed off the cast on her wrist, tried to hide it behind her right forearm as she crossed her arms on the table. She shouldn't have worn her Louboutins—too flashy. She regretted the low-cut blouse as well. Coming to Interpol had sounded exotic, but this was anything but.

"I was told to come to this office for an interview," Del said. "Six Hundred East Street Northwest. Seventh floor."

"That was how you came to be here, not why."

"I'm sorry, but—"

"Do you always apologize?"

"I am here because I was asked to be here."

"That is still not *why*."

Del took a deep breath. Her way of centering her mind—always return to the breathing. Feel the air coming into the lungs, exhale slowly, and repeat.

"Because I called your office last year."

The woman flashed a tight smile that said, *that's right.*

Just before the holidays, Del had contacted the National Central Bureau—Interpol Washington—for help trying to locate a suspect who had fled the country. A shot in the dark, but one that hit the target. Interpol had been able to identify and track the man on his return to the United States and helped avert what could have become a bloodbath in the center of Manhattan on New Year's Eve.

Del said, "Ma'am, could I ask your name?"

"Katherine. With a *K*."

With a K. Del wondered how many times a day she used that. Like *Bond—James Bond.* Except that instead of "James Bond," it was "with a *K*."

"And . . ." Del hesitated. This was a test, and she disliked games. No choice but to play along at this point. "So, you are Director Dartmouth, yes? Katherine Dartmouth?"

The director's tight smile eased. "Most of the recruits assume that my colleague, Marshal Justice"—a nod of her head indicated the man beside her—"is the one in charge."

Score one point for Del.

Most of the recruits.

So they were interviewing many people. Not just her. "Ma'am, you are the one who called me, correct? We spoke on the phone last year. You offered me a job."

"I believe I said we were interested. Which is why we asked you here: to see if we still are."

"Yes, ma'am."

The opening salvo apparently over, the director looked to the man beside her. "I'd like to introduce Boston Justice, chief deputy US marshal for the Eastern Virginia District."

"A pleasure," Justice said, his Southern accent drawling out the last syllable.

"Congratulations on solving your case last year," Director Dartmouth said to Del. Her accent sounded more prep-school manufactured, but with lingering elongated vowels persisting beneath the polish. "Your" came out "yoor." Not New York. Maybe Philly?

"Couldn't have done it without your help, ma'am."

"I'm sure you could have. And perhaps *should* have. Almost everything about your methods went against the book, from what I was told."

Del remained silent.

"The rules, Detective Devlin. Ruffled feathers with the New York Mayor's Office—even your own Commissioner Basilone of Suffolk County."

"I was doing my best."

"To serve and protect, or ruffle feathers?" Katherine didn't wait for an answer. "So, you're an idealist?"

"More of a practicalist." Was that even a word?

"Is that why you pushed the boy off the roof?" Katherine opened a file folder on the table and leafed through a few pages. Pictures of someone in hospital.

The woman was trying to needle Del now. It was obvious enough that she didn't need to rise to the bait. "He fell. I tried to save him."

"Nobody would have blamed you. I saw his file. At best, he was a month away from overdosing. At worse, he could have hurt someone—killed someone, even."

Del inhaled and felt her lungs fill. "I tried to save that young man. Risked my own life." She brushed the cast on her left wrist again. Felt it twinge in pain. Broken in the fall. Lucky it wasn't her neck.

"And yet he suffered what might be a mortal injury."

"He's not dead."

"The family is suing Suffolk County."

Del had sailed off the rooftop because she refused to let go of the kid, but she probably should have. They fell forty feet onto the grassy embankment out front, but she landed on top of him. If she had just dropped him, he still would probably have suffered broken legs falling onto the sloping wet grass from that height. But her body weight landing on him had crushed ribs and fractured his skull. He was in a coma now, though the family claimed he had said that she pushed him off the roof and he grabbed her as he fell. Del exhaled long and slow. They had known all this before they asked her here.

She repeated, "I risked my life to try and save him." She hated being defensive.

They had found drugs on the kid—a stash of coke from the evidence room, but it wasn't much. Maybe he was in a hurry. The thing he had waved at her in his right hand was a piece of circuit board, something he had taken from the technical services office. Something from the 3-D printer.

And how had he known her name?

She had the ID tag pinned on her blouse. From the career day event.

"Do you know what the difference is between lying and bullshitting, Detective Devlin?"

"I'm not lying."

"I'm not saying you were. I'm asking you a question."

Del's hackles eased. "They're both dishonest."

"I'm not sure they are. A bullshitter believes his own bullshit. They're not lying, because they believe it's the truth."

"I still think it's lying."

"Can you tell if someone is bullshitting?"

"As well as anyone, I guess."

"And how about gaslighting?"

"Pardon me?"

"Gaslighting."

Del took a moment to collect herself. "This is an abusive behavior to alter information in such a way as to make a victim question his or her sanity, make them doubt their memories or perception of reality."

"Cult leaders, serial killers—"

"Politicians," Deputy Marshal Justice cut in.

Katherine said, "Is this really the same as lying? What if the liar believes their own lies?"

Del said, "I believe the root cause is a desire to manipulate."

"Manufactured reality—that's what we're talking about."

"And how does this relate to me, ma'am?"

"Because I've been told you're something of an expert on lying. Your eyes. You see differently than I or Deputy Marshal Justice. Is this correct?"

"In a way, yes."

Katherine leafed through more papers on her desk. "A mutation? An abnormality?"

"It doesn't affect my visual acuity, ma'am." She had perfect vision. More than perfect.

"This enables you to detect if people are lying?"

"It's a skill that I believe all law-enforcement officers can and should train themselves in."

"Not like you can do, from what I understand." Director Katherine Dartmouth closed her files.

Silence for a few seconds. Del resisted the urge to fill the empty space by saying something.

"Do you have questions for us?" Katherine asked.

Del's father told her that you always needed to be prepared in an interview. Sit down and write out a list of your own questions. Make sure you knew why you were going and what you wanted to find out. Assume they want you more than you might want them.

"What, exactly, is the job, ma'am?" Del said.

Not exactly probing, but when the director's office had called, they were vague. Then again, when Interpol Washington requested the appearance of a law enforcement officer, it wasn't exactly elective.

"It's not so much an offer as an assignment." The man, Deputy Marshal Justice, joined in again.

Del turned to him. "If you don't mind me asking, sir, what does a US marshal have to do with this? Is there an investigation involving me somehow?"

"I'm here only as part of the interview process."

"Deputy Marshal Justice," Katherine said, "is my second in command."

"I would be working for Deputy Marshal Justice?"

"You would be working for me," Katherine replied. "In Lyon, France. The headquarters of Interpol."

In France? Del rocked back in her seat. This had taken an unexpected turn, but at least it wasn't confrontational anymore. "Why me?"

"You speak French?"

"Of a sort." Her Louisiana Creole mother had made her take courses in high school.

"You have a college degree?"

"In Arts, from NYU. And finishing a law degree at night."

Not exactly Ivy League. She didn't want to be a lawyer, didn't even plan on taking the bar exam. She was just burnishing her credentials to get into the FBI. She had submitted her application and taken the entrance exam two months ago.

Katherine opened another file on the desk. "A policewoman with a degree in fine arts."

"Doesn't exactly uniquely qualify me."

"It might." The director looked up from the papers. "I called you last month because I was impressed with your initiative on the Lowell-Vandeweghe case."

"I was lucky."

"Which is an acquired skill, in my experience. I'm also looking for someone . . ." Katherine paused. "A little more representational, shall we say."

Representational? Del absorbed the word before replying, "I believe the best person for a job is always the best qualified."

As a brown-skinned woman in what was typically a white man's job at the Suffolk Police Department, she hated it when she felt they were promoting her based on anything but skill.

"So this"—Del paused to choose her word—"*assignment* would be with Interpol? As an Interpol agent?"

Deputy Marshal Justice said, "No such thing as an Interpol agent, Detective Devlin. Law enforcement officers are 'detailed' to the Interpol office—in effect, loaned from their department for a period of time.

Katherine added, "What we need is someone who can act as legal attaché."

"Legal work?"

Del watched the director's eyes.

She didn't see colors the same way normal people did—the director was right about that. With her acute and unusual vision, even though the director's skin tone was the same across her face, Del saw variations related to heat, which caused different colors to fluoresce. People's noses were darker—less blood flow—while the area around the eyes and forehead, with more capillaries close to the surface, was brighter.

"It's not legal work, not in the sense you're thinking," Katherine replied. "Shuffling paperwork, but it requires a certain intelligence."

The shade of skin around her eyes flashed and then faded. An unconscious reaction, a tiny flicker of induced stress. It usually indicated a lie.

"Interpol is a club more than anything else," Katherine continued. "One with a hundred ninety-two member countries. It's not really a law enforcement agency; it's an information-sharing network. Its charter forbids it from undertaking anything political or military in nature."

"We are focused," Deputy Marshal Justice said, "on international organized crime, cybercrime, human trafficking—that sort of thing. When it comes to taking action, we interface with National Central Bureaus in each member nation."

"I still don't see how this relates to me."

"We have an opening as legal attaché. It's the only position we can fill given our current mandate at the General Secretariat, but we need someone with a different skill set. A person who can act independently. *Think* and act."

4

Past seven at night, and the sky was still twilight blue. Daylight savings time had finally rolled the clocks forward by an hour.

Thank the merciful God.

Del was more than done with winter.

The branches of the oak and beech trees lining Eighth Avenue were bare, but the organic, earthy-wet scent of spring was in the air for the first time. The sun had been bright in the sky today, warm enough that Delta came out at lunch to sit on the picnic tables in front of the Fourth Precinct offices. She had spent half the time with her face up to the sun, the other half stealing glances at the top of the six-story structure, reliving the forty-foot drop onto the grass embankment the month before.

Lucky she hadn't killed herself.

At the end of the day, her new shift boss, Sergeant Joss, had dropped her at Jamaica Station and she took the train into Atlantic Terminal, then the subway to Seventh Avenue Station in Brooklyn. Tuesdays were family day. Dinner with Mom and Dad.

She turned onto Eighth Street. She loved the orderly row of brownstones just off Prospect Park. She had grown up here, played stickball in the streets with the local kids.

The last rays of the setting sun cast a cheerful glow along the ornamental moldings at the top of the three-story homes lining the right side of the street. Mr. Thompson, two doors down from her parents' place, was busy doing spring cleaning in his tiny front yard. He waved as she passed. She opened the three-foot-tall wrought iron gate and jogged up the wooden steps to the entrance.

She reached for the doorknob, then paused.

The door was ajar. Her parents never left it open unless they were doing work in the front. She looked up and down the street, then at the windows.

Lights off. No glimmer at all from the kitchen or living room; nothing upstairs, either. The shades were pulled. But she had just called her mother, who said dinner was going to be served at seven sharp. Seven ten now. She was late. Del glanced up and down the street again. Was there a power cut? Mr. Thompson's front light had already come on. He'd gone back inside.

She pushed the front door gently open. "Mom? Dad?"

The warm scent of cumin and sage and cayenne from a slow boil of gumbo filled the air inside, but the interior was quiet. Dark. Cold, as if someone had left a door open. Maybe a window? But it wasn't that warm out. When she had called her mother, not ten minutes before, to say she was running late, they had had jazz playing loudly in the background, her dad saying he needed help in the front yard and for her to hurry up.

A tingling dread settled into the pit of Del's stomach.

Her parents were elderly, her father still on the force but well into retirement age. She unclipped her holster and put her hand on her Glock. There had been a rash of break-ins this side of Prospect Park, and some areas on the other side were still a bit sketchy, even now.

She pushed open the inside door of the entrance. The hinge squeaked.

Dark inside.

Deathly quiet.

Maybe they had to leave. Hospital? Some emergency? But her dad's aging Crown Vic was parked out front. She unholstered her gun and crept inside. She held the weapon down and away, but with her left wrist in the cast, she couldn't hold the gun properly. In her peripheral vision, she caught something darting sideways through the living room.

She raised her Glock. A blinding flash of light . . .

"Surprise!"

Del blinked in the sudden glare. A crowd of people filled the living room with their hands held high. A broken symphony of groaning, off-key party horns filled the air with a sinking noise that was broken by the squeal of a frightened child.

"Jay-sus, Murphy, and Joseph." Del's father ambled in front of her, his hand up and pushing the Glock gently aside.

"I . . . uh . . ." she stammered.

Strung across the opposite wall, a Dollar Store sign in gold lettering announced, "Happy 29th Birthday!"

Awkward laughter.

Del put the gun away. "Sorry, I just . . . I wasn't . . ."

"Can we put our hands down?" asked Coleman, her old partner from the Second Precinct.

Everyone still had their palms up, now in mock surrender. Giggles and snorts as Del shook her head. "Yeah, yeah, you got me."

"Please, Officer, don't shoot," someone called out, which got a laugh.

"Bag of nerves today?" Del's father wrapped her up in a bear hug.

"Birthdays make me twitchy." She laughed.

Half her father's precinct, the Second of NYPD on the Lower East Side, seemed to be crammed into the living room. Many of them were as Irish as her dad. Most, she had known since she was knee-high. One by one, they wished happy birthdays and stacked gifts by the door. A lot of whiskey, her father joked—and that was "whiskey with an *e-y*," he added, as he always did.

"Oh, Missy, you didn't need to come," Del said.

Her sister was here as well, with her two kids and her husband. Two years older, her only sibling had taken a job in network security in Atlanta four years ago. She had been a rebel as a teenager, probably stayed out of jail only because dad was a cop, but she had settled down. Something their mother never forgot to remind Delta of each Tuesday.

"You know, haven't been up in a while," Missy said as she handed over a neatly wrapped gift box. She looked around the room. "No boyfriend yet?"

The room was embarrassingly filled with Del's mother's and father's friends, a few people from Suffolk PD like her old partner, and Tommy and Susan Thompson, childhood friends from up the street. Her sister wasn't asking a question, but making a statement.

"Be nice," Del replied, and kissed her sister's cheek.

"This *is* me being nice."

They both laughed and embraced. Del felt herself relax for maybe the first time in months. Her sister grabbed her cast and offered to sign it and then, with a serious face, told her what an idiot she was and how she had almost come straight up from Atlanta when she heard.

Her mother's friends hung back in the kitchen and waited for Del to make her way around to them. They laughed and shrieked in a happy mob around the bubbling pots of gumbo—still the bohemian group of painters and sculptors who had made up the other half of Delta's life as a child. Her mother's friends kissed her wetly on the cheeks and squeezed and hugged, in contrast to the handshakes and quiet conversation at the other end of the room.

The two halves of Delta's life: Irish one side, Creole the other.

"Happy birthday," someone said from behind her.

Del turned with a spoonful of jambalaya halfway to her lips.

A squat, powerfully built Latino man grinned. He had a young boy in the crook of his left arm, and a taller, pallid-faced man had his arms around both of them together.

"Angel." Del put the spoon back into the pot. "You're out of the hospital?"

"Happy birthday." Angel Rodriguez lifted his right arm to hug her but winced.

Del took a step toward giving him a hug but settled for a cheek kiss. The big, pale, chubby-cheeked man behind Angel—Charlie—bent over to give her a kiss as well. Angel was a private detective, a former Navy SEAL, who had been almost killed just before the holidays. He'd been instrumental in solving the Lowell-Vandeweghe case.

"What are you doing here?" Del said.

"We got that place around the corner."

"Oh, right. Hey, congratulations."

Angel and his partner, Charlie, had bought a fixer-upper townhouse a few blocks away. They had also just adopted Rodrigo, a little boy from Colombia.

"But we'd be here no matter where we lived," Charlie added. He was a veterinarian. "You saved my Angel's life."

"No, I didn't."

"Yeah, you did. Take credit where credit is due."

Del's mother and her art pals had gone quiet as they eavesdropped. "You see?" her mother piped up. "She does have friends." She shared a boisterous laugh.

"Angel, Charlie, and Rodrigo, this is my mother, Amede"—Del enunciated *Ah-meh-deh*—"Bechet."

They greeted and exchanged hellos.

"And the one last mystery we all need an answer to," Amede said, quieting everyone down with her hands upraised. She retained an almost Jamaican-sounding cadence and inflection after growing up deep in Louisiana.

The room went quiet.

Del relented after a few seconds and asked, "What's the mystery?"

Amede pointed at a gift basket on the dining room table. "Who is this Mr. Boston Justice?"

***

"No, he's not a boyfriend," Del said. She took a sip of the whiskey and winced.

Her father took a somewhat bigger slug of his. "Little odd for someone you just met to send you a gift basket at home. Someone who *interviewed* you?"

She still listed her permanent address as her parents' house. It suddenly felt juvenile, as if she wouldn't fully become an adult until she had her own place. She did have an apartment in Manhattan—her mother's old loft on Bleecker Street, in Greenwich Village—but that was only because it was rent-controlled, passed down, and she wasn't sure how much longer she could hold on to it. Real estate prices anywhere in the five boroughs had long since passed into such nose-bleeding heights that anyone under thirty without a trust fund didn't have a chance anymore.

"It is a little odd," Del agreed.

They sat on the back balcony together, just the two of them, while her father sneaked a cigarette he'd bummed from one of his officers.

"You know you shouldn't do that," she said as he lit up. He'd already had two heart attacks and had sworn off smoking—at least, to her mother.

"And you shouldn't take swan dives off buildings." He took a puff, his face lit by the glowing ember. "So what kind of a name is Boston Justice?"

Del laughed. "He did say his parents must have had a sense of humor."

It was odd. Was it a conflict of interest? She wasn't sure what to make of it. Sending her a birthday present with a personalized card?

After the interview in Washington, he had shown her out, but instead of saying goodbye with a handshake at the entrance, Boston had proposed going for a walk to discuss some more. She had wanted to see the new National Museum of African American History at the Smithsonian, the massive inverted ziggurat at the edge of the Mall. They had walked together the four blocks, down past Pennsylvania Avenue, while he explained the mission of Interpol, what she could expect, and why she would be so useful to their project.

"He's a US marshal," Del said. "*Chief deputy* US marshal for the Eastern Virginia District."

Her father's eyebrows rose, the corners of his mouth curling down. People often said he looked like Al Pacino, complete with a mole on his left cheek. He'd been told so often that he now did impressions of the man every time he wanted to look comical. This was his version of Pacino's impressed look.

He said, "The US Marshals Service is the oldest American law enforcement agency, founded by George Washington himself in 1789." Her father took another puff. "They ensure the integrity of the Constitution itself. They want to hire you into the USMS? Now, *that* would be an honor. Imagine, the daughter of an Irish immigrant—"

"No, no," Del said. "It's not even a job."

The impressed-Pacino look slid away. "I don't understand."

"It's a posting—a *detailing*, as they call it. I'd still work for Suffolk County PD."

"That's clear as mud."

"They have a job with Interpol in Europe they need help with. I caught the director's eye after my stunt of calling their office last year."

"Sounds exciting."

"I turned them down."

"You did what?" The "what" came out as a broguish "*wot?*" He dropped his cigarette. "I thought you said you wanted to move up in law enforcement."

"This is moving sideways. Or some other direction I can't even figure out. And I'm not ready to move to Europe. I mean, you're not well—"

"That's an excuse, and you know it."

"It's not what I want."

"Interpol, eh?" her dad said. "The current president is Hui Meng, the deputy minister of public security of China. And the secretary-general is Propochuk. A Russian, if you can believe it, right out of the FSB. That's a nest of vipers. I looked it all up when you went to Washington."

"So, you agree with me."

"I do not. This is the sort of thing you said you always wanted. International intrigue, an opportunity to use that big brain of yours—"

"But there's no security. It's not a job offer, not really."

"Was security what you were looking for when you fell off the top of that building?"

"That was different. It was instinct. Reaction."

"So what's your instinct now?"

"They suggested I attend a meeting this week. The Ukrainian president—"

"Is speaking at the UN day after tomorrow. My squad has been assigned as part of the security detail. The Kiev police chief is attending and asked to visit One PP."

"I'm not sure."

"Why not? The chief even mentioned asking you to come."

"Me?"

"You're a celebrity. All that newspaper coverage from the Lowell-

Vandeweghe case. One thing New Yorkers can't resist is anyone who gets on the front page of the *Times*."

Celebrity? Del had been stuck ass-deep in paperwork behind a desk the past three months, apart from two weeks off after breaking her wrist falling from the roof. Now she was under two internal investigations at the same time. Not that anyone thought she had done anything unethical, but being a cop was a lot more about rules and paperwork than anything else. There were procedures that had to be followed.

She said, "I'll think about it."

"Don't think too hard. Pretty sure that's your weakness."

"Thanks a lot, Dad."

The old man laughed and raised his glass.

Del had brought out the gift box from her sister. She undid the bow and peeled off the tape, unwrapped it, and lifted off the lid. An inch-wide green-yellow ball of what looked like putty rolled around inside. There was a card below it. She picked it up and read: "This is genuine raw Indian yellow, supposedly extracted from the boiled urine of emaciated cows fed on poisonous mango leaves. Not even kidding. Gross, but I know you'll love it."

She laughed. Her sister knew her exactly. The ball of putty was a rare pigment, something Del had been trying to find.

The porch door squeaked open behind them.

"Delta," her mother said excitedly. "Come inside, child. There is something for you."

"I don't need any more presents."

Her mother gave a sly grin. "But I think this one you will."

***

The back of the envelope's address said it all in neat blue letters: "J. Edgar Hoover Building, 935 Pennsylvania Ave., Washington, DC."

"Why didn't you give it to me earlier?" Del said.

"I only just checked the mail. Usually nothing but bills and junk."

Del didn't believe her mother. She would bet this had been sitting on the kitchen counter all week. This was planned. She had waited until Del's surprise party to have everyone here.

Del had written the FBI entrance exam back in January. After getting her detective's stripes with Suffolk PD—one of the youngest ever to do so—she had spent most of the past two years preparing for this. Between that and night school for law, she hadn't had time for anything resembling a personal life.

She sat at the dining room table. The crowd of partygoers pressed around her.

"Don't open it now," her mother said. "This is too personal."

Del rolled her eyes. *Sure.* After stage-managing getting everyone here for a surprise party, finished off with opening her acceptance letter to the FBI, her mother wanted her to put it away?

"I'll open it," Del said.

Her mother clapped her hands with glee. Nina Simone's voice crooned in the background.

Taking a deep breath, Del ripped open the corner and slid a finger down to tear open the envelope. She took out the letter and held it up to the light.

5

The full-body scanner at the UN entrance wasn't like the ones in US airports. No rotating arm whirring around. This device was two squat rectangles you stood between, feet on the yellow footprints in the middle. Silent. The simplicity of the technology felt exotic, as if Del had stepped into some future world.

"Please, step to one side," said someone behind her. She had her hands over her head, held straight up in surrender. Yesterday, she had finally gotten her cast removed.

"You're good." The dark-skinned young woman in a navy-blue uniform with a yellow "United Nations Security" symbol waved her forward.

Del put her hands down, rubbing her wrist, and stepped past the machine.

"You have trouble finding the place?" her father asked in greeting. Of course, with a lopsided grin.

It would be hard to miss the hundred-story glass monolith bordering the East River, situated on its own private eighteen-acre estate, donated by the Rockefellers in the 1950s. It stood apart from the cluster of midtown skyscrapers. She had valet-parked her father's Crown Vic by the fluttering row of two-hundred-plus national flags in the entrance crescent. She was late after almost deciding not to come.

Her father wasn't asking whether she'd had trouble finding it, but needling her about showing up late. Del was usually punctual to a fault—something else her father had drilled into her.

"Brighten up," her dad said. "Come on, let's go into—"

"*sir*," said that same voice from behind Del, "please, I said step to one side."

"Do you know who I am?" answered a man's voice in a curious British accent.

The hundred-odd people in the entrance hallway stopped and turned to the source of the commotion: a dark-skinned man with black-rimmed spectacles and a flowing cream-colored robe that stretched to the floor.

"This is outrageous," said the man, his voice rising in volume. "I have already been searched once on the way in. I am the Kenyan envoy, and you cannot—"

"I don't care if you're the king of England." Del's father strode over to the other full-body scanning machine. To the security officer there, he said, "What's the problem?"

The UN officer replied to Del's father, "Please, you stand back as well."

The young man turned to one of his computer screens and pointed out an object to the man in the robe. "There are four black disks blocking out the scanner. They didn't trigger the metal detectors. Please open the bag for inspection."

He refused. "That is a diplomatic pouch."

"Then you cannot enter." The young security officer stood his ground.

Del's father held back. His squad was here only to assist outside on First Avenue. This wasn't his jurisdiction.

What most people didn't realize was that the eighteen acres of the UN headquarters in New York made up an entirely different country, within but not part of the United States. Technically, it wasn't part of *any* country—it was extraterritorial, not subject to the laws of New York or even the United States. It had its own police force, its own fire department, and even its own postal service.

Outside the entrance were police with dogs, trained in detecting explosives, and a security team that did random physical searches. After that, a phalanx of two metal detectors and two different millimeter-wave full-body and property scanners. Del had never seen such tight security. The Ukrainian president, Yulya Voloshyn, was speaking, and a dozen groups from all sides weren't happy about it.

The man continued to protest. "I am most certainly not—"

"Then you must leave," the security officer repeated. More security arrived and encircled the man.

Del took a protective position beside her father. Today she was here as a guest, not in any official capacity, and she felt exposed without her sidearm.

The man looked back up the entrance hallway. The hundred-plus dignitaries waiting to get in were focused on him, everyone silent. "They are Rangers hockey pucks," the man practically whispered.

"Excuse me?"

The man relented and unzipped the pouch in his bag. "Ice hockey—you know, the pucks from the New York Rangers hockey team. They are a gift for my nephew."

Del's father was close enough that he reached in and retrieved one, held it up to his nose, and sniffed. Then laughed. "Right you are. Why didn't you just say so?"

"Sir." The UN security officer took the puck from Del's father and inspected it himself before returning it to the pouch. In a louder voice, he called out to the security staff and crowd, "The situation has been resolved. Please continue."

He turned to Del's father. "Please do not do that again, sir."

"Just trying to help," Del's father said. He turned to Del. "Can you believe that?" He led her forward to the General Assembly Hall. "They got this place locked down tighter than a nun's—"

"Dad, please," Del protested.

"Right, sorry."

"That could have been a bomb. You should have let them handle it."

He laughed. "I know a puck when I see one."

"You're Irish. You know literally *nothing* about hockey."

***

"Ukraine will be a leader of the Fourth Industrial Revolution." Yulya Voloshyn slapped the marble podium.

Her face was magnified and projected onto the two huge screens flanking the gold United Nations symbol—the world map encircled by a laurel wreath—at the center of the UN General Assembly Hall. Her skin glowed ethereal white in the spotlights, her golden hair in a braid wrapped all the way around her head.

"Our largest trading partner is now the European Union, and tonight I am announcing a new initiative and partnership that will lead Ukraine into the next century and beyond."

Two dozen rows of stadium seating sloped down to the center of the hall, each row ringed by green-topped tables adorned with nameplates. A large TV camera on a huge metal dolly was focused on Voloshyn from the back of the hall, where Del was allowed to sit with her "visitor" credentials. The delegates had earpieces in, their feeds instantly translating the Ukrainian president's speech. She spoke excellent English.

Del noticed that the country nameplates at the back, closest to her, were "Estonia" and "Eritrea." At first, she thought it was alphabetical, but then she realized that the United States had mid-row seating halfway up, like the box seats at a sports stadium. Best seats in the house. There wasn't even a common alphabet between all these countries. Their position was set by some tribunal according to their perceived importance, she guessed.

"Instead, however"—Voloshyn again slapped the marble podium hard enough that the crack echoed through the chamber—"our country is divided and beset by political forces from outside our borders. On one side, the East, our Russian brothers and sisters, and on the other, our Western cousins. I am here today to say, *no more*."

A smattering of applause from around the chamber.

Voloshyn had been nominated for a Nobel Peace Prize—she hadn't won—the year before, for negotiating the Minsk III accords, which had maintained a fragile peace within Ukraine's borders. This managed to stop fighting between pro-Russian separatists, mysterious invading forces that denied being from Russia, and Ukrainian military and internal militia.

In the middle of the conflict, several years before, the commercial airliner MH17 had been shot down.

"I am proposing a new Eastern Allies common defense initiative that will be separate from NATO," Voloshyn said. "And independent from the Russian sphere of influence."

A collective inhalation from the assembly. Papers scattered. Delegates in the middle of checking their email picked up their earphones. Voices broke into urgent hushed conversation.

"We will be suspending the American Maritime Operations Center in Ochakiv," Voloshyn said.

An angry man's voice called out, "What about Oleksiy?"

Catcalls from around the hall encouraged the outburst. Blue-shirted UN security officers hustled to where the red-faced man heckled Yulya again. "Where are your true allegiances?"

Staccato applause broke into a steady thrumming and banging on the tables.

The Ukrainian president wasn't fazed. She held up her hands, palms out. "We will not forget Oleksiy, but we *must* not forget *ourselves*. I am joining the EU in condemning the withdrawal of Russia and America from the intermediate-range missile ban. We will be carving a new path for Ukraine. One that is independent."

6

The official speeches over, the assembly moved downstairs to the ballroom for a reception. A large screen on the opposite wall announced, "Leadership in the Fourth Industrial Revolution."

The circular ballroom of the United Nations building reminded Del of the Pantheon in Rome. Almost a football field in diameter, and half that to the peak of the domed ceiling. If Del's memory served her correctly, the hole in the center was called the *oculus*—a thirty-foot circular gap for occupants to observe the heavens or, maybe more to the point, for God's eye to look in.

For *the gods'* eyes to look in, she mused. The Romans had a whole circus of them.

She had visited Rome once—a gift for finishing undergraduate school, from her grandfather, a man she'd never met, who lived in Ireland. Her dad and he must have had a terrible disagreement when her father left Ireland thirty years before, because her dad never spoke of him. He had only barely allowed her to accept her grandfather's gift of the trip, and only let her send a written note in thanks. It was strange, but Del had learned not to press on this topic. It was the one thing her father never wanted to talk about.

One day soon, she would have to force the subject with him, but not yet.

She returned her attention to the great round eye in the ceiling. The similarity to the Pantheon was no accident—the dome even copied the same inset hexagonal patterns she remembered from the original—an example of humanity's earliest use of compressed concrete, made almost two thousand years ago and still standing.

They didn't make stuff like they used to.

Built for the emperor Hadrian, she remembered—the same guy who built the wall across England to separate it from Scotland. Should have built one to separate the two halves of Ireland, her father liked to say—would have saved a lot of the Troubles.

"Beautiful, isn't it?" Del's father said.

They weren't the words she would have used. Incongruous, perhaps, or maybe derivative. Imitation was the sincerest form of flattery, but from an artistic perspective, this was outright plagiarism. From the outside of the thousand-foot glass tower, you would never guess that something like this ballroom was inside. Then again, it was funded by the Rockefellers, who weren't known for their subtlety.

"Yeah, it's nice," was all Del could offer.

She and her father sat alone at the table farthest from the presentation screen, she with a glass of red wine, he with his whiskey, a plate of crackers and cheese and caviar between them. Recessed blue and orange lights illuminated the neoclassical columns describing the circumference. The round tables set with floral arrangements and numbered tags had the feel of a wedding.

"Why does everyone have such an obsession with ancient Rome?" Del mused. "I was in Washington last week and couldn't help noticing how it looked like a copy of the Via Appia. The conquerors' way."

"Is that a translation?"

"Just what it represents."

"Still in a bad mood?" Del's father took a sip of his whiskey.

"I don't understand. What did I fail?"

"Sometimes, things just aren't meant to be." Del's father looked away.

She'd been going over and over it for the past two days. When she opened the letter from the FBI, she had been telling herself not to expect anything, but really, deep down, she felt she had aced the entrance exam.

She had stellar credentials—according to what she had read, everything they were looking for.

Rejected.

That was the end result of the very gently worded letter. She hadn't failed the exam, however, and her credentials weren't in question.

She had failed the background investigation. That was what it said.

Without any more explanation than that.

It felt as if Del had hit a brick wall. Years and years of dedication to a single aim. Her dad had always said to set expectations low so you were never disappointed, but she hadn't. She expected.

She had called and demanded additional information, but no one returned her calls. Failing a background investigation wasn't something she could improve on. It felt like struggling against a choking fog—something insubstantial yet inescapable and suffocating.

"Do you think I should just apply again?" Del said.

"I think you should drop it."

The words felt like a kick to the solar plexus. The first time in her life she had ever heard her dad tell her to quit something.

"You've got a wonderful career with Suffolk PD. Or you could join the NYPD, come work with me for the last years I'm on the force."

That was exactly what Del had been trying to avoid. Not because she didn't love her dad, but because she adored him *too* much. The man was the center of her universe, had always been her hero. She would be following him around all day. But she needed to be her own person, to stand on her own two feet, and that was what her dad wanted, too.

She poked at the caviar. "I should get going."

"Why? You got a date?"

"Now you're being mean."

Her father winced. "I was just—"

"I'm not in the mood."

"Can't you stay with your old man? For dinner? I wanted to show you off a bit." He glanced behind Del. "Ah, and speak of the devil."

"Are *you* not the Devlin?" replied a thickly accented Russian voice.

At least, it sounded Russian to Del's ear.

"Delta, this is Grigory Georgiev." Her father got up and extended his hand.

She turned and stood. A bear of a man, six-six and three hundred pounds, pumped her father's fist. His meaty grip enveloped her outstretched hand next, with just as much vigor. Sweaty hand. Powerful grip. She appreciated that he didn't soft-serve her with his shake. She did her best to squeeze back.

"This is the guy I was talking about," her dad said. "Commissioner Georgiev of the Kiev Police Force. I've been assigned to give him a tour of One Police Plaza tomorrow."

"So you are the famous daughter Mr. Devlin cannot stop speaking about," Grigory said.

She extricated her hand from the great paw. "The same."

"I can join you?" he said to her father, and then looked at her and the table.

There were six empty chairs.

"Of course," Del replied. So much for making a quick exit. "So you two have met before?"

"Yesterday," Grigory replied. "We went over security outside. And had a few drinks. Have you ever heard your father singing his rugby songs?"

Del did her best not to roll her eyes. "Who is this Oleksiy that President Voloshyn referred to?" she asked.

The man's bushy eyebrows raised high. "A Ukrainian freedom fighter killed by the Russians. Assassinated in Moldova."

"Assassinated?"

"No one but the Russians would be so bold."

She hadn't heard of it. "Freedom fighter," Del said. "Isn't that code for *terrorist?*"

"Depends on your side."

"And wouldn't a Ukrainian freedom fighter be on the side of Ukraine?"

"This is hard to understand."

"I thought Ms. Voloshyn had ended the conflict."

The Ukrainian police chief's body convulsed into something that became a laugh, but nothing about it suggested humor. "You think the

Middle East is difficult? Put yourself in the shoes of Poland and Ukraine, sandwiched between East and West. Russia invaded Georgia, a NATO ally, and nothing was done. They invaded Crimea and still retain part of our country, and yet, nothing from the West."

"What I know about Ukraine could fit on the back of a matchbook."

"Imagine if Russia announced a partnership with Mexico and started installing missiles on America's southern border. How would your White House react?"

How would *Texans* react? This was Del's first mental image. Men and women in Stetsons, weighed down with bandoliers of ammunition, on the bank of the Rio Grande.

"So you're saying this is a proxy war between America and Russia?"

"Between East and West, same as has been happening for hundreds of years. One we sadly lose each time, no matter who is the victor. Which is why President Voloshyn said what she said today."

Del replayed the speech. "Withdrawing the American Maritime Operations Center?"

"And Russian initiatives as well. Creating a Slavic and Baltic independence block. Of course, many inside Ukraine, many in Russia, many everywhere oppose the—"

"Ms. Devlin," said someone.

She turned. Dark skin. Sleek dress.

"Director Dartmouth," Del said, rising from her chair. "Commissioner Georgiev, Sergeant Devlin, this is Katherine Dartmouth of Interpol."

A bald man in a dark-blue suit and open-necked blue shirt stood beside Director Dartmouth. He excused himself without being introduced.

Everyone exchanged handshakes.

"Please, sit," Katherine said.

"I'll leave you two to talk. Grigory, want to join me at the bar?" The two elderly men headed off together.

"I'm glad you could make it," Katherine said to Del. "Are you still considering our offer?"

"I haven't made a decision yet."

"Ukraine is our top priority. I was hoping—"

A commotion at the front interrupted them. A man in a blue UN security services uniform stood on the stage and waved his arms. "Ladies and gentlemen, there has been a bomb threat, and while there is no immediate cause for alarm—"

The effect was immediate. The assembled guests, hundreds of them, streamed for the exits. A group of security personnel had crowded around President Voloshyn.

Del scanned the bar area to her left for her father. She caught a glimpse of him behind the big Ukrainian, both of them making their way straight toward Voloshyn. Katherine got up and made for Voloshyn as well.

"Dad, goddamn it," she growled under her breath. "Let them do their—"

A loud crack echoed, the sound compressed and reflected by the domed roof. Screams. People scattering. A knot of UN officers near where Voloshyn had been were now making for the exit. The security staff amassed in a swarming drove, flooding in from outside the ballroom against the tide of screaming people headed for the exits.

Was that a gunshot? It sounded hollow, like a cap gun Del used to play with as a kid. The commotion was right where her father had been heading.

"Call an ambulance," she heard someone screaming.

In a daze, she crossed the fifty feet and shoved through the crowd. She expected to see the pale-white face of Voloshyn lying on the marble floor, but . . .

Her father lay facedown, a dark pool seeping across the marble below him, a dark hole in his back, left of the spine.

7

"I'm so sorry, Detective Devlin," Commissioner Basilone said.

Del shook his hand. He was her boss—her boss's boss—but she stared straight through him without really seeing.

All the color seemed to have drained from the world. The images before her eyes seemed unreal, everything two-dimensional, as if she could stick a finger through the paper-thin veneer of reality. Through twenty-foot windows lining the city-block-long hospital corridor, she looked eight stories down onto the East River, where sweating chunks of the season's last ice meandered past.

The sky was clear but darkening, two bright vapor trails from jets high overhead, the horizon purple as the sun set beyond Presbyterian Hospital's newest wing. It cast a shadow a thousand miles long, right out over Queens and into the distance.

The spacious area felt more like a fancy hotel lobby than a waiting room.

"So sorry," Basilone repeated as he let go of her hand.

She mumbled something in reply. He was here only for the media. At street level, the carnival of news trucks that assembled yesterday had grown into a tent city on the parking lot tarmac.

How the hell did someone get a gun in there? The question circled around and around in her head. The place had been locked down tighter than Fort Knox. Nothing like this had ever happened before. No one had the balls to try to assassinate someone in the UN headquarters. Someone was trying to send a message.

And Del's father had ended up being the messenger.

Her sister, Missy, asked, "Did they say anything yet?"

She had just returned with her two kids. They had stayed here most of last night, until Del finally said she should take the little ones back to the house. Her husband had stayed with Del's mother in one of the waiting area's couch corners, which they claimed as theirs. A steady stream of Amede's friends appeared with food over the night, through the day, and now into night again. On the next couch was Del's father's Second Precinct squad, along with a few of her own colleagues from Fourth Precinct in Suffolk County. Chief Alonzo had come by to give his condolences.

The assemblage was almost the same as at Del's birthday party, except for Director Dartmouth and Grigory Georgiev, who had come in the ambulance with Del and stayed the whole time. They sat with the United Nations security detail on the other side of the hall.

Director Dartmouth had been the one to find the shell casing of the bullet. The UN security team had requested it, but she had turned it over to the NYPD.

Grigory said that Del's father had taken the bullet for him, had placed himself in front of the shooter as Grigory tried to protect President Voloshyn. It was just like her dad. She could never stop him from getting into the middle of things. Lost in thought, she stared at that pile of ice making its way out to the sound, melting away to merge again with the endless ocean.

"Del?" Missy shook her gently. "Did they say anything?"

"No, I haven't—"

A man in scrubs opened the double doors from the surgical unit. Everyone turned.

***

"I'm not supposed to have this," Officer Coleman whispered.

Del squeezed in beside him on the couch and took the offered ballistics report. The ragtag bunch of unwashed officers in yesterday's clothes and two-day stubble closed ranks around her.

"I got a copy from Esposito, who grabbed it from the servers in the operations center at One PP," Coleman continued, his voice low. He stole a glance at the two United Nations officers across the corridor. "Nobody's seen it yet. God forbid this gets to the press."

Last night had almost sparked another international incident when doctors pulled the bullet from where it had lodged in her father's fourth thoracic vertebra. The UN security team claimed it as their evidence and tried to take possession. The crime had been committed on their territory, they said, not on US soil. Whatever the legal ramifications, the NYPD officers almost started a brawl with the hapless doctor in the middle, holding the tiny blood-covered prize in a Ziploc bag overhead.

Before any lawyers could intervene, the bullet was spirited away.

Possession was nine points of the law, as Del's father liked to say. A dagger twisted in her stomach at the thought. She couldn't help it. Everything she saw, the way she thought about things—it all came back to her dad.

She leafed through the technical report.

Every gun was unique. Each was constructed from dozens of parts, and even if they were made with the same tools, the metal dies wore over time, accumulating chips and microscopic fractures. The assembly machines vibrated and were subject to use, abuse, and corrosion.

When a gun was fired, the firing pin made its distinct mark on the cartridge's primer, and as the bullet left the casing, it accumulated scrapes and marring unique to that weapon, from the rifling in the barrel. Details included direction of spin, width and depth of the lands, microscopic scratches, and more. The class characteristics could identify the type and even make of weapon, and once a suspected firearm was found, a forensics examiner would use a Leica comparison microscope to split-view a test-fired bullet against the original.

Del frowned. "I don't understand."

She backtracked through the report. She was no expert in ballistics, but this was strange.

"Clean as a whistle," Coleman said. "No markings. You're not reading it wrong."

The section on class characteristics was blank, not because they hadn't finished the analysis, but because there simply were no grooves or scratches on the bullet. The .38-caliber round had entered through her father's back, hit the fifth rib, and ricocheted into his vertebra, grazing his heart en route. The bullet was dented from the impacts but had zero microscopic scrapes from the barrel.

"How's that possible?" Del said.

"I think I know."

Director Dartmouth pushed her way through the crush of NYPD officers crowded around Del, holding her phone out in front of her. Pictures of the UN ballroom's marble floor, spatters of dried blood, yellow numbered markers.

Something else in the images.

Del took her phone and swiped through them.

"What is that?" she said.

Katherine squeezed onto the couch next to Coleman. "We think it's a plastic casing."

"Of what?"

"The device used to fire the bullet."

"So, a *plastic* gun?"

"We weren't sure," Katherine continued. "Just a suspicion, but something we feared might start happening. I needed to look at ballistics first."

Del scrolled left and right on the image, back and forth, then zoomed in. It was cracked bits of a triangular plastic chassis—didn't look like anything to her. Could have been a child's broken toy. That would explain how the weapon had made it past security, why it hadn't set off any metal detectors.

"We're only about to start analysis," Katherine said.

"We?"

"Interpol is handling forensics. The samples were flown to France this morning."

"Are you kidding?"

"They have better facilities than here."

Del noticed the switch from "we" to "they."

"Better than the FBI's?"

"This isn't an internal investigation for the United States," said Katherine. "As you know—"

"I know, I know. Extraterritorial."

"An attack in the United Nations headquarters. I handed over the spent brass to the NYPD, but the plastic parts were recovered by the UN teams."

Del said, "Can you get your UN friends to release security camera footage of the inside of that ballroom?"

"They're saying there is a lot of confidential material not related to the investigation—world leaders having private conversations on topics they can't let leak to the media."

"We're not the media."

"They have their own rules."

Grigory pushed his way through the knot of people around the two women.

"Did you see this?" Del asked, holding up Katherine's phone. "They're saying it was a plastic gun. What did you see? Please, anything. Think."

She had asked Grigory a dozen times already.

"He saved my life. This is why I am here. But I did not see anything. I had my back to your father. I was looking at President Voloshyn . . . but maybe I did see something."

Del got to her feet. "What?"

"Please, can we have some privacy?"

"Anything you want to tell me, you can tell everyone here."

"Please."

Del relented, and the group of NYPD officers grudgingly moved aside. She edged her way through them. The men felt like her big brothers as they watched her retreat with Grigory to the next couch.

Grigory waved to the two UN security officers, who brought Katherine with them. She spoke in hushed tones with the officers as they passed her a tablet screen.

Katherine sat next to Del, with Grigory on the other side. He put the tablet down between them and hit Play.

The images were grainy, the room dark, but it was the ballroom. The video had been enlarged, and focused on a table of African men in flowing robes.

Del said, "I'm sorry, but what is—"

"Just wait."

As if on cue, the tinny sound picked up the announcement: "Ladies and gentlemen, there is no cause for alarm . . ."

The robed men got up from the table, and the video froze.

"There, you see that man?" Katherine pointed to the edge of the frame and zoomed in on a figure in a suit and tie. The image was a little fuzzy, but the face in full view.

"Okay, yeah, sure."

Del took a closer look at the face. Screens displayed colors only in RGB—red, green, blue—not the full spectrum of wavelengths her eyes could see. On screens, everything looked muted to her, as if she were looking at black and white instead of full color.

Katherine pressed Play again. A tight knot of men moved through the frame, the unmistakable blond braid of President Voloshyn in their midst. Grigory was right behind them, and then, there: Del's father, his hand on Grigory's back.

The video stopped again, this time by itself just after a tiny bright flash in the lower left corner. Katherine zoomed in on the frame. The same man at Del's father's side, appearing to grapple with him, the man's arm straight out. Something in his hand.

"That's the gun," Katherine said.

"Is he shooting at Voloshyn?" Del asked. She frowned.

"I think he's trying."

"So, who is he?"

"We were waiting until we could get verification," said the senior UN officer. "The man in that video is Yuri Korshunov. He was attending the event. We have video of him entering and exiting the building."

"Where did he go?"

"This is what we have begun work with the director on."

"We should have had this information yesterday," Del said.

"We have it now," replied Katherine.

"And who is he?"

"Russian. Ex-FSB. You have to understand how dangerous this is. The politics involved . . ."

"I don't care—"

"Miss Devlin?" a young woman's voice called out.

Del stood up. It was a nurse. "I'm here."

"Your father has woken up. He's asking for you."

***

"Dad?"

Del fought to hold back tears.

At least, the breathing tube was out of his mouth. When she came in a few hours ago, a white plastic nub had been inserted between his teeth, with a blue hose like a giant straw snaking out to a machine that was inflating his lungs. The nurse said that he was breathing on his own now. That was progress, right?

His eyes fluttered but didn't open.

"What's wrong?" Del turned to the nurse. "I thought you said he was asking for me."

"He's still somewhat sedated. Propofol at ten milliliters an hour."

Del had no idea what to compare that to. Wasn't Propofol the drug that killed Michael Jackson? She pushed the thought from her head.

"Just give him a minute, dear," Del's mother said, standing on the other side of the bed. "Just wait."

The ICU room was as big as a hotel suite—twenty feet wide and thirty long, with its own bathroom and shower. From the ceiling in the center of the room hung two huge metal arms, dangling equipment from their swiveling fingers—monitors displaying heart rate and blood pressure, a battery of controls for eight different intravenous drips, the ventilator, and things Del couldn't identify.

The place had that antiseptic reek of bleach and floor cleaner.

Her father's hands looked puffy. She noticed his nails, discolored from a fungal infestation she had tried and tried to get him to fix. He always said it was nothing, that they had always been like that. Maybe she could do it now, while he was incapacitated, so he would have nice nails when he got better. That would be a—

An alarm sounded, high pitched and urgent. It came from the heart monitor device.

"What's wrong?" Del stepped back.

The nurse seemed unconcerned as she punched a blinking light on the display. "His heart went into atrial fibrillation. Nothing to worry about."

Nothing to worry about? Del glanced at the readout. Her father's heart was thumping away at 150 beats a minute. His resting heartrate was more like seventy. At this speed, he should be sprinting up a hill, not lying motionless in bed. Was he having a heart attack?

"Delta?"

She pulled her eyes away from the racing line on the display and forced a smile onto her face. "Dad. You're fine. Don't worry." The way it came it out, it sounded as though he *should* be worried. "The doctor, she said, well—"

"I am *not* fine," her dad replied. His voice was hoarse, weak, barely above a whisper. "But I will be. Anything that doesn't kill you, right?" The edges of his mouth crept into the faintest of grins.

"That's right."

"Come closer."

She leaned in.

"I need to tell you something."

"About the shooting? Did you see the man who did it? We have a video."

He shook his head, not more than a half inch each way. His eyes closed. "Not about that."

"Not about the shooting?"

"Come nearer. It's . . . it's . . ."

She put her ear almost to his chin. She smelled last night's whiskey still on his breath.

He forced out a whisper, "It's about . . . our family . . ."

"Missy? Amede?"

He shook his head. "Not . . . I need to tell you . . ."

"Something about me?"

His hand slid back down over his chest. The alarm started up again, and this time the nurse jumped around the corner from her observation desk. Moving between Del and her father, she began pushing buttons on the IV drips. Two more nurses—men—appeared from the hallway, and a doctor was there a second later.

"Dad? What did you want to say?"

"Ma'am, you'll have to step back," said the nurse.

8

Del weaved left but kept her eyes locked on him.

When he swung back, she jabbed, jabbed again, then planted her left foot and uncoiled her midsection to launch a right hook. Her opponent staggered back. Before he could regain his balance, she transferred her weight to her right and fired a roundhouse kick, her shin delivering a gouging blow just under the left pecs.

She stopped and bent over, heaving air in and out.

The heavy bag creaked and shook on its steel chain. She'd named the bag "Mickey" years ago—not for the mouse, but after an old boyfriend.

Good old Mickey. At least, she could punch back now.

Midday sunshine streamed in through the eight-by-eight metal-lattice window of the front of her apartment on Barrow, just off Bleecker in Greenwich Village. Not *her* apartment, she reminded herself. Her mother's. It was the last unit in this block still under rent control, dating all the way back to the seventies, when Amede had used it as her own art studio. The building's owner wanted to turn it into condos and had filed the legal paperwork.

She probably couldn't hold on to it much longer.

She raised her fists and confronted Mickey again, then dropped them.

Del was pulling her left jabs. The cast had come off her wrist only two days ago, and she couldn't really use it properly yet. And her left shin flared in pain from that last roundhouse. She looked to her right. Against the old radiator leaned an inch-thick wooden dowel—a gift from her kickboxing instructor. She was supposed to sit and grind the dowel up and down against her shins every day. He said that eventually it would kill the nerve endings.

There was always a way to numb the pain—if you could take it. Today, she'd already had about all she could manage.

She decided against another round with Mickey and began unspooling the cloth wrap around her knuckles and thumb. She didn't use boxing gloves. The wrap was there to align the wrist and hand, keep the bones from shattering and the skin on the knuckles from tearing, but gloves did nothing, really, except cushion the blow. She uncoiled the long strips of black wrap and let them fall onto the paint-spattered floor.

What had her dad wanted to tell her?

She had spent the night in the hospital. Stayed all through the small hours until a blinding sunrise blotted out the purple twilight over the East River. Her mother had slept in the daybed in the corner of the ICU room, bundled up under a blanket, while Del sat next to her father, holding his swollen hand.

Missy had taken the kids to their parents' place in Brooklyn, then came back in the morning. She shooed Del out of the ICU at daybreak, told her to get some sleep and a shower.

Del had taken the subway to Greenwich and laced up. Pounded Mickey a few times.

They had to insert the breathing tube again. Her father's body had gone into septic shock, they said, and because it was his second intubation, they would have to leave him in an induced coma till they could perform a tracheotomy.

His heart had kept going like a jackhammer all night.

A hundred thirty beats per minute.

Then a hundred fifty.

That damned alarm went off every five minutes. The nurse turned it off each time and said not to worry. So why not turn it off altogether? They had drugs going into him to stabilize his heart—he'd already had two heart attacks, as she must have told the staff a dozen times—and chemicals to bring his blood pressure up, pushing and pulling and keeping him alive like some failed science experiment.

The doctors were optimistic but said it was possible he could "succumb" to this. *Succumb*. Who used a word like that? They meant he could die. Part of her refused even to let the thought exist in her mind—told her that it was defeat even to think the words. He was a rock. He had a lot of good innings left in him; no way he would go like this.

But she had seen people die.

Everyone had to meet their maker one day. Another of her father's sayings. She couldn't help it. His sayings. That voice that everyone has in their head—Del realized that the one in her head was her father's. Irish accent and everything.

The bullet had torn part of his stomach and gone through his spleen. They removed that last night and had to suture the pancreas. It leaked fluid into his chest cavity, which was now infected. Septic shock. Blood infection. Touch and go.

She was about to get in the shower when her doorbell rang.

***

"You didn't have to come in on a weekend," Del said to Lucius.

The diminutive head of Suffolk PD's technical services wagged his head from side to side. "I kinda did."

"You didn't."

"Anything you need—know what I mean?"

Del hated it when people used expressions like that. Were they really asking a question? What if she didn't? The only thing worse was saying, *it is what it is*. A complete nonstatement. Young people used stuff like this more and more. Lazy, in her opinion. She groaned inside. She had just turned twenty-nine this week, and she was already grumping about *these young people nowadays*. She exhaled slowly and counted the beats. Her father always said, when you're upset at someone for no good reason, it's because of something in you, not them.

"You okay?" Lucius asked.

"Fine."

"When my wife uses that word, it doesn't mean what it means. You didn't just grunt or something?"

"I'm fine. I mean, I'm good."

"'Cause you're sweating."

"I was working out."

Lucius was fully five years her senior, but he seemed ten years younger in his Converse All Stars, white-and-black checked flannel shirt, and jeans. It was Saturday, but he always dressed like this.

"How's your dad?" he asked. "I'm going to pass by after, you know . . ."

"He's okay," she lied.

A white lie. What was the point of making it uncomfortable?

It wasn't even really a lie. She was the expert in lie detection, but they both knew she was not telling the truth and, at the same time, telling the truth a different way—that she didn't want him going there right now but didn't want to say it.

But she added, "Maybe you should wait a few days to visit."

"Whatever's best for the family."

She changed topics. "Did you get it?"

He reached into his jacket pocket and produced a slab of white plastic. Two inches thick, triangular, with a snub muzzle protruding, and trigger and handle beneath.

"You made it that fast?"

"Took a few hours. Scanned the image you sent me, matched it to some online drawings, and printed it out this morning. You want?" He held the object out to her. "It's not loaded."

She took it. Cool to the touch. Weighed less than her sidearm, but chunkier.

"Can I come in?"

"Of course. Sorry." She stepped from the doorway. "You want a coffee or something?"

"That would be great."

Walking toward the kitchen in the back, she asked, "So, how does it work?"

"Same as a regular gun. Firing pin, barrel—just made from plastic. Single use. In this case, very single. The one that hit your dad exploded getting the bullet out."

The fragments had been taken to France for analysis, but Del had taken a picture of the images on Katherine's phone and sent them to Lucius.

"I heard about your place," he said as he followed her. "About your paintings. All white, or sorta white."

He stopped to inspect one of the row hanging from the exposed sprinkler system pipes. The frames lined both sides of the sixty-foot-deep, twenty-wide apartment—the top floor of a five-story walkup. The walls were red brick, and the only natural light came from the twelve-foot window at the front. At the other end were a small kitchen and the fire-escape door. A Murphy bed—stowed—was halfway down on the left.

"I see colors differently than you do," Del explained. The words came out automatically.

To a "normal" human, her paintings all looked like a mishmash of white and off-white shades, but Del mixed her own pigments that phosphoresced in wavelengths only she could see. Her own very private art collection.

"Four different kinds of cones in your retina instead of my three," Lucius said.

"That's right."

"Very cool. So you can see ultraviolet? I've always wanted to ask."

"A little. It's hard to explain."

"Like dogs have two types of cones in their eyes," Lucius said. "They're color blind. So they see about ten thousand shades, whereas I have three cones, so I see about a million shades. With your four cones, you see a hundred million colors?"

"Been doing some homework on me."

"So you see ninety-nine million more colors than I do. Damn."

"Dogs do perceive color," Del explained, "but a lot less than you. Instead of seeing the rainbow as violet, blue, blue-green, green, yellow, orange, and red, dogs see it as dark blue, light blue, gray, light yellow, darker yellow, and very dark gray. If dogs could speak, they wouldn't be able to name orange and red. In the same way, it's hard for me to explain *ishma*, the word I came up with as a kid to describe a color you can't see."

"I read that dogs have three hundred million smell receptors in their noses versus, like, a few million for humans. So your vision compared to mine is like a dog's sense of smell to mine. And dogs can smell out drugs and bombs, or even if someone has cancer. So your sense of sight has got to be pretty spectacular."

"A curse and a blessing." She put some coffee on and sat down to look at the plastic gun. "This is the same model? The Liberator?"

"As far as I can tell from the images you sent me. Named after a design the United States OSS—the Offices of Strategic Services—built in World War Two. The OSS tried to mass-manufacture them and drop into Europe ahead of D-day. Not sure how effective they were as weapons, but the goal was more psychological, so the enemy would know that just about every civilian could be armed during liberation."

And now anyone with a 3-D printer could have one on demand. Guns manufactured traditionally could be tracked, but these were completely untraceable. Maybe. "Is it the same design?"

"Not really, but sort of, and still single shot "

The OSS. Del knew the group's wartime origins before it became the CIA.

"The design was uploaded by Leonardo Bondar, self-proclaimed leader of the Black Army—basically a hacker group, or used to be. Now the buzz is that it's actually an offshoot of an anarchist group based out of Ukraine. The State Department banned the design days after it was released on the internet, but you can find it on servers on the dark web. Hard to stop stuff on the net once it gets out. There are dozens of designs now from different sources."

"But someone decided to use this one. So anyone with a 3-D printer can make it?"

"Just download the design."

"It's that easy?"

"Whether it works is another story. How tough the plastic is, the tolerances, a dozen other things that depend on the device that made it."

"How many 3-D printer machines are there? I mean types?"

Lucius looked up and to the right. "Maybe ten different processes. Extrusion and fused deposition—that's just a single print head. Those are cheapest and most common. Then stereo lithography. Those start with a tank of resin. And then there's powder sintering, and the most sophisticated is material jetting."

Del took a second to absorb it all.

She said, "So each machine has its own distinctive plastic and manufacturing process? So even if we can't trace the gun, we can trace the type of machine used to make it." And there had to be ways to trace individual signatures and even manufacturing irregularities to specific machines. So it wasn't hopeless, just a new frontier in forensics.

The coffee machine gurgled, then beeped that it was done, so she filled two cups and got the milk out. She didn't have sugar, so she didn't bother asking. He took it black anyway. "Would this one fire? A bullet? If we tried it?"

Lucius shrugged. "Pretty sure."

"And you made this one at our offices? With that new machine?"

He puffed up like a proud parent. "The new Strataform Replicator. Got it this month—just about every police department and government office did. Uses parallel jetting heads, like an inkjet on steroids. Six different materials, including a conducting metal, and it's fast."

"Do a lot of consumers have these?"

"Used to be 3-D printers were cool but nerdy, like PCs were back in the eighties. But then, boom. Suddenly, PCs were everywhere. What if, instead of buying stuff, you could just make it in a Replicator? That's the new Strataform device. They sold a few million last month. They say they're going to get one in every home in America."

"So that everyone can start making their own guns?"

"I mean, from another point of view, you can look at it as a symbolic act supporting resistance to world governments. They're shipping these things worldwide." He took a sip of his coffee. "But most people will be printing lampshades or toothbrushes or whatever."

Del's phone pinged. A text from Katherine. A link to the Interpol file on Yuri Korshunov.

The man who shot her father.

She said, "Lucius, I appreciate your help, but I gotta go."

"Like I said, anything I can do." He gulped down the last of his coffee and stood. "But if you're that interested, there's the Maker Faire going on in Queens this weekend."

"What is it?"

"The Annual World Maker Faire. Insanely nerdy, lots of pop-up tents and cosplay, but Strataform is sponsoring this year. There's a whole conference on 3-D printer tech going on. And your boy Lenny Bondar is going to be there."

"Lenny?"

"Leonardo. The guy who originally uploaded that gun design to the web. NYPD already picked him up and questioned him."

He held up his phone. An image of a huge man with an equally imposing red beard.

***

"Damn it, damn it."

Del got up and paced around her kitchen table before getting back in front of her laptop.

TSA and DHS had just reported Yuri Korshunov getting on a flight to Kiev at 9:00 p.m., three hours after her father was shot. Katherine's file included a picture of Yuri at passport control in JFK, then another from Sofia Airport in Bulgaria. By 5:00 a.m. New York time, he had left the airport and disappeared.

If the assholes from UN security hadn't taken so long with the facial recognition, they could have stopped him. Why did he go to Bulgaria? One opinion linked him to mafia there, but the same report stated that he could just as likely still be working for the Russian FSB. The porous borders in Eastern Europe provided an easy way for someone to disappear.

His name hadn't been made public yet. But that hadn't stopped the rumors.

That morning, a skirmish had erupted in Kharkiv between the Ukrainian Ninety-Second Mechanized Brigade and a group of pro-Russian separatists, which turned into a three-way pitched battle when a Ukrainian separatist group joined in. It was confusing. Del couldn't quite keep track of who was fighting for whom, where, and why.

Yuri Korshunov.

There were only a handful of pictures of the man. One of them from two years ago. Sixty-two years old, his face looked hewn from a weathered block of Siberian granite.

She pulled up a web browser and did some searches.

Ex-FSB. Ex-FSK. Even ex-KGB.

Back during perestroika in 1991, when Yuri was a freshly minted officer of the Soviet secret police, Boris Yeltsin had disbanded the KGB and reformed it as the FSK. It changed title again in 1995, to the FSB. She always figured it was just an initialism shift to go with a cleansing of the leadership. The rank and file must have remained the same. Each name change was just a variation on the wording for "internal police investigation."

How many times had the Russian secret police changed names? She brought up a Wikipedia article and counted. Twenty-two times in the past hundred years.

Out of curiosity, she brought up a page about the FBI. That was the roughly equivalent organization, right? The Federal Bureau of Investigation? The United States federal internal police? Founded in 1908, as the FBI; with zero name changes since that time.

She had never thought of the FBI as a sort of secret police, but it performed basically the same function. Same way we didn't call Guam or Puerto Rico "colonies" anymore, but "territories." It sounded better.

It wasn't just that, though.

She guessed it depended on who was in charge of the internal police. If you had a dictator in charge, then it was secret police. With a democratically elected government, it became more of a self-policing internal force.

In theory.

Which raised the next question: Did she trust the politicians in charge in Washington?

Del picked up her phone and called Angel Rodriguez, her private detective friend.

He picked up on the first ring. "Are you okay?"

"Not really. I need help with something."

"Anything."

"Could you investigate someone? Look for anything unusual. Not sure what."

"Of course. Who?"

"Me."

9

The dragon belched a roiling fireball, rearing its head back as it opened its jaws. Del felt the heat on her cheeks. Curved horns cut a black silhouette against the blue spring sky. Two men in vests and chaps—one with a bowler, the other a top hat—and copper-fringed goggles blocked her path. They gawked at the flaming lizard and clapped.

"Excuse me," Del said.

A woman in a leather corset and thigh-high boots tapped one of the men's shoulders.

"Oh, sorry," the man mumbled, and stood to one side.

The metal dragon rolled forward and this time farted a conflagration from its backside. A freckle-faced kid with a half-eaten wisp of cotton candy laughed and pointed. Del pressed forward, squeezing her way between the spectators. On closer inspection, the dragon was built atop a GMC camper van, its chest a mesh grill covering the windshield. A man in a Kiss T-shirt operated the fire lizard's flexible neck from the roof of the vehicle.

The crowd thinned as Del made her way to the entrance of the New York Hall of Science, a glass-topped cylindrical structure. A phalanx of ten-by-ten white tents lined the walkway, the booths and their enthusiastic occupants hawking everything from robotics to glitter glue. Flanking the front doors, two flagpoles bearing the Stars and Stripes stood sentry, and between them stretched a forty-foot banner of a red robot announcing, "Maker Faire."

The New York Hall of Science shared Flushing Meadow Park in Queens with the Tennis Center, where they played the US Open in the fall. Del had flashed her badge at the attendant when she drove up, said it was official business. The young kid had looked at her ID, then at the green Zipcar logo on the door, then back at her badge before raising his eyebrows and indicating the staff parking at the back.

Del picked up a Maker Faire program as she entered the building. Just past 1:00 p.m.

Adam Petty, the CEO of Strataform, had already started his talk in the main auditorium, but the guy she really wanted to talk to was right in front of her. A twenty-foot poster of Lenny Bondar, founder of MakerArmy—one of the world's leading 3-D printer companies—towered over the interior foyer.

***

"We are poised on the edge of the Fourth Industrial Revolution," Adam Petty said from the stage. "The ability to make tools is one of the key traits that make us human, and the ability of our tools to make *their own* tools is the first step on a road that will make us *more* than human."

With his right hand, he flipped back the mop of gray-streaked hair that had fallen over his eyes. Thick, black-framed glasses hid half his face, and a cleft chin with two-day stubble completed his self-consciously hipster look. He wore a logo-printed T-shirt with long-sleeved denim overtop, open. Jeans and sneakers. Not your typical CEO.

"Nobody is printing titanium turbine parts on a desktop yet . . ." he paused theatrically. "But soon?" He raised an eyebrow.

The crowd of true believers murmured and laughed. Of course it would be soon.

"Nobody is printing themselves a new kidney on their kitchen table yet—"

This time, he didn't need to pause.

"But soon," the crowd replied as one.

"Could you give him my card?" Del asked a young man by the stage. "Get him to call my cell phone as soon as he gets off the stage?"

"We're not doing any more interviews."

Del held out her badge. "I'm not a reporter."

The young man squinted and looked at her card again before replying, "I'll see what I can do."

***

Del inspected a metal bracket that seemed to grow up out of the desk it rested on: branches and fingers of steel entwining delicately to grasp a cylinder.

"We aren't bound by old manufacturing constraints," a young woman said. She was working the Metal Labs booth. "An artificial intelligence models a three-dimensional stress map and builds material only where it's needed. Looks biological, right?"

"Can I hold it?" Del asked.

The young woman nodded. "It's a bicycle neck—the front part that holds the handlebar. Uses a third as much material and is twice as strong as a traditional part."

It looked almost alien, as if it had been created by an aluminum-based insect from another planet. "You can print in metal?"

"'Printing' is a bit of a misnomer. 'Additive manufacturing' is more accurate, but yes, we can *print* in just about any material." She indicated a gantry structure surrounding a ten-foot metal cylinder on the other side of the room. "We're making an aluminum fuel tank for a rocket during the show. It used to take months to manufacture, cost millions."

Del put the part down. "Now it takes a weekend?"

"And a few thousand dollars."

"I can understand rocket engines," Del said, "but how can you expect to compete on bike parts? I mean, how do you go up against mass manufacturing?"

"We *do* mass manufacture. They're called print farms. We have one in

Lowell, just outside Boston. A textile mill building that had been empty for a hundred years, and now we have a thousand of our desktop machines on each of ten floors. A cloud manufacturing service. Send in a CAD file via internet, and we churn out thousands of parts a day. Almost completely automated. We're bringing manufacturing back to America."

Cloud manufacturing. A few years ago, half the words out of this girl's mouth wouldn't have made any sense. Del thanked the enthusiastic staffer and meandered to the next booth, Strataform Medical.

A young man held aloft a dripping sliver of pink goop. "This is my skin," he explained.

"*Your* skin?" said an onlooker.

"We cultured my skin cells in vitro, then deposited them one at a time through the bioprinter head, into scaffolding. This can be used as a skin graft for burn victims. Skin is the simplest example, but we can print larger organs—like ears, for example."

He indicated the next plastic dish, where a semitranslucent blob of something ear-ish looking quivered. "We're working on liver and kidneys, even ligaments. Soon even smaller, like printing molecules for individualized vaccines."

Del stopped and listened.

It reminded her of a recent case: the infamous Dr. Danesti and his encephalitic monkeys. Danesti had gotten all the funding he needed, and more. He had been talking about 3-D printing internal organs as well. Her mind automatically twisted, trying to find some connection.

The next booth was sponsored by the Massachusetts Institute of Technology's Self-Assembly Lab. A woman in a lab coat held in her hand a single lightbulb, attached to an extension cord. On the table below her was a flat sheet of grayish plastic. The woman waved the lightbulb an inch above the sheet. Tendrils reached up from the table and tried to grab the light as it skimmed past them.

"It's a biomimetic polymer," the woman explained. "It responds to heat and light, in much the same way that a plant does."

Del watched the woman pass the bulb back and forth a few times. The plastic looked alive.

Behind the woman stood a twenty-foot-square table bordered by a three-inch barrier. What looked like hundreds of miniature toy cars raced around on its surface, bumping into each other. She walked over to get a better look. In the few seconds it took for her to get there, the little cars had organized from a random bumper-car melee into flowing, collision-free movement.

"This is an example of emergent behavior," explained a young woman. She couldn't be more than a teenager. "Like a shoal of fish, or a murmuration of sparrows in the sky. With minimal sensory apparatus and intelligence, teams of bots can achieve sophisticated higher order . . ."

"Detective Devlin?"

A tap on her shoulder. She turned around.

"You wanted to speak with me?" Adam Petty said. "Is it something urgent?"

Up close, the plastic rims of his glasses were almost cartoonishly chunky. It had to be his signature look, Del decided. Was it urgent? Damn right it was, but while the attack at the United Nations had been made public, the details had not. "I'm looking for some help."

"With what?"

"One thing is that I'm looking for ways to backtrack what was created with a 3-D printer."

She had asked his assistant to call her phone, but instead he had found her directly. Had they been watching her? Tracking her movement?

"I'm not sure I understand," Petty replied.

She watched his face. For a second, he looked afraid. His forehead flushed bright in her vision. "General forensics research," she added.

The heat in his face dissipated. "With no disrespect, I'm really busy today. Perhaps we could schedule something for another day? When I have more time?"

"I need help tracking the makes and models of plastic and materials used in 3-D printers, across all models and manufacturers," Del explained. "It's urgent."

"All models? We make most of our business printing turbine engines for Boeing, and other large-scale processes."

"More interested in the output of your desktop models. In plastic."

"I'm sure I have someone on staff who can help." He gave her a searching look. "Why come to me?"

"Partly convenience. I saw that the show was here today. And we have a new Strataform Replicator in our office, so it's the only model I'm familiar with."

That was a bit of a stretch. Del had barely stood within ten feet of the device.

"Ah, so a customer."

"You could say that."

"I'll send you all the technical data we have on our product, and what information we have on competitors, if you can email me more details of what you want." He paused. "You said 'one thing.' Is there a second?"

"I was hoping you might be able to tell me something about that guy."

She pointed across the hall to a stage getting set up. A projector displayed the name "Leonardo Bondar" on a ten-foot screen.

"Lenny?"

The heat in Adam's face cooled some more.

"You know him?" Del asked.

"Who doesn't know Lenny?" Adam beamed a grin that Del didn't return. "He's a character, I'll give him that. We have . . ." He looked up. "How could I describe it? Maybe, a *conflicted* relationship?"

"He says he's the leader of the Black Army. What do you know about them?"

Adam snorted a laugh. "Wait, wait. Lenny and I might not see eye to eye, but that Black Army stuff? Did you see all the people dressed up in cosplay gear here today? It's like Black Hat—hackers—but he does physical stuff in atoms instead of bits and bytes. He headlines each year at Defcon in Vegas. He founded MakerArmy, his 3-D printer company, and the Black Army is his troops of kids that like to play hacker."

"So, just a slinger of bits and bytes?"

"But no guns or bombs."

"He did upload a gun design to the web."

"Ah, right. Back to that again."

"*Back* to that?"

"Sorry, but we've all been painted with a broad brush."

"But Mr. Bondar was the one who uploaded a 3-D-printer gun to the internet, correct?"

"That was more to provoke a point."

"Provoke what?"

"Just provoke. You haven't met Lenny, have you?"

It wasn't really a question. Del glanced at the stage. "I haven't, but could you . . .?"

The burly redhead himself was testing a microphone by the podium. Adam shrugged—*why not?*—and led her over.

"Lenny," he said. "I want to intro—"

The big man cut him off in midsentence. "What do you want, Petty Thief?"

Adam was unfazed. "This young lady would like to meet you."

Leonardo's eyebrows furrowed. "You a cop?" he said to Del.

It was rare that people surprised her. His face was cool, almost blank. How did he know? She was in civilian clothes. "Detective."

"I already spent two hours with the police this morning."

"I work for Suffolk PD. Delta Devlin." She held out her hand.

"We're not in your jurisdiction. What can I do for you, Officer?" He tested the microphone. "One, two, one-two." He didn't offer to shake.

She lowered her hand and waited for him to finish. "Mr. Bondar, I want to know if you can track who downloaded your gun design."

"You gotta be kidding me. Cops were all over my ass this morning. I was here in Queens all day yesterday. And the State Department got me to take that gun file down, but you can't control the people. That was the whole point."

"Did your design need modification to work on different 3-D printers?"

"I'm done talking."

"I'm just gathering information for future forensic analysis—same reason that I'm talking to Mr. Petty."

"Forensic analysis?" Lenny stopped playing with the microphone.

"Manufacturing methods, and so on."

"You want to talk manufacturing, then Petty's your guy."

"We are bringing manufacturing back to America," Adam said to Lenny.

Lenny got down off the stage. "Maybe America, but not the rest of the world. You're making centralized factories controlled by corporations. This was supposed to be about bringing power back to the people."

"We're putting Replicators in every home in America," Adam countered.

By now the two of them had just about forgotten that Delta was there.

"And where are you getting the money for that?"

"At least I can raise funds," Adam said.

"In exchange for what?" Lenny held his arms wide. "That's what we'd all like to know."

"For future profit."

"Profit," Lenny scoffed. He turned to Delta "You want to know what this guy really wants? This guy wants to be the Steve Jobs of the Fourth Industrial Revolution. Bringing manufacturing back to America."

"And you don't?" Adam's hair had flopped over his eyes again. He swept it back. "MakerArmy is filing for an initial public offering on NASDAQ, I heard. You'll be a billionaire. You're telling me you're not in this for the money?"

"You want to talk guns?" Leonardo pointed at Adam. "This guy's team has twenty different firearm schematics loaded up for his machines."

"On private servers," Adam retorted.

"Of course private." Lenny turned to face Delta again. "You want to get up someone's ass? Give this guy a proctology exam, not me."

10

Delta wandered out of her apartment in Greenwich Village, walked down Bleecker to the Starbucks on the corner of Leroy. Morning sunshine angled through the fire escapes overhead. She waited ten minutes in line at the coffee shop.

The young woman behind the counter took Del's credit card and handed it back after charging more than six bucks for a cup of hot milk and a few coffee beans.

"Have a nice day," the girl said as she handed the card back.

Del watched her face and earnest smile. *Have a nice day.* That was what she said, but did she mean it? Del went to retrieve her card but hesitated, hovered an inch from getting it. The girl held it out farther.

Was she lying? Did she really want Del to have a nice day? Was she really the least bit concerned about what kind of day Del was having? Of course she wasn't. It was automatic, perfunctory, part of the process, and part of her job to tell this small lie. The girl's forehead didn't register the slightest glimmer of heat, the soft tissue around her eyes relaxed and cool. She was lying, but the lie was so practiced and had so little impact, it set off no biometric markers.

Del took her card, thanked the young woman, and waited by the counter.

Not all lies were the same.

Zealots who believed their own lies, and young men and women wishing you a nice day at the coffee shop, had more in common than just trying to sell you something.

Del thought about the article she had read last night, about a psychological test in which people were asked to pick a number from one to six, remember the number and not tell anyone, and then roll a die. If that number came up, they announced whether they had picked the number, and if they had, they were awarded ten times the roll in cash.

Unsurprisingly, the players seemed to always beat the odds.

When hooked to a lie detector, the machine would register the faint signals of lies being told, which made consistent sense.

The experiment was repeated, but this time, instead of going to the test participant, the winnings went to charity. Again unsurprisingly, the players beat the odds—but this time, the lie detector didn't pick up anything. So lie detection was less about detecting the lie than about whether the liar would *benefit* from the lie, or thought the lie was for a good cause.

Detecting lies wasn't a simple thing.

Del's grande non-fat latte arrived, and she went out in front of the coffee shop and sat down. A steady stream of Villagers ambled by on their way to Washington Station to take the ACE train uptown—digital zombies, each with their own white cardboard cup in hand, head down, eyes on their tiny phone screen.

After leaving the Maker Faire yesterday afternoon, Del had spent most of the evening back at Presbyterian before going home to attempt sleep. Early this morning, she had called her sister, who said their dad was still unconscious but stable. The doctors said he was recovering. Del wanted to do something but wasn't sure what. She couldn't sleep, couldn't paint, and there was only so much beating on Mickey she could do without refracturing her left wrist.

Another question had loomed as she lay in bed, awake in the small hours.

What did she want to do with her life?

That had never really *been* a question before. Her life had been set, the world's cogs moving in their orbits around her—but now she'd been rejected by the FBI. This apartment wasn't even hers, and she still spent half her nights at her parents'. Her mom had been talking about moving to Atlanta, selling the place in Brooklyn when her dad retired.

That had always been years away.

There was no way her father would go back to work in the NYPD. At minimum, this was forced retirement. Did she really want to follow in his footsteps? A career in local enforcement? Be like one of her dad's buddies—spending weekends sucking back beers and barbecuing sausages in the backyards of Brooklyn and Queens?

She had seen Suffolk PD only as a stepping-stone.

Had she been lying to herself? Had she ever even been honest? She had become a cop because it made her dad proud. Not *only*, but mostly. She had always wanted something more.

Guilt burst free of its moorings. Why was she even thinking this? Pure selfishness. She was worried about how her life might change while her dad was fighting for his. What the hell was wrong with her?

Straight in front of Del rose a white-brick wall, ten stories high, inlaid with stained glass guarded by wire mesh. A domed steeple topped with a cross towered into the clear sky. "Our Lady of Pompeii," read the sign over the colonnaded entrance.

She hadn't been to church in years.

Its massive front doors were open, so she walked over, ascended the steps, and entered the calm coolness of its cavernous nave. The place was deserted. Catholic. Familiar. Del walked between the pews and chose one at random, sat down, and placed her coffee cup on the floor. She clasped her hands and bent her head.

Please, help me. Please, help my father.

When had she last gone to confession? She couldn't even remember.

Forgive me.

She had always had a conflicted relationship with church. Both her mother and her father were Catholic, and both observed the traditions on the surface, yet both held the faith at arm's length.

Growing up, her mother had spent as much time teaching Del about

Catholicism as she had about the *loa*, the spirits of the Louisiana Creole. It was a heady mixture of ancient African spirits and deities, old European lore and myth, and Catholic symbolism and litanies.

The religion, if it could be called that, had been brought to America with refugees of the Haitian revolution at the beginning of the seventeenth century—the Haitian revolution distinguishing itself as the only slave uprising that led to the founding of a state that was both free from slavery and ruled by nonwhite former captives. It was something her mother proudly told her when she was growing up.

It was a part of Del's blood every bit as much as Ireland was.

So, as she sat in the silence of the Catholic Church, she also said a prayer to the *ghede,* the voodoo spirits of death. She sat in the silence and waited. For what? A sign? And then . . .

In her head, she heard a voice.

God helps those who help themselves. It spoke in an Irish accent.

***

On her way out, Del tossed her half-full Starbucks in the wastebasket by the entrance, vowing never again to spend six bucks on a coffee. She headed back up Sixth Street toward her apartment, when her phone chirped in her pocket. It was her sister.

"Is Dad okay?"

Missy exhaled and made a funny keening sound. "Ahh, I'm not sure."

Del's heart jumped into her throat. "What do you mean?"

"You best get over here."

***

Del walked out of the elevator on the seventh floor and rounded the corner into the block-long waiting room. By the entrance to the ICU stood three off-duty NYPD officers she recognized, all of them talking to a doctor in blue scrubs. Angel Rodriguez stood to one side, also listening, and was the first to see her.

He waved her forward.

"What's wrong? What happened?" she said breathlessly.

The officers and Angel parted to each side of the doctor. "Ah, Ms. Devlin. Your father is awake. You should go in and speak with him."

"Speak with him? I thought he was getting a tracheotomy."

From what she'd been told, he wouldn't be able to speak. The tube inserted into his neck would bypass the vocal cords.

"That wasn't necessary," the doctor replied.

"So the infection is gone?"

Everyone looked down at the carpet.

"What?" Del looked at the ICU entrance and then back at the doctor. "Is he okay?"

"He's recovered, yes. Why don't you go in?"

"Yeah, you should go in and talk to him," said one the NYPD officers. Frankie. One of her father's best friends.

"What's wrong?" Del asked again. Why did they look so uncomfortable? She scanned the hallway. The UN security officers were gone. Just these three New York cops left. None of her mother's friends. The hallway was almost empty.

"Del, honey, don't take this the wrong way," Frankie said, "but we got word you were down at that show yesterday. Talking to Lenny Bondar. We got people watching him. You don't need to do that."

Don't need to? Or we won't let you? It wasn't her case, and even if it were, it was her father. She wouldn't be allowed anywhere near the investigation.

"Why don't you go in," Angel Rodriguez said. He motioned at the door.

"Come in with me?" Del said.

He nodded and followed her. Del flashed a pink card at the attending nurse—usually they had to call in to the ICU room to make sure visitors were allowed, but the pink pass granted immediate entry. The double doors opened.

"Charlie rook Rodrigo home," Angel said as he followed her. "Anything I can do. You know that—"

"Can you dig a little on this Leonardo Bondar?" Del asked. "And don't, you know, the guys . . ."

"Just between you and me."

The doctor had gone in ahead of them, but he stepped into a different room. Del halted at the corner of the corridor to her father's room. "What aren't they telling me?"

Angel ran a hand through his hair. "Go and talk to your dad. I'll go and see what I can find out about this Bondar guy."

***

Her father was propped up in the bed, surrounded by pillows. Plastic tubes ran across his chest and into both arms and coiled together up into the beeping machines arrayed around him. She glanced at the heart monitor. Seventy-two bpm.

Not in fibrillation anymore.

Her own heart came down out of her throat a little.

"Del, sweetie," her father croaked.

His voice was stronger than when she last heard it, on Friday. His cheeks were sunken, but the color had returned. His eyes wide open. Del's mother and sister sat in chairs to either side of his bed, each holding one of his hands. Her sister looked at Del and smiled but then looked away, her eyes red and swollen.

Her mother shifted her seat to one side. "Come sit."

Del stepped carefully to the bed. Two containers on the floor collected fluids from his chest drains, and cables snaked out from him and into the machines. She kissed her father's forehead. He was clammy, sweaty, his hair matted to his scalp.

"You okay?"

"Right as rain." He coughed.

"You look so much better. When did you wake up?"

"A few hours ago."

"And you didn't call me?"

"You needed your rest, sweetheart. I heard you've been in here all hours."

Del took a seat and held her father's hand. "They didn't need to do the tracheotomy?"

"The infection's gone."

"That's good news." She looked at her mother and sister, who both looked away. "What? That's good news, right?" She looked back at her father. "Is it something with your heart?"

"The old ticker's just fine."

She waited, but he didn't add anything.

"Did you see the guy who shot you?" Del asked. "Did they show you the video?"

"I didn't see much of anything, to be honest. One second, I was behind Grigory; the next, on the ground."

"Did you see the video? It seemed like you were looking right at him. Yuri Korshunov. An ex-KGB officer."

"I saw the video. They showed me the pictures. Maybe I saw him."

"Maybe?"

"Not sure."

"I met the guy who designed the gun that was used."

Her father said, "You did *what*?"

Del's mother and sister both shifted in their seats. "You're investigating?" her mother said.

"Leonardo Bondar. He was at a trade show in Queens yesterday. It was his gun design that Yuri used to shoot you."

"So you think a gun manufacturer is a good place to start looking for a shooter?" her father said.

"He didn't manufacture it. Designed it. I was hoping he might be able to help me track where it was created. Maybe by who."

"They have people for this," her mother said. "The FBI? They said the UN security are investigating. We have other concerns now, Delta."

"God helps those who help themselves," Del said to her mother. Then to her dad, "Isn't that what you always tell me?"

"She does have me there, Ammy."

"It's not just the gun," Del said. "It's a whole weird world. 3-D printers. The Fourth Industrial Revolution. Metal dragons. Spaceships. They're even manufacturing organs and skin that can be used in surgical procedures. Said they could revolutionize stuff like cancer treatment."

Silence in the room.

Absolute silence.

Her mother's eyes fell to the floor again. "Your father has something he needs to tell you."

"What?" Del turned to her dad. "Is this what you wanted to tell me before? On Friday, you said you needed to tell me something about our family."

Her father looked surprised. "Ah, no, no—"

"What was it you wanted to tell me?"

"Just that I loved you."

Del didn't need her special skills to spot this straight-up lie. "Dad. Come on."

"It was nothing, Del. I was delirious."

"You were *not* delirious."

"What I needed to tell you is that me getting shot is a blessing in disguise."

"*Blessing?* Dad, you almost—"

A voice interrupted. "Delta?"

It was Angel. He hung his head in through the ICU door.

"What is it?" she asked.

"I just got word from your NYPD buddies. About Lenny Bondar."

"And?"

"He skipped town. Right after you left yesterday—didn't even do his planned speech. He went out to JFK this morning. Got on a flight to Europe."

"And they didn't stop him?"

"For what, exactly, would they do that?"

"I don't know. Damn it." Del got halfway up out of her chair.

Her father's hand grabbed onto her wrist. "Delta, honey, I need to tell you something."

"What is it? Dad, please, tell me."

"I've got cancer."

11

Flower petals glowed in the sun, with an iridescence Del had had to make up words to describe when she was a child. *Ishma*-purple and glow-blue, dotted with glittery fireflies of light. The closest she could compare it, if asked to describe, was to neon speckles of lint on a sweater under a black light. Composite flowers like daisies and sunflowers had the strongest pollen fluorescence in full sun, but the most beautiful were often little surprises like the orange and blue glow of a cucumber blossom, or the tiny wild buttercups she stared at now.

Spring flowers were beautiful to everyone, but for Del they were spectacular.

It was her first time visiting France, and so far, so beautiful.

A bee buzzed lazily by in the sunshine and alighted on a delicate stem for its morning nectar. Del felt an affinity for insects and arachnids, like the tiny bright red-and-black scorpion that scuttled beneath the bee. They sensed some of the world the same way she did. Maybe enjoyed the same way of settling into warm, dark corners.

She checked her watch. She was late.

Over trimmed hedges stood an imposing five-story, glass-walled building. Rectangular concrete columns rose at ten-foot intervals to the full height of the structure. They reminded Del of the flying buttresses of medieval cathedrals, but these weren't for support or decoration. Maybe to block a physical attack?

That made more sense.

The architecture of the place felt muscular. Cameras and sensing devices bristled from the columns and walls and lined the twenty-foot double steel enclosure ringing the compound. Five layers of high-voltage wire were strung above the fences.

***

"Welcome to the International Criminal Police Organization," Director Dartmouth said from the other side of the entryway.

Katherine dusted off the pant leg of her suit and folded up a brown paper package before standing up from her perch on the marble balustrade.

Del hadn't expected her outside. She'd been lost in her thoughts. Of her father. She strode the ten feet over and shook hands. Nice, firm grip.

"Were you waiting for me?" Del asked.

"Nice day for it. Having lunch outside, I mean. Your first time in Lyon?"

Del nodded. Only her second time in Europe, after that disastrous trip to Italy with Mickey when she graduated from college.

Behind Katherine blossomed a thicket of pink roses. A manufactured varietal, they had a solid pink hue in her vision, not like the spectral explosion of the wildflower beds on the way in.

Katherine deposited her brown wrapper in a garbage bin. "I'll show you in. I got a call that you didn't take the car we sent." She opened one of the glass doors.

Interpol headquarters was on the southern bank of the Rhone, toward the north of central Lyon, at the edge of the Tête d'Or park, which housed the city's botanical gardens. It was far enough from the city center that few visitors came on foot.

"It's five minutes from the Marriott," Del said. "I walked through the gardens." That had to be why Katherine was waiting for her. Del had sent the car back.

They passed through security and two sets of metal detectors and scanners. In dramatic contrast to the squat, almost cubical glass-walled exterior, the inside was organized around a three-step-down sunken octagonal meeting area with the Interpol logo at its center—a blue Earth, pierced through its axis by a sword and flanked by the scales of justice. The sun beamed down through a skylight high overhead.

"This way," Katherine said, walking toward one of the glass elevators located at each corner of the octagon. It looked like a 1970s hotel lobby. It smelled like a hospital.

Del felt unsteady, and it wasn't just the jet lag. The shock wave of her father's cancer diagnosis had flattened her emotional landscape, leaving her feeling unmoored. Was she running toward something, or just away?

***

"Where are the forensics labs?" Del asked as they stepped into the elevator. What did one do on one's first day at Interpol? She felt awkward, like a kid starting at a new school.

"Fifth floor."

"Can I take a look?"

Katherine checked her watch. "We have a few minutes."

They got out on the top floor and walked past a brightly lit common area with purple walls and impressionist prints. Through open doorways, Del caught glimpses of paper-strewn desks with monitors and keyboards. The soothingly familiar feel of a police station.

Katherine made a few introductions before she stopped and knocked on a door near one of the octagonal interior structure's corners. A small brown-skinned man with a white short-sleeved shirt and oversize pocket protector opened the door.

"Yes, hello, Director Dartmouth." The man's accent was South Asian—Indian?—and his smile was instantaneous, as if this was the best surprise of his day. "What can I do you for this wonderful morning?"

Katherine said, "Officer Jatt, this is Detective Devlin."

Jatt's head wobbled ever so slightly from side to side. He shook Del's hand. "Please, call me Suweil. This is my name."

"And call me Delta." Limp handshake, but his enthusiasm made up for it.

The whites of his eyes grew even wider. "Did you want to come in?" He swung the door wide.

"Jatt is our resident expert in everything from digital forensics to facial recognition, 3-D printing, and everything in between," Katherine said.

One wall was a rack of computers and electronic equipment. No exterior windows, just a single large pane looking out on the interior courtyard. Del noticed a large square structure at the back of the forty-foot lab—a Metal Labs additive 3-D printer, and beside it, on tabletops, two Strataform Replicator machines. She had seen billboard ads for the machines on the taxi ride from the airport.

"Do we have time?" Del asked.

Katherine checked her watch again. "Perhaps later."

They thanked Suweil, and Del promised to return. She followed the director back to the elevator.

"There's something I want to request."

"Already?" Katherine pushed the button. "I realize why you want to talk to the forensics team. You're free to do so as long as you maintain confidentiality internally."

"It's not that."

The elevator's doors opened.

Katherine waited. "So, what is it?"

"I want to join the mission to Ukraine. For the election monitoring."

The elevator door started to close, and Katherine held out her hand to keep it open. "Come on. I need you to meet your new partner."

***

"Detective Devlin," Katherine said, "I am pleased to introduce you to Officer Jacques Galloul of the Police Judiciaire."

A compact man with coffee skin, in khakis and a crisp blue oxford shirt, sat at a conference table in the ten-by-twenty-foot meeting room. A silver tray and coffee urn stood on a credenza, the only other furniture in the room besides the chairs.

He was on his phone and held up his finger. *One second.* He spoke in French while Del and Katherine waited. Eventually, he put the phone away, stood, and stuck out his hand. No tie. No jacket. Head shaved. A sheen of perspiration over his face as if he had just run over.

"*Un plaisir,*" Del said.

"So you speak French?"

"*Juste une peu.* My mother is Louisiana creole. I'm not sure if it counts as French." She took another look at him. "Have we met before?"

"I don't think so."

Del couldn't quite place his face, but he looked familiar.

"Already better than the last recruit," Jacques said to Katherine. Then to Del: "It is a real pleasure. I'd like to offer my sympathies about your father. Terrible."

"Thank you," Del said. "Director Dartmouth said you'll be my new partner?"

"'Partner' is not the right word," Jacques replied.

"Officer Galloul offered to give you an orientation session, do some Q and A," Katherine explained.

They sat across from Jacques, and the director indicated he had the floor.

"*Bon.* Let's start with some basics," Jacques said. "The secretary general of Interpol, Alexei Propochuk, is our chief full-time official, responsible for the day-to-day running. This is the equivalent to a CEO in the private sector."

Del had read that Propochuk was the police chief of Moscow in his previous life and had worked with Gorbachev to dismantle the KGB during perestroika. He was well respected and had earned unanimous election as head of Interpol. *Still a Russian,* some grumbled.

Jacques continued, "Our president, Hui Meng, China's deputy minister of public security, occupies a part-time and unpaid governance role, whose primary responsibilities are to chair the annual General Assembly. More like a chairman—again, to borrow a private-sector analogy. Any questions so far?"

Del shook her head. She had done her reading on the flight. The Chinese Ministry of Public Security was roughly equivalent to America's FBI. As Jacques continued with his introduction, she glanced at Boston Justice, who was busy answering an email on his phone. Why was he sitting in on this?

"Interpol has no police powers per se," Jacques said. "Our main weapon is information, and our key challenge is fighting *dis*information. In a world where more and more people believe that the Earth is flat, this is no so small task."

Del nodded. She understood. Information was why she had come.

"All investigations and arrests in each Interpol member country are carried out by the national police in accordance with national laws. We are banned from engaging in any political or religious disputes. Our main work is disseminating information on international criminal organizations. We do not investigate individual crimes."

Jacques paused, perhaps to see whether Del was paying attention.

"Understood," she said.

"Interpol is often nothing more than a bulletin board where national police forces post wanted notices."

Jacques began detailing the ways in which the organization exchanged data, which made Del wonder: How had she passed the background check to become part of Interpol's Washington Bureau? Whatever happened to the FBI background check that had disqualified her from their recruitment process? Del had her friend Angel looking into her own background, but so far, he hadn't found anything unusual.

Katherine stood up with her phone out. "Excuse me, I need to get on something." To Del, she added, "Come and see me when you're done?"

Jacques waited for Katherine to leave before continuing, "Some nations give Interpol Red Notices legally binding force, but most do not. And we are not involved in extradition requests, nor can we make such requests—these are made on a bilateral basis between national authorities. Do you have any questions?"

Del's notepad was out, but she hadn't written anything. "So if you're not my partner, what exactly is our relationship?"

"Now, that is a good question." A bloom of prickly warmth appeared on Jacques's forehead. Was he upset? The heat map of his face radiated anger, but his smile and eyes remained calm. "To answer, I have a question of my own."

"Go ahead."

"Why is a Long Island detective at Interpol headquarters?"

"Same reason as you, I imagine."

"I doubt that."

Del put her pen down. "I'm sorry, I don't follow."

"Tell me why you are *really* here."

"To catch criminals."

Which was half the truth. Officer Jacques Galloul's question wasn't really a query; it was an accusation. He wasn't her partner, he explained, but her babysitter. He wouldn't let her out of his sight. From one law-enforcement professional to another, it bordered on an insult.

It was her first day in school, and the bully had declared himself. Del had been bullied before, beaten down. Not anymore.

She was here really for one single purpose.

Russia had just issued an Interpol Red Notice for the arrest of Yuri Korshunov, the man who shot her father.

12

Del clicked the side-table lamp on and inspected the brown alligator skin. "*Damn it*," she muttered, running her finger over the scaly smoothness.

The nick in the side of her only pair of Vuitton heels was small but new, and unmistakable. She had gotten them last week from Bentley's in Manhattan—a gift to herself for this trip. Almost stole them at the price she paid, but this mark, this gouge near the toe, wasn't there when she bought them.

Was it?

Maybe that was why they were so inexpensive.

She put them down gently next to her red-soled Louboutins and black-and-white Nikes and New Balance and twins of Jimmy Choos— two sets of sneakers, four of sensible pumps, and three of precious heels she might or might not get a chance to wear. Those were just along for the ride. Maybe she should have packed more, but her mother had said to bring as little as possible and go shopping in Europe.

With the shoes taken care of, she unzipped the other side of her case and pulled out a stack of blouses, inspected them one by one. She hadn't had time to unpack in the morning after taking last night's red-eye from JFK.

The Marriott Lyon hotel room was smaller than the American counterparts she'd been in, but it felt sharper, the design aesthetic sleek and minimalist. She picked up a bottle of Côtes du Rhône from the circular glass dining table by the window and poured a cup. She dropped herself into one of the zebra-striped chairs, below a lamp that hung over on a long cantilevered base, and looked out the window.

The Rhône River meandered slowly by in the darkness.

She took a sip of wine. Now she was literally on the *côte du Rhône*—the bank of the Rhône. She hadn't bothered with dinner, despite invitations from Katherine, but had picked up a baguette, a small wheel of Camembert, and the bottle from a neighborhood grocer.

Why had Russia issued an arrest warrant for one of its own officers? Yuri Korshunov was still listed as a member of the FSB. One problem with Interpol was that it treated all its members equally and therefore assumed that all their requests for help were equally valid. That was a reasonable assumption to make about Canada, Japan, the United States, South Korea, the UK, or even Poland. But it wasn't reasonable to suppose the same about places like Venezuela, Cuba, Iran . . . Del hesitated but then capitulated, adding Russia to that list. Dictatorships had learned a long time ago that they could skirt Interpol's constitution and use it to harass innocent dissidents, businesspeople, journalists, and opposition leaders.

So why had Russia issued an arrest warrant for one of its own?

Unless Korshunov wasn't.

Or they didn't want the West to think he was.

She turned on her phone and scrolled through her in-box to the message from Grigory Georgiev, the commissioner of police in Kiev: *Sources have informed us that Yuri Korshunov has been spotted in southern Ukraine.*

***

The commissioner had written in secret, he said, in strict confidence because it wasn't yet confirmed. He implored her to keep this to herself, at least for now.

They were trying to find Yuri, he said, but the area was unstable. That whole region of Ukraine had been overrun by pro-Russian separatist forces. He said he owed it to her father to let him know, and wished her family all the best.

Russian forces.

After hanging up the last of the clothes from her suitcase, Del lifted out a bag of white and gray plastic rods and cubes. She dropped it into another bag, which she had gotten from the hardware store next to the grocery, and took them out to the balcony, along with the wine bottle and glass.

Unlatching the patio door, she watched it fall outward like a window. Not a design she had encountered at home. It took her five minutes to figure it out, but eventually she got the glass door to slide open, turned on the outside lights, and sat at the wooden table. She took another sip of wine and opened the hardware-store package to take out the small butane blowtorch.

***

Her father's medical prognosis wasn't good, but he remained a rock. The whole family had sat in with the doctor when he described the stage-three cancer that had infected her father's lymph nodes. The doc had said it was lucky because this might not have displayed any physical symptoms for some time.

Del did her research. "Lucky" translated to an average survival rate of eighteen months.

Her father had been almost cheerful about it. Said he always knew that a shoe would drop, and now, at least, he knew which one it was.

She had gone with her father to his first chemo treatment, nine days after the initial diagnosis. He refused the wheelchair, so she had hovered by him as he walked, proudly although slowly, into the clinic on the third floor of Presbyterian's west wing. After checking him in with the nurses, she had slathered her hands with antiseptic gel, then sat nervously reading the pamphlets on breast and ovarian cancer.

The nurse came and ushered them into a quiet room filled with reclining chairs, each occupied by a frail-looking person attached to an IV bag. Many wore head scarves.

Del had feared the worst, but her father weathered the first treatment with no real ill effects and became stronger the following week. The new drugs were much gentler on the system, the nurses told Del. They sent him home.

Missy took him for his second chemo session.

Del took leave from work the first week, but her father had implored her to return the week after. She hadn't checked her email in almost two weeks, and the first thing she saw was a message from Adam Petty, CEO of Strataform. He had sent her all the technical data sheets on the Replicators. He had heard about her father and sent his sympathies—said he would connect her with Strataform Medical, where they had clinical trials under way for advanced treatments.

The UN forensics investigation had ground to a halt.

Interpol Europe hadn't shared any information at all in the first few weeks and then had sent data to the FBI. Del wasn't allowed to see the report—just the results, which were inconclusive.

She went into the office and did her research. Lenny Bondar's Black Army wasn't as harmless as Adam Petty, CEO of Strataform, had made it out to be. A slew of online investigative articles linked it to the Ukrainian Black Army, a Russian revolutionary group long since extinct but now in revival. It had no stated leader, no base of operations except on the web. Now the media were suggesting that Bondar was head of a resurgent Black Army faction—not just hackers, but armed terrorists as well. As the election approached, there had been a surge in social media and websites linked to the Black Army in Ukraine.

And Bondar had now disappeared. Interpol was tracking him, but the trail had gone blank.

***

Week by week, her father had regained his strength. Del had hovered around him, but the one thing that bothered her father more than anything else was being mollycoddled.

After a month, he had taken her out to their local Irish pub and had a whiskey, chemo or no chemo.

A bird didn't fly because it wanted to fly, he told her. It flew because it had wings. He told her that battling the cancer was his fight—she had to go and face her own. He said this thing with Interpol was a once-in-a-lifetime opportunity, and he wanted her to help find the bastard who had shot him. "Don't look a gift horse in the mouth," he said.

Last week, she had called Katherine and accepted. With one condition.

***

Del dropped one of the white plastic strips onto a ten-inch square of sheet metal. After taking another sip of wine, she used a lighter to ignite the blowtorch, then picked up the metal sheet with a pair of pliers and heated its underside.

The only confirmed information she had from the Interpol forensics team was that the gun used to shoot her father had been made using an additive technology—a printer that put down layers of material one on top of another. To do that, they had to melt down the plastics before squirting or oozing them into place.

She had ordered samples from all the major manufacturers. Strataform, of course, and Metals Labs and Bondar's company, MakerArmy, plus a dozen smaller ones.

The lump of plastic melted on top of the heated metal sheet.

In her vision, the sheet of metal glowed hot in infrared. The oozing plastic glistened in sparkling shades. It was one thing to study something over the internet, but entirely another to see it with her own eyes.

13

"How was your first week?" Katherine Dartmouth asked.

Dartmouth's office was on the fifth floor, on the other side of the building from the forensics lab. The glass wall looked onto the botanical gardens over the Tête d'Or park and the low-lying urban sprawl of Lyon into the blue-shifted distance.

"It was good," Del replied.

Boring was a better description. At least, Interpol had the same mountains of paperwork in common with regular policing. After making Jacques's unpleasant acquaintance, she had been inundated. She already had a stack of paperwork to sort through—requests from the FBI and other US agencies regarding persons of interest in Europe.

The role of legal attaché was primarily one of coordination, not the actual gathering of foreign intelligence, or counterintelligence investigations. It involved coordinating information from US embassies in Europe and sharing investigative leads and information from organizations stateside that submitted a request.

The position was normally filled by a senior-ranking law-enforcement officer, often from the FBI. It was more than a little unusual for a lowly Suffolk County detective to be here. She had spent the past three days mostly alone in her cubicle, surrounded by empty cubicles in a large open room. She felt that she was being isolated on purpose. Or ostracized.

"How's your father?" Dartmouth asked. "And please, call me Katherine."

"He's doing as well as can be expected."

Dartmouth sat on the edge of her desk and looked down at Del. "You're getting along with Officer Galloul? Important that we maintain strong bonds between police forces. Between nations. It's one the goals of Interpol."

"He's an interesting character."

"Character?"

"He was . . ."

"Go on."

"Unpleasant."

"In what way?"

"He accused me of having some ulterior motive."

"But you do."

"I'm not hiding it, so it's not ulterior."

Not for the first time, coming here felt like a mistake. Several times already, she had resisted the urge to take a taxi to the airport and catch the next flight back to New York. Del wasn't concealing anything, but she wasn't volunteering, either. She had gone two more times to the forensics lab and had even requested that the samples of the gun used to shoot her father be brought up from storage. A request like this couldn't have gone unnoticed.

Katherine said, "I know you've been talking with the forensics team, and I realize you've been looking into your father's shooter."

"That was my condition for taking the job."

"We agreed you could look into Leonardo Bondar."

Del watched Katherine's face. Had the director been truthful in saying she would let Del investigate?

Dartmouth's face remained cool. "There's a limit to the latitude we can give you as a new part of Interpol."

"There's a connection between Bondar and Korshunov," Del said.

"They both were in New York at the same time, and both left right after the attempt on Voloshyn."

Dartmouth slid off the desk and sat in the chair, facing Del. "I also know that Grigory Georgiev sent you a message regarding Yuri. You didn't share this with us. With *me*."

Del felt her face heat up. "Georgiev said it wasn't official."

"You still should have communicated it. This is your main job as attaché: communicating all information you gather. FBI and CIA both have cases open on Mr. Korshunov." She paused and looked down at her desk. "Perhaps this is too close to you."

What had they expected? This was about as personal as it could be, but that wasn't why she had kept Georgiev's message to herself. She still had the habit of holding things close to the vest—the instincts of a detective on the prowl.

Dartmouth took a folder from the desk and opened it. "We've had a formal complaint from Officer Galloul."

Del straightened in her chair. "For making requests to the forensics team?"

"Officer Galloul has axes to grind. The last person to occupy your position was removed for breaching guidelines, which is why Korshunov and Bondar are potentially troubling. I agreed to give you some leeway, but this goes beyond a simple crime."

Del didn't follow.

"Because these were politically motivated," Dartmouth explained. "Linked to the Ukrainian elections in three weeks."

"Surely, an assassination attempt is more than *just* politics."

"It's still guesswork that Voloshyn was the target at the UN meeting in New York."

Guesswork? Del couldn't help raising her eyebrows.

Katherine continued, "The Russians are still contesting whether it was Korshunov in the video, even though they were the ones who issued a Red Notice through Interpol for his arrest."

"Wouldn't we have issued an arrest warrant anyway?"

"But they did first. Which makes you wonder why." Katherine looked at her notes. "So you've been investigating 3-D printers? We have a strong relationship with Strataform. Adam Petty—you met him at the same event in New York, correct? The one where you met Bondar?" Dartmouth put the folder back on the desk.

"He's the one who introduced me."

"Did Mr. Petty suggest getting your father's case submitted to the clinical trials with Strataform Medical?"

Del nodded.

Katherine closed her folders. "You're sure you want to go to Ukraine? Fighting has spread beyond just the south and east."

"I don't want to step on any toes, but yes, I'd like to see the place myself."

"The fighting there is not restricted to the physical world. This is a war being waged as much in the mind as on the battlefield. A struggle to define reality. You need to be careful who you listen to. You will have no gun, no badge. No contacts, no friends."

"I have a personal relationship with Grigory Georgiev. I think I can contribute."

"Even President Voloshyn. Is she telling the truth? Or is she bending reality to try and fit a narrative she is creating? Trying to cut through all that—this is our primary mission. Information."

"I understand."

Del watched her boss intently and waited for a response. Katherine closed her eyes and rubbed her eyebrows, then the edges of her eyes and temples. Her eyes opened, and she stared into space for a moment before replying, "I'll consider your request. But there would be something I need you to do for us in return."

***

It had been stupid to try keeping the message from Grigory a secret, even though he had requested that she keep it strictly confidential. How had Katherine found out? She was head of the Washington Interpol office, so who knew what access she had? Maybe even to Del's personal telephone and messages. Katherine hadn't volunteered, and Del hadn't asked.

It didn't matter.

What did matter, Katherine had told her, was that from this point on, Del share any least thing she could pick up on. Her first task was to write down a detailed résumé of her meeting with Officer Galloul, including anything he said.

After that, Katherine needed Del's impressions of Grigory Georgiev, the message he had sent her, and any details that came to mind, no matter how small. Katherine said to be careful of Georgiev, but she didn't say why.

***

"How's Dad?" Del said into her phone. She had just dialed her sister.

"He's good," Missy replied. "We finished his fifth chemo this morning. One more left."

"How's he holding up?"

"You know how he is."

"Missy, come on, please. He's not feeling well?"

Del had bought her dad one of those fitness trackers before she left. The wristwatch ones that tracked how many steps you did each day. It could even tell when you were asleep. She had a matching one on her own wrist. Each day, they had to do at least ten thousand steps, she told her dad, and she could track him on the app.

For the first few weeks, he had been logging twelve thousand to fifteen thousand steps a day. She let him win just about every day, taking off the tracker before going for a run, so she wouldn't log too many steps. Like the games they used to play when she was a child, except that now *she* was the one letting *him* win.

Last week, he had averaged eleven thousand steps. This week, it was down to seven thousand. The past two days, half that.

"He's resting," Missy said.

"He never rests."

"Now he is."

"How's Mom?"

"How do you think?"

Del was doing two things at once. She finished writing up the report on Grigory's message and sent it over to Katherine, then closed her laptop. "I wouldn't ask if I knew."

"You should be here, Delta. Not out wherever the hell you are."

"I'm here because it's what Dad wanted."

"Because he knows it's what you want."

"Did he say that?"

Silence.

"Missy, I'm coming back this weekend before I go to Kiev." One of her conditions for accepting the job was regular visits back to the States, paid for by the bureau.

"You're going to . . . Del, are you sure you know what you're doing?"

"Is Dad there? Can I speak to him?"

"He's sleeping."

Del exhaled long and slow. A message popped up on her phone—from Suweil, the forensics guy on the fifth floor.

"I'll call back later," she said. "I love you."

***

"So that's it?" Del said.

Suweil had just laid two eight-by-eight-inch bags down on the aluminum worktable. Inside each clear bag were two large, splintered bits of whitish plastic.

The remains of the gun that had shot her father.

Del paused a moment before asking, "Can I open them? Take the parts out?" She had just put on nitrile rubber gloves.

"Please be careful." Suweil stepped back.

She emptied the contents onto the table, picked them up, and inspected them in the bright sunshine streaming in through the lab's south-facing windows. The two largest chunks fit together more or less, with the other fragments fitting in the gaps. She had traveled a long way to do this.

"So no fingerprints, no DNA residue?" Del didn't need to ask. She had read the reports. "Is there anything else we can do?"

"Not with the plastic," Suweil said.

The parts looked the same as the pictures—but, of course, different in Del's vision. The plastic wasn't uniform, the colors striated at the pressure fractures where it had come apart.

"It was glued together," Del said. "Have we tracked down the composition?"

"This is still being investigated. But I have sent all the spectrographic details of the resins used. It has the chemical signatures of sourcing from Helico Corporation, with polymer traces of manufacture on the West Coast of the United States."

"So it was made on the West Coast?"

"Or shipped from there. This company is the largest manufacturer of 3-D plastics."

Del said, "You're an expert in digital forensics, right?"

His head waggled from side to side.

"Is there any way to get a list of who downloaded the file used to create this?"

"I'm afraid this is beyond even our abilities."

"If we brought in a machine we thought might be involved, would it be possible to see if it was used to create the gun?"

Suweil thought about it for a second. "If the data resided somewhere, yes, even if it got erased. And perhaps some manufacturing anomalies."

Del reached into her handbag and took out the blowtorch and the sheet-metal plate. She'd had to explain for some time to the security people at the entrance before they let her in with it.

"Can I destroy part of the sample?" she asked.

Suweil's eyes widened at the sight of the blowtorch. "For what purpose?"

"I need to see something. With my own eyes."

He knew that Del's father had been shot with this thing. He agreed but spent the next twenty minutes photographing the pea-size fragment from every angle, then requisitioned a form from the Interpol central servers, which she had to sign.

***

"Can you turn off the lights?" Del asked.

She closed the blinds. It wasn't dark, but dim enough.

Suweil provided a pair of pliers, and Del placed the scrap of plastic atop her metal plate and heated it. Within a minute, the crumb drooped and then oozed across the plate. Del watched intently. Did anything seem different? Similar?

What was she hoping for? She wasn't sure.

The metal plate glowed dull red, and the plastic streaked in a rainbow of shades in Del's vision. "What colors do you see in that?" she asked Suweil.

His thick brows furrowed together as he considered her question. "In this light, gray, perhaps? White? The metal of the plate is glowing ever so slightly orange."

Still holding the sample with the pliers, she turned the plate and applied the torch directly to the plastic. It flared in a yellow blaze with bluish edges, giving off an immediate stench of burnt rubber.

She turned the blowtorch off.

"Did your experiment get any result?" Suweil asked.

Each plastic and resin had its own signature. ABS made a blue flame with yellow edges and smelled more acrid; cellulose acetate had an almost vinegary stench as it flared with tiny sparks. Acrylics, for some reason, smelled fruity and floral when they burned.

He looked toward the lights, and Del nodded. He turned them back on.

She inspected the plastic one last time before putting the metal plate down. "Not anything useful, I think."

"Then I am afraid we have hit a dead end. We can tell nothing more than where this plastic was manufactured, not where the gun itself was made. Whoever created it was very careful in removing any evidence we could track."

Del watched the cooling metal and didn't say anything.

"I do have one request," Suweil said.

"What's that?"

"The shell casing from the bullet—could you get us this? The New York police have it in their possession. They have been very resistant about letting us look at it."

14

"My name is Igor. Welcome to Kiev!" said a man with a shock of black hair pulled halfway back across his skull, so that he looked somehow bald and shaggy at the same time. He wore a too-large black sport jacket over a navy-blue shirt. He opened one of the passenger doors to a worn red Lada with a faded tan leather top.

"Really?" Jacques said.

He stood next to Del at the entrance of the Hyatt Regency Kyiv.

"Sorry, sir," said the concierge. "This is rush hour. Another taxi will be ten minutes."

***

"How are you enjoying Kiev?" Igor said from the front bench. "You are married? Honeymoon? Yes?"

Del couldn't help laughing at that. "We work together."

"I am joking. I can see. Your friend isn't smiling. We need to smile."

"It's a beautiful city," Del said. "But terrible what's happening in the south."

The fighting had gotten worse.

Igor waved a hand in the air. "Every fifty years, the Russians attack the Germans and destroy Ukraine. And then, fifty years later, a different set of Germans attack the Russians and wreck our motherland all over again. And so it goes throughout the millennia—a back-and-forth power struggle between East and West, with us stuck in the middle."

"So, what do you do?"

"I would do anything for my country." The taxi swept through an intersection and past a billboard of President Voloshyn. "She is trying to stop this. That is why this election is so important. But I'm afraid history is already re-creating itself."

Igor pulled off the road into a driveway. "And here we are. This is your stop?"

***

A syrupy yellow liquid fell in ropey loops into a foot-wide cylindrical glass container. After it filled to the top, the cylinder began to rotate slowly. A bright light clicked on, illuminating the tank of goop in an intense flickering beam. Within a few seconds, ghostly lines and edges began to form within the fluid.

Del edged closer and leaned down to get a better look.

Ten seconds more, and the outlines became more definite. An object began to form within the yellow tank, appearing from nothingness at the urging of the shimmery rays emanating from the machine.

"This new process can take as little as thirty seconds," the young man said. His name was Artem, but just "Art" was easier, he'd said when introducing himself. "We can manufacture objects up to a cubic feet in volume."

"Foot," Del said, her face just inches from the spinning cylinder. "Cubic *foot*, not *feet*."

His English was good but not perfect. Jacques and Del were the only two people on the "tour," and she sensed that they had been the only people to come in the front door today. No one but them would dare push through the angry mob outside.

"Of course—a cubic foot in volume," Art replied nervously.

Last week, Del would have said his accent was Russian, but after four days in Kiev, she had become familiar with the brogue when Ukrainians spoke English—which almost all of them under thirty did. This young man wore a tracksuit top over a blue T-shirt. The faintest wisps of a mustache shaded his upper lip, and his cheeks were an almost translucent pink, like a baby's. He couldn't be more than eighteen and was the official tour guide for the Strataform Kiev manufacturing facility.

The three of them were still in the lobby, a twenty-foot-square room with high ceilings, and walls adorned with the same Strataform posters and advertisements Del had seen on the billboards lining the highway from the airport. The air inside was faintly acrid with an undertone of rotten eggs, which, she supposed, was from processing acrylonitrile and polyphenylene plastics somewhere in the building. Not a scent that would be popular with tourists.

The machine before them was a gray box three feet high by six long, with the receptacle at its far end. It stopped, the light shut off, and the amber solution drained from the tank, to leave behind a glistening transparent jawbone, complete with teeth. Not even a minute ago, it had been empty space, and now it was half-filled with an intricate and flawless object that rested in the middle of the cylinder. A short blast of hot air, and the cylinder descended.

"Can I pick it up?" she asked.

"You can have it."

Slightly warm and tacky to the touch, the hardened resin was surprisingly clear compared to the amber liquid it had been formed from. The teeth and bone were smooth and glasslike.

"The intense light depletes oxygen molecules in the liquid, which causes it to harden," Art said. "This process isn't commercial yet." He waved them forward to a stairway up. "On the next levels are our production floors."

Del turned the polymer sample around and around, then offered it to Jacques.

The Algerian Frenchman crinkled his nose and gave the tiny Gallic shrug that Del was sure they must teach in every nursery school in France.

Shoulders up, he said, "*Non, merci.* I wonder whose jaw that is. You have to wonder, no? Why would they choose such a thing? Why not go with a whole skull? Would be more macabre." He smiled to indicate he thought this was funny.

"You didn't have to come," Del said under her breath. "It's Saturday. A day off. This has nothing to do with the election monitoring."

"Which is exactly why I am here."

"I just want to know more about 3-D printing. Consider this my personal time."

"This job should *not* be personal."

Jacques had been shadowing Del the whole four days she had been here, even inviting himself to the meeting with the Ukrainian bureau chief when Del introduced herself to the local staff. Three meetings so far with election officials.

Del was exhausted.

On Friday, she had gone back to New York, direct from Lyon, on a 2:00 p.m. flight that got in at 5:00. She went straight to Brooklyn to see her father. He was starting his sixth week of chemo and radiation, and for the first time, she saw it in his face. He looked gaunt and tired, his skin yellowed with jaundice from the drugs affecting his liver.

She had gone to his afternoon chemo session the next day and offered to stay.

He didn't want her there, he said. A part of her felt that he wanted to be alone, but then, he had Missy and her mother there. Did he just not want *her* around? She kept asking him questions, but he always deflected, as if he was hiding something from her. She felt ill and had almost canceled her return flight on the Sunday night red-eye, but Monday morning she found herself back at Interpol headquarters.

Wednesday, she had taken a connecting flight through Frankfurt to Zhuliany, the Igor Sikorsky Kyiv International Airport on the outskirts of the capital—right next to the Antonov Aviation Museum. On approach, she had pressed her face against the window and watched the rows of cottages roll by between green trees, and just before landing had crossed over a jumble of the massive namesake Antonov aircraft parked at the exhibit.

The Kiev airport had the same glass-and-metal-modernity feeling as many in America, but it was filled with Costa coffee shops and Vodafone ads instead of Starbucks and T-Mobile. All the signs were in English along with the Cyrillic characters, and on the taxi drive to the hotel she had noticed road signs with Stop on them. It felt alien but familiar, as if the whole world was converging into one homogeneous modern form.

One thing stood out more than any other: advertisements for Strataform. They were in the airport, on billboards, even on bus stop benches. Even more than back home, Strataform seemed everywhere.

Jacques might have been shadowing her in Europe, but he hadn't come to New York.

Going to see her dad hadn't been the only reason to go back home.

She was stopped at JFK security and asked to explain why she had a packet of .38 ammunition in her checked luggage. Official Interpol business, Del had told them, and produced her ID. She had also stopped off at the evidence room at One Police Plaza.

***

The main manufacturing room of the Strataform facility thrummed at a frequency at the low edge of audible. The vibrations came up through the thick rubber mat covering the concrete slab floors, into Del's pumps and up her tarsals and tibiae, femora and pelvis, to her spine and brainpan. Row upon row of boxy, gray Strataform machines, their orange lights glowing through their transparent covers, hunched like linemen in a grid stretching the width and length of a room the size of a football field. Each machine was busy grinding out something.

In the channels between the Strataform sentinels scuttled dwarf three-wheeled robots, each with a single multipronged arm that dangled overhead, carrying some plastic part regurgitated from one of the machines.

The smell of rotten eggs was stronger here.

"There are three levels to this print farm," Art explained as he walked ahead of them. One of the three-wheeled bots angled straight at him and then, at the last instant, darted around. "A thousand Strataform Replicator machines per floor—the operation almost completely automated, as you can see. Manufacturing a cubic-foot object takes ten to twenty minutes.

This facility can produce millions of parts a day, depending on their size and complexity, and all completely customizable. We are bringing manufacturing back into the hearts of industrialized nations."

"Are these the same as the home version of the Strataform?" Del asked.

Art wagged his head from side to side. "More and less. They have the same three-color pigment—"

"Acrylics," Del completed his sentence for him. "And ABS? And they print out conductive copper strips? So they can lay down circuitry?"

Art nodded. "That is right."

"And it smells nice," Jacques said.

"This is the Rayton polymer,' Art said. "It has UL94 V-0 flammable rating and is chemical resistant, with very tight manufacturing tolerances at heat. We are the only ones capable of using it. Almost like metal."

"Polyphenylene sulfide, PPS—that's what gives it that smell," Del said.

"That is right."

"Why not just make things the normal way?" Jacques asked.

"A good question." Art's face brightened. 'Across the street from us is the National Museum of Ukrainian History. It is filled with artifacts stretching back hundreds and even thousands of years of our motherland. Each object has been digitized into 3-D."

When Art paused theatrically, Jacques said, "And?"

"If anyone wants *any* of those objects, you can simply order one on your visit. The command is sent here, and one of the machines will replicate it for you. Within an hour, any of those thousands of artifacts will be custom delivered in a box as you leave. Complete manufacturing on demand."

No Gallic shrug this time, the corners of his mouth bent down while his eyebrows went up. Jacques was impressed.

"This is the future of manufacturing," Art said. "There is no—" His phone chirped, and he picked it up and frowned.

"Something important?" Del asked. "It's fine; we can leave."

"Yes, an important message." He held the phone out. "But it's one for you."

15

"I received an alert that you were visiting one of our facilities," Adam Petty said on the fifty-inch flat screen on the wall.

His signature foppish hair half-obscured the black glasses, his perennial two-day salt-and-pepper beard hipster-matching a printed T-shirt and army jacket.

It was past noon here, so about 5:00 a.m. on the US East Coast, and the middle of the night on the West Coast, but who knew where the CEO of Strataform was now?

Jacques and Del sat in a ten-by-ten staff room just off the main lobby. From the mess of scattered cups and the stained table by a two-pot stand, it had to be the break room. The countertops were filled with fantastical curving shapes and mythical creatures in plastic, with swords and imitation jewelry that she assumed had been created from the artifact collection in the museum next door. The acrid sulfurous smell of the upper floors gave way to a more mundane odor of office carpet.

"An alert?" Jacques said, his eyebrows raised once again.

"Detective Devlin is a person of interest to our organization," Petty explained, "after everything that happened to her father, and her and my meeting at the Maker Faire. I sent all the materials to your lab and to the FBI, as requested."

Jacques's eyebrows somehow rose even higher.

Petty continued, "I'm saying we are cooperating. When your credentials logged into one of our facilities, I got a note. This one felt personal, so I messaged."

Del said, "I appreciate it, and thank you for all your help. Where are you, if I may ask?"

"Singapore."

Del did a mental calculation. Five hours ahead of Kiev—about 7:00 p.m. "I've got to congratulate you," she said.

"You like the facility?"

"You know how many signs I saw for Strataform on the way in from the airport?"

"Eastern Europe is a big market for us."

"How many of these facilities do you have?"

"In Ukraine? More than a dozen. I'll have Artem give you a list." His smile faltered. "I assume you're tracking down Yuri Korshunov? And Lenny?"

"Any information you have would be useful."

"Not to mention legally required," Jacques added.

"I'm afraid that Lenny's . . . dalliances . . . with the Black Army weren't as harmless as I assumed. Not from what I'm seeing online now. Have you heard anything?"

Jacques's curious expression turned to a frown.

Del shook her head.

"I've enrolled your father in our Strataform Medical early trial program for cancer," Petty said. "We've begun to get involved in his primary care. I'll be happy to keep you updated."

"Thank you," Del said. "Very much."

"And I sent a gift to you."

"A gift?"

"At your hotel."

***

Jacques pulled out his Interpol badge and held it out, yelling, "*Merde! Putain!* Move away!" at the surging crowd outside the Strataform facility entrance.

Del had stopped on the stairs and had her camera out taking pictures, and not just of the Dnieper River flowing by in the distance. A buzz-cut young man in a tracksuit, with a placard in his hands, ran straight at Jacques, screaming something in Ukrainian. Del couldn't understand what he said, nor could she read the sign.

The man yelled, "Workers of the world unite!" as soon as he heard Jacques speak English. The man's face was apoplectic red as he spat the words out.

"Move aside," Jacques said, holding out his badge. He made an opening and pulled Del after him.

She put her phone away. When they arrived an hour ago, there had been a few loiterers, but the mob had grown to hundreds now, half of them waving signs and chanting in Ukrainian. She noticed a rotund man with a Mohawk, and a crisscross tattoo on his neck.

"Nice day you chose to visit this place," the Frenchman said. "Did you do this on purpose, to antagonize?" They pushed through the edge of the crowd.

"I had no idea," Del said.

It was the first of the month—May Day. A major Ukrainian national holiday, one of the most important on the socialist calendar. Today was the day to honor workers' rights and achievements, here and all over the world. A day for the worker.

The Strataform facility had almost none.

A nearly completely automated manufacturing facility that could pump out a million parts a day and yet run with just a handful of people on-site. Not popular on May Day, apparently, and Del doubted that the billboards all over town—literally all over Europe, as far as she could tell—were helping keep a low profile. A squad of riot police with plastic shields and rubber truncheons had arrived.

Jacques held up his badge again, and they let them through the forming police cordon.

"So he is sending you presents, hey?" he said as they crossed Redutna

Street to the Ukrainian Museum of History. The entrance there was empty.

"I have no idea what he's talking about," Del replied.

"You and Mr. Petty seem close."

"I met him once in New York."

"You make friends easily, it seems."

They stopped at the corner of Lavrska, the main thoroughfare, four lanes wide, that the winding Redutna led down to. The Ukrainian National History Museum was grandly named, but its appearance didn't live up. A gray corrugated metal roof angled over the arched structure that looked more like an abandoned aerodrome than a national landmark.

The tarmac of the road was weathered and cracked, the sidewalk uneven. The intersection of the two roads was marked by three truck tires, painted in alternating stripes of gray and white and potted with small shrubs and earth in their centers. It was the most cheerful thing on the street.

It was warm—hot in the direct midday sun—and Jacques wiped a hand across his bald brown pate. "You should not be messing with this Black Army. I know that in America this must be like a harmless joke, for people to join and post memes for the workers of the world. But here"— he pointed at the crowd, chanting as they faced the police—"this is a whole different thing. Ukraine is my specialty.'

"I don't need a babysitter."

Even as Del said this, she wondered how she could get a taxi back to the hotel. Could she flag one down? Did Uber work here? Google maps did, she already knew. A taxi from the hotel had dropped them off, and it was just a few miles, so at worst she could walk, but was that even safe?

"I'm making sure you don't suddenly decide to go off on your own," Jacques said, wiping perspiration from his brow. The armpits of his shirt were already dark. "Come on. Let's have a coffee."

He led her up a flight of stairs to a café. A fresh breeze blew in off the Dnieper River, visible beyond a massive figure that rose above the trees, shield and sword held high.

"That's the Motherland Monument," Jacques said of the robed sculpture gleaming in the sun. He had a habit of acting as tour guide. "Taller than the Statue of Liberty." He took another glance. "Better looking too."

They sat down at an open-air table overlooking the park. *Two espressos,* Jacques signaled to the waiter.

On the way out, Artem, the Strataform tour guide, had given Del a list of all the company's print farms in Ukraine. Sixteen of them, and half in the south. Several were near Melitopol—odd given the political instability and running battles in the area.

Jacques said, "Do you know the motto of the Black Army? *Death to all those who stand in the way of freedom for the working people.* Not very catchy, but clear enough. With a skull and crossbones on top. This is no joke."

"The Black Army hasn't existed in a hundred years," Del said. "Disbanded in 1922 when Nestor Makhno was executed." She had done her homework.

"But now experiencing a renaissance. Did you *see* those people outside Strataform?"

"That's why I took pictures—they might be members."

Del watched Jacques sizing her up. He alternated between being dismissive of her to the point of being rude, and then suddenly trying to be helpful, opening doors for her, explaining how this and that worked, making sure she had everything she needed. She responded in kind. A kind of cat-and-mouse game—or cat and dog. Today he was the chivalrous tour guide.

"In 1918," Jacques continued, "the Black Army carved out its own part of Ukraine, the Free Territory, and held on to it for years. In the south and east of the country—same place they are fighting now. The Russians with the ethnically pro-Russian locals against the Ukrainian forces, but now we have also separatist Ukrainian forces and a resurgence of the Black Army. It is more now than just an online splinter group that your friend Bondar was involved with. The situation is becoming very complicated. You are poking your nose where it could get cut off."

The coffee arrived, and Del thanked the waiter. "What would you do if it was *your* father who Korshunov shot?" She put the printouts of the Strataform locations in the front pocket of her backpack.

"I would be home with him." Jacques took a sip of his coffee and looked out at the Dnieper.

Del followed his eyes out to the broad blue-gray expanse. A tugboat pushed a long barge upstream. She had read that this was an important trade route in the Middle Ages, between Byzantium—the reformed Roman Empire—in the south, and the Baltic Sea in the north. Kiev itself was here mostly because of the rapids between the islands she saw in the distance. In medieval times, these had been impassable, and so a village, then a city, had sprung up. Difficult passages often yielded beautiful results.

"I read your files," Jacques said. "What I could find. Congratulations on the Lowell-Vandeweghe case. You stopped a serial murderer. But I warn you, this is another world, with different rules—sometimes none."

"Director Dartmouth picked me because she thought I had the right tools for the job."

"Be very careful of that one," the Frenchman said. "A viper in sheep's clothing."

Del had read that Director Dartmouth gutted one of the French Directorate's programs, showing how the data collected was useless. "She does her job, like I do."

"You are an expert in spotting lies, yes?"

"As well as anyone in law enforcement."

"Now I think you are telling a small lie yourself, no? Tell me, in the faces of the people in that crowd outside Strataform, did they look as if they were lying?"

"They were yelling in Ukrainian."

"Your trick, your special vision"—he waved a finger around his face—"does it not work in any language?"

"It's a combination of a lot of factors."

"Like what?" When Del didn't answer right away, he added, "Perhaps that they don't even know that they're lying. Those people outside that factory—they want jobs back for workers, but we know that is impossible. Technology has passed them by. We all want cheaper televisions. Even they do. We can't get prices like that from factories filled with people."

"They're expressing anger."

"That is true, but then they go home or to the pub and start telling stories about how jobs should be brought back to workers. They quote 'facts' that are wrong, and they may even know they are wrong."

"That's what politicians do too."

"It's still lying."

"They're demonstrating for workers' rights," Del said.

"I have great sympathy for the unprotected masses." Jacques snorted and affected his best Gallic shrug. "Workers' rights. Human rights. This is all a myth. None of it is real. Purely imaginary." He tapped his temple.

"I'll have to disagree."

The Frenchman tapped his espresso cup. "This, and this"—he slapped the table. "This is reality. The physical. Everything else is a myth. Created by, and existing only in, the mind. France, the United States—these are all fictions."

"The United States is not a fiction," Del countered.

"Nationhood is a fairytale created by politicians, one designed to bend our minds. What is happening here, right now, in the Ukraine is—"

A thumping concussion shook the concrete gallery beneath their feet. A moment later, a rush of air and screaming. Del jumped up from the table and ran to the railing behind them. A churning maelstrom of dust and papers billowed up a hundred feet into the air in front of the Strataform facility.

16

Kiev's night skyline glittered through the open curtains of Del's fifth-floor room at the Hyatt Regency. The tiny coffeemaker sputtered as it finished making a cup. It hadn't taken her long to get used to living in a hotel room. They all looked more or less the same: bed, dresser with a television over it, a small table with guidebooks to local restaurants and the in-room dining. The ritual of packing and unpacking.

What she wasn't used to was *that*.

A Strataform Replicator, the size of a small refrigerator, squatted on a table in the corner. The mysterious gift Adam Petty had promised. Arrived yesterday, Tuesday, since Monday was the May Day holiday. Del had almost forgotten he said he had a gift for her. She had expected maybe a coupon for a steak restaurant, not an entire self-contained manufacturing system. Looking at this new toy, she had to admit, though, as an artist she was fascinated with the possibilities.

Del removed the packaging and started to look through the documentation. She turned it on and connected it to her laptop, then to the hotel internet after a few minutes. The login prompt popped up on her screen, and the Strataform began formatting itself. Its single orange light turned on.

She had already been in Kiev a week. As part of the Interpol contingent, she had attended more than a dozen meetings with elections officials. The constant worry was Russian influence. Only ten days to the elections, and the country was starting to come apart like a matryoshka doll thrown from a window.

Suweil's team was monitoring the digital spaces around the campaign. He sent in reports of possible influence vectors and suspicious bot networks in social media. An attempt to bend reality of the collective mind, Jacques kept telling her, and it wasn't just the Russians.

She opened up the Word program on her laptop. It took about fifteen minutes to finish writing her report, which she sent directly to Katherine. Eyes only.

"At the meeting today," she typed at the end of the report, "Mr. Rostislav was not entirely honest when confronted on mounting irregularities."

***

Official duties took up half of Del's time. The rest she spent sightseeing.

The outline of the Budynok Mytropolyta, the palace that was home of the Kiev Metropolitans for almost a thousand years, was just visible through her hotel window. The word "metropolitan" came from the Old Latin *metropolitaus,* meant "resident of an ecclesiastical city." In this case, the Kyiv Metropolitans were bishops of all Russia under the pope of Constantinople—modern-day Istanbul—the seat of the Roman Empire in the early Middle Ages.

A deep sense of history permeated the city in a way Del had never experienced before. The millennium-old Mytropolyta was just across the street from her hotel, next to St. Sophia's cathedral and surrounded by so many art galleries and museums per block that she had to remind herself she was here for work.

On her first night, the taxi driver who picked her up—Igor again— was supposed to take her to a restaurant, but when the young man found out that it was her first time in Kiev, he took her on an impromptu drive around the city to point out all the landmarks.

Del had a large corkboard on one wall of her room, with a map of

Ukraine stuck on it. In the center was a picture of Yuri Korshunov, pinned to the approximate location of the city of Melitopol. Del had requested to go to southern Ukraine as part of the monitoring process, but she'd been refused. It was unsafe, the Ukraine Bureau said. She would be out of her depth.

They weren't wrong.

She couldn't just go out on the street and interview people the way she did as a detective in New York. She had other people pinned on the corkboard, too. Bondar, for one, the mysterious head of the MakerArmy corporation, now somehow affiliated with the resurgent Black Army. She had other suspected leaders of the Black Army up there with him on the board.

But it all centered on Yuri Korshunov, the Russians, and their commanders.

Back at the UN Building in New York, had Voloshyn even been the target?

What was Korshunov doing in Melitopol?

The city was on the southern coast of Ukraine, close to the Sea of Azov, near the border of Crimea, which had been annexed by Russian invasion in February 2014, in very recent history. To most outside observers, the main purpose of the invasion was to gain control of the massive naval base at Sevastopol. West of this was the naval base that America was building with the Ukrainians—the one Voloshyn wanted to cancel construction of.

Control of the Black Sea—and, by extension, the entire region—hung in the balance.

The whole area south of eastern Ukraine was now disputed territory, centered on the city of Donetsk, where the ill-fated Malaysian airliner had been shot down in 2014. Del drew notes on her corkboard—the Ukrainian Seventeenth Armored Brigade had been sent into Melitopol and Donetsk, along with the Ninety-Third Mechanized Brigade. Russia had amassed its Spetsnaz brigades just over the border in Rostov, as well as along the border of Crimea. Pro-Russia separatists were in open conflict with Ukrainian forces, but freedom fighters were now attacking both sides, and from reports, these forces had fractured further, into internal fighting within cities and districts.

It was difficult to understand what was going on.

The area to the south and east matched closely with the zone that the Black Army had claimed and maintained as the Free Territories in the Ukrainian revolution in 1918, about a hundred years ago. In America, the Black Army had now become a popular rallying call in online circles for civic freedom, but in the same way that soccer moms put "Free Tibet" stickers on the bumpers of their Priuses.

Here it had a different, more direct meaning.

When Del was having coffee with Jack outside the Strataform facility, there had been an explosion in front of the factory. A homemade bomb. Two people injured. The Black Army hadn't claimed responsibility, but the incident had moved the organization closer to the status of international terrorists by Interpol's reckoning.

She stared at her corkboard and tried to make some sense of what was happening—to this place and, maybe more importantly, to herself.

What did she think she was accomplishing? What was the goal? That she was going to find and arrest Korshunov, an ex-KGB assassin hiding in a war zone, all by herself? With no weapon and no real authority here? And was her motivation purely revenge?

Her father hadn't even been the target. It was just a mistake, maybe just like her being here. Interpol already had a warrant for Korshunov, as it did for Bondar, who was now classified as an international terrorist linked to the Black Army. What was she hoping to accomplish by being here?

Her phone beeped.

***

Suweil's face appeared in the chat box on Del's laptop screen.

"Nice Replicator," he said.

Del turned to look at the muscular box, with its glowing orange light, on the table behind her. The laptop's camera pointed toward it. "A gift from Adam Petty," she said.

"Was it your birthday?"

"A few weeks ago."

"My attempt at humor. Seems you are good at making friends."

The same thing Jacques had said. Odd.

"I sent you some pictures. These are from in front of the Strataform facility the other day, just before the bomb went off. You think you can match them to any members of the Black Army?"

"I am on it."

Strataform had submitted security footage from outside cameras, but Del figured her camera's pictures might have better resolution.

She said, "And can you keep it confidential?"

"The pictures?"

"I mean, not secret, but don't go telling everyone I took pictures at Strataform."

It wasn't on her list of official duties, and she wanted to keep her profile as low as possible.

"What I really want," Del said, "is to know if you can find an area where some of these people may be congregating. Places where they tend to be found."

Suweil's eyebrows furrowed together and parted a few times, as if they were chewing on an idea. Finally, he said, "I can try to match backgrounds of these people in other pictures online, to vacation pictures. But if you go to one of these gatherings, you will stick out like the spicy thumb."

Del let the butchered simile go. This place was so chaotic, as long as she kept her mouth shut, she should be okay.

"If you are going to be investigating these Black Army people," Suweil said, "perhaps we should switch to communicating via a back channel. They have excellent cyber skills—very good at intercepting regular channels."

"Whatever you think," Del said.

"I've begun working on the shell casing you gave me from the NYPD. I will be soaking it in a batch of chemicals that should be able to get more DNA out. Of course, we've already found Katherine's."

The director was the one who picked up the casing.

"Send me any information as soon as you get it," Del said.

She sat on the couch, opened up the Strataform instruction manual, and leafed through it. "Can I print a 3-D image of a fingerprint with this thing? One that will fool a biometric device, like a phone fingerprint reader?"

"It takes some skill. Most people are making toys with it, for their kids. That is the biggest market in America. You can make shoes, too."

"Shoes?" The Replicator's orange cyclops eye seemed to be looking back at her.

Manufacturing on demand, the kid at the Maker Faire show in New York had said, was the beginning of the Fourth Industrial Revolution. No need to bring shoes or even have them delivered. Just download a file and print out and, when done, insert into the refabricator at the top, and the machine would melt down and reuse the plastics via its own built-in recycling system. Maybe the answer to the mounting environmental crisis. This was part of Strataform's marketing avalanche.

"I could print a gun with this thing?"

"You know this is illegal."

"I'm saying hypothetically."

"Hypothetically, you could download a file from the dark web. Should I send you a hypothetical link?"

Del checked her watch. "I better get going. Big meeting with Dartmouth tomorrow morning." The director was flying in from New York for Del's second meeting with the Russians.

17

Del woke up early the next morning and took a limo to meet the director at the airport.

After a slog through rush-hour traffic, they reached the southern edge of Kiev. The limo left the main highway and coasted to a stop on a side street dead-ended by a pile of concrete blocks and straggly low bushes. Thin yellow-striped metal stanchions bordered the empty sidewalk, and a basic wrought iron fence with a wooden backing surrounded the building. On the street corner was a billboard with yet another Strataform ad.

The divider window of the limo slid down, and the driver said something in Ukrainian. Director Dartmouth spoke back and pointed toward the pile of concrete blocks.

"I told him we will be about an hour," she said to Del. "Before we get out, I want to be clear. You are here as my assistant. Observe and watch. Pay attention. You understand?"

Del nodded. "Got it."

The building looked nondescript, not what she expected for the Russian consulate. She had imagined large concrete dividers, rows of security fencing, and police dogs. Outside central Kiev, the buildings became drab, more uniform. "Soviet-era" was how the cabbie Igor had described them on their excursion a few days ago. Everything was in gray concrete, which matched the cloud-covered sky. Just past the low scrub ahead, a squarish-looking apartment block rose up with the hill.

They got out of the limo together and walked around the corner, then straight about two hundred feet. The area was deserted, no other people on the street at all. No other cars parked. A small guard shack of gray corrugated steel sat at the corner of the building. Director Dartmouth walked up to the window. It slid open, and she offered her credentials and indicated for Del to do the same. The guard inside looked at them, checked the pictures on their cards, and looked at the computer screen.

They waited.

The man said something in either Russian or Ukrainian and handed back their papers.

"Let's go," Dartmouth said.

A double set of metal doors opened, and they were ushered into a hallway. Inside were men with automatic weapons slung from single-point harnesses. Impassive faces. They went through a set of metal detectors, after which they were asked to take out all their electronics and everything from their pockets. Next, they went through a millimeter wave scanner.

They were not given back their cell phones and devices. "Leave everything," said one of the guards. Buzz-cut hair. Muscular.

When Del took a step forward, the guard put out a hand and pointed at her ears.

"Everything."

He meant her hoop earrings. She undid her belt as well, then took off her shoes. They provided blue slippers.

Before being led through the next set of double doors, they went through one final physical search. Del almost expected to be shown into a separate room, given a gown, and told to undress.

***

Pink folds of fat spilled from the voluminous Russian ambassador's tight shirt collar. Katherine introduced Del as her assistant, and he waddled around his desk and offered his hand.

"Anatoly Ushakov," he said, giving Del a damp handshake and a wide smile. "You are from New York?"

"That's right."

"I love the Yankees. My daughter is at NYU. I have heard of you. That famous case in Long Island. The serial killer? Yes, that was you?"

Del glanced at Katherine, who shrugged with her eyes. "Yeah, that was me," Del replied.

"Can I take a picture? I post it to my Facebook? My daughter will love it."

"Sure, I guess."

Ushakov offered his phone to Katherine, who gamely took a picture of him squeezing Del to his side. When he took his phone back, he said, "Security coming in was not offensive? Not too invasive? Very sorry we had to take all your electronic devices. One cannot be too careful."

"Of course not," Katherine replied.

Del looked around the office. Faded green carpets, potted trees with shiny plastic leaves to each side of the dark wood desk. Peeling wallpaper, pictures of the premier of the Politburo and the FSB chief behind the desk. The heavy stink of cigar, with an undertone of sweat from the man now ambling back to the other side of the desk.

Del noticed something unusual. On each of the electrical outlets along the walls, the white plastic seemed smudged in a rainbow. The patterning stood out in her vision—something fresh, like an oil slick, within the *ishma*-tinted shades that she was sure only she could see.

Del and Katherine took two chairs in front.

"Ambassador," Dartmouth said, "we have a long list of infractions using social media accounts, and complaints from polling officials charging intimidation."

The man spread his arms wide. "We are not interfering in any way."

Del watched the heat pass into his forehead. He was hot and sweaty to begin with, and a terrible liar to boot. His periorbital area flared.

Catherine said, "Are you funding or supporting the Black Army?"

The heat signature in his face cooled. "Not at all."

Some truth. "Not in any way?"

"Yuri Korshunov," Del blurted out.

Catherine clucked and frowned at her.

Del persisted. "Is he still working for the FSB?"

She watched him closely.

"We are the ones who issued the arrest," the ambassador said.

Almost no heat in his face.

"So he was not sent to America by the security services," Del said.

He either didn't know the truth or had suddenly become a very good liar. No change in the blood flow across his face as he shook his head and said, "Not by us."

Katherine said, "I apologize for—"

A concussion *whumped* in the distance.

An alarm rang out, followed by a piercing shriek from the corner of the office. A juddering explosion shook the walls. Plaster chunks and dust fell from the ceiling. The door opened, and a man yelled in Russian. Two more came running in and grabbed the ambassador. A bright flash before a shower of glass shards fell over Del.

The shock wave knocked them to the floor.

18

The setting sun cast angled rays through the blinds, illuminating glowing dust motes in the wake of the two dark-suited men who had just deposited a heavily laden, paint-spattered bedsheet onto Commissioner Grigory Georgiev's desk.

Katherine and Del stood side by side with the commissioner in his cherrywood-paneled inner sanctum. An ornately carved antique desk dominated the space, and a copper-studded brown leather couch and chair bordered the expensive Persian carpet in the center. It had more of the opulent feel of the Mytropolyta—nothing like the drab, purely functional space of the Russian embassy.

All three of them stared at the rumpled bedsheet. With a thumb and forefinger, the commissioner pulled it back.

"I am very glad neither of you was hurt," Grigory said. "Would you like a drink?"

Del's suit jacket and pants were still covered in drywall dust.

"I'll have one," Katherine said. "The US is recalling all nonessential staff."

The commissioner flicked open the sheet.

"So, this is it?" Del said.

"One that didn't explode," Grigory replied.

The makeshift attack drone looked like a toy. Four-foot wingspan and three-foot fuselage, with a model airplane gas engine at the front. The wings and body were transparent grayish plastic. The composite parts looked taped together.

"It uses what my technical people call a Raspberry Pi computer engine," Grigory said. "We have notified your father that you are all right—through official channels."

The attack had inflamed an already volatile mix. The Russian embassy had been one part of coordinated assaults on government buildings across Ukraine, at the same time as cyber events. Government systems and mobile networks went down for the first few hours in the chaos.

Sixteen attack drones had hit the Russian Embassy, one of them blowing straight through the window of the ambassador's office, where Katherine and Del were having their meeting. They had scrambled downstairs and jumped straight back into the waiting limo.

The Black Army had initially claimed responsibility, but confusingly, another message was relayed denying its involvement. The intelligence services said this indicated a possible split in the faction.

"May I take a part?" Del asked. "Of the wings, as a sample?"

The police commissioner frowned but then shrugged. *Why not?*

Del pulled free a piece and held it up close to her eyes. From her pocket, she took out a lighter. Holding one corner, she clicked on the flame and let it burn. The plastic gave off a vinegary-acrid smell with flame, yellow sparks, and black smoke.

"Cellulose acetate," Del said. "This wasn't made with a Strataform Replicator. More of an amateur type of technology, like something from a MakerArmy device."

The commissioner was impressed. "The same thing our forensic team said."

"Can we send this back to Lyon?" Katherine asked.

Grigory nodded. "Our team is saying they must have a production facility in the south, somewhere in the disputed territory."

"Who is 'they'?" Del asked.

"Has to be related to the Black Army."

Grigory went to a cupboard in the corner of the room and got out two glasses, pouring three fingers of amber liquid into each—one for himself and one for the director.

"So you think they have a . . ." Del paused before using the word. ". . . *print farm* in the south?"

"They're using it to build drones, weapons," Grigory replied. "Melitopol would be our guess as their center of operations."

"I'd like to go down," Del said.

"I think perhaps you should go back to Lyon," Katherine said.

When Del didn't reply, Grigory said, "You think it's coincidence that two members of your family have almost been killed by the Black Army?"

Del hadn't thought of it that way.

"I'm saying it is a possibility. We are still working on guesses."

"Perhaps your father was an accident, but they are now following you. It was no accident that the attack on the Russian embassy occurred within minutes of two members of the Washington Bureau arriving."

Grigory took a drink of his Scotch. "Ukrainian media is sympathetic to the attack. Retaliation for Russian assassinations. I can't argue with that. Hundreds of killings gone unanswered. And then we have the assassination of Markov by poisoned umbrella tip on Waterloo Bridge, and Litivinko by polonium in London."

"Assassination by Russian security forces in Ukraine is a sad reality," Katherine said. She took a sip of her drink. "Violence has become normalized. In the past two years, the Kremlin has supplied arms and funding that killed fifteen thousand people here. Mundane now. For a few thousand dollars, people are executed all over the country, and this technology is making it worse. The same kind of gun used to shoot your father had been recovered from fourteen incidents the past month."

"My dad was the first? With a 3-D-printed gun?"

"It has sparked copycats. This dog is out of its bag."

Del needed somewhere to start if she was ever going to unravel this snowballing mess. An itch started in the back of her mind. "Was there anything . . . anything *unusual* before any of this started? Maybe involving Americans?"

Grigory put thumb to lip and leaned back in his chair. "There was an art dealer."

From the corner of her eye, Del sensed a flash of heat in Director Dartmouth's face.

Grigory continued. "An American disappeared at the Persian Palace Hotel. Hutchins."

Del let the name float around in her head for a few seconds. "Wait, *Timothy* Hutchins?"

"That's right."

He was a New Yorker. Not someone Del knew personally, but who might be within her mother's wider circle of acquaintances. She had read in the *Times* about him going missing back in March. She remembered going to one of his exhibits at MoMA a few years back. The worm of the memory grew as she recalled his fantastical, alien-like works of art.

"He was shot?" Del said.

"We are not sure."

"You don't know how he died?"

Grigory finished off his scotch. "To be honest, it is hard even to describe."

***

Del uncorked last night's half-finished bottle of wine and swung open the patio door of her hotel room. She had a message on her phone from Suweil—something urgent but not that urgent, he said in the subject line. The news of the attack at the Russian Embassy was front page in the news cycle all over the world.

Why had the ambassador taken a picture with Del? Katherine said it was a way of getting a clear image of her for their security apparatus. He hadn't lied about putting it up on his social media feed. Del had brought the picture of the two of them together up on her phone—him beaming, her looking distinctly uncomfortable.

She sat down at the patio table, looked down at her pants, still covered in bits of plaster. She returned inside, changed into jeans, and put the dust-covered clothes in a hamper bag in the closet and marked it for dry cleaning. Back on the patio, she opened her laptop. Purple twilight faded into night, and the lights of the city bathed the clouds from below.

Del clicked a button on her laptop and turned on the video of Lenny Bondar.

"The Black Army had nothing to do with the attack on the Russian Embassy," Lenny said, "and the MakerArmy 3-D printer was not used in the construction of the drones used in the attack. We challenge the authorities to send us parts for analysis."

He went on and on in the video, describing myriad reasons why his group had nothing to do with the attack. The details seemed a little damning, the level of knowledge feeling as though it implied too much knowledge. He stood in front of a chipped concrete wall with no other markings.

Why was Bondar suddenly the front man for the Black Army? He'd been connected with them, sure, but his MakerArmy 3-D printer company was mostly a commercial enterprise, not a social one. He had an affiliation with the Black Army online, but that was a far cry from posting videos representing them—especially after a major terrorist attack.

Del closed the video and texted Suweil. A few seconds later, a box popped up on her laptop screen with a soft beeping sound to indicate an incoming call. She accepted, and the forensic scientist's chubby brown face appeared in a video on her screen.

"Are you very okay?"

Del said, "I'm fine."

"It seems to be a very dangerous time to be where you are."

Speaking to Suweil had a way of lightening up any situation. She smiled. "What have you got for me?"

"Did you see the video of Bondar today?"

"Just now."

"That concrete wall he was standing in front of—I've made a match. I ran a cross-correlation with pictures you took from outside the Strataform facility." An image popped on Del's screen: the heavyset man with a Mohawk. "I matched the backgrounds with pictures that people are posting on Instagram."

"People?"

"Young people. I think you would call them 'club kids.'"

"You have a location?"

"I've got an area. I'll send you everything I have."

An email popped up on Del's screen. She thanked Suweil and closed the connection. She looked at the glittering city lights and took another sip of her wine. Her laptop was almost out of power, so she retrieved the cord and plugged it in.

Still bent over holding the plug, she knelt to inspect the wall socket. Its color was rainbow patterned in faint *ishma*-red, just like the ones in the Russian embassy. Strange, but perhaps this was merely a by-product of the manufacturing here.

Del made another call. It was still lunchtime in New York.

"Hello?"

"Angel, this is—"

"I know who this is. My God, are you okay?"

"I'm fine," Del recited. How many times would she have to say the same thing today? "The cell phone networks were down, and I couldn't call for a while. How is Rodrigo?"

"He's good."

"And Charlie?"

"Good. You sure you're okay?"

"Listen, Angel, I have something I need some help with."

There was a pause on the other end before he replied, "Sure, anything."

"I know the last time you got involved in one of my cases, it didn't end well."

"Come on, just ask."

"You think you could go look in on my parents?" Not that she didn't trust her sister, but she knew her. Missy wouldn't want to tell Del anything bad when she was away, when there was nothing she could do. "When I was back there two weeks ago, he was doing great, but . . ."

"I understand."

"And you think you can ask my mother about Timothy Hutchins?"

News stories from six months ago were that Hutchins had gone missing on a European trip, originally thought to be missing in France but never left the Ukraine, eventually linked to a botched investigation by Kiev police. His only family was a sister who was seventy-three. Del had mentioned Hutchins before, but Grigory bringing him up again was unusual enough to warrant more investigation.

"That art dealer guy that disappeared, right?"

"He had a sister in Queens. Maybe you could go have a talk with her, too?"

Someone knocked at Del's room. She thanked Angel, hung up, and opened the door a crack. "Hello?"

It was Jacques.

"You okay?" he asked.

"I'm fine," she said yet again. "Thanks for asking."

They exchanged small talk for a few seconds before Jacques excused himself. "If I were you," he said as he walked off down the hallway, "I wouldn't go out anywhere tonight."

She waited until she heard his door close before she grabbed her jacket, stepped out into the hallway, and took the elevator down.

***

The dented red Lada raced to a stop at the curb. The driver's window already open, Igor's head of black hair popped out. "My favorite customer. Hungry? I got some good places you can get late-night food."

Del ignored his question and opened the passenger-side door. She slid into the technicolor backseat and held up her phone. "Igor, you know where this is?"

His black hair formed a halo around his prematurely balding head. He frowned. "You don't want to be going there."

"But I do."

"It will be mostly empty at this hour."

"Empty?"

"I mean, it will maybe just be getting going."

"Then let's get going."

"Maybe it is not a place for a person like you."

"You mean a policewoman?"

"You're not from here. I don't mean because you are a woman—"

"You'll be with me, right?"

Igor gave a gap-toothed grin. "That is right. You are correct."

***

They drove past the spotlighted gold domes and sparkling musical fountains of Independence Square, which was already teeming with wandering bands of tourists this early in the season. It was warm, almost seventy, and Del wore a simple black tank top and her Nikes.

She opened her phone and followed their progress. They went down past the Olympic sports complex, curved around the St. Nicholas Cathedral and down toward the southern end of the city. The architecture flattened out, from tall buildings into individual homes and cottages, and then into warehouses, half of them looking derelict. Crowds of young people wandered the streets in knots. Thumping music floated through the air in the distance.

"I guess they have started early," Igor said.

Del checked her watch: 8:00 p.m.

The taxi slowed as the crowds grew thicker. In a side street, a bonfire of wooden pallets roared, its flames rising thirty feet, sooty black smoke snaking up into the black sky. Police stood on one corner, not so much policing as simply standing their ground.

The car stopped.

"This is it," Igor said nervously from the front. "You are sure?"

Del craned her neck forward to look out the window. "Stereo Plaza," announced a sign high up on the side of the red-brick warehouse. Heavy bass shook the concrete beneath the Lada's tires.

"I'm just going to go have a look around inside," Del said. "Five minutes."

Igor repeated, "You are sure?" The easy smile was gone from his face.

Del handed over a wad of twenties, US. The taxi driver took it and held up his phone. "You have my number?"

She clapped his shoulder for encouragement, his more than hers. He looked as nervous as she felt.

Del walked down a halfpipe tunnel of concrete covered in layers of graffiti, toward the entrance of the Stereo Plaza. Propped up behind a guardrail at the top edge of the halfpipe, a threesome of hooded teens, wreathed in marijuana smoke, watched her walk by. A woman in a tight pink tube top with long blond hair and dark sunglasses, with a studded glass choker collar, danced by herself in slow motion to a different beat from the one thudding out of the Plaza ahead. The woman's white sneakers had three-inch soles.

Del advanced toward the end of a loosely assembled lineup.

What did she want? To find Lenny? She just wanted to talk to him. He hadn't seemed dangerous when they met back in New York. Then again, after what happened today, half the Ukrainian police force had to be on the lookout. If she didn't find him first, she wouldn't be having a conversation with him anytime soon.

She reached the end of the line—at least a hundred kids, none of them more than seventeen years old, dressed in a kaleidoscope of mismatched fashion. Up at the front, she thought she saw a guy with a Mohawk, and she was about to step out of the line to have a better look when someone grabbed her from behind.

"Excuse me," said a male voice.

He pulled on her arm and tried to spin her around.

Del turned and crouched, not quite alarmed but definitely on edge. She half expected to be offered drugs, and ten years before, she might not have been ready to say no.

Two feet from her, a man with a weathered face stared back. Sixty. Maybe more. Homeless? He was dressed in ragged clothing. Those features were old, Del realized, but they were hardened. And those eyes.

She knew those eyes.

Blood drained from her face. She grabbed instinctively for her gun, then swore under her breath, realizing she was unarmed.

The man was Yuri Korshunov.

She lowered into a fighting stance. Scanned his hands for a weapon. Checked her six and left and right.

"I just want to talk," he said.

Del didn't reply and backed up two paces. He was maybe six feet, two hundred pounds. One punch to the throat would drop him in his tracks, but then, he was KGB trained. He'd be ready for something like that. Maybe sweep his feet? Get low?

Without saying another word, he turned and walked away. Del advanced, then hesitated. A trap? Drawing her in? Who else was he with? As he began to disappear into the crowd, she jumped forward.

What should she do? Grab him?

Wrestle a trained assassin to the ground? Maybe she should . . .

Before she could even complete the thought, two men emerged from the crowd. One of them put his arm around Yuri's neck; the other bent down and wrapped a huge arm around both his legs. They lifted him like a sack of turnips.

19

Had the men seen her?

Del pushed past three young guys in nylon-net tops, ropes of gold chain around their necks. One of them said something as he staggered back. His eyelids drooped, face slack. Drugged, spaced out, all three of them.

She mumbled an apology and focused on the men wrestling with the squirming and cursing Korshunov. Their captive kicked free, and the man holding his feet yelled, grabbed him by the collar, and slammed a fist the size of a roast chicken into his face. Blood spattered onto the ground. The first man muscled Korshunov to the concrete and put something—a rag—over the meaty pulp of his nose.

No one in the crowd seemed to notice. Were these policemen?

The attackers—thickset, in dark suits, bald heads rising neckless from wide shoulders, matching armbands in fluorescent green—could have been clones. Which gave her another thought: maybe they were bouncers.

To anyone in the crowd, it looked like doormen taking out an unruly patron. No one paid any attention. Either these men were working for the Stereo Palace, or they knew the armbands the staff used. Del slotted the theory away. No way these guys were staff—which meant this was a planned abduction.

They had known that Yuri Korshunov was going to be here.

Another kid loomed in front of Del.

Del said, "Excuse me," as she stepped around him. The two men had Korshunov back in the air and shuffled along the concrete half-pipe, toward the street.

A young woman now blocked her path.

"Excuse me," Del repeated.

The woman stumbled into Del. She tried to shove her away. Del took her eyes away from Korshunov for a second to look at the girl. Woman? Maybe. On second glance, she wasn't sure. Maybe it was a young man. No, definitely female.

Four stiff braids shot out like helicopter wings from the back of her head, which was otherwise shaved except for a single tuft of black hair in front. A torn net tank top covered with a tiny coat of faux fur in black with a short skirt, frayed nylons, and scuffed Doc Martens. Three blue dots of paint—one on each cheek, and one between the eyes—and bright red eye shadow around recessed dark eyes.

The girl said something in Ukrainian—Russian?—and Del said that she was sorry and tried to hold the girl upright while keeping her eyes on Korshunov. His captors had reached a white panel van by the curb. The side door slid open. They chucked him unceremoniously inside and climbed in after him.

The door slammed shut.

Del sprinted the next fifty feet as the van squealed away. She rapped on the Lada taxi, driver's side. The window rolled down. Thick smoke curled out, accompanied by a twanging Bollywood beat.

Igor singing along with a joint between his lips. "Everything o—"

Del opened the door swung into the backseat. "That van. See it?"

It turned a corner up ahead and disappeared.

Igor blew out a mouthful of smoke. "Yeah." The joint dangled.

"Christ, Igor, is that weed?"

"It is a party, no?"

"Follow them. Get that van."

"Get it?"

"Follow it. Come on, hurry up." She resisted the urge to jump into the front seat and shove him aside.

Igor squinted and leaned forward over the steering wheel. Even in the dim light, his eyes looked bloodshot. He pointed. "That van?"

Del nodded urgently. "Go, go, go."

Igor threw the joint out the window and put the Lada into gear. It lurched forward before juddering to a stop, almost throwing Del over into the front seat. The heavy Indian Bollywood beat dropped into a bass rhythm.

"Sorry," Igor said.

He fumbled and finally got into the right gear, and the Lada pulled into the street. They had to weave left, then right, between revelers on their way into the rave. Del pointed up the street, making sure Igor's red eyes kept focus on what they were chasing.

Were those men Interpol?

Possible. She had never seen the agency in action, but then, Interpol didn't arrest people. They—*we*, she corrected herself—relied on local law enforcement. So maybe these were Grigory's guys, undercover men. That would make sense.

Except that the van had turned away from downtown.

The Lada squealed around the corner of a gas station and onto the empty street the van had gone up Del's stomach felt as if it fell through the rusted floorboard, until she saw the white flash of a panel in the distance.

"There!" She jabbed a finger.

"I am on it." Igor turned up the booming Bollywood tune and shoved down on the accelerator. The Lada's lawnmower engine screamed with everything it had.

Another thought chilled Del.

Was it the Russians?

They looked like what she imagined FSB would look like, and the Russians certainly wanted to get their hands on Korshunov. Would they kill him? Or was this something else?

She was out of her depth.

They sped up the potholed street, past a disintegrating brick building with exposed metal beams. Spotlights illuminated a billboard for Saxon

Radio 96.4. The crumbling sidewalk was paneled with green siding. The Lada raced after the van, almost going up on two wheels as it took the curve at speed.

It was an on-ramp for a highway.

Del checked her phone's map. The highway was E95. It led straight east, over the Dnieper and toward Russia. She did a quick check. The nearest border was three hours away, right next to Belarus.

Igor's head was down, his eyes almost at steering wheel level. He was as stoned as those kids at the party. The car lurched as it threaded its way through the evening traffic. The young cabbie was no expert in surveillance. How could whoever they were following not see them?

Del's eyes went back to her phone. Her finger hovered over the message app. Should she call Jacques? In retrospect, it had been dumb to leave without him, but he wouldn't have let her come out—then she wouldn't be here at all.

Should she call the director? Better to leave a message. As a car swerved around them, she pushed a connection button for her boss and began to text.

Up ahead, the van dropped onto an exit ramp.

"They're heading north," Igor said. "Onto Ukrainky Boulevard."

Del changed back from the texting app to the map. That street led back into the center of the city. Maybe these *were* Grigory's men.

Or maybe American?

Was this an extradition? The Justice Department was still angry that Korshunov had shot someone on US soil, and positively fuming that the United Nations had taken over the investigation.

Traffic slowed as they followed the van down the ramp. It was only four cars ahead now.

"Can you turn down that music?" Del asked.

Igor nodded and turned the dial low. He glanced at Del, who raised her hands in defeat. He turned the radio off.

Up ahead, the van slowed to a normal pace. Not a hint that they suspected a tail—least of all from a faded red Lada trailing marijuana smoke. Ukrainky Boulevard was a six-lane road, three each way, bordered by twenty-story apartment blocks in concrete the color of raw hamburger.

Nice touch, Del thought. Did they think the pink would brighten the place up?

The van took a side street.

"Hold back a bit," she said.

They stopped at the corner and let the van continue another half block before following it. They kept their distance. The van weaved, ducking up streets but never quite disappearing from view. A construction crane loomed overhead.

The neighborhood looked familiar.

"Are we near the Motherland Monument?" Del asked. That was next to the Strataform facility she had visited two days ago.

The van ground to an abrupt stop beside a small overpass. Exhaust curled from the tailpipe. The body's metal had rusty patches. Not exactly CIA material, but then, what did she really know of the CIA?

The van's back door slid open.

20

Three men tumbled out of the van. One stood up, pointed at the other two. A gun in his hand. The two on the ground recoiled, their hands coming up in both protection and submission.

Del expected the crack of gunfire.

Nothing.

It was Yuri Korshunov holding the weapon. It must have misfired, or perhaps it wasn't loaded. Or he simply hadn't fired. Whatever the reason, he threw the pistol at one of the men's heads before turning to run.

"You know this man? Igor asked. "An old boyfriend? He hurt you?"

The overpass the van was on covered a concrete culvert half hidden in chest-high grass. Korshunov ran down the edge of the concrete wall and into the grass. The two men were already back on their feet and scrambling down after him. The van's tires squealed as it accelerated down the street.

"Did this man hurt you?" Igor repeated.

They disappeared into the darkness at the bottom of the small ravine. It would be suicide to go down there in the dark. Even for Del. She needed to call for backup.

"I'm just saying, maybe, like you hired those men to hurt him?" Igor said.

Del finally caught on to what the cabbie was getting at. "No, no, it's nothing like that."

With an eye on the semidarkness at the bottom of the ravine, she turned on her phone. The battery was redlining but still had at least fifteen minutes. She considered calling Grigory but brought up Katherine's number again. In the end, she texted Suweil.

Something rustled the grass and bushes near the bottom of the culvert. Korshunov reappeared from the bushes. The men had run straight past him.

Igor saw what was happening. "You have a gun?" He opened the glovebox.

Del said, "You stay here."

Korshunov said he wanted to talk, right? She could grab him, shove him into the cab, and get the hell to somewhere safe.

Glancing over his shoulder, Korshunov walked into the tunnel beneath the overpass. He hadn't seen Del or Igor in their car. The kidnappers' van turned at the far end of the street, the two men running after it, and disappeared from view.

Del opened her door and stepped out into the dim night. She listened. Wind fluttered the leaves overhead, and crickets chirped. The sky was cloudless. The stars had already come out, the Big Dipper high overhead. At least that was familiar. She didn't hear any other cars.

She stopped to send her text message to Suweil, then hit Katherine's number. It went to voice mail. She hung up.

"Damn it."

She sidestepped down the embankment and into the wet, tall grass. Her Nikes sank into the squishy, marshy mud at the bottom of the ravine. It smelled earthy and wet, with a faint sweet stink of rot. Cold oozed into her socks and between her toes. She made her way gingerly toward the tunnel's entrance.

"Yuri, this is Delta Devlin." She held up her hands, palms out in surrender. "I'm Sergeant Devlin's daughter." He had to know that name, right? "You said you wanted to talk."

Silence. Just the sound of the crickets.

"I don't have a weapon," Del said, turning on her cell phone's light.

The entrance to the tunnel wasn't high enough for her to get through without crouching. She heard skittering in the darkness beyond and played her light back and forth over the opening. She hated rats.

She hated the thought of tunnels even more. Of being *enclosed*. In the dark.

"God . . . damn . . . it." Raising one muddy Nike, she stepped through the round black opening.

"Yuri," she called out again, "I just want to talk. That's what you want, right?"

She took one step and then two, then stopped and flashed her light back and forth.

This was insane.

Yuri didn't have a gun; otherwise, he would have used it up on the road. *Right?* She shined her light into the darkness. Two tunnels led away from the entrance. Del had no idea, so she chose the left one.

The tunnel stank of gasoline and sulfur, like rotten eggs. Something rumbled in the dark distance. A power plant? The stench was gag inducing.

"Yuri?"

She lit the few feet ahead of her with the cell phone. Maybe this was the wrong way. After a few minutes of creeping, she decided to change course and reverse back down the tunnel. Noises echoed. Small scuttling sounds. Like a whole plague of rats behind her in the blackness, but she hadn't seen even one dart through the dim cone of light she played over the silted floor.

This was too much.

The hairs rose on the nape of her neck. Another minute, and she reached the connection with the other tunnel. She turned toward the entrance.

But there was none.

***

Take a deep breath.

Calm. Keep calm, Del told herself. Panic was the enemy in any tough situation. She inhaled, then exhaled. *Go back to the breath.* Her hand holding up the cell phone light trembled as she surveyed the dirt-and-rock wall where the entrance had been.

Or where she *thought* it had been.

You just took a wrong turn.

How was that possible? It didn't matter.

She retraced the last few minutes in her mind. One step through the entrance, she remembered putting a muddy Nike in front of her, then scanning left and right with the light. Then she had gone left.

Right?

The darkness seemed to devour the feeble rays from her cell phone. The smooth curved concrete walls seemed to constrict around her, as if she were in the belly of some monstrous snake.

She looked again at the wall where she thought the entrance was. Dirt and pebbles sloped up to the ceiling, closing off the tunnel. But she was just here a minute ago.

It was her mind playing tricks on her. Already she was panting. The air seemed sucked from her lungs.

Chuk, chuk, chuk . . . Something scrabbled behind her, and she swung the light around, her stomach coming up into her throat. Beyond the thrum of distant engines reverberating against the walls, it was so quiet that she heard the thump of her own heart in her ears.

A sign of anxiety. *No kidding.*

Breathe. Just breathe deep.

She coughed violently. Gagged on the smell and bent over, hands on her knees.

"Igor," she called out, then screamed: "*Igor?*"

She checked her cell phone for reception. Nothing. She closed her eyes. The entrance had to be just a little farther down the tunnel. It was the only explanation.

Holding the light out ahead of her, she scanned the floor. The beam pierced only fifteen to twenty feet into the close, fetid air. Just a smooth, curving concrete wall, and a floor littered with garbage. She stopped to pick up a wrapper. Chocolate bar.

That meant other people had been at least this far.

And the fumes. These tunnels had to be attached to something. She walked forward carefully, step-by-step.

"Yuri," she called out. "Yuri, are you in here?"

Her voice echoed. Nothing.

She should have taken the gun Igor offered her.

Ahead, she saw a dim monochromatic flicker. The tunnel split in a Y. She hadn't seen this before. Had she? Her mind felt as if it was ungluing, the tunnel walls closing in, her breath coming in panting gasps, a headache pounding behind her temples.

Left. Right? Turn around?

Her light dimmed.

Or maybe it was just her eyes.

With the back of her hand, she wiped them, smeared away the sweat and accumulated grime. She had gone left when she first entered the tunnel, so she decided to go right. She tried to picture how this would look from above. The van had stopped on the overpass, and there was solid earth to the left and right, and houses beyond that.

She stepped forward and turned right, her pace now picking up, her light sweeping up and down, left and right. As her feet scuffed against the dirt, again she heard behind her the scrabbling of many little feet.

But the moment she stopped and turned and swung her light around, the noises stopped. Just the panting of her own lungs sucking nasty air in and pushing it out. She broke into a jog, the panic uncorking a jolt of adrenaline and cortisol into her bloodstream.

She skidded to a stop.

This wasn't right. She never came this far. The fumes permeated through her sinuses and deep into her brain, the headache now pounding, the fear tightening its grip, squeezing her mind.

This can't be right.

Del slowly and deliberately turned around and began walking back the way she had just come. Maybe some dirt had slid down and covered the entrance after she came in. That had to be the right tunnel. There was no other option. She checked her cell phone. Still no signal. And now only a sliver of battery remained.

Her light grew feebler.

Her feet crunched against gravel, her toes scattering a mound of it. With one trembling hand, she held the light up. The floor sloped up. The walls closed in, a pile of dirt and sticks and gravel closing off the tunnel straight ahead of her.

She moaned.

She had just come this way, hadn't she? Hadn't she just turned around and come back on her path? She hadn't turned, hadn't . . .

Her light flickered off. She shook it back on.

Whimpering sounds in the darkness, and her mind jumped before she realized those noises were hers. The patter of little feet behind her. She spun around with her dim light but saw nothing.

Just go forward. You shouldn't have turned around. The machines, the engines, the fumes—this was connected to something.

Del broke into a jog again, one arm up in front with the light.

Again she skidded to a stop.

The tunnel ended, this time in a flat concrete wall with a scrawled red graffito of a skull and crossbones. Her light winked out.

"Igor!" she yelled. "God damn it, Igor, can you hear me?"

Pitch black. Absolute oily darkness.

She was trapped.

21

Minutes passed.

Maybe longer. It was hard to tell.

Del tried her phone again, pushed the buttons, but it was dead.

Her breath came in quick gulps. She consciously tried to slow it down. *Think. Breathe. Deep and slow.* She felt as if she were suffocating. Her left hand felt for the sloping wall—cold, clammy dirt stuck to it—and she knelt and then sat with her arms wrapped around her knees.

Squeezed her eyes shut.

Calm. Long breaths.

There had to be an explanation. Scuffling noises all around her now. Her eyes opened and stared into the pitch blackness.

Except not quite black.

Red dots appeared around her. Not red, but toward the infrared band in her vision. Smudges of heat. Rats? Circling for a kill? Waiting for her to stop moving?

She tried to stop shivering and focused on a single reddish dot. It didn't look like the body of a rat. Wasn't big enough. Then they moved again in a coordinated shifting sea, in perfect synchrony. Was it her eyes?

"Get away!" she screamed.

She took a deep lungful of air and almost retched from the fumes. She leaned to one side and opened her mouth to throw up.

Then stopped.

Another sound. Louder, scratching to her right. A bright beam stabbed through the murk, and the red smudges scampered away. The ray of light widened, illuminating the graffiti-covered wall to her left.

Voices.

She got shakily to her feet. "Igor?"

Another beam of light played out, the two beams crossing. Enough illumination for Del to see long shadows coming out of a hole in the sloping gravel wall to her right. Whoever it was didn't respond. From her crouched position, she rotated and brought her hands up.

"Who is it?" she said.

"Do not be afraid," answered an unfamiliar voice with a heavy Ukrainian accent.

Multiple sets of hands scraped away at the dirt and gravel, and chunks of it slid down to Del's feet. Didn't sound like Korshunov.

"Come. Come here," said the voice.

A hand beckoned through the growing aperture. Now a body could fit through.

Del didn't have much choice. She scrambled up the embankment and felt warm hands grab under her armpits and pull. She slithered through and balled up, knees to her chest, and yanked free on the other side.

She kicked out, and someone yelped as her foot connected.

The gruff voice that had talked to her through the opening cursed.

Del scrambled to her feet. Lights scissored up and down, and someone grabbed her from behind. She got a glimpse of a Mohawk haircut before a bag was yanked down over her head.

***

They dragged her out of the tunnels and back into the mercifully sweet, cool air outside. She felt her feet sliding through the mud of the bottom of the culvert, felt the tall grass against her arms. She tried to fight back at first but gave up. Saved her energy. If they had wanted to kill her, she would already be dead.

Or they would just have left her in the tunnel.

The headache persisted, the nausea bad enough that she almost threw up in the vehicle they stuffed her into. It wasn't a van. She felt her knees against the back of the seat in front of her. One body to each side of her, pinning her in the middle. It wasn't Igor's Lada, either. The fabric under her jeans wasn't the cracked vinyl of his old car. It stank of cigarette smoke, not marijuana.

They weren't gentle but weren't unduly rough, either. Hands tied behind her back, but not too tight. What happened to Igor? She hoped he wasn't lying on the side of the road with a bullet in his head.

They pulled away without squealing the tires—not in a hurry. Del counted the turns in her head. Left, left, then right. A sweeping turn a minute later, and she heard the thrum of the wheels picking up speed. Onto the highway. A few minutes later, they pulled off, turned left and right and right again.

She spat out bits of fiber from the bag over her head. Rough on her skin. Burlap? Some kind of natural fiber. Not manmade, nothing like polypropylene.

The vehicle skidded to a stop.

***

"I'm an Interpol police officer," Del said.

"We know," answered a voice. An American voice.

Her captors had walked her up three flights of stairs and sat her on a wobbly chair in a brightly lit room. Her hair was in her eyes, the burlap sack still obscuring her vision, but through its coarse weave she could see maybe a dozen people in front of her. They talked in Ukrainian. Russian? She wasn't sure. The voices lowered. Dim shapes moved away. Most left the room.

"Take it off," said the American-accented voice. "And untie her."

The hood over her head came free. Del pulled her hands loose.

She rubbed her eyes, swept her hair back, and blinked. The room was twenty feet square, with dusty wooden floorboards and warped, cracked plaster walls. Two windows in front of her, both boarded up. The air damp.

Whoever was behind her reached into her jeans pocket.

She grabbed the wrist, twisted, and heard a crack and squealing yelp. Del held on tight and swung around out of the chair, wrenching the arm into a hammerlock as she slid back behind the kidnapper-turned-captive. Del glanced behind her. Nobody there. She hooked her left arm around the young man's throat and forced his right hand, the one that had gone into her pocket, up.

"Not nice to stick your hand in a lady's pants without asking," she said, tightening her grip around the man's slender throat. He either had no concept of fighting or chose not to fight back at all. He gasped and gurgled, limp in her grip.

She held up his hand to see what was in it.

"That's a tracking tile," said a hooded man sitting across the room.

"Lenny?" Del said.

"Nice to see you again, Detective Devlin."

Leonardo Bondar sat on a large chair woven in tendril threads of plastic to form a crown above his head. It looked like a giant marine arthropod that had somehow crawled into this drab room.

Bondar wore a thick brown fur coat that reached the floor, with a hood up around his head. His wild tangle of beard looked like some hairy animal clinging to his chest. His face was haggard. Deep lines under his eyes. His cheeks were smeared with dirt.

To his left was the girl from the rave—the one with the helicopter braids, bright red mascara and lipstick, and blue dots of paint on her cheeks. To her left was a young man with vivid red hair, a single lick of it curled and stuck to the middle of his forehead, and lipstick matching the girl's. He had on a rumpled green suit and white shirt with a thin pink tie.

To Lenny's right sat two kids with yellow-green hair, in nylon net tops with gold rope chains around their necks. They sat hunched forward on their chairs, looking at Del from the tops of their eyes, in what they must think was a menacing pose.

The effect was more that of a comical intervention circle.

"We used the tracking tile to follow you," Lenny said. "We thought they were going to grab you, too." He glanced left and right. "And you've already met my friends."

Del remembered one of the dyed-hair kids falling against her at the Stereo Palace. If they had planted something on her, that was when it happened. She had thought they were stoned, and had tried to help him up. Stupid. She needed to be more careful.

"What happened to Igor?" Del said.

"Who?"

"The taxi driver."

"Scared off. Said the Russians were coming back, but he showed us where you were when we got here."

What the hell had just happened in there? She was shaky, her mind still echoing with the memory of suffocating blackness.

"You're free to go," Lenny said. "We had to keep you tied up until we got clear. For your safety as much as ours."

Del let go of the young man and pushed him away from her. Just the seven of them in the room, but more were outside the closed door. "You know it's a crime a kidnap a police officer?"

"We *rescued* you," Lenny said. "You should be thanking me."

"Did you . . . did you close off the tunnel? Bury me in there?"

Lenny shook his big head, his Taliban-worthy beard sweeping back and forth over his fur coat. "We heard you yelling. We dug you out."

"Yuri. Yuri Korshunov. You have him?"

Lenny ignored her question. "You shouldn't be here, Detective Devlin."

"Did you grab Yuri? At the event?"

"He was there to see you, apparently, not us. We did not abduct him."

Bondar leaned forward into the light and gave Del a good view of his face. His eyes were steady, his facial muscles slack. The heat in his forehead was even and unchanged when he spoke, the periorbital blood vessels cool. Either he was a sociopath, or the man was telling the truth and wanted Del to know it. She sensed he was showing off, that he liked the spotlight.

Del asked, "Do you know who did grab Yuri?"

"The Russians?" Bondar shrugged. "They seem to want him, but then, a lot of people do. This is not your fight. You should not be here."

"And you *should* be? You're as American as I am. Stanford educated, grew up in Queens. Your MakerArmy company was on track for an IPO. You could have been a billionaire next year. This isn't a good career move, Lenny. A better question is: What are *you* doing here?"

"My family is Ukrainian, like you are Irish," Lenny said. "We have a special, hidden bond, you and I."

"Like what?"

He paused. "One way is that we both have been forced here. Please tell me, what do you think *you* are doing here?"

"I'm looking for truth."

"'Revenge' might be more accurate."

"Why did you attack the Russian Embassy?" Del asked.

"That wasn't me."

"Me?"

"Us."

"The Black Army, or you and your friends?" Del put her hands out wide enough to encompass the five young people in front of her. They didn't look like much of an army. A stiff wind might blow half of them over.

Del said, "I saw your online video claiming you represent the Black Army. How did you become their spokesperson?" When Lenny didn't respond, she added, "I tested the plastic. From the drone airplane. I was in Grigory Georgiev's office, the police commissioner—"

Lenny interrupted. "I know that Russian traitor. Did he mention another American who was forced here? Timothy Hutchins?"

"What about him?"

"That's for you to find out."

Del didn't want to play games. "Grigory showed me a drone that didn't explode. I tested it."

"*Tested?*"

"Lit part of it on fire. It was cellulose acetate."

"A lot of machines use that."

"But your MakerArmy 3-D printers are the main ones."

"Which means they're framing us."

"Who is 'they'?"

"I think that's what you"—he pointed a sausage of a finger at her—"should be trying to find out. A good place to start would be our mutual friend Adam Petty."

"Georgiev said that the attack came from Melitopol, that they were able to track where the airplanes came from. That's the historical center of the Free Territory."

"You've been picking up a little history while in Kiev, I see."

"Why did you run?" Del said. "From New York?"

"Your father's shooting was pinned on me. I saw what was coming. Reality is manufactured here just as much as in America, and they were creating a reality that would have ended up with me in jail. After all, this is my business, isn't it?"

"Manufacturing reality?"

"We take ephemeral ideas and give them substance. Like this." He slapped his plastic chair.

"Why not come in with me? To Interpol Bureau in Kiev? You can explain it all to them."

"I am explaining it to you."

"You kidnapped me."

"You have no idea what you've been caught up in."

"Enlighten me?"

"Go home." He indicated the door. "Leave." When Del didn't get up from her seat, he said, "The reason you're here is entirely manufactured."

"Which means what?" She was getting tired of this game. She was tired, period.

"Isn't it a bit odd that a Suffolk County detective has been hired as attaché for Interpol? In your headlong rush for revenge, did you ever stop to wonder about this?"

Del had wondered, but as her father told her, it didn't do to pick apart every stroke of luck that went your way. Hearing this out loud, however, she suddenly felt foolish, and she could see he was gloating. She felt a sinking sensation in the pit of her stomach.

"When you get back to your hotel, read your email."

"Why should I trust you?"

"You are no more than a trained bear in a circus. Your boss is using you as a human lie detector. All those meetings you attend, all the questions they ask you to ask? No electronics allowed inside the Russian embassy? No problem. They send you."

Del didn't respond. All those meeting summaries, even the ones internal to Interpol—Katherine had asked for résumés, for her eyes only. Del had been trying to help, trying to fit in.

Was she doing anything illegal? No. But was it ethical?

"Check your email," Lenny said. "You'll see a complaint filed, a second one by your coworker Officer Jacques Galloul. He's trying to get you sent home."

Del took a beat to absorb this. Bondar was saying he had access to internal Interpol communications? "Do you have Yuri? Did you get him from the tunnel?"

"One thing I can tell you."

"What's that?"

"Yuri Korshunov was not the guy that shot your father."

"I saw the video."

Lenny laughed—short, quick hiccups that bounced the beard up from his coat. "Have you really looked at that? I mean, had it analyzed?"

"Of course I've looked at it."

"That's not Yuri in that video. It's pure, uncut manufactured reality."

22

The rusted Honda Civic pulled away in a plume of blue exhaust, one hand out the passenger window waving goodbye. Whatever the Black Army might be in the cyberworld, its meatspace needed an upgrade.

Del pulled a hand through her hair, trying to impose some order on the knotted mess. She picked out wisps of burlap fiber and shivered. The sun had just come up, and there was a chill in the air, low clouds dark and threatening rain.

Lenny's boys had dropped her off at the observation platform over the Dnieper, near the center of town. The tops of trees beyond the deck obscured parts of the river. To her left stretched the rest of central Kiev, three candy-striped smokestacks rising up from the low-lying factories in the distance, tugs and barges at piers along the water, and two bridges that crossed the waterway's branching forks. Straight in front of her, on the other side of the Dnieper, was a sandy bank, and trees that went almost to the horizon.

Del didn't have a watch—she'd left her fitness tracker at the hotel, and her phone was still dead—but it couldn't be much past 6:00 a.m. She didn't want to ask any of the visitors who had already arrived to watch the sunrise, didn't want to draw any more attention to herself. The tourists, all dressed in sensible jackets with daypacks, stole glances at her in her tank top and jeans and sneakers, looking as if she had just come back from the rave she attended last night.

Crossing her arms to retain some warmth, Del turned and began walking to the Hyatt.

Even though Lenny had insisted she was free to go, before she could walk out the door they had forced her to wear a blindfold and hood. It felt as if they were playing at being gangsters.

The two young men with the Day-Glo green hair and nylon-net tank tops had driven her around the city for two hours before dropping her off. After telling her she could walk home from this spot, they had started to drive off, then stopped, and one got out to make sure she knew the way.

Not exactly criminal masterminds, but they were technical wizards. At least Lenny was.

He said the video of Yuri shooting her father was a *deepfake*. By now it had become common, even available through phone apps—a technique that used artificial intelligence to map someone's body and face onto a video of another person. Make it look as if one person were doing something when it was really someone else. Techies had started the craze, using it in porn to put celebrities in compromising positions, but it had spread, and the fear in law enforcement was exactly this sort of thing.

Hadn't someone checked it? Wouldn't this be standard practice to verify? That it might be a fake hadn't even crossed Del's mind. Then again, it might not be. Lenny might be trying to deflect, to draw attention away.

The way he said it, though—he made sure she was looking right at him. She believed him.

So, what did that mean, exactly?

Del walked away from the river, through a huge arch 150 feet high, built of cinder block. Everything in this city was built of cinder blocks. Arms still wrapped tight around herself, she laughed when she read the inscription on the brass plaque. This was the Friendship of Nations Arch.

Lenny's kids had a sense of humor, at least. They clearly knew all about Del. Her background, her special vision.

She still felt high from the fumes in the tunnel. Her headache had subsided, but it was still there. Which led to another thought: When that kid fell against her, did they drug her?

The memory of the tunnel still turned like a screw in her mind. A fulminating fear of being trapped, buried, the walls closing in. How was it possible that the tunnel entrance closed up like that? And then the tunnel itself seeming to shut up behind her again? Was she hallucinating? What had happened?

Or . . .

Did Lenny and his kids stage it all? Did they know she was claustrophobic? What could she believe? And where the hell was Yuri?

They're framing us. That's what Lenny kept saying, but he couldn't say who "they" were. He seemed to think the Russians had snatched Yuri. The "Russians," whatever that meant. When she mentioned the police commissioner, Lenny had snorted and called him Russian. He meant *ethnically* Russian.

Del had asked Lenny about the contagion of 3-D-printer guns sprouting up all over the Ukraine. Grigory said they had been used in more than a dozen shootings in the past month.

Lenny had replied by asking whether she saw the list of people who were shot. Corrupt politicians, he said, and that he had nothing to do with what happened, but if the masses chose to make weapons with his technology, wasn't that what America was all about? Empowering the masses, enabling everyone to defend themselves?

He kept pointing the finger at Adam Petty.

At Strataform.

She had tried not to let incredulity creep into her voice when he started talking about Petty, but it wasn't easy. The simmering animosity between them had been hard to miss when she met them in New York—the two competing wannabe Steve Jobses of the Fourth Industrial Revolution. His implicating Petty felt like a simple misdirection.

Was it possible the commercial fight between the two leaders in 3-D printing would spill out onto a *literal* battlefield?

The thing was, Lenny had looked as though he was telling the truth, and that was more worrisome. Del could usually spot a lie. So maybe

Lenny was mixing truth and lies. Bullshitting, in other words. Using some truth to cover the lie.

Or, worse, a zealot. Someone who believed their own created reality, their own lies, so that they didn't even know they were lying, not even to themselves. Like a form of psychosis. If he really believed his own bullshit, then it would be impossible to tell whether he was lying—not by talking to him, at any rate. He might even convince her of his imagined reality.

That was what cult leaders did.

And on reflection, those kids around him—it did have the feeling of a cult.

She was so out of her depth.

Del walked up the hill through the arch, along a tree-lined footpath past some open dumpsters, and down a stone staircase by a building with blue stone and red-framed windows. It was the National Philharmonic of Ukraine building, Del read as she passed. Normally, she would be excited, thinking about coming here for a concert.

Lenny's kids had been following her.

When he said she had been picking up a little history here, he knew she had been sightseeing. So these kids weren't harmless and without skills—their skills were just geared more for watching and observing.

Was it possible they had tracked her digitally? She looked up at the building, at the security cameras sticking out over the doorways and corners. These cameras were everywhere.

But maybe they didn't even need that.

Del got her phone out of her pocket. Could Lenny be tracking it? At the Suffolk Police Department, they had consulted the FBI on a few cases to tap the Google Sensorbank, a commercial database tracking where each person went, what they did. Police used it all the time.

But the problem with any database was that it could be hacked. She knew enough about cybercrime to know that.

Del reached the end of the pathway, where it met a busy four-lane throughway. Cars hissed past as a light drizzle began to fall. She waited for a break in the traffic.

Lenny claimed to have intercepted internal Interpol documents, said he sent one to her email. She hadn't verified this yet, but he said it was a report from Jacques Galloul, requesting that Del be barred from Interpol duties, saying she was spying internally at Interpol, spying when she went to meetings with the Russians.

That this was political interference—something that anyone working at Interpol was forbidden to engage in.

Political.

Across the street was a billboard with President Voloshyn's face, her blond hair in a braid, with some Cyrillic text beneath. Del couldn't read it, but she would bet it said something about change for the better. That was what all political campaigns promised.

The election was in exactly a week.

A dull thud in the distance, followed by three loud pops. Gunfire?

Del crossed the street and climbed up an incline around what she called Tchaikovsky Street—she couldn't pronounce the longer name—that led straight to her hotel. At the top of the hill, the gates to St. Michael's Monastery were already open. As she passed, she looked over her shoulder at the gold domes and stopped.

***

The rain started in earnest and spattered against the pavement outside.

Del bowed her head and held her hands together, still trembling from the wet cold, a puddle of droplets forming below her on the pink-and-white marble floor of the monastery.

"Please, please take care of my father," Del prayed.

After passing through the modest front entrance, between white columns topped with gold, the interior of the church was an explosion of reds and blues and pinks, every inch of wall and archway covered in paintings of angels, saints, and men and women with spears and armor. The place felt familiar but different—the crosses were square, and everything covered in gold leaf.

Del searched for a corner where she could sit, a pew to pray at, but the monastery didn't have any chapels. So she lit a candle and placed it in one of the copper urns before a painting of a saint. She couldn't decipher the name, so she picked the second one. People were searching for her, she knew, but she needed a second to herself, to regroup.

She said a prayer for her family and for her father.

She didn't want to believe that anything could happen to him. A part of her just wanted it to be over, wanted to come home and find everything magically fixed.

Her father was her bedrock.

Part of him didn't want her there, in Brooklyn, either. Her mother and sister were different. They were the caregivers. She was the hunter, like him. He wanted them there, but not Del. He didn't want her to see him weak.

Now she was the one being weak. She was being *used*.

At first, at the interview in Washington, she had thought Katherine wanted her because she was a woman. Perhaps because she was a woman of color. Certainly it was because of her success in solving that last case, but still it had a whiff of affirmative action. Del hated the idea, but when she failed the background screening for the FBI . . .

She didn't want to be a beat cop. That had never been her dream. She was doing it for her dad.

When Katherine asked her to report on all her meetings and sent her questions to ask at those meetings, Del knew then what was happening, even though she wasn't being honest with herself. She knew she was being sent in to spy on people, to use her gift to report back on who was telling the truth and who wasn't.

Her skill wasn't perfect. She kept telling people that, but she also kept telling them about her abilities. She was to blame. At the core of it, Del wasn't confident enough in her own abilities, so she needed her little trick like a crutch, and she used it, over and over. Now someone else was using her for it, and she went along.

That much she could believe from Lenny.

But her father? If Yuri hadn't shot him, then who had? And why? The video—*the created reality*—might have been manufactured, but in the physical world there was a bullet, and a hole in her father.

She had to remind herself that she was here for a good reason—it was the only way to get inside the UN investigation into who shot her father. To bring justice for the most important person in her life. Del's back straightened up at that realization.

Now there was a faked video, too. All that had to leave a trail of some kind.

If Lenny Bondar was telling the truth.

He might be lying. Worse, he might not even know he was lying.

23

The hot jets of water against her frigid skin were steaming bliss, knowing fingers that soothed away the fear and confusion of the past twenty-four hours. She let her mind go blank and stood in the shower, just letting herself breathe and enjoy the heat working its way into her muscles and bones.

This place had good water pressure, at least.

Before getting into the shower, she'd plugged her phone in. She had almost stopped to check her email, but she was dirty and beyond tired—hadn't slept in two nights—and getting clean and warm was what she needed first.

It didn't take long for the questions to creep back into her mind.

Why would Lenny Bondar be tracking me? What's my position in this?

She had been a nobody until a few weeks ago, until she decided to take up with Interpol. She guessed it was her father. Had to be. She needed to speak with Yuri, find out what he needed to tell her.

Having Del show up in Kiev made her an obvious target.

Where was Bondar's base of operations?

Del remembered the story of another tech guru, John McAfee, founder of the famous antivirus software, who had taken his millions and disappeared into Belize. He constructed a Heart of Darkness–style compound in the jungle and assembled his own cultlike army of followers. Even after getting charged with murder and hoisting himself onto the FBI's most-wanted list, he had escaped back to America and managed to extricate himself from all charges. He even ran for president in the next elections.

A tech genius in the grip of psychosis, losing his grasp on reality. Lenny Bondar wouldn't be the first.

Those kids in that room with him—they weren't soldiers. That young woman and the others were dressed up like cartoon characters. Fantasy. Make-believe.

MakerArmy—that was Lenny's company. Before this mess, it had been on track for an IPO on NASDAQ. Lenny would have been a billionaire, but that dream was shattered. Always follow the money—that was what her friend Angel said.

MakerArmy.

Black Army.

Like Black Hat, the famous hacker conference, "black hats" were the bad guys in movies. These kids weren't messing only with the digital world, but with the physical as well. Turning make-believe into reality.

Manufactured reality. That was the phrase he kept repeating.

He had said to stay away from Melitopol—the same thing Director Dartmouth had told her. This was the center of the historical Free Territory of the Ukrainian Black Army a century ago. It was where Yuri Korshunov was first spotted when he entered Ukraine. The whole area was fast becoming a full-blown war zone.

Del got out of the shower, put on a thick bathrobe, and rubbed her hair with the towel, scratching the back of her head, trying to get at that itch inside. One thing for sure: she didn't want to get caught without a weapon again. She should ask Grigory for a permit, but first run it by Katherine.

She glanced at her luggage. When she brought back that shell casing from New York, she brought a box of .38-caliber ammunition back with her. No gun, just the cartridges. She had told security at the airport that it was for Interpol. What she really wanted was to test the Strataform—she glanced at it in the corner—to see if it could create a 3-D gun downloaded from the web and then successfully fire a bullet from it. See with her own eyes.

Enough. She took a deep breath in, counting to five, then out, counting to six, and repeated nine times. First things first.

She picked up her phone, now charged.

There was the email from Lenny, along with a dozen others from Suweil, Jacques, and Katherine asking for status updates. Her last message to Suweil was that she had found Yuri Korshunov. She even left coordinates from a GPS pin on her phone.

She clicked open the email from Lenny and scanned it. It seemed to be exactly what he had said. An email from Jacques to her boss, Katherine, and the General Secretariat, requesting again that Delta be removed from Interpol for reasons of conflict and political interference.

Jacques hadn't said anything to Del. Wasn't he supposed to be her partner?

Was the email real?

She cursed. Maybe she shouldn't have opened an email from a known hacker. That was stupid. Halfway through sending a group message to Suweil and Katherine, someone thumped on her door hard enough that it shook the walls.

"Devlin!" yelled a voice from outside her hotel room.

The accent was French. Jacques.

She closed his email to Katherine and yelled, "Hold on a second."

Still in her bathrobe, she crossed to the door and opened it a crack. The security chain was on. He tried to force the door. The chain snapped tight.

"What can I do for you, Officer Galloul?" Del said.

"We've been searching all night." Jacques's voice was equal parts anger and relief. "I received a message from Kiev police that your phone was turned on in the area of the hotel. What happened? Can I come in?"

His face was pressed into the three-inch opening.

"I just got out of the shower. I'll file my report."

"Can you tell me now?"

"You can read the report. If they give it to you."

"If they . . . What game are you playing?"

Del unchained the door and pulled it wide. "I saw that complaint you filed."

"You found Yuri Korshunov last night?" Jacques's voice was quieter.

"Someone snatched him from a warehouse district. I followed but was grabbed by Lenny Bondar's people. They released me, and I just got back. I'm fine."

She tried to close the door.

Jacques stuck his foot in. "*Leonardo* Bondar? You found him? Where is he?"

"Can I get dressed?"

"He abducted you? What did he say? Where?"

"A multistory building. I think in the north of the city . . . Look, I'm fine. I'll file my report. I need to think."

She pushed his foot back and closed the door, went to the bed, and slumped onto it. She took a deep breath and let her shoulders relax.

Three loud fist thumps against the door. She threw her head back but got up and opened it again. "Jacques, look, I don't—"

Two men in Kiev police uniforms with serious faces. Jacques was ten feet behind them.

"As I told Officer Galloul, I'm okay," she said.

"Yuri Korshunov," one of the men said in a heavy accent. "You met him last night?"

"Can I please get dressed? As I already told Officer—"

"You need to come with us. Commissioner Georgiev will see you immediately."

"What's this about?"

"We have him."

"Who?"

Del's mind was still hazy from the fumes, but she sensed something off with these two blank-faced young men. They wanted to bring her to Grigory? She had just found out that perhaps Yuri didn't shoot her father. If that was true, then who did? The closest person to her father when he was shot was Commissioner Georgiev.

She suddenly felt very exposed. "I'll come only if Officer Galloul comes as well."

"Yuri Korshunov," the young Kiev officer repeated.

"What about him?" Del said.

"We have him."

She was speechless for a second before saying, "Can I see him?"

The young man shrugged. 'I think, yes."

"And talk to him?"

"That, I think, no."

"Why not?"

"Because he is dead."

24

The skin was already mottled bluish pink, the mouth agape as if he was trying to say something, some final words swallowed in time by death. The man's naked body was laid out on a dented stainless-steel table with a two-inch lip to stop fluids from slopping, and a sink at one end, fitted with a spray hose.

Located in the basement of Kiev's main hospital, the morgue was a huge room, a hundred feet long and fifty wide, with eight identical stainless-steel tables staggered along its length. Each was topped with an exposed body in varying stages of clinical examination, some flayed open in a giant Y, others already crudely stitched back together like a Christmas turkey. A dozen gurneys with blood-soaked sheets lined the walls. At the other end of the room, two technicians worked a pair of shears, crunching through ribs to open a chest cavity.

Del stood shoulder to shoulder with Commissioner Georgiev and one of his officers, the same young man who came to collect her from the hotel. The coroner stood to the other side of the table. Korshunov's body was half covered by a green cloth. Both eyes were open, but one was darker than the other.

Del leaned in to get a better look.

"We think a fox got to him," said the coroner, a gaunt sixty-something man in blue scrubs, with a hairnet over gray curls. His eyes were a pale brown—too light, somehow, for his dark skin. "The body was found at 6:24 a.m. by a jogger, down by the river near Volodymyr."

He pulled back the rest of the sheet covering the dead man, revealing a deep-purple bruise near the hip. He quickly covered back up the shriveled penis.

"I do not think Mr. Korshunov's modesty is at risk," Georgiev said to the coroner. He turned to Del. "Is this the man you saw last night?"

Grigory was in full police commissioner's uniform, cap under one arm. Formal and stiff, not like the times she had met him before.

Del wanted to be sick but did her best to contain it.

It wasn't the morgue and dead bodies—not *just* that, anyway. Her head still ached from the fumes she had breathed last night. What was it about morgues and green ceramic tiles? They were the ice cream to the apple pie of nose-burning preservative chemicals.

After a pause to gulp a breath of air, Del said, "You sure that's Yuri? I think that's the guy I saw last night, but . . ." She took another breath through her mouth.

"Verified digitally," Grigory said, "with Interpol. We took pictures an hour ago and sent them in. There is no mistake."

"We have been busy—sixteen bodies last night," the coroner said with a nod to the sheet-covered gurneys by the walls. "But we have a regular list to watch out for, especially the ones on the Russian shit list."

"You mean hit list?" Del said.

He shrugged—*as if it made any difference*—and pointed to a collection of printed mug shots on the wall. "Our Russian cousins probably put him in here."

"Was the bullet from one of their weapons?" Del asked. How could the coroner already have an opinion? Had they already retrieved the bullet and done forensics?

"I am apologizing," the coroner said quickly. "My English is not practiced very much often. I said probably, yes? We have not begun an internal exam."

"Sixteen bodies?" Del said. "Was there a gunfight?"

"Not with Mr. Korshunov. He was found alone. Most of the other bodies are from fighting in the east of the city."

"Most?"

The coroner frowned. "Something very unusual happening in the past weeks. Some bodies we are having a hard time determining cause of death. There was a big—"

"You must have heard gunfire this morning?" Grigory said to Del.

She nodded, remembering her walk back to the hotel. "I saw Yuri at the Stereo Palace, a rave club in a warehouse district."

"We know it. And then?"

"Like I said, Lenny Bondar's kids grabbed me when I followed Yuri into that tunnel under the bridge, at the coordinates I left with Katherine."

"We searched there and found nothing."

"No footprints?"

"As I said."

"You can ask my taxi driver. Igor. He's usually in front of my hotel."

The officer beside Grigory made a note in his pad.

"Why would they leave him in the bushes?" Del said. "I mean, if it was the Russians, why wouldn't they just take his body back to Russia?"

"They leave bodies everywhere here," Grigory replied in a gruff voice.

"Why is his nose so purple?" Del asked the coroner.

"Lividity changes up to six hours after death," he replied. "He must have been facedown for the first hour or two, and then moved. Blood has pooled toward his back now, the way he was found. Bruising on wrists before death, but vibices on his neck indicate constriction after death." The coroner pointed things out as he spoke.

White spots around his neck, against graying skin. "He wasn't strangled?"

"That was after death. I believe they dragged him like this."

"And you didn't find anything in the tunnel?" Del said to Grigory. "No drag marks?"

"Nothing."

"And cause of death?" Del asked.

"Single gunshot wound in the back, which is cause of this bruising near the hip." The coroner lifted the side of Korshunov's midsection toward them and pointed at a small black hole just visible near the center left of his back. "Close range, but unusual."

"How?"

"Low muzzle velocity, from what I can tell. I will add more detail once I finish my examination."

"He was alive when you last saw him?" Gregory said.

"I already said he was," Del replied.

"I am making sure there is no misunderstanding."

"I told you, somebody grabbed him. Two big men, bald heads."

"Could you identify them? We have a book with pictures of known Russian operatives."

"Sure," Del said, and then after a pause: "At least we have Korshunov's DNA now. Are you sending a sample to Interpol?"

"Already done."

Del had intended to ask the commissioner for a permit to carry a firearm, or to get her a weapon she could carry, but seeing the look on his face, she just said, "Can I go back to my hotel?'

***

Past lunchtime, and Del hadn't eaten anything since the day before. She ordered up some room service—a club sandwich and Diet Coke. The afternoon sun cast bright rays onto the bed, the sheets and cover still untouched. Something else she hadn't done lately: sleep. Two nights ago, she had tossed and turned before giving up at 5:00 a.m. and going for a run, but in the past twenty-four hours she hadn't even gotten into bed.

She yawned and shook her head, tried to shake out the cobwebs. An email from Katherine to call her as soon as she got back from the coroner.

But first things first.

She turned on her laptop and dialed the video app. It picked up on the second ring.

"Dad?"

Her father's face appeared in blocky pixels. "Delta. Hey, sweetheart, are you okay?"

The image stabilized. Even on the small screen, he looked gaunt. Withdrawn. Two-day stubble on his cheeks. She couldn't remember him ever not being clean-shaven. A point of pride—his shirts always clean and pressed, shoes shined, necktie in a Windsor knot with the dimple done just so. Today, his shirt was rumpled, with what looked like a smudge of food near the lapel.

"I'm great," she said after a pause.

"Because your boss called us this morning." He coughed, then coughed again, deep and phlegmy.

She waited until he cleared his throat before she said, "My phone died. That was all. They were worried when they couldn't find me."

"No need to tell me stories. Just glad you're okay."

"How are you doing?"

"Great."

His voice was hoarse, but he smiled. *Great.* It was the same word she had just used, and she guessed it was just another mannerism she had gotten from him. Never say how you really felt. Seeing him, she felt a claw dig into the bottom of her stomach.

"One more week of chemo and we're done," he added. "Been doing radiation every day—well, weekdays. I get weekends off."

"When did you start that?"

"A few weeks ago."

"Nobody told me."

"We don't want you to worry."

After two seconds of silence, she said, "I should come back. I'm *going* to come back."

"No, you are not. I'm fine. This treatment just knocks you back a bit. Next week, I'll be done and you can come home and see me when I'm getting better." He coughed and spat something into a handkerchief. "And your friend Adam Petty—from that Strataform company?—he was in touch with my doctors. They're helping with my treatment."

"I'm not sure what I'm doing here," Del said.

"Just keep at it."

"Dad, do you remember anything else about when you were shot? Are you sure it was Yuri Korshunov?"

"I never said it was. I didn't see who did it. I saw the video, though; it seems right."

"What do you remember?"

"That Grigory fellow—he was the one that grabbed me. Right after."

"After? You're sure it was after?"

His brows furrowed. "Why?"

She waved a hand in the air and dismissed it.

"You tell me when you're ready," he said. "And you don't come back here, you hear me? Not till you're done with what you're doing. Take the opportunities in life; make the most of them. Second chances don't come often."

"Second chances?"

"I mean, look where you are now. Who needs the FBI? This is better, no?"

She promised that she wouldn't give up, and her mother came on. It was dinnertime on the East Coast. She told them that she loved them before ending the connection.

What had Yuri wanted to talk to her about?

***

"Suweil, Lenny Bondar sent me an internal Interpol document last night," Del said. "The Black Army has access to our communications."

As soon as she got off the phone with her family, she dialed the forensic tech at Lyon.

"How do you mean?"

"They intercepted a document from Jacques. Sent yesterday."

"Perhaps they have access to his accounts."

"Is that possible? Access to Interpol?"

"Anything in the digital world is possible. Bondar is well connected with very good hackers. He is talented himself. And do not forget, you are in their—how would I say it? Backyard? Territory? Do not use the hotel wireless, for starters. Was this document encrypted?"

"I don't know."

"Did you not ask Mr. Jacques?"

"Is there any way to improve security? Communications, I mean?"

"An easy way would be to switch devices. If they have snooped something you are already using. I'll send a temporary phone to your hotel. Something new. Just between us."

"Thanks, Suweil."

"You are very welcome."

"Bondar said that the video of my father getting shot at UN headquarters in New York was faked."

"Faked? You mean the whole of it?"

"Not all of it. Just Yuri shooting my father. He said it was a 'deepfake.' That it was really someone else."

Silence on the other end while Suweil processed. "I see."

"Is there a way to analyze this? See if he's telling the truth?"

"Even in the best fakes, there is always the eyes. They are difficult to get right, because most pictures of people are with their eyes open. In simulation videos, the person tends to not blink—not something that's obvious at first glance."

"Shouldn't this already have been analyzed?"

"Usually, this is standard procedure."

"And what's Jacques's story? Do you know how he ended up at Interpol? He doesn't seem to want me here."

"I think this is more than just Mr. Jacques. This is the French government."

"Do you know why?"

"They believe you are interfering in politics, I think. Americans, anyway."

Del let that sink in. "One more thing. If you're sending me a package, could you add something to it?"

"I am listening."

"See if you can get all the video, from all cameras in the UN headquarters from that day. At least eight hours before and after."

"That is a lot of data."

"Could you put it on a disk? And don't send it to my name."

"What name should I use?"

"Ghost."

***

The next call was one Del both dreaded and couldn't wait to make.

Director Dartmouth picked up on the third ring. "Detective Devlin, I can't tell you how relieved we are that you're unhurt. Officer Galloul and Commissioner Georgiev were up all night looking for you."

"I met them this morning."

"Jacques? Or the commissioner?"

"Both. Georgiev took me to the morgue to identify Yuri Korshunov's body. Not really identify"—they had already done that, with Interpol, he said, so Katherine had to know—"but to see if this was the same man I met last night."

"I assume it was?"

"The Black Army has compromised our communications."

"What did Yuri say to you?" Katherine asked.

"Did you hear what I said?"

"I want to know what *he* said. Why did he track you down?"

"I assume something with my father."

"Assume?"

"He didn't have time to say. I'll put all the details in my report. He was killed by a single gunshot and lay facedown for two hours before being moved to the park where he was found."

"We have the coroner's preliminary report," Katherine said. "They're sending the bullet to our labs. Suweil will analyze. So you'll have full access to information as soon as we get it. What about Bondar? You said he abducted you."

"I got trapped in the tunnels. He got me out."

"Trapped how?"

How? *I'm still not sure.* "I think he's playing some kind of game." She hesitated but added, "He said Yuri wasn't the one who shot my father. The video from the UN is a fake. Suweil is supposed to look at it."

A pause on the other end. "Delta, I think you should come back to Lyon on the next flight."

"Bondar brought up that art dealer, Hutchins. Commissioner

Georgiev mentioned him as well. I think I should investigate more."

"All consular staff from the US embassy have been recalled," Katherine said. "Sixteen people were killed in Kiev last night from fighting. More than a hundred dead yesterday across the Ukraine. You need to come back."

"I need a few more days."

"No more interviews for the elections. The monitoring mission is finished."

Del felt an anxious edge rise in her throat. What did Bondar say she was? A trained circus animal? "He sent me an email, a file of a complaint filed by Jacques yesterday. Sent to you and the General Secretariat. Claiming that I'm a spy."

"This is the leak you talked about?"

"So, it's true?"

"How did he get it?"

"He didn't exactly tell me."

A pause.

"We all have our gifts, Detective. 'Spying' is a dirty word. I prefer 'special talent,' which is why I contacted you in the first place."

Which meant both that the leak had happened and that the content was true as well.

"So, you're using me as a human lie detector?"

"What other kind would you be?"

"No electronics allowed in those meetings with the Russians." Del wasn't really asking anything, just speaking out loud. "That's what this was about? Using me?"

"I gave you a job. You accepted. You did it—and performed admirably given the circumstances. Now I need you to come back. We'll deal with this together."

Del's phone pinged. She held it back from her face to look at the screen. It was a text from Angel Rodriguez. She clicked the button to switch to speakerphone while she opened the text message screen.

"I just need a few more days," Del repeated.

You asked me to investigate you, said Angel's text message, *and I found something.*

She texted back, *What?*

"I heard your father isn't doing well," Dartmouth said.

This zeroed Del's attention back on Katherine. "What did you hear?"

"That he's having a difficult time with the treatment. I'm very sorry. I think it is in all our best interests if you come back to the States."

Angel's message came back. *Can we talk?*

Not right now, she texted. *Just tell me.*

When Del didn't respond, Katherine added, "You'll need to check in with Interpol in Lyon before returning."

"I haven't slept in two days."

"Then take the first flight tomorrow."

Angel's next message appeared: *Did you know your dad changed his name? When he came to America? Someone had been poking around in your past.*

Del felt her face flushing. *I didn't know.* "Sure, yes," she said to Katherine. "Good."

A link appeared on Del's screen, to a story from thirty years ago, about Jonathan Murphy. The *Guardian* article detailed an attack on British troops stationed in Belfast.

Jonathan Murphy, it said, was the ringleader of the attack.

"Jonny" Murphy. An IRA terrorist.

Someone knocked on the door.

25

Del stared at the man.

Black balaclava over his head, the two top corners of the sewn-together fabric sticking up from the top-like comical ears. There was nothing funny about the weapon he gripped close to his chest, one hand on the barrel's handguard, the other on the grip, forefinger resting against the trigger guard. He wore a camouflage jacket, the business end of the carbine held high, his eyes glaring at the camera through fabric slits.

The image was black and white, dated 1987.

Four years before Del was born.

A caption identified the man as Jonathan "Jonny" Murphy, leader of the Belfast Massacre later that year, and the gun as an ArmaLite AR-18. An American weapon, supplied by sympathizers across the pond. Most IRA weapons were Russian, channeled through Libya and Muammar Qaddafi, the article said, but at the time there were many in the United States who sided with the Republicans.

She couldn't take her eyes away from his.

This image was real, Del was sure of that. She stared at the man's eyes. What was he thinking? And who was this man to her?

Remains of her half-eaten club sandwich and fries were scattered on a tray next to her laptop on the bed. She was starving an hour ago, but the moment the waiter appeared at her door with the room service, her stomach had shriveled into a knot.

When the rap came on her door, she had almost jumped out of her chair.

She checked her phone. Just past lunch. Too early in New York to call her father. She wasn't even sure she wanted to. She needed to be positive first.

She needed a lot more than that.

She needed another drink.

An empty one-shot bottle of Jack Daniel's stood next to the can of Diet Coke.

For someone who was supposed to see things that no one else could, whose special talent was telling whether someone was lying, who was here spying for her country, she hadn't spotted this at all.

Her own father had been lying to her—not just lately, but for her entire life.

What had Bondar said? That we all lived in manufactured realities?

She went to the minibar for another Jack, poured it into the remains of her Coke, and took a sip. It was awful, the chemical sweetness not doing the sour-mash whiskey any favors. Again she clicked the email Angel had sent her, and stared into another face.

Was it her father?

A scanned image of a Northern Ireland driver's license, this one dated 1982, five years before the picture in the paper. Irish driver's licenses at the time, unlike British, had photos on them. The image was grainy, the face black and white and tiny, but there was no mistaking it.

That was her father.

He was twenty-five in the photo, but she would know his face anywhere. Knew every nook and cranny, that dimple at the edge of a smile looking back at her from a decade before she was born. The license identified him as Sean Patrick Murphy. Brother to Jonathan Richard Murphy, Angel said in the email. Both of them son to Lilly Devlin and Patrick Murphy.

Angel provided all the background information he could find from the Irish registries and from a friend at DHS. It seemed her father had changed his surname—reverted to his mother's maiden name—when he arrived in America in 1987, the same year his brother was captured after the Belfast Massacre.

Lilly Murphy, her father's mother, had died in the early 1990s and Jonathan Murphy, the brother, had spent eleven years in jail until he was released in 1998 after the Good Friday Agreement ended the Troubles.

She took another mouthful of the diet cola and whiskey. Winced but swallowed.

Her whole life came into focus. Her dad had always shrugged off her attempts to talk about her grandfather, about his family in Ireland. He said he didn't talk to his father anymore, but never explained why. He said that before he left, his brother was dead, his mother as well, and there was nothing there for him anymore.

But "Jonny" Murphy wasn't dead. Not as far as Angel could tell from a brief investigation. The digital trail went cold soon after his release from prison. This was why her father never wanted her to go to Ireland, why he never took her, why he never wanted to talk about it.

What had her father done? Why had he run?

A cold realization crept up from the pit of her stomach, tickled the back of her neck and the back of her mind. When her dad had thought he was dying, when he was gasping for air on the hospital bed, he said he had to tell her something about their family. This was it. Had to be. The awful truth was too clear in her mind, the pieces fitting together.

And later, when her father had said to drop pursuing the FBI application after she was rejected due to a background investigation—it had struck her as odd because he'd never told her to quit anything in her life. He was always the one pushing her never to give up. Even now, even a few hours ago, he had been pushing her forward.

"*Second chances don't come often,*" he'd said to her.

Where was Jonathan Murphy now?

Angel had no idea.

A screw wormed its way deeper into her gut. Was this why Bondar said they shared a hidden connection? Who was he talking to? Was he talking to Jonathan Murphy?

The video from the UN Building—Bondar had said it was fake. She had it on her laptop, opened it and played the file. Zoomed in and paused. She studied the face of the man with his arm out, holding the yellow plastic gun. That was definitely the same person she had just seen laid out on the stainless-steel table in the Kiev morgue. She slid the video play button forward, watched the flash of the muzzle, her father falling forward. Grigory catching him.

If that was a fake, then who was holding the gun? Who shot her father?

She rubbed her eyes and decided to try a different tack.

She looked up Timothy Hutchins, the art dealer who went missing in Kiev. She knew of him, had been to see one of his exhibits at the MoMA in New York. She clicked a link to the stories of his disappearance. For three weeks, they didn't know where he'd gone during a solo European trip this past January. It was only in the second week of February that they identified his remains.

The same coroner she saw this morning had filed the report.

The remains were found at the Persian Palace hotel, not far from where she was. The article in the *New Yorker* was light on details of exactly *what* was found. Vague. Alarmingly vague. The cremated remains were flown back to his sister, it said.

She clicked through related articles, to images of his latest shows. Installation artworks in Europe, at the Travesía Cuatro gallery Madrid, the Modern in Poland, and two galleries here in Kiev. Del selected one of the images, of a flowing waterfall-like glass structure lit up from all sides. It had an organic, biological feel.

Like the chair Bondar had been sitting on last night.

She clicked more links. Hutchins had been an avid proponent of 3-D printers, had been using MakerArmy devices to create his artworks.

MakerArmy.

Black Army.

Irish Republican Army.

Del rubbed her eyes again. The alcohol hitting her bloodstream, on top of two nights without sleep, had turned her brain into cold molasses. She considered shoving her laptop and the room service tray off the bed and curling up under the covers. She needed some shut-eye.

The Strataform Replicator's single orange eye stared balefully from the corner of the room.

Del pulled up web pages about MakerArmy and Strataform, the heavyweights duking it out in the 3-D-printing world.

Strataform was the gorilla in the room, the multibillion-dollar company that had already supplied aerospace and government and automotive services. Millions of consumers had bought the Replicator, its website claimed.

When personal computers first appeared, everyone thought they were for nerds—interesting but not something for the masses. A few years later, they were in every home. Now, 3-D printers were making the same transition.

She clicked a video of Adam Petty, talking again about the coming Fourth Industrial Revolution. A combination of artificial intelligence, 3-D printing, bioelectronics, and more. Ukraine was trying to position itself in the forefront of this revolution, President Voloshyn had said at the UN meeting. Dozens of print farms, like the one Del had visited with Jacques, were already in operation across the Ukraine. This was the new wave of manufacturing.

Adam Petty and Lenny Bondar were competing to be the Steve Jobs of the next technological revolution to transform humanity. What was that worth? Was there a connection? Billions of dollars were at stake. Maybe trillions.

Bondar was now being painted as a terrorist, a crazy tech millionaire who had wandered off the farm. His company had suffered, but he was only the symbolic leader—a position the company had already relieved him of as it distanced itself from him. The young man had fallen far from grace. Why had he done it?

Del held the rumpled sheets of her bedspread longingly and imagined crawling under them. She had promised Katherine she would be on the first flight out to Lyon. The American embassy had issued a warning that all its citizens to leave Ukraine, that consular services were suspended. Violent unrest was spreading across the country, and the preelection rhetoric had ratcheted up from all sides.

Russian forces were rumored to be amassing on the eastern frontier.

*****

Two Mercedes cabs waited in a line at the front of the hotel, but Del walked past them and banged on the roof of the tan-topped red Lada. Igor leaned over to manually crank down the window and grinned sheepishly. "My God, Detective Delta!" he said around a mouthful of salami sandwich.

"You know where the Persian Palace is?"

It wasn't really a question. The Palace was one of the big hotels. Del could walk to it by herself if she had fifteen minutes.

Igor put the sandwich down on his multicolored bench seat. "I'm so glad to see you are safe. When the police arrived, they told me to leave. There were others. They said they knew you. I went down with them to the tunnel entrance, but it was blocked off. I said I was sure you went into it—"

"Thank you for staying as long as you did."

"Shouldn't you be resting?"

"You know the Persian Palace?"

"Of course."

She opened the back door. "Then lets—" Someone grabbed her wrist. Jacques stood on the sidewalk and pulled Del back from the Lada.

26

The manager's bald dome reflected a patchwork of late afternoon sunshine, the slanting rays filtered through intricate carved-wood patterns hung over the Persian Palace's restaurant windows. The perspiring man smelled as if he had bathed in cologne, then downed a shot for good measure. A haze of apple tobacco from a hookah pipe on the bar wafted through the damp air.

"Interpol?" the manager said.

He studied Del's identification, turned the card around, and inspected both sides as if it were a museum curiosity. He wiped his brow. He looked like someone who was always perspiring. Maybe always nervous too. A tic in his left eye.

Del said, "We'd like to talk about Timothy Hutchins."

"I'm a very busy man."

She looked left and right. The only other person in the cavernous space was a bartender, busy staring into his phone while he smoked the hookah. Behind the wall of colorful drink bottles, accessible by a winding staircase, was a mezzanine level, its private lounges strewn with gold pillows and half-obscured by gaudy red sashes. A crescent opening behind the bar led to a domed hallway to the elevators.

They had waited a full ten minutes for this guy after paging him. He gestured to a cushioned bench across a carved wooden table. He moved the hookah pipe to one side.

"I have already spoken to a dozen officers."

As Del slid in beside Jacques, she noticed the bulge under the left side of his suit jacket. A Glock 22 in .40 caliber, just like the one she had at home. First time she had seen him armed since they arrived in Kiev.

At first, he had refused to let her leave the hotel. He had physically pulled her back from Igor's taxi, his fingers digging between the triceps and biceps of her upper arm. She had dropped and blocked, pulled her arm free, and damn near throat-punched him in an almost automatic sequence, only stopping herself just in time to ask him whether she was under arrest.

He had said, of course not.

She had told him that Bondar gave her a lead and that she didn't have much time. Jacques had eventually relented but insisted on coming with her. He asked questions on the way over, but the answer he got was that Bondar had spoken about Timothy Hutchins. She needed to see things with her own eyes, to talk to whoever had discovered Hutchins's disassembled parts.

Bondar had said she was a circus animal, here to do tricks for her masters. Maybe. Maybe she hadn't seen it, had been too hemmed in by all those trees to see the forest that surrounded her. It was time to strip away the leaves, dig down under the bark. Maybe bulldoze an acre or two.

"It took ten days before we noticed the smell," the manager said. "Meanwhile, we had four other guests stay in the suite. I reported all this to the police."

"So, he didn't check out?"

"It is not uncommon with Americans. You just leave, yes? Assume we have a credit card on file? We did not."

"But he left his luggage?"

"He left some clothes."

"You didn't report it?"

"He was due to leave that day, as I said. I'm not the police."

"Did he leave anything valuable?"

This time, the flicker in the eyes was joined by a flowering bloom of blood-heat around them. "Nothing."

Plain lying. Refreshing, in a way, to see something so obvious. Naked and simple. This was no criminal mastermind, no wild-eyed freedom fighter. Just straight-up larcenous self-interest. The manager had taken something of value that Hutchins left behind.

Del didn't press for now. "Who found him?"

"Him?"

"Hutchins's body."

The man's face cooled. "I wouldn't say what they found was a *body*. And unless he did it to himself—"

"Himself?"

"Nobody else went in that room. That I can tell you with certainty."

***

A wiry old man, not more than five feet and a hundred pounds, hovered in the hallway by the elevators. His face was weathered and creased. He didn't offer his hand as he said, "Vasily."

"I'm Detective Devlin, and this is Officer Galloul." Del didn't offer hers, either. "You found Timothy Hutchins's body?"

The old man glanced left and right. His stained dungarees hung loose under a clean denim jacket, and his flat cap, also blue, was too big for his head. "Which man?"

How many bodies had been found in this hotel? "They didn't inform you?"

The old man looked as if he was going to spit. Del took a step back.

"You mean ten-oh-four?" he said.

"That's right. The Czar's Suite."

"What kind of police are you?" He said it to Delta without looking at Jacques.

"American."

"The man was American?"

"He has a sister in New York. Where I'm from. Your English is very good."

His shoulders straightened, and he seemed to grow an inch. "I have a daughter in New Jersey."

"The Garden State. You visit often?"

"Just once. I like it better here." The inch of height diminished.

"Can we look at the room?"

"Ten-oh-four?"

"That's right."

He paused to size up Jacques, then said to Del, "It is empty today."

"The room?" she asked. "So we can open it? Right now?"

Vasily gave a shrug and led them around the corner of the main elevators to a smaller hallway. He put a card from his pocket into a reader, stuck his chin forward, and opened his eyes wide in front of a black glass square on the wall.

His identity accepted, a number pad appeared on the glass display. He glanced down at a fob attached to his card and entered a sequence. "The code changes every hour," he said.

"Facial recognition?" Del asked.

"Retinal scanner."

The words seemed alien coming from this old man. They entered the elevator together. This close, Vasily smelled of onions, sausage, and cigarettes. The elevator was spotless, with a strong whiff of pine cleaner. New. Stainless-steel walls. It accelerated smoothly upward.

Del said, "How did you find the body?"

"All in the reports."

"I'd like to hear it from you. You found him?"

"Cleaning staff said the room stank like a rat was caught in the ventilation." After a pause, he added, "It happens. Quite often."

"Finding bodies in a room?"

"Rats in the ventilation, I meant, but yes, from time to time."

Jacques asked, "Is security like this common?"

The elevator slowed and opened.

Vasily answered, "Military-grade security systems for important guests. Filtered air. Even electronically isolated. I have been trained in the—how do you say?—sales talk." The old man strode down the plush-carpeted hallway to 1004. Del followed with Jacques in tow.

At the door, he inserted his security card and submitted again to an eye scan. This time, a voice asked something in Ukrainian. Vasily answered, sounding annoyed. The door unlocked and hissed open.

Vasily put out his hand and invited them to go ahead.

Jacques said, "What else is in the sales pitch? Air sealed?"

"Exterior windows are triple-layered polycarbonate, bulletproof—can resist anything up to the rocket-propelled grenade attack."

Not exactly standard at the Hyatt.

Del walked in first. Twelve-foot ceilings. Thick ivory wall-to-wall carpet adorned with embroidery, bone-colored furniture bordered in gold leaf. What the hell was Timothy Hutchins so afraid of to warrant renting his own private luxury bunker? He had to be terrified of something—only someone scared would rent a place like this. Or maybe it wasn't unusual on this side of the world

"Where did you find the body?" Del asked as the other two joined her.

Vasily made his way into the bedroom and nodded at a ventilation panel on the opposite wall. "Someone had unscrewed the panel and . . . put the remains into it. Jammed them in."

Del felt woozy. The air seemed to suck itself from the room, and her vision went flat, as if she were removed from the scene. She held on to one of the bedposts to steady herself. The setting sun shone straight through the window opposite the bed and onto the wall below the ventilation register. The wallpaper seemed to glow.

She had noticed the same rainbow-colored pattern on the wall sockets in her room, the same as in the Russian embassy. Had she seen the same pattern on *all* the wall plugs in Kiev?

"You okay?" Jacques whispered.

She said to Vasily, "It took a month to find him?"

"After one week, I found the remains. It took a month for the police to decide who it was."

Del steadied herself and took a step closer to the ventilation duct, shifted her head left and right to get a better look at the rainbow hue against the wallpaper. "What happened there?"

"Must have been dirty hands against the wall," Vasily said, looking at the smudge. "We tried to clean it."

"And the carpet?"

A black caked-on grime at the edge of it, below the vent.

"We are replacing it soon."

"Did the police get any leads?" Jacques asked Vasily.

"You are asking me?" the old man replied.

"Please," Del said.

"He went in at 9:32 p.m. and never came out," Vasily said, sounding as if he had repeated this a dozen times. "There is a private security contractor who monitors all doors and windows. Nobody else came in or out for two days until the next guest checked in. No windows or doors opened. Totally secured."

"And cleaning staff came in?"

"The next day."

"And didn't see anything?"

"The police have all the security camera footage." Vasily sniffed. "I am surprised it took so long for them to find out."

Del inspected the rainbow-hued smudge on the wall again. "Why is that?"

"Mr. Hutchins left without paying his bill."

"He didn't?"

Vasily hesitated.

Del turned to him. "What does that mean?"

The old man's face darkened. "You want to know the truth? About this Russian running the place? I'll tell you the truth."

***

"Get some sleep," Jacques said. "I'll talk to Commissioner Georgiev about Hutchins."

"Please don't," Del replied.

They had returned to Hyatt. She felt as if she might pass out. 7:00 p.m. She hung halfway in and out of her hotel room door. A waiter slipped past them carrying a tray loaded with stainless-steel platters. Del wasn't sure whether she was hungry or wanted to throw up.

"Why?"

"I'm not sure." She hadn't shared what she'd seen on the wall. What Jacques couldn't have seen. To him, it was just a dark smudge; to her, a rainbow of color.

"Our flight is 10:00 a.m.," Jacques said. "Do not leave this room."

"Are you serious?"

"This is for your own safety." The Frenchman's shoulders slumped. "For what it is worth, I am sorry. About the complaints. I had to."

"Had to?"

"I have bosses, too. This has been an ongoing fight. It's not about you."

It's me, not you. How many times had she heard that? It was how her relationships tended to end. *It's not you*, they'd say, when really they meant, *it's* all *you*. Hearing it from Jacques felt depressing for more than one reason.

"Please, Detective. For your own safety."

She watched his face. Saw him watching her *watching* him. She looked away guiltily. She had been doing it again. Reading his colors, seeing whether he was telling the truth. *A spy.* That's what he had called her. And now she was spying on him, but he held her gaze. He was telling the truth or was a hell of a good liar. She decided on truthful.

"I won't go out," Del said.

"At 8:00 a.m. I will be back. If you need anything, I am just a few doors down."

She let her door close.

Lies. Truth. Bullshit.

Everyone seemed to think she had some superpower, when the truth was less dramatic. It was a skill, a perception, nothing more or less. The truth was, she'd had enough. She wanted to go home.

She needed to talk to her father, ask him about Jonathan Murphy. Was that why Bondar had contacted her? Because she had a family connection to the IRA? Was he in touch with her *uncle*? Was he working with the IRA? Did this stranger know more about her family than she did? She had to call her father first thing tomorrow morning.

No.

She would talk to her mother. She had to know. If she didn't, then Del might need to step more carefully. This wasn't just a case anymore. This was her life. Her family's life.

Del's room had been cleaned, the sheets back to perfect. Her clothes and shoes arranged.

That rainbow smudge on the wall in the Czar's Suite at the Persian Palace was the remains of melted plastic, she was sure of it. The same shimmering colors she had seen when she melted the combination of cellulose acetate and polyethylene that came out of the Strataform machines. She looked at the Replicator sitting in the corner of her room.

Hutchins had had one, too. In his room at the Persian. That was what Vasily told them. The big secret. The manager had taken the printer and sold it, used it to pay the bill when he thought the man had skipped out.

That was why he didn't report the man missing.

Whoever had stuffed Hutchins's remains into that ventilation shaft didn't want him to be found, not right away. They had to be desperate. Maybe they couldn't sneak a body out past all that security. That made sense. So they cut the body up. Hid it.

Somebody had to have been in there. Vasily said the ventilation duct was unscrewed. Someone did that. Someone cut up the body and stuffed it in there. All that fancy security meant someone was lying.

She opened her laptop and searched for Maker Faire. And there it was. Mid-January. She knew she'd seen it before. There had been a Maker Faire conference here in Kiev that week. Bondar had to have been here. Adam Petty as well. That was the conference Hutchins had come here for, Vasily said. The hotel was full of Americans that week, attending the show.

What the hell was going on?

She was too tired to form ideas out of the murk swirling in her head. In two steps, she collapsed onto her bed, grabbed one side of the covers, and pulled them over her as she kicked off her pumps. She closed her eyes.

***

Del ran down the rain-soaked sidewalk. The air was thick with acrid smoke. She was too slow, so she left the ground and floated forward into space, high enough that she could get a view of the curling black clouds over Belfast in the distance. Wicked flames licked the sky.

"This way." A man in a black balaclava waved her forward.

He crouched and swept his automatic weapon left and right to clear the hedges before motioning for her to follow.

Behind them came the creatures.

She couldn't turn her head. Was it fear? Did she not want to see? She couldn't turn to look, but she felt them. The spiders, crawling up her body, up the back of her neck. Faster—they needed to move faster.

***

Del awoke with a start, panting.

It was pitch-black.

She tried to move but felt a crushing weight on her chest. Not just her chest. Her face, her arms pinned down against the bed. *You're still asleep, she told herself. This is just a nightmare. Wake up. Stay calm. Just breathe.*

27

Calm.

Return to the breath.

Panic is the enemy in any situation.

Are you sure you're still not asleep? Del inhaled slowly on a five count, then exhaled to a six. She didn't try to open her eyes. Didn't try to move. Her mind filled with half-memories of mindscapes, waking into a dream and then into another, fever-fueled nightmares of monsters from when she was a child.

Return to the breath.

Her heaving chest slowed.

She couldn't move her arms or legs. *What happened?* Sharp edges pressed against her face and the exposed skin of her hands. What did she last remember? Getting into the bed, her eyes closing, and the heavy darkness of sleep almost before she hit the sheets.

This was no dream.

Bile rose up and burned the back of her throat. She squirmed and then cried out. Something hard and angular wedged into her mouth.

Adrenaline hit her bloodstream like chilled rocket fuel.

She wriggled in panic, and her left arm came free. She wrenched it up and scraped at her face, pulling away debris, and shoved herself sideways, scrabbling and pushing.

And fell into open space.

She hit the floor hard. A carpeted floor.

Del rolled away and sprang to her feet, staggered, and banged into the table and chairs, almost falling over before she put a steadying hand against the patio window. She turned. The nightscape of Kiev's skyline shimmered beyond the glass.

Quiet and serene.

She turned back. Her bed . . .

The bed was covered in a dark mound rising in a cone three feet high—a mosaic of dark fragments and angles. She took a wobbling step and bent down to pick up what looked like a plastic business card, featureless and dark. Her shaking hand dropped it.

"What the f . . ."

She was still dressed. Her head throbbed. A jolt of jet-fueled panic shot her running around the foot of the bed. She skidded to the floor again before scrambling to her feet and banging into the door, opening it, and running into the carpeted hallway.

**

Del slammed the meaty part of her fist into the door. It swung open and jammed against the chain lock as she was about to pound it a fourth time. Jacques's face appeared in the gap, his blue dress shirt unbuttoned. He was barefoot in rumpled suit pants.

He lowered the Glock in his right hand down to the side.

"What's wrong?" He peered carefully forward but retreated, his eyes still on her. "Are you alone?"

"I need to come in."

Jacques rocked back, mumbled a curse in French, and disappeared for an instant as he closed and unlatched the door. It swung open a foot, and Del pushed her way past him. Two room service trays were on the floor by the foot of the bed. The desk by the window was strewn with papers secured by his laptop.

The room smelled musty, sweaty with an undertone of french fries.

"What is it?" Jacques peered into the hallway before closing the door. She sat on the bed and put her head in her hands.

"What?" His voice softened. He buttoned up his shirt and sat next to her. "Detective Devlin, what happened?"

"I . . . I was . . ." The words were not forming. She still wasn't sure. *Buried in plastic?* "Something in my room."

She fought back tears, but it wasn't just the shock of the moment. Images flooded her brain—her father, his sickness, him pushing her away even as he lied to her. Did he lie? Or did he just leave out the truth? She fought a sensation of claustrophobia, of chasing a ghost to the other side of a world that squeezed and pressed in on her mind.

Jacques said, "Some*thing*? Someone? Tell me. Should I call the police?"

"I was buried." She reined her emotions back in. "Buried alive."

No tears. She was not going to cry. Del gritted her teeth and let the fear transform into anger.

"Buried? Where? Last night, in the tunnel? I'm sure it—"

"Just now."

"Just *now*?"

"Are you going to repeat everything I say? In my bed. I was buried in my bed." Her voice was calmer, but the words seemed to come from someone else's lips. She realized how ridiculous it sounded. *Buried alive in my bed.*

Inhale. Exhale. Hands steady now and to each side of her. She explained, "Someone dumped a load of . . . I'm not sure. Plastic disks? A whole truckload of them, right on top of me. In my room."

"Are you serious?"

"Do I look like I'm joking?" She used the line he had used on her earlier in the day. Stupid. She shouldn't be sarcastic. This wasn't the right moment. You had to be careful with sarcasm, her father always told her. Another dagger lodged in her throat.

"You look . . ." Jacques paused to choose his words. "Do you want a glass of water?"

"Somebody just attacked me while I was asleep."

"*And* you were kidnapped last night."

"What are you saying?"

He affected the Gallic shrug she found so annoying. "Let's go, right now. To your room." He bent over to put on his socks and pulled his shoes from under the bedside table. The digital clock on top of it read 3:02 a.m.

Del was still dressed in the business slacks and blouse of the day before, but no shoes. She remembered kicking those off when she hit the covers. She stood and patted her pockets. "Damn it."

"What?"

The doors closed automatically when you went out.

***

"Twelve sixteen," Del said to the young woman behind the reception desk.

She had her hair done up in a bun and wore a black business suit and white shirt. Pale skin. She smiled a perfunctory grin and asked, "Mrs . . .?"

"Miss. Devlin. Delta Devlin."

"You have identification?"

"I left it in my room. With my key. Which is why I am here." *Easy with the sarcasm.* Del did her best to smile. "This is an emergency."

"Emergency?"

Why was everyone repeating what she said? *Inhale. Exhale.*

Jacques produced his Interpol identification. "Please, we need the key immediately."

The young woman's eyes widened. "Just one moment, yes?" She turned and disappeared into the back room.

Del inhaled again, counted the breath out, and leaned on the white plastic countertop. It was polished, curved, highly engineered. The lobby was three stories high, its four rows of white leather couches empty, the bank of elevators clad in amber glass, with floating amber glass chandeliers, reminding her of Timothy Hutchins's artwork, flowing and biological.

Del studied its form. It had to be 3-D printed. there was no other way to manufacture something like that. She had started to notice a lot of this sort of stuff scattered in nearly every corner of Kiev.

The young woman reappeared with another woman. Same uniform, older face.

The manager inspected Jacques's ID herself while working at the computer terminal. "I recognize Miss Devlin. There is no problem."

The younger one raised a finger, as if she needed to be called on before speaking in class.

"Yes?" Del said.

"Your name is Devlin?"

"That's right."

"Ghost Devlin?" The younger woman retrieved a package from behind the counter.

Del nodded, which got a confused frown from Jacques.

The woman handed over a manila envelope maybe two inches thick. Jacques tried to get a look. "What is it?"

She tucked it under her arm. "From my parents. My old nickname."

His eyes narrowed, but he didn't pursue it.

"Here you go," said the older woman from behind the counter, handing her a plastic key card. "Sorry for the delay. Our computers had a glitch."

Del took it. The key looked like a white version of the mass of thousands of black plastic cards that had covered her on the bed—that had almost suffocated her.

"And I will need to see the video camera logs from the last two hours for the sixteenth floor," Jacques said, his Interpol ID still up. "Please have security prepare them for me."

***

Jacques took the key card from Del and pressed it against the door handle. The light flashed green, and the lock clicked. He depressed the handle and swung the door, then held it open, holding his Glock out in the other hand. He edged into the hallway, glanced into the bathroom on the right, and walked into the bedroom.

Del followed him in, her eyes on the bed.

It was empty. Not empty, just no massive pile on top of it. The sheets were rumpled as if she had slept on top of them. Which she had before being immersed in a three-foot-deep sea of plastic. Which wasn't there anymore.

How long had she been gone?

The digital clock on the bedside said 3:10 a.m. Eight minutes since they were in Jacques's room. Not more than ten minutes since she left. Could someone have cleaned it up that fast? It was possible. But . . .

"The patio door is locked," Jacques said after testing it.

No adjoining doors. So whoever staged this trick had to have come in from the hallway.

"I'll check the security cameras," Jacques said, thinking the same thing she was. He put his weapon away. "But you are, I mean . . ."

"I'm sure." Del flipped up the sheets and looked under the bed. Nothing. Nothing at all.

***

Had she been dreaming? Drugged?

Five a.m. now, and the sky was brightening, the sun just over the horizon, and the city lights fading. Jacques offered to stay, but she told him she was fine. She wasn't. He checked the security cameras. No one had come down that hallway after 1:00 a.m., and nothing was on the exterior cameras, either.

Del searched the room but found nothing.

No black plastic cards, no other entrances or exits at all except a ventilation duct under her bed, against the wall. She had shined a light into it, smelled the air. Remembered Vasily's story of pulling bits of flesh from it. Remembered the glint of the rainbow smudge against the wall in the Czar's Suite. Burnt plastic. What did it mean?

While Jacques looked at footage from the hotel's security cameras, Del stayed in her room and searched security footage as well, but not from the hotel—from the UN Building the day her father was shot.

Suweil's package had a hard drive with the six hundred gigabytes of UN video that she had requested from him yesterday. He had sent it by courier, along with a new phone, which he said was unregistered with the Interpol system.

A favor, he said. Just to be sure. He wasn't sure how it was possible that someone had compromised the Interpol internal communications network, since everything was encrypted end to end, but if the attacker had inserted a middleman attack . . . The details became more technical, and Del couldn't follow it.

A note, scrawled in careful block letters, was inside with his package.

Suweil said he had reviewed the video of her father being shot. He said that it did look fake. This sort of thing was analyzed as a matter of procedure at Interpol, to see if videos had been tampered with, and he wasn't sure how it had escaped review. Korshunov didn't blink at all in the sixteen seconds he was in the video—not quite impossible, but almost.

Why hadn't anyone else spotted the deception?

Del began reviewing security footage from the UN meeting, starting first with the cameras by the entrance. She tracked forward to the time her father arrived, then cycled back and forth, watching the faces that came in past security.

If one person could be faked, then why not more than one? She needed to see Korshunov coming in. Watch who was with him. Again she reviewed the recording of the shooting. Suweil said the fakes were the ones who weren't blinking. She stared at the eyes. Who in those frames wasn't closing their eyes?

She rubbed her neck.

Just past five. Ten at night in New York. She was procrastinating. She had to make the call.

***

The phone picked up on the first ring. "Mom?"

"Delta, honey, how are you?"

Her mother's lilting Southern accent sounded melodic. Tender. Delta was tired of not understanding most of what people said, of the fragmented English and rough accents. She wanted to crawl through the telephone connection and curl up on the other side.

"I'm fine."

A pause on the other end. "When you say that, you never are."

Now a pause on Delta's end.

"What's wrong? Did you talk to your sister?"

"I need to ask you something about Dad."

"He's not doing very well, honey girl. He's in for surgery. They need to put a stent into his throat."

"Is he okay?"

"Very sick."

The way she said it, Del heard the strain. Could feel the lump in her mom's throat even from five thousand miles away.

"I'm coming home," Del said. "Today. I'm leaving Kiev. I'll find the first flight back to New York from Lyon."

Her mother sobbed once on the other end. "That is so good to hear. I'll cook up—"

"I need to ask you something."

"About what?"

"About Dad. Did he change his name? When he came to America?"

"What do you mean?"

"I'm not kidding. Did Dad change his surname from Murphy? Is his brother *Jonathan* Murphy?" As she forced the words out, the skin on the back of her neck prickled.

Another pause. For one second, then two. "Mom? You still there?"

"That was a long time ago."

Del let those words sink in. *A long time ago.* Not a denial. Not a confused reply, asking what she was asking. Her mother understood. She understood and said it was a long time ago, but what exactly was *it*?

Her mother continued, "He was trying to start a new life. He had nothing to do with any of that. Your father had to separate himself, you understand?"

"I'm trying. Did he ever . . . I mean, was he—"

"He never had anything to do with it," her mother repeated. "He wanted a fresh start."

How would her mother know? What had he told her? Del had so many questions, she wasn't sure where to start. Her whole life felt as if it had just fallen out from under her. Who was she really? Who was her family? The floor sank into the earth, swallowing her up.

Something pinged. Then pinged again. It wasn't Del's phone.

She glanced at the Strataform Replicator in the corner of the room, but it was off, its orange eye dark. Another ping. It was something on Del's bed. She scattered some papers. It was the new phone Suweil had sent her.

His text read:

> I have initial results from DNA testing
> on the Korshunov shell casing.

"Your father wanted to get away," her mother said on her other phone. "It was a different time, honey."

> The coroner's report says it was a low-
> velocity entry, just like your father's wound.
> The bullet is .38 caliber. I wanted you to
> know first, but it's your DNA on the shell
> casing. I had to send in the report.

"Mom, I'm sorry, but I need to go."

"You're coming home?"

"I'm on my way."

She told her mother that she loved her and to tell dad the same thing, but her mind had already slipped sideways. The sick feeling in the pit of her stomach was gone, replaced with something more toxic. She hung up and looked again at the Replicator.

Del got up and went to the machine and turned it on, entered her security access code, and cycled through some menus. She found the one for print jobs and scrolled down.

Scrolled down.

She hadn't even used the machine yet.

What were all these jobs it had been used for? She checked the dates. A whole collection of them were yesterday. And there. One of them was a print job for parts of the 3-D gun file she had downloaded two days ago. She hadn't done that. Not printed it out. Proof that someone had been in her room.

She wasn't imagining it.

She was being set up.

Her face flushed, and she crossed over to her dresser, rummaged through the clothes, and found the bag with the ammunition she had brought to test the device. It was a plastic strip loaded with eight rounds.

One was missing.

She pulled her clothes from the drawer. Nothing.

"Damn it." She knelt and grabbed her suitcase and threw her clothes into it, went to the closet and took everything off the hangers. She grabbed the remaining seven rounds of ammunition on the plastic strip and pushed them into a side pocket of her bag, scanned the room quickly, grabbed her coat, and made her way out the door, grabbing her laptop bag and Suweil's new burner phone.

With her regular phone, she texted Jacques and said she would meet him at the airport.

But she didn't even make it to the elevator.

One of Grigory's men, the same young man as the day before, held up his hand to stop her. "Miss Devlin, I'm afraid we are going to need your passport."

28

Concrete chips from the pockmarked walls littered the floor. The stairs up were painted red. The room's single door was roughly welded steel framed in wood. The edge near the lock looked as if it had been chipped away by fingernails. The walls, too, were littered with scrapes.

It smelled of fresh bleach—the chemical strong enough to wash away blood, break down DNA, and erase any trace of a person.

Del was a long way from home.

The young officer had brought her down here, smiling the whole way in the police car, telling her not to worry, which, of course, had the opposite effect. They had come in through the back entrance, through doors with inch-thick steel bars, to a stainless-steel table and chair in the basement. They brought her luggage, left her with her cell phones, but took her passport.

Then left her alone.

If the goal was intimidation, it was working. Neither of her phones worked. For two hours, they sweated her without answering any of her questions, without telling her anything. No one searched her, though, or her luggage.

Footsteps down the stairs, and the steel hinges creaked as the door opened.

"Miss Devlin, I do apologize," Grigory Georgiev said.

He closed the welded-steel door behind him. He was alone.

Delta said, "Am I under arrest?"

"Why are you here?"

He took the chair opposite her, across the table.

"For the election monitoring."

"Have you not seen the news? Russian forces amassing on our eastern border. All American service staff have been recalled. Why are you *still* here?"

"I was trying to leave. I have—*had*—a flight this morning." That flight, if it was on time, was leaving in fifteen minutes. No chance now.

"Which explains the luggage. And the rush. Yes?"

The commissioner smiled in a blank-faced way that felt more threatening than comforting. When Del first met him, he had seemed like a big teddy bear, his large hands and huge shoulders and slab face the archetype of a Slavic strong man. Down here, alone with him in this basement, she wondered why the place had just been scrubbed down with bleach. The teddy now looked more grizzly.

"I'm being set up," Del said.

"By who?"

A good question, which she didn't have an answer for. This big Slav sitting across from her, smiling a menacing grin, was one very real possibility. He was the one standing closest to her father when he was shot. But Adam Petty was the one who sent her the Strataform Replicator—the one used to print 3-D gun parts that would surely match the one used to shoot Korshunov. And then there was Bondar.

"I don't know."

"For what?"

"Korshunov."

"I heard your father is in surgery today. Please, wish him my best."

"I'd like to go home and do that in person. I might still be able—"

"I'm afraid you won't be making any flights today."

Del glanced at the green metal bars of the door behind him. She'd been a police officer for six years, but she had never been the person on this end. Locked up. Freedom taken away. The gulf between her and her family felt like a light-year and growing wider by the second.

"I have great sympathy for you, Detective Devlin," Grigory said. "But you know how this must look."

"Why don't you explain it for me?"

"We have security camera footage of you chasing Yuri Korshunov into a tunnel. Grainy, admittedly, but you yourself admitted to going in there after him. We have your own confession."

"He was the one who approached me. He was then kidnapped."

"So you say. In this same tunnel, we find a shell casing that we sent to your own Interpol labs for analysis, and it comes back with your DNA." He looked at her luggage. "Should we search you? What would we find, Detective?"

She repeated, "Am I under arrest?"

"Not yet."

"Then why am I here?"

"Because we need to get to the bottom of this before we can allow you to leave. A lot of strange things have been happening since you arrived." He shifted in his seat, putting both forearms on the table, and leaned toward her. "Yuri Korshunov was a Russian FSB piece of crap. The world is better off with him dead; on that we all can agree. Did you shoot him? If you did, this can solve my problem." He shrugged. "We just say you were defending yourself."

"I didn't shoot him."

"Do you work for the CIA?"

"If I shot him, how did he end up in a park miles from that tunnel? Do you think I dragged him there? By myself?"

"Did you? Maybe you had help. You also appear on video cameras coming from that park that morning. I ask you again, do you work for the American CIA?"

Del paused and then said, "Did *you* shoot my father?"

The big man sat back in his chair and gave a big snort of laughter that came from deep in his belly. He slapped both hands against his knees. "And here I thought I was the one asking questions."

"The video from the UN was faked."

"Faked?" The bear's smile slid away.

"It wasn't Yuri who shot my father. Did you see Yuri? With your own eyes? You were the closest person."

Deep furrows on the Ukrainian's face. "I had my back to your father. I turned when I heard the shot, and caught him."

"Did you see Korshunov? Actually see his face?"

The commissioner's eyes went up and to the left—a tell for when someone was trying to remember. Up and to the right was when they were trying to invent. "I did not. No, I did not see him. I only saw the video."

"Did you shoot my father?" Del asked again.

"I did not."

His face remained cool, no blood pumping into the edges of his eyes or forehead. Either he was a master liar, or the lie had no personal impact for him. He could be thinking this was somehow for a greater good. He might not have done it for himself.

"Do you work for the CIA?" he asked again.

"I do not."

"I believe you." He put both palms onto the steel table. "You see? Progress. Why were you at the Persian Palace Hotel yesterday?"

"Investigating the disappearance of Timothy Hutchins."

"But *why*?"

"Because Leonardo Bondar told me to."

The commissioner's head nodded. "We will need the access codes for the 3-D printer in your room."

"It was used to print a 3-D gun, I can tell y—"

Noise in the stairwell interrupted her. Someone yelling and then cursing. In French. Jacques's voice echoed down the hallway, followed by scuffling noises and someone else yelling in Ukrainian. The Frenchman appeared behind the steel grate of the door to the stairs leading up.

"Delta, are you here?" Jacques said.

"I'm fine," she called back.

A Kiev police officer tried to haul him back up the stairs.

"It's okay, it's okay," Grigory said. "Let him down."

A second later, the door creaked open and Jacques pushed his way into the basement. "I must strongly object, Commissioner Georgiev.

Detective Delta Devlin is here on official Interpol business and—"

"You can object all you like, but I need Detective Devlin's help."

"With what?"

"Finding Leonardo Bondar."

"I don't know where he is," Del said.

"But you do you know what his people look like, yes? From the rave party?"

She nodded.

"We are lucky it's a Saturday night. We're going to sweep the club areas."

"You think they would be dumb enough to go there now?"

"You would be surprised how dumb people can be. Once you help us find Bondar, you will be free to go." He turned and nodded at Jacques, then looked back at Delta. "Now, is there anything else you haven't told me?"

Del glanced at her luggage, the cartridges in the front pocket. An image formed in her mind, of the man—*her uncle*—in the black balaclava mask, holding the AR-15.

"Nothing else," Del said. Not right now, anyway.

***

Thumping bass rattled the Lada's windows even a hundred feet from the entrance. This wasn't Igor's Lada. This one was even older and more decrepit, if that was possible. The officer in charge of the stakeout used them to keep a low profile, he said. No one believed that police would sit in cars like these.

The kids who went to these parties spent half their time outside, buying and selling and consuming drugs, among other activities. Del watched a young couple making out in the car ahead of them.

She sat in the backseat, next to Commissioner Georgiev. Del kept one eye on the stream of young people going into the Dacha nightclub, while glancing back and forth at another stream on her laptop. Video playback from all the cameras at the UN Building the day her father was shot. She was steadily fast-forwarding through hundreds of hours of footage but unsure what she was looking for.

Her luggage was in the trunk.

As soon as she spotted one of Bondar's people, as soon as they captured them, she would be free to go. That was what they said. She wasn't so sure, but on this, at least, their interests aligned—she, too, wanted to speak to Bondar again.

They had spent the rest of that morning and into the afternoon working with sketch artists to come up with ideas of what Bondar's "men" looked like. Georgiev's officers kept using that word, "men." As if they were soldiers, which they weren't. That much, Del was sure of. At least one of them was a woman. She thought. That, she wasn't quite as sure of.

The problem was, most of what she could remember were their outfits. Maybe they were cleverer than she thought. At the time, she had assumed they were just colorful kids, dressed up for an evening out, wearing costumes that let them blend into the streaming masses of youth in these clubs. And all she could remember now were the costumes.

Effective.

It was already almost midnight, and Del was heading into a fourth night of almost no sleep. She had managed to sneak in about two hours at the end of the afternoon, before they set off. Once the sun went down, they began the rounds, starting at the Stereo Palace.

Del's phone pinged, and she picked it up.

An image was texted to her.

She opened the picture and zoomed in. She squinted. A young man with red hair.

"Is that one of them?" the commissioner asked.

Del shook her head and texted back. No, not anyone she recognized.

The commissioner's officers had looked at the sketches and listened to her descriptions, and the younger ones were now prowling the clubs, taking pictures and sending them to her. Finding Bondar had become Georgiev's focus—and Del's, if she wanted to get out of here.

She had called her mother and said she missed her plane today, but that she would be on the first one tomorrow. As of four hours ago, her father was still in surgery. Something had gone wrong, but she had no more information than that. They promised they would text her when they knew. Nothing yet. Del said a small prayer every time she thought of her father. Imagined him in some surgical bed, tubes coming out of him. Why was she here, so far away?

Del shook her head to clear it, then scrubbed fast-forward on the video of the UN entrance. She didn't see anything unusual but wasn't sure what she was looking for. She tried staring at the images, hoping to see anyone who wasn't blinking, but that was an impossible task to undertake by hand.

She glanced up from her laptop at a new knot of kids going into the club. Nothing and nobody familiar.

"These assassinations need to stop," Grigory said.

Del looked back at her UN video. "I didn't kill anyone."

"I'm not saying you. I'm thinking out loud."

"I'm listening."

"Korshunov might have been an FSB asset, and I don't regret him being gone—but the Russian government is crying foul. There have been six Russian agents assassinated in the past month, since Bondar arrived here—and he's never lived here before. He's American. And speaking of that, four Americans have died in Kiev under suspicious circumstances since the start of this year. The East and West are gearing up for a war over it, and Ukraine is caught in the middle. Again."

Del decided to switch to a different camera feed at the UN Building, one in the hallway leading to the main reception. "What about Olek . . . what's his name? The one they were shouting about at the UN meeting."

"Oleksiy Bozhena. The Ukrainian freedom fighter killed in Moldova."

"What happened to him? Was he shot?"

"These murders, if we can call them that—the coroners are having a hard time coming up with cause of death. Often, it is something internal, bleeding, as if the attacker had a knife inside their body. Often much stranger."

Del said, "*Inside* their body?"

"That's right."

She fast-forwarded the image on her laptop, and a stream of people walked up into the main reception. She was hardly paying attention, but something that Grigory had said tweaked her mind.

"What kind of injuries?" Del said as she looked up, then looked back down at her laptop. Two people had just fast-forward sprinted up the stairwell and stopped to talk, then disappeared. Who were they? She hit the rewind button.

"Do you want to see some of the coroner reports?" Grigory asked.

"Yeah . . ." Her voice trailed off as she looked up.

On the other side of a pack of kids, two stiff braids of hair helicoptered above the others.

"That's her," Del said. "That's the one that was with Bondar." The same blue dots of paint on her cheeks and forehead, same four braids of crazy hair sticking up from the back of her head.

"You're sure?" Grigory picked up his walkie-talkie and spoke into it.

Del looked back down and froze the image on her laptop screen.

And there *they* were.

Adam Petty and Leonardo Bondar, speaking together in the stairwell outside the reception at the UN event. Neither had mentioned he was there. She checked the time stamp. Ten minutes before her father was shot. In fact, the NYPD had questioned Bondar. He had said he was in Flushing Meadows that day. So Bondar was lying. He had been there when her father was shot.

Unless this video was also a fake.

29

The keening squeal of a trapped animal reverberated in the enclosed space, the screech echoing dully off the damp concrete. How many pleading wails had these walls absorbed over the years? Too many to count, Del imagined. The building looked most of a century old and had to date from deep into the decades when Ukraine was part of the Soviet Union. Was this a regular police headquarters back then, or part of the secret police?

Was there a difference? Even now?

They had returned to the same precinct she was in yesterday. This time, Del wasn't the captive. She hoped. They said she would be free to go once she helped them find one of Bondar's people, but now Grigory said he meant once they found Bondar himself.

Shifting goalposts.

Not that Del had any options. There was no escaping to an American consulate. All US staff had been evacuated as Russian forces threatened the eastern border two hours' drive away. Fighting had intensified in the south, and it was rumored that armored forces had already breached through from Crimea. Del wasn't even sure there were any more flights to the west. The airport was canceling commercial flights.

As much as she wanted to speak again to Bondar, Del felt nothing but pity for this poor thing zip-tied to the chair in the middle of the ten-by-ten room. The young woman's helicopter braids had come undone in a stringy mess now matted to her sweat-streaked makeup, and tears were rolling past the blue dots under the girl's eyes. She was eighteen but looked younger.

They had identified her as Bondar's cousin Irina.

"You know this woman?" One of Grigory's men held Irina's chin in a hand as big as her face. He had been questioning her in Ukrainian but switched to heavily accented English for Del's benefit as he pointed his other hand at the detective to make the point.

Irina managed a small nod.

"You abducted her at the Stereo Palace?"

The girl whispered something in Ukrainian.

"She said they saved you," another of Grigory's officers, Dany, said into Del's ear.

It was the same young officer who had retrieved her from the hotel yesterday. He had been assigned to shadow Del; that much was obvious. He said to call him Dany, but his real name, his Ukrainian name, was Danya. It meant "God's gift." Blue eyes, square chin, broad chest. It wasn't hard to imagine what he was thinking as he told Del what his name meant. The young man had a high opinion of himself.

She had to be careful of him. Of everything. She was on her own.

The big officer with the dinner-plate-size hands slapped Irina hard enough that she almost fell sideways from the chair she was tied to. He returned to questioning her in Ukrainian.

"I'm going next door," Del said back to Dany. She couldn't watch any more of this. It didn't take much to imagine herself in that chair.

***

Del opened her laptop in the main lobby of the basement.

Yesterday, she had thought that maybe Bondar's people were dressing up like club kids, using this as a disguise to melt into the underground of Kiev's young population. But the ease with which they had found and captured his cousin, the young girl in the next room, reinforced Del's earlier opinion that these were just kids playing at being soldiers. Then again, kids playing at being soldiers often got people killed, usually themselves first.

"What's that?" Dany asked from over her shoulder.

"Video recordings from the United Nations Building in New York."

"Security cameras?"

"That's right."

The young man leaned closer. "That's Leonardo Bondar. Who is he talking to?"

"Adam Petty."

"The founder of Strataform."

"That's right."

"What are they talking about? Do you have audio?"

"Wish I did."

"What about lipreading?"

"I can't read lips."

She wished she could have seen this live, though. The image was clear and in color, but recorded in RGB—red, green, blue—not in the full color spectrum her eyes could see. She couldn't see the blood flow in their faces, couldn't use her crutch of seeing what others couldn't see. It felt like boxing with one eye closed.

"But isn't there software that can? Some type of algorithm? You are Interpol, yes?"

This kid wasn't just a pretty face. Del hadn't thought of that. Why wouldn't there be?

Another slap of skin against skin, and Irina yelped in the next room.

Del rummaged in her pocket and took out her two phones. She selected the burner from Suweil. She texted him to ask about reading lips using software and gave him the coordinates of the video on Bondar and Petty.

She added that she had an idea. She wanted to send an email in clear text into Interpol and see if he could trace the leak, if there was one. There was no signal down here, so the messages didn't send.

She needed to get aboveground.

"Why do you have two phones?" Dany asked.

Del lied casually, "Most Americans do."

She couldn't talk to Bondar yet, but Petty didn't know she'd found this video of him. He had never said he was at the UN Building—in fact, had lied about it, telling the NYPD he was in Queens when her father was shot. She emailed him and asked whether he had time to speak again, and left her laptop on and put it into her bag. She needed to tether its wireless to her phone when she got a connection.

"Dany, that was a good idea, the lipreading."

The young man's face brightened. Another hard slap and yelp came from the next room.

"Do you think you could help me again?"

"We cannot leave the building."

"The coroner is two floors up. We wouldn't need to go out."

He pouted duck lips for a second, then said, "Let me check with the boss."

***

The morgue door yawned open and exhaled a sharp whiff of preserved death. The cadaverous coroner, the same one with the pale-brown cat eyes, snapped off one rubber glove and held his hand out. "Detective Devlin, how can I help you?" he said with an accent that sounded vaguely British.

Behind him was a pallid body with a freshly opened chest, the ribs spread wide like a scavenged clam. Del hesitated but took the coroner's moist hand and pumped it twice. The bony fingers, practiced in cutting and squeezing, had a strong grip. Green-sheeted gurneys jammed the floor space between the four autopsy tables.

"Busy night?" Del asked.

"You could say that."

"Can we speak out here?" The sight of decomposing bodies made her think of her father. Her throbbing headache had returned.

The coroner glanced over his shoulder and said something to his assistant, who turned on a bone saw with a high-pitched whine. The door closed behind the coroner, the noise abating into a low squeal as the instrument bit into a rib.

Del said, "You autopsied Timothy Hutchins?"

"Hutchins?"

"The American."

"You'll have to be more specific."

How many dead Americans were there? "From the Persian Palace."

Through the closed door, the saw's pitch seesawed as it ripped through sinew and bone.

"Ah, I remember. Hutchins. They brought in parts of him in Ziploc bags. Interesting. The blood had congealed before death."

"Before? Any idea of the cause of death?"

"The man was cut into a dozen pieces. More than a dozen."

"You just said the blood had congealed before death."

"My best guess. Some type of clotting agent. I imagine so they wouldn't create a mess sectioning the corpse."

"You think he was murdered inside the hotel room?"

"Why else stuff him into the ventilation duct? This is only conjecture, however. You are the detective; I merely catalogue my observations."

"What kind of tool was used? Any idea?"

The coroner squeezed his eyes shut. He shook his head and then opened his eyes, almost like a lizard, the paleness of the light-brown irises oddly disconcerting. "My feeling is that this is not just one blade but dozens."

"Dozens?"

"The large bones were left intact, the femur and so on, but the meat cleaned off as if by a scavenger. Extremely sharp. Tiny blades, like a food processor. And I've had more cases." He waved a hand at the morgue door. "I am not sure what to make of it. I need to get back."

Food processor? Del's stomach churned at the image of bones and blood in a Cuisinart. Was he serious? "Can I get a copy of your report?"

He glanced at Dany, who nodded. "If you read it here."

The coroner had to return to his work, and Del sat at a table in the hallway. Another green-smocked man delivered the report, and she asked Dany to read it out to her in translation. Just what the coroner had said. There was cell phone reception on the second floor, so with Dany looking over her shoulder, she tethered her laptop to her phone's data and sent out an email to Suweil, texting him on the burner phone as well.

A body stuffed into a ventilation duct. Herself getting trapped underground and then buried alive in her hotel room. Bodies cut up from the inside out. Del opened up her web browser and looked again at the images of Petty and Bondar yakking away at the UN Building.

If someone had altered the original video to make it look as if Korshunov shot her father, how could she have any faith that this was real? If either of these two was implicated, why would they be left in the video? She replayed it again, watched their faces. She saw Bondar blink, very clearly, and then again.

***

Del pushed open the basement door. The girl Irina's face was smeared with blood.

"Did she say where Bondar is?" Del asked. "Anything about Korshunov?"

"She says that Korshunov was working with them," the interrogator with the meaty hands replied in a thick accent. He paced around Irina, rubbing his knuckles. "She says he had left the FSB. That's why the Russians were after him."

"He did not shoot your father," Irina said to Del in halting English. She spat out a mouthful of blood.

"Who did? Do you know?"

The young woman shook her head.

The interrogator grabbed her flyaway braids and yanked her head back. "Where is Bondar?" he growled.

Del stepped forward and gently put a hand on his forearm, urged him to let go. She pulled up a chair beside Irina. "I need to speak to Lenny again," Del said.

Irina looked at the interrogator and then back at Del and shook her head. "Korshunov was at the UN meeting trying to *talk to* Voloshyn, not hurt her."

"What did he want to tell her?"

The girl shrugged.

"Was Bondar there? At the UN?"

Another shrug, but this time her head nodded as well.

"So he was at the UN Building when Korshunov was there?"

"When your father was shot. I don't know about Korshunov."

Another small piece of the puzzle fell into place. So Bondar was at the UN Building. The video wasn't a fake—not that part of it.

"Did he shoot my father?"

She shook her head.

"Look at me and answer," Del said.

Irina's head slowly came up, and she looked Del in the eye. "No."

"Was he planning something with Adam Petty?"

Another shrug, this time with no head nod.

The interrogator snorted and retreated to the corner of the room behind Irina. He unfolded a cloth sheet to reveal a set of metal tools. He selected pliers. Irina shifted in her seat and tried to look behind her.

Del held up her hand. "Tell me where Lenny is. I really need to talk to him." To the interrogator, she added, "She's telling the truth." Back to Irina, she said again, "Where's Lenny? We're going to find him somehow."

"I don't know," Irina said.

The interrogator advanced with his pliers.

Del held her hand up to hold him back. "I need to talk to him."

"Somewhere in Melitopol," Irina said. "Please, that is all I know. He left Kiev."

Del's phone buzzed in her pocket.

She got up from the chair and had quiet, urgent words with the interrogator, asking him not to hurt Irina, saying that she could get more out of the girl by speaking quietly to her.

There had to be some weak reception in this corner of the basement.

Two text messages were on the burner phone, one on her regular. One message was from Suweil, saying they had matched DNA on the shell casing from the UN meeting to Korshunov. The next was scraps of text he had managed to reconstruct from the lip-read conversation between Bondar and Petty. She didn't open it, because the message on her regular phone was from her father.

He had woken up from surgery.

***

"Dad?"

Scratchy throat sounds and forced breathing.

"Delta," whispered a reedy voice.

Dany had brought her up to the precinct lobby so she could use her phone. Georgiev had come up as well and ushered her into a cubicle at the side of the entrance, but still behind a set of thick green metal bars and a locked gate. When she called the house, Del talked to her mother first. She said they had finished the operation but that her father's vocal cords were damaged. He had insisted that he wanted to talk to Del.

"Don't force it," Del said to him. "You're going to be okay."

A second passed before he replied, "Thank you," in little more than a sigh.

"For what?"

"Your friends."

He sounded high, which was probably accurate given all the meds he had to be on. Was he delirious?

"My friends? You mean Angel? Did Angel Rodriguez come by?" She had asked the private detective to drop by on her father.

"Patty."

Del paused while her mind searched. "I don't have any friends called Patty."

"Adam Patty."

"Petty. You mean Petty? He came by the hospital?"

"They helped," her father's scratchy low voice said. "They put something . . . in my . . ."

A tingling blossomed at the base of Del's spine.

"What do you mean they put something? Where?"

"They put something, from one of those printers, into my throat."

Prickling dread crawled its way up Del's spine and exploded like a hatch of spiderlings across her scalp and into her brain.

She felt like screaming but kept her voice to a tremulous whisper. "Dad, don't let them . . . You didn't let them put anything into you, did you?"

30

"You have what you asked for!" yelled a familiar voice.

Jacques barged in through the front door of the precinct. Cool night air, scented with distant fires, swept in around him. He scanned the lobby, and his eyes zeroed on Del. With one arm, he motioned for her to get up, and with the other he waved a paper over his head.

He said, "Commissioner Georgiev, this is a directive straight from President Voloshyn, ordering you to release Detective Devlin."

"Dad, I have to go," Del whispered into her phone.

***

"Thank you," Del said to Jacques.

The Frenchman sat facing her on the opposing bench of the black limousine. He said something in Ukrainian to the driver. The divider window buzzed and slid shut, and the limo pulled away from the curb.

"You're welcome. I heard your father woke from surgery."

"How did you hear that?"

"We have a flight tomorrow morning. First thing." He handed her passport over. "What happened in there? Did they hurt you?"

"We found Bondar's cousin, a young woman named Irina. She says

Lenny left the city and went to Melitopol." Before she left, she had Georgiev promise not to hurt Irina. She had been honest, had given them all the information she had. Georgiev would release her, or at least promised he would.

"There's intense fighting in that area. The Black Army is mobilizing."

"She said Korshunov didn't shoot my father."

"You believe her? Korshunov's DNA was on the shell casing. Your NYPD confirmed it."

Del nodded slowly as she studied Jacques's face. He was flushed, blood pumping under his eyes and into his sweaty forehead. Stressed.

"What else?" he said.

The limo swerved around a corner.

Jacques was at the UN meeting when her father was shot. Korshunov didn't shoot him; of that Del was now certain, which meant someone else did. Irina said Korshunov was working with the Black Army, had become a rogue agent, which explained why the Russians were hell-bent on getting him, maybe even were the ones to kill him. But his DNA was on the shell casing.

"What else?" Jacques repeated.

"That's it," Del replied.

Buried alive. Bodies cut up as if they'd been in a food processor. The weirdness had an otherworldly feel to it, as if this were a film, the dark streets of Kiev sweeping past the limo's window like frames of celluloid.

She wanted to tell Jacques that Bondar and Petty had been at the UN meeting, that Bondar had lied about it to the NYPD, but there was still the matter of a leak inside Interpol. She eyed her suitcase on the floor, the rounds of ammunition in the inside pocket. One round missing. She was being set up. Right now she couldn't trust anyone.

The creeping dread had formed into an idea more terrible than any Poe nightmare. When her father was shot, he had been brought into a special surgical wing at Presbyterian. Brand-new. One that she now knew was sponsored by Strataform.

And they had put something from their machines into his neck.

***

"What are you doing?" Jacques asked.

"Messaging my family."

It was about a ten-minute drive back to the hotel. Del turned on her laptop and balanced it on her knees, tethered its network connection to her cell phone. While she waited for the laptop to boot up, she reread the second text message from Suweil.

In the past hour since she sent him the request, he had sent her back fragments of the conversation between Bondar and Petty at the United Nations. Bondar used the words "nickel titanium" at least three times in the heated conversation. In her research, she had seen this term before.

Nickel titanium was used as an artificial muscle fiber.

It wasn't listed as one of the materials used by Strataform, but Suweil had identified several capabilities of the device that weren't listed.

Adam Petty had just helped her father. Why? Why the sudden interested in Del's family and Del herself? When she first talked to Petty at the Maker Faire in New York, his face had flashed bright red. As if he was surprised to see her. He hadn't mentioned that he had been in the UN building when her father was shot. And when Lenny Bondar and Adam argued in front of her, Bondar had asked Petty where he got his money.

Del couldn't talk to Lenny, but she could find Petty. Her laptop finished booting up, and she emailed Adam Petty asking him to call her as soon as possible.

She checked her email in-box.

A message from Angel, who had gone to speak with the sister of Timothy Hutchins in New York. Angel said that Hutchins was working with Strataform, had been working directly with Adam Petty on his artwork. Exactly what Del had suspected. Petty seemed to be at the center of everything. Angel was a former navy SEAL and had some friends he said he could send to help her in Ukraine, if it came to it. Del replied that it wasn't necessary.

Not yet.

She did a search and opened up videos on robotic applications using nickel-titanium shape memory alloy actuators as artificial muscle fibers.

Another article on used magnetized rubber. A flat sheet printed out and folded up by itself into a complex shape like a spider, then began to crawl across a table. In another, an insect-size drone levitated from a counter, driven by ionic thrusters with no blades or moving parts. Not just 3-D, but objects created with an extra dimension of time and movement baked into them. The website called it "4-D" printing.

The Fourth Industrial Revolution.

That was what Adam Petty kept talking about. What the presentation at the UN meeting was about. What would it be worth to be the Steve Jobs of the Fourth Industrial Revolution?

Del went back to websites she had visited before and watched again the video of a printed object folding and twisting itself like a flower opening and closing. Like something biological. The same way that Timothy Hutchins's art felt biological.

Nobody went in or out of that room at the Persian Palace—that was what the security contractors said. What the police said. And yet, someone had unscrewed the ventilation duct, cut Timothy Hutchins into many pieces, and stuffed him in. She might not have trusted the security contractors, but that old man, Vasily . . . He was sure. She had absolute confidence he knew that place inside and out.

A new message pinged her in-box. From Adam Petty. He said he was still in Singapore, five hours ahead. That would make it 7:30 a.m. He said he could talk anytime on Skype. She messaged back that she would call him in fifteen minutes.

Jacques got up from his side of the limo and slid into the seat beside her. "You sure you have nothing else to tell me?'

Del slapped her laptop shut.

"Emailing relatives. Sorry, but it's private."

***

"Detective Devlin, are you all right?"

Delta adjusted her laptop screen so it focused squarely on her face. She sat at the small round table near the glass balcony door of her hotel room. She checked her watch. 2:24 a.m. Jacques was coming back at 7:00 a.m. to get on the flight to Lyon with her.

"Thank you for taking this call at such short notice," she said.

"But you are still in Ukraine?"

"For the foreseeable future," Del replied.

Petty still had the same mop of streaked gray hair casually flopped down one side of his stubby black-framed glasses. Dark circles under his eyes. More than two days of stubble this time—more like the start of a beard, though not in any well-kept hipster sort of way.

"You aren't leaving?"

"Why do you ask?"

"I just heard . . . I mean, the situation."

"What did you hear?"

Del waited. Had he heard that she was detained? If so, why? What was he tracking her movements for? Who was talking to him? Georgiev?

"Nothing, just that the situation was degrading. All American consular staff recalled. It doesn't seem like a place to stay in."

"Thank you for helping my father."

The edges of his smile faltered, twitched. His eyes narrowed ever so slightly. Through the video link, only the red-green-blue spectrum was transmitted, so Del couldn't sense the blood flow in his face, but even without that, the guy looked uncomfortable. Exhausted.

"The surgery was a success, I heard," he replied.

"You seem to know an awful lot about me and my family."

"Just trying to help."

"I'm sure."

She looked off to one side of her laptop and pretended to shuffle papers.

"What's this about?" he said after a two-second pause. He looked as though he was sweating bullets.

Behind him was what looked like a hotel kitchen with a mural on the wall by the table. Del clicked two keys on her laptop, took a screenshot, and emailed it to Suweil. All the lights were on—the ceiling lights, the lamps, the light over the stove.

"I'm quite busy," Adam said when Del didn't respond.

"So you're in Singapore? What's the time? It's the middle of the night here."

"That's right." He looked up and right. "Seven forty-five in the morning."

"How many print farms do you have there?"

"Just one so far."

"And how many in the Ukraine?"

This time he looked up and left—the sign of searching memory, where up and right usually meant fabricating something. Creating a fiction. Lying.

"Two dozen. Maybe more. I sent you that list."

"And you're not here? Not more worried about your investment?"

"What on Earth could I do?"

"Speaking of investment," Del said, "the reason I called you—well, really a few questions."

"Go ahead."

"How does Strataform finance itself?"

Adam Petty visibly sat backward. He hadn't expected this. "Ah, um, well, we are the world's biggest commercial manufacturer in 3-D printing. We have four billion dollars a year—"

"I mean on the consumer side. I've read online that people estimate you're charging only half the cost of your Replicators. Why is that?"

"Selling below cost? Well, we're making a market. Been done before."

"In the Ukraine?"

"In marketing speak, we call that a beachhead."

"You were in New York when my father was shot."

He blinked. "You met me at Maker Faire."

"So, you were in Queens when it happened?"

"I'm not sure where this is going. I'm very busy, Detective. Could we hurry this along?"

"One last question."

"Sure."

"Nickel titanium. Why is it in the Ukrainian Strataform machines? It's not listed as a specification."

He inhaled and exhaled. The same stress-relief practice that Del used.

"Future proofing. It's common in the tech world. The first 'smart' speaker included a microphone on the first generation of millions shipped, without listing the feature. But when the corporation added their voice assistant, suddenly those millions had an extra feature they hadn't even known they had."

"Right. But those millions of people also didn't know they were being listened to."

"They weren't."

***

Del closed her laptop and gazed out at the twinkling lights of Kiev. Almost three in the morning, and her mind felt like sludge. Barely any sleep in four days, yet she was still terrified lying on the bed. Had that really happened?

Her father.

What had they done to him?

She didn't get a chance to ask him about Jonathan Murphy, about the IRA, about changing his name. She trusted that her mother was telling the truth. She glanced at her luggage and tried to decide whether to dispose of the ammunition still in it, but that carried its own risks. Someone was setting her up in more ways than one.

The IRA connection linked her directly to the Black Army. This was no coincidence.

She rubbed her eyes and looked at the other side of the room. The Strataform Replicator machine was still there, the orange light on its top subdued. In low-power mode.

Del took a deep breath, slowly to a count of five, held it for two seconds, and then counted her exhalation. She repeated and then repeated again, her mind relaxing. Coming to a decision.

Was it even possible?

She had to find out.

Del flipped open her laptop and composed an email to Katherine, Commissioner Georgiev, and Jacques, saying she had discovered what Korshunov was doing at the UN Building. She said she had found out exactly what was going on, that it involved Adam Petty and Strataform but that it was too sensitive to send electronically. She had the file in her room, she said—had written it all down and had it out on her desk. She said she would bring it to Interpol on the flight in the morning.

She pushed *send*, then set an alarm on her phone and positioned it across from the Strataform machine. She checked the fitness tracker on her wrist and made sure it was working. She put on a T-shirt and shorts, turned down the lights, and sat on the bed—but after a moment, she got back up and went into the bathroom to grab every towel she could find. She pulled the bed away from the wall and dropped the towels in a pile against the ventilation duct, then pushed the bed back.

Only then did she sit back down on the bed, slide under the covers, and close her eyes.

***

Del watched her father's heart rate monitor, the number climbing from one-thirty to one-forty, then one-sixty. The thin green line pulsed and quivered. He was in arrhythmia again. How much could he take? What hadn't he told her? Why was he keeping secrets?

A blaring horn cut through the darkness. The spiders scattered to the corners of the sky. Del fought against the light, wished the klaxon would go away, but she knew she needed to escape.

***

Del's mind swam back from the dream. Her body and mind had sunk immediately into a deep slumber the second her head hit the pillow. Her cell phone's alarm brayed from the corner of the room.

Why had she set it? What was going on? Her mind reassembled, and she shook her head, the jolt of adrenaline sharpening her senses. She clicked on the lamp by the night table.

And heard a scuttling sound in the darkness beyond.

She took a deep breath and swung her legs over the edge of the bed, got to her feet, and went to the corner of the room and turned the alarm off. Her phone said 4:02 a.m. It was still recording video. Her hand holding the phone was shaking. Nausea wormed away at the pit of her stomach—a combination of waking up too quickly from a deep sleep, and a wave of vertigo from jumping up. She held one finger over the phone, hesitated an instant, then pushed *stop* on the recording and played the video.

A steady image of the Strataform machine appeared. The lights were out when her phone was recording, so Del put it into low-light mode. The image was grainy and blurry. She scrolled right to advance through time. It had recorded an hour of video. As Del swiped the time marker to the right, the image remained steady and unchanging.

Except . . . What the hell was that?

She stopped the video and scrolled back. Played it again at regular speed.

The Strataform machine hummed to life in the recording. A layer of material slithered from its output tray. After ten seconds of nothing, the sheet of plastic quivered and then seemed to come to life. It folded up on itself, parts of it sectioning off and coming free like spindly legs.

Ten more seconds of grainy video, and what looked like a gangly insect skittered away from the machine and down, out of view.

31

Pounding footsteps thudded in the corridor beyond Del's hotel room.

She stuffed the phone into her shorts pocket, ran to the entrance, and squeezed against the wall behind the door. Voices yelled in the corridor. A man and a woman. Del braced and waited for the door to crash open.

This time, she wasn't going quietly.

More loud voices.

The woman screaming.

They weren't being covert. A door slammed. Footsteps padded away, this time slowly. Del unclenched her jaw. It didn't sound like an attacker— not one focused on her, at any rate. Her shoulders relaxed an inch. Sounded more like a married couple having an argument. In the sudden silence, she felt her heart thumping in her chest, her breath coming and going in quick gasps. She realized that her fingernails were digging into the palms of her balled fists.

Remaining against the wall behind the door, she reached for her phone and replayed the video. She paused it and zoomed in. Reversed and played it again. Paused.

Her hand holding the phone shook. She put it back in her pocket, blinked, and looked around the room, then ran to the bed. Squatting, she flipped the whole king-size bed onto its side in one motion. The mattress and frame did a lazy half cartwheel, stopping on end against the patio window-doors. The pile of towels was still under the bed, blocking the ventilation duct. Nothing moved under there.

It took a week to find Timothy Hutchins's remains, then another *month* to identify him. Why so long? Was the coroner that backed up? Nobody had sounded the alarm when Hutchins disappeared, because he had no family except for a sister in New York. He hadn't been very close with her and didn't talk much. Whoever murdered him—and someone must have—had to know that.

The question had been, why kill Hutchins? What did he know that made him such a threat? There were too many connections back to Adam Petty. Everything led back to Adam Petty, and it had to be about this, this *thing*.

The Strataform machines could print whole little machines, miniature drones, whatever they could be called. Machines that could, perhaps, attack a person. Skin and muscle removed from the bone—that's what the coroner said. And there were millions of these printers in people's homes and businesses all over the world.

And nowhere as many as in the Ukraine.

***

Del rewound the video once again. Zoomed in. The first thing to come out looked like a stick insect. Was it sent in to harm Del? Her suspicion was that it had been sent to find her written notes. She had said she left them on her desk because they were too sensitive to send via email. The second sheet that came out of the printer looked like a little snake as it rolled into a cylinder and wriggled away. A shudder ran through her.

Her little test had been more of a crazy speculation than anything else, and she had half-expected to hear someone crashing through her door in the middle of the night.

Del could hardly believe her eyes.

Whatever the hell these things were, they were still in the room. And not just one of them.

As the video played, another sheet and then another came out of the Strataform. Two more stick-bots folded up and scuttled away from the machine. Four of those things were still in the room somewhere.

Del grabbed the TV remote, turned it on, and jacked up the volume. She pulled the curtains shut on the patio doors, then went to the Strataform printer and pulled its cord out of the wall. The orange light in its print bay stayed on.

Damn thing had a battery. She pulled off the cover and considered ripping it apart, then stopped herself.

Instead of tearing out the guts of it, she plugged it back in and went through the print logs on the small display. The print jobs for stick-bots weren't registered, but the previous print job—the one designed to set her up for Korshunov's shooting—was still in memory. She selected each of the items from that job and set the machine to reprint.

***

Del had sent the email on a hunch, wondering whether it would elicit anything, but the speed of the response was breathtaking. That message went to Katherine, Grigory, and Jacques, so either one of them was part of some conspiracy, or Interpol's communications were compromised. Or maybe it was someone else inside Interpol.

Maybe her hotel Wi-Fi had been hijacked. It could be that simple.

She was in the Black Army's backyard here, and while she doubted their fighting capabilities, she didn't question their hacking credentials. The more she thought about it, there were a dozen ways her digital information could have been intercepted, and she was no expert—there were probably more ways she didn't even know about. Suweil was still looking into it, but Del didn't have the luxury of time.

Whoever sent these things knew by now that they had failed. Did they know that she knew? That she had a video of the creatures crawling out of the machine? What was their backup plan? What came next? Del needed to get ahead of this somehow.

One thing was clear: they were ready to kill over it.

Maybe those things were even sent to kill *her*.

Was she being watched or listened to right now? She had set her phone's alarm for an hour and had purposely let herself go to sleep. Somehow, whoever sent the instructions to the Replicator knew that she was unconscious, asleep. So one way or another, she was being watched.

***

Del methodically ransacked the room.

Pulled the dresser from the wall. Took all her clothes from the closet and ripped out the shelves. She pulled out each drawer from the dresser and peeled away the paper lining the bottoms, ripped the refrigerator from under the cabinet and emptied the minibar, pulled out all the bottles and cans and chocolates and peanuts. She put her Interpol phone and laptop in the bathroom and covered them in towels.

They had demonstrations of things like these stick-bots at the Maker Faire. Swarms of tiny robots that worked together. Could they operate independently? Didn't they need some kind of operator? Did they have their own cameras? They had to have some form of sensing and communications equipment.

What were their capabilities?

"Where the hell are they?" Del muttered to herself.

She dragged the dresser into the middle of her room. The flat-screen TV tottered back and forth on top of it, still playing Europop videos at high volume. After being checked and rechecked, everything in the room was piled into the center—the bed on its side, the night tables upended. The Strataform machine had finished the print job for her, and she unplugged it and ripped the cover off, then jammed wet toilet paper into its print bay.

***

Waxy gray light bled around the corners of the curtains. Almost 5:00 a.m.

Del sat on a chair and surveyed the room. She held a plush toy in her hand. A small nightingale stuffed animal, a national symbol of Ukraine.

They left one on her bed each morning. Del had ripped it apart and found a small device inside, attached to one of the beady eyes. It had to be a webcam and microphone. Battery powered. Probably communicating with the hotel Wi-Fi. So someone *had* been monitoring her.

She hadn't found anything else. No sign of the devices that had crawled out of the Strataform machine.

When she was buried in the plastic shards, it couldn't all have come from her printer. It simply didn't have enough volume of material. So something must have come in from outside, and her door had been locked. The only other way in that she could think of was the air duct under the bed.

She swiveled on her chair and took a closer look at the wall near the ventilation duct that was still piled with towels. She walked over and pulled the towels back. Could these things have wriggled past the obstruction and squeezed themselves through the quarter-inch grating like some kind of octopus-bot? She had no idea of their capabilities.

Near the edge of the duct, she noticed a small bulge under the carpet. A rainbow smudge was against the wall just under the socket. Del got onto her hands and knees, her eyes almost level with the floor. She picked at the carpet, felt a mound underneath it. Del found the room service tray, took a fork, and used it to dig at the edge and rip back the carpet.

A small mound of melted plastic lay on top of the wooden underfloor, wedged against the molding. She prodded it. It was still warm to the touch, with tiny wires sticking out. It had to be one of the stick-bots. Maybe two or three of them together? Unable to escape, they must have burrowed like giant bedbugs between the edge of the carpet and the molding, where they melted themselves down.

Using the fork, she scraped the glob of plastic and wire from the floor.

With her other hand, she took out her burner phone and dialed a number. After four rings, it picked up.

"Igor," Del said. "I need you to do something."

***

"Detective Devlin?"

A muffled voice from beyond her door, accompanied by gentle knocking. It wasn't Dany, which meant it wasn't the Kiev police, about to march her off. It was Jacques.

She yelled back, "Give me a minute. I'm finishing in the bathroom."

Bright sunlight streamed in through the open patio doors. 6:00 a.m. She held up the lump of melted stick-bot and inspected it once more before pocketing it.

The bed and dresser were back in place, but she had torn up the edges of the carpeting all around the room. She tried to push it back into place, but it looked ragged. The cupboard shelves were stacked up by the minibar refrigerator, the bottles still scattered across the floor. She had ripped open the Strataform device and, using the much-abused fork, torn out the interior circuit boards and arranged the bits and pieces across the carpet.

With her burner phone, she took pictures of everything inside it.

A louder knock. "Detective Devlin, please open the door."

She got up from the bed and grabbed her backpack and suitcase. "One second," Del said as she advanced to the door and unlocked it. She tried to squeeze herself through into the hallway, but Jacques barged past her into the room. The door clicked shut behind him.

He surveyed the damage. "Anything you want to tell me?"

Jacques was dressed in a light-gray suit, freshly pressed. Del was in jeans and sneakers and a T-shirt, with her backpack on. "Couldn't sleep," she replied.

"Are you taking drugs?" From the way he said it, he wasn't even being sarcastic. He looked at the bottles on the carpet. "You've been drinking?"

The orbits of his eyes shone bright with intense blood flow. Something was going on. The man was beyond tense. Tiny flecks of lint fluoresced in the direct sunlight on his blue shirt, as if he'd been rolling on the floor. Or lying on a carpet.

Del stared at him and said, "Have you been monitoring me?"

32

The limo accelerated down Volodymyrska Street through Old Kiev. Almost six thirty in the morning. The first Monday-morning delivery trucks clogged the streets. Through the trees out her left-side window, Del watched the two-hundred-foot-high brick-and-wood structure of the Golden Gate slide past—a reconstruction of the medieval city gate of Kiev a thousand years before.

A gateway from another world.

When Del was stuck in the underground tunnel, when she became trapped chasing Korshunov, she had seen smudges of red heat in the darkness. Hundreds of them. They weren't rats. They had to be these bugs, these tiny machines. Maybe thousands of them, working in unison as she had seen in the demonstrations at Maker Faire.

That tunnel entrance wasn't more than two blocks from the Strataform printer farm. It must have been connected underground.

"Whose car is this?" Del asked Jacques.

He sat across from her on the limo's bench seat facing backward, their luggage on the floor between them. For the past week, they had been taking city taxis from one place to the next, but now they were being ferried in this sleek black Mercedes.

"Government," Jacques replied.

"Which?"

"You know how far up the food chain we had to go to get you out of here? This is the only flight out to Europe today. Maybe the last."

"Who is 'we'?"

"Interpol." He exhaled. "I'm going to need some answers, Detective."

At the hotel, he had denied any knowledge of her being monitored. An obvious lie that he didn't try to explain away, even when he knew she could read his face. He wasn't good at lying. He was, however, genuinely surprised when she showed him the plush toy. He said he had no idea who put it there, and she believed him, which only confused her more.

He wanted to take the surveillance toy, but she insisted on keeping it in her luggage.

Del watched Old Kiev slide past her window.

Jacques said, "Of course we were monitoring you. I asked to have two of Georgiev's men outside your door all night. Dany—you know him, yes? For your safety. What about your email last night? You said you found out what Korshunov was doing at the UN? That it involves Adam Petty?"

"For Director Katherine Dartmouth's eyes only. The file is in my luggage. We can look at it once we get to Lyon. All together."

Jacques's eyes flickered down at her carry-on bag. He said, "Georgiev said they've tracked Bondar. The Black Army is mobilizing; his people have been tracked going south. If you have information, it is critical—"

She noticed the Glock under his coat. "I need to speak to Katherine first."

As if on cue, Del's phone rang.

"Director Dartmouth," Del said into her phone. She glanced at Jacques. "I'm on my way to the airport right now with Officer Galloul."

"Care to elaborate on that email last night?"

"When I get there."

"I would prefer now."

"I have reason to believe our communications are compromised, ma'am. That's why I didn't want to send anything electronically."

A pause for a beat. "I heard your father is in recovery. Adam Petty was personally involved, from what I heard. What's going on between you two?"

"I would prefer to elaborate when I get to Lyon, ma'am. Are you going to be there?"

"I flew in yesterday." Another pause. "I had to vouch personally for you with Georgiev just to get you out of Ukraine. Lucky they have bigger problems right now. But there is something else I need to talk to you about . . . your father . . ."

"Something to do with Strataform?" Fear knotted in Del's stomach. "What did they do to him?"

"We received a background security check on you."

"From the FBI?" Del had been waiting for this shoe to drop.

A pause. "Why would it be from the FBI?"

Now Del was confused. "I don't know. Don't they do security checks for you?"

"It was sent in anonymously. Something from before you joined us. It came to light when a staffer did some research after your meeting with the Black Army."

"I was kidnapped."

"Did you know your father changed his name?"

She'd been waiting for this. A fluttering in her stomach. Del switched the phone from her right to her left ear and turned away from Jacques. She whispered, "I only found out about this last week, ma'am. I know that sounds—"

"We will talk when you get here. I just wanted to give you a heads-up. The General Secretariat's office is concerned. When you arrive, it won't be a meeting with just me."

"Understood."

"One more thing," Katherine said. "We also found out why Bondar and Korshunov tried to assassinate President Voloshyn. At the UN meeting, she was about to announce a major contract with Strataform. It would have destroyed Bondar's MakerArmy commercially. His IPO would had been canceled, billions of dollars lost. That's why Bondar went rogue. Your father got caught in the cross fire. This was all about money."

They said goodbye, and Del hung up the phone.

"Everything all right?" Jacques said from the other bench.

The limo took a hard swerve to the left. About twenty more minutes to the airport.

***

"*Tak*," said the young woman in the Securitas uniform.

Del returned her Interpol ID and passport into her pocket. The airport was almost empty, the security lineup only six people deep, but they went through the diplomatic line anyway.

She passed through the metal detector ahead of Jacques and went to the scanner conveyor belt to retrieve her carry-on suitcase and backpack. She returned her Interpol laptop to the front sleeve of her suitcase and made sure Jacques saw her doing it. He had been watching her every move, shadowing her. It had been difficult to arrange a drop-off in the flower pot at the entrance, but she had sat down to tie one of her sneakers.

He hadn't noticed. She hoped.

The departure board was half empty, and of those flights listed, more than half were canceled. No flights to Russia, she noticed. Their flight to Frankfurt was on time at gate B2.

Still midnight in New York.

News on the TVs at the empty gate waiting areas all played images of flaming trucks, gray clouds billowing out from grubby buildings, and men in balaclavas crouching with assault rifles behind crumbling brick walls

Director Dartmouth knew about her family. About her father's brother. Jonathan Murphy. She hadn't said it directly, but Del knew. This was no coincidence. Someone was setting her up—the same person who set her up with Korshunov. The same person who arranged getting her father shot.

But who?

The TVs switched to an image of President Voloshyn's face with voter statistics below. Del couldn't read the Cyrillic script, but the numbers and the faces said it all. Voloshyn was barely ahead but sliding in the polls. The election was in four days. Del couldn't believe they were still going ahead with it, in the middle of a full-blown conflict.

Jacques and Del stopped together at gate B2.

"Forty minutes till the flight," she said. "I'm going to get a magazine and hit the head. You want anything? Water?"

The Frenchman sat down heavily. "Don't go far."

Del put her work cell phone into her suitcase. She still had her backpack on. She walked a hundred feet down the concourse, to a retail shop, where she made a show of leafing through the magazines before selecting *Elle* and paying for it along with a bottle of diet soda. Jacques kept an eye on her the whole time. Slowly, she walked back toward him and stopped in front of the restrooms. An announcement came on.

Jacques looked away for an instant.

Del slipped into the restroom entrance, but instead of going left, she ducked right, into the men's room. Just one guy inside at a urinal, who didn't look around. She locked herself in a stall and squatted on top of the closed toilet lid.

She checked her watch. It was 7:42—thirty-four minutes till their flight.

Bondar wasn't part of any fighting force. That wasn't why he had gone to Melitopol. Del was sure of that. He had obviously had words with Adam in that video, but was it an argument? They weren't on the same side. Or were they? Were they arguing? Or plotting? Neither of them had admitted he was there when her father was shot. A conspiracy between the two of them?

Was Commissioner Georgiev in on this? His group was the one in charge of Hutchins's body's identification, which took over a month. Something seemed off. Why had he been so interested in her father when he came to New York?

When she admitted that a 3-D gun was printed from her machine, he didn't search her luggage, didn't force her to give up the machine, or come and confiscate it. Was he the one who put monitoring devices in her room? A plush toy that was a symbol of Ukraine had the camera inside it. That seemed like something the Kiev police force might use.

More to the point, what was the point of all this? Why her?

***

"Delta?" called out a voice.

It was Jacques. She checked her watch. Ten minutes exactly since she came into the bathroom—7:52. Her plane was boarding.

"Delta, are you in there?"

She listened in silence. He called out twice more before she heard his footsteps, and she waited until the sound of him knocking on stall doors in the women's restroom before she stepped onto the floor and opened the latch of her door. As fast as she could without running, she exited from the bathroom and walked quickly up the concourse, past the security checkpoint and into the check-in area beyond. At the plant pot by the bench, she reached in and grabbed the small bag she had left. Five rounds of .38 ammunition and the plastic parts for a 3-D-printed gun.

Igor waved from his Lada outside.

She signaled back at him—*one second*—stealing glances left and right for any sign of Georgiev's men as she pushed through the double glass doors.

"Where to?" Igor asked as he rolled his window down.

She had to trust someone. She texted Suweil on her burner phone:

> Please don't tell anyone about this
> phone or our communications.
> Please give me a day. Please.

She thought about it for a second and added,

> My life depends on it.

She held out a fistful of American hundred-dollar bills to Igor.

33

Del slouched in the backseat of the Lada on the way out of the city. Eight in the morning, and they were stuck in crosstown traffic.

"Are we being followed?" she asked Igor.

"Who would be chasing us?"

A long and twisty list. "Do you see anyone?"

"Same as two minutes ago. I don't think so. It would help if I knew what to look for."

Del stuck her head up. She didn't see anything. It didn't mean they weren't being tracked. This wasn't like the old days. Ninety-nine ways someone could be following them, and only a few of them by car.

Early this morning, she had gone to the hotel ATM and withdrawn as much cash as it would give her. It offered American dollars, so she managed to get out a thousand before it hit her daily limit. Igor accepted five hundred for the drive to Melitopol, but was going only because they were friends, he said, and because he had grown up down there. The drive would take nine or ten hours, he warned, and there would be police checkpoints.

Maybe worse than police.

Military, and who knew whose.

They might not be able to get there at all, or in one piece.

The fighting in the south had frayed into a disjointed conflict between armed militia, Ukrainian regular forces, and pro-Russian separatists. She was heading straight into what had become a war zone—all those burning cars, men in balaclavas, and smoking wreckage of buildings on the airport TVs. Del had gotten rid of her Interpol laptop and the work cell phone by leaving them in her suitcase, and ditched all her clothes except a change of jeans in her backpack.

She was never good at letting things go. Once she got hold of something, she was like a dog with a rag toy. By now, the alarms had sounded from Interpol to Kiev. One thing she hated was the feeling of being pushed around, of being led into a corner, and going back to Lyon right now had exactly that feeling.

That sensation of being trapped.

What were the odds that an outside security report on Del had just made its way to Interpol? Straight into Katherine's hands.

Zero.

Katherine said it wasn't from the FBI, so then who sent it in? Now Interpol and the Kiev police had to know about her family's connection to the IRA, and an offshoot—the New IRA—had been blamed for a shooting in Belfast last month.

Did Bondar think she was a fellow terrorist?

The taxi stopped at a light, and Del slid deeper in the backseat.

Adam Petty wasn't in Singapore; of that much she was certain. He had the curtains closed and all the lights on when they video chatted. She texted Suweil and asked if he had any luck with the images she'd sent him of Petty from her video interview last night.

What exactly was her plan?

Del felt her future slipping away. Someone had set this all up, and up until now they had been leading her by the nose. She couldn't go back, not with her tail between her legs, and she had a feeling that whoever was propping her up as the fall guy had worse in stock for her.

A bigger problem was Korshunov's murder. Katherine might have gotten clearance to get her out of Ukraine, but Del had a feeling the murder of Korshunov might still be pinned on her. If she left now, she would have no way to defend herself.

The truth about her father would come out.

He hadn't told anyone in the NYPD about his past, unless *everyone* was keeping a secret from her. His connection to Jonathan Murphy would come as a surprise to everyone. How would they react? Realistically, that djinni was already out of the jar. Nothing she could do about it anymore. He was set to retire, anyway, if he lived through this cancer.

Or survived whatever Adam Petty had stuck in his neck. Was it one of these *things*?

She held up the lump of plastic and wires. She needed to confront Petty but couldn't yet. First, she must speak to Bondar, find out what he and Petty were arguing about. Find out why he lied about being in the UN building when her father was shot.

Her father had tripped and fallen in front of the shooter.

So, who were they really trying to kill? Georgiev? Voloshyn?

She'd bet money that Bondar or Petty was behind it. Or both. Everything came down to a struggle between these two, and Strataform was the prime suspect.

Petty had had his people stick something into her father's neck. Could one of these things be activated through the internet, come to life, and shred her father's insides like a buzz saw? She imagined wrapping her hands around Adam Petty's neck, wiping the smirk from his face.

Del had dumped her cell phone and laptop, so no one could contact her through the usual channels—which meant no one could issue her a threat. She half expected a call on her burner phone, telling her to come back now or they would hurt her father.

She needed more information, needed some leverage, and this lump of plastic was a start. She needed to find Lenny Bondar before anyone else did. Bondar had singled her out to talk with her, pointed her in the right direction. Was he the one pulling the strings? She didn't think so, but with what she knew now, she had more leverage.

That was her plan. Find Bondar.

She knew he was somewhere in Melitopol. He contacted her before.

He felt some connection to her. If she could just get herself into Melitopol, make it known she was there, he would find her or she would find him. She would find out what he knew.

Then she would go after Petty.

***

Traffic cleared as they neared the city's southern edge. Red-and-white-striped towers belched smoke into a blue sky dotted with high, scudding clouds. The Lada began to tremble as it hit its top speed of about fifty miles an hour, its engine rattling like a lawnmower on the edge of failure.

"Is this the Dnieper?" Del asked Igor.

An expanse of blue streaked with whitecaps stretched under a suspension bridge.

"We have to head east before we go south," he replied from the front.

Her burner phone from Suweil pinged. A message from him:

Are you okay?

She dialed his number.

"Delta," he said right away. "What is happening?"

"I'm fine."

"All craziness is breaking loose here."

"Are you in Lyon?"

"They are saying you were kidnapped again." He added, "Your family was calling to find out what happened."

"I haven't been kidnapped."

Silence for two seconds. "This is exactly what kidnappers would tell you to say."

"Have you heard anything about my father?"

"What would I hear?"

"I don't know."

"I have not heard anything. Delta, you need to come back."

"How did my family find out?" It had been only an hour since she left the airport.

"The office alerted them."

"The office?"

"Kiev airport has been shut down," Suweil said. "Commissioner Georgiev has—"

"Suweil, I know this is a big ask, but you can't tell anyone I'm talking to you."

"You sure you are not kidnapped?"

Silence on her end.

"I could lose my job."

"We suspect there is a communication leak, yes?" Del said. "Or a mole?"

"I suspect a leak."

"You said yourself that the Interpol office should have detected the fake video, correct? As a standard part of any investigation?"

"Korshunov's DNA is still on the shell casing of the bullet that shot your father."

"But until we find this leak, please, just give me a day."

Suweil exhaled loudly. She could imagine him rubbing his eyes on the other end. "Twenty-four hours. Maximum. Then I need to tell them."

"Thank you."

"Twenty-three hours and thirty minutes. It was half an hour ago this started."

"Who sent Katherine the background security report on me?"

"I have no idea what you are talking about."

Del weighed her options. "Never mind. Were you able to do anything with those images of Adam Petty I sent last night?"

"The background image matches social media posts of tourists in a hotel in Tokmak—"

"Tokmak?"

"In southern Ukraine."

"You're sure?"

"With a very high degree of probability. You knew he was there?"

Del said, "I knew he wasn't in Singapore."

"Katherine said you sent an email last night. You have a secret dossier explaining what Korshunov was doing? That implicated Adam Petty?"

Del watched the riverbank pass by as the Lada entered a low forest on the other side.

"Please, if I am to be keeping a secret, then tell me."

"You're not going to believe this," Del said.

"You might not believe what I might believe."

She pulled the lump of plastic and wires from her pocket. "Strataform Replicators bring a whole new meaning to having a bug in your computer."

***

A spider with dangling wires and a gleaming nest of camera eyes marched over a muddy pockmarked moonscape of craters. In the distance, more of them moved, whirring and clicking and feeding on the shattered bodies of fallen soldiers. Delta hovered unseen in the air above them and watched and waited . . .

***

She awoke from a half slumber. She was laid out on the back bench of the Lada, her head on her backpack as she rubbed her eyes with one hand, a jolt of adrenaline sharpened her senses. Igor was turned around, shaking her gently.

"Miss Delta?"

"What's wrong?" She pushed herself upright with one arm and blinked.

The cabbie pointed at the horizon ahead. Over rolling hills into the distance, thick smudges of black smoke against a clear blue sky. He took his foot off the gas. The Lada stopped whining, but the side panels still vibrated as if the wheels were working their way off the axles.

"How long was I out?"

"A few hours."

The sun was high, but Del sensed a switch from midmorning to midafternoon.

Igor asked, "Can I ask if this official Interpol business?"

"More personal."

"How personal?"

About as much as it could get. "Do you know the area?"

"Are the police looking for you? I heard you talking—"

"Why?"

The Lada slowed. A Mercedes whipped past them in the fast lane.

"There will be checkpoints. Soon. I called some friends while you were asleep."

"I didn't tell you to contact anyone. Who did you call?"

"To see what the situation is ahead."

"What kind of friends?"

Igor kept looking straight ahead. "I thought we might need some."

"Did you use my name?"

"I said only I was coming."

"These are good friends?"

"I have known them all my life and would trust them with it." He put his foot back on the gas.

Del spent a few seconds weighing her options. "Can your friends ask around about Leonardo Bondar? See if they know where we might find people associated with the Black Army?"

Igor shook his head.

"You won't ask?"

"This Black Army isn't a real thing. Not like you are imagining. Not in the last hundred years, anyway."

"Bondar is real."

Now Igor nodded. "He is."

"Can you see if any of your friends have heard he's there?"

* * *

While Igor made calls and drove, Del connected her personal laptop, which she had tucked safely in her backpack, to her phone to get onto the internet. It was painfully slow, but she managed to do a few searches. She looked up "soldiers" and "bugs" and "Ukraine." Most of the results made no sense, but she clicked on one page that autotranslated from Ukrainian to English. A story from a few days ago, a social media post, of a freedom fighter at the southern edge of Ukraine who claimed to have been attacked by a giant insect in the middle of the night.

Del checked the location of the soldier on a map app and saved the image of the young man on her laptop.

"Nobody has heard anything of Bondar in Melitopol," Igor said from the front seat. "But there are rumors. I have a name of a place we can try."

Del rummaged in her backpack and pulled out another two hundred dollars. "Can you get me to Tokmak?"

Igor pulled his foot off the gas again. "Are you being serious?" He held up a hand and refused the money.

"I'm serious."

"Why do you want to go there?"

"I have information that says that Adam Petty is in a hotel."

"I thought we were chasing Leonardo Bondar. Where did you get this information?"

"My friend Suweil."

"Can you trust this person? I mean, with your life?"

Del didn't reply.

"The last time I dropped you off, you were kidnapped. You understand my concern."

It wasn't as if Del hadn't thought about it. A leak somewhere at Interpol. That video file not being checked for authenticity. Suweil was the constant intermediary and the one person she had chosen to trust. She didn't have much choice. Still, she didn't know.

Del had dumped her Interpol phone at the airport, but she still had the burner Suweil gave her. He could be tracking her. Maybe even listening to them. She considered throwing the phone out the window, but then she might be completely cut off. Then again, Suweil was the one who gave her the address of the hotel Petty was in. Either she had to trust him, or not.

The two-lane highway topped a ridge. A line of slowed traffic, brake lights glaring, snaked down the other side of the hill. Igor slowed. "We need to go onto the back roads from here, wherever we are going," he said. "Police checkpoints ahead."

He turned up the radio.

The way he listened so intently Del had to ask, "What are they saying?"

"Russian tanks have crossed into Ukrainian territory from Crimea."

A dull thudding of artillery in the distance.

Del said, "The Vesna Hotel on Central Street in Tokmak—do you know it?"

Igor turned to face her. "And I ask again: this Suweil person—do you trust them?"

34

In any fight, you had to be adaptable. You couldn't be set in your ways. That was what her dad always told her. Del rubbed her left wrist, the one she had broken falling from the roof because she wouldn't let go of the kid who broke into the police station. Sometimes, she also needed to know when to let go.

"Do you know the hotel?"

"I have friends in Melitopol, but Tokmak, I don't think—"

"Can you take me?"

"This is fifty kilometers toward Donetsk. Near the center of the pro-Russian forces. And you heard on the radio; this is very dangerous."

"Please. Get me there." She tried again to hand the money over to the front seat.

He waved it back. "Tell me, why are you risking your life for this?" With two fingers, he indicated the black smoke on the horizon.

"Something is happening in Ukraine," Del said.

"What is it you say? Tell me something I don't know."

"When I went into that tunnel, the guy I was chasing got killed."

"Again, I know this."

"But not by the Russians."

"You know this how?"

"I think someone is trying to make it look like they did it."

"And why *you*? Why are you here?"

"I think they are trying to blame me."

"Will this help stop that?" He pointed again at the smoke on the horizon.

"I'm not sure anything can stop that."

"But it might help?"

"In some small way. Maybe."

Igor flicked the turn signal and switched lanes. He took the next exit.

***

Dry scrub, straw yellow from the winter it hadn't yet recovered from, lined the potholed road into Tokmak. The railing across the Tokmach River bridge had fallen apart from some long-ago accident or simply rusted away. The waterway reflected a rainbow-hued chemical slick from its surface, bordered by a bare forest of birch trees—fingers of white bark between naked gray branches. Squat concrete apartment blocks rose up as they entered the town.

It seemed deserted.

Igor slowed the car. They passed a gas station. Empty. No lights. No people. A single car met them going in the opposite direction. The Lada crept onto the main street, creviced with potholes still brimful of water from last night's rain. The broken asphalt of the road deteriorated into mud at its edges. The town center was two- and three-story white brick buildings, the ground-floor windows covered with rusted metal bars.

A dog barked at them from an alleyway.

"Where is everybody?" Del said.

"They are still here but keeping inside. You heard on the radio, the Russians are coming."

In the next alleyway, Del saw a line of schoolchildren in matching blue uniforms—girls on the left, boys on the right—being marched along by adults. The parents turned to watch Del watching them. Fearful. Del and Igor were strangers. The locals kept their eyes on the Lada until it was out of sight.

"There." Igor pointed through the windshield at a four-story building that rose above the others, its sidewall littered with peeling pasted-on advertisements. "That's the Vesna, beside the hospital."

"Hospital?" Del surveyed a crumbling three-story structure to its right.

Igor shrugged and pulled into a parking spot. A series of shops lined the ground floor of the hotel. Del couldn't read Ukrainian, but she interpreted a "24" sign as meaning the shop was open all day and night. It was closed.

Del asked, "Is that the entrance?" She pointed at a red sign over a set of double doors.

"That is reception, yes."

Some detective she was. She couldn't even detect where the hotel's front desk was. In Kiev, half the signs had been in English for the tourists. Things had felt familiar, her hotel the Hyatt, an American oasis she could hide in. Out here, she was exposed in an alien landscape. She hadn't thought this through.

"You're going to have to come inside with me," Del said.

Igor was already out of the car. He opened the entrance door for her.

The lobby was dimly lit. Two plastic potted plants stood on either side of a window with "reception" stenciled over it. It was deserted. One of the white acoustic ceiling tiles hung loose, about to fall. Igor hit the reception bell. Its ping echoed.

A young woman appeared through a doorway behind the glass. She frowned but slid open the reception window. "*Vitayu?*"

Igor smiled and said something in greeting. He then said to Del, "Show her the picture." He continued speaking to the girl in Ukrainian. She shook her head and pointed at the entrance.

Del held her phone up with a picture of Adam Petty. "Have you seen this man?"

The girl looked at the phone, then at Del with an equally blank expression.

It suddenly occurred to Del just how foolish this errand might be. Suweil had been so confident when he said that Petty had been at this hotel. How could he know? How could she even really trust him? What on earth would a billionaire tech guru from Silicon Valley be doing in this broken-down village at the edge of a war zone? The lobby floor wasn't even tiled, the yellowing linoleum peeled back at the edges of the molding. She looked up the stairs off the main floor. Mold spread in several dark patches on the ceiling.

"*Tak*," said the young woman.

Tak. That meant yes. Del had learned enough Ukrainian to know that word. She turned back to the girl. Igor had put a C-note down on the counter.

The woman pointed toward the stairs and said something to Igor.

"She says he is here, in room one-twelve," he translated. "She says they are closing the hotel. Everyone is going home. Everyone is gone."

"But Petty is still here?"

"She says yes but that we should hurry."

"Because they're closing?"

"Because his other friends just went up to get him."

***

Del advanced down the second-floor corridor. She had told Igor to go back to the car and watch to see whether anyone came out. The overhead fluorescent strip lighting flickered. The carpet underfoot was stained in blooming patches. She passed room 106. Petty's room had to be in the next hallway. Even rooms on the opposite side.

She peered around the corner.

The hallway was maybe a hundred feet long, ending in a fire escape. Ten doors down each side. One of them open. She counted in her head. That had to be 112. She listened for any voices. Nothing but the growl of a truck in the street out front.

Del crept forward, one step at a time, and squeezed herself against the opposite wall. Someone was in there. Rustling sound of papers. She peered around the corner.

Adam Petty sat cross-legged on the bed, a pillow in his lap, staring straight ahead.

The room wasn't more than ten by fifteen feet, with an old cathode-ray TV on a stand in the far corner. Orange curtains were half-drawn, most of the room still in shade. A man in a suit was at a chipped Formica table near the foot of the bed, bent over, his back to Del. He leafed through papers in an open briefcase.

Should she hold back? Follow them?

The man in the suit turned. Shaved head. Gun in his hand.

Del dropped and rolled backward away from the door. Chips of particle board showered down. Two sharp cracks and then another. Holes punched through the thin walls of the hallway, just above her. She hit the carpet and pushed herself back up, hands and feet together, and bounded back the way she came, just making the corner as another shot splintered the wood paneling behind her.

She ran straight into someone.

Igor.

He grabbed her and pushed her behind him, then stretched one hand out around the corner. Two more loud cracks, these from Igor's gun. He knelt and pulled Del down with him. "Not going into a war zone without my Sokol," he said, grimacing. "Did I mention I was Ukrainian infantry when I was younger? Where is your gun?"

"I don't have one."

"*Navizhenyy.* Are you crazy? How many are there?"

"At least one."

"The one shooting?"

"Maybe two. Maybe three. I didn't get a good look."

Footsteps thudded down the hallway. Someone banged into the fire escape door at the end. Two seconds later, they heard it squeak shut. Was that one set of footsteps, or two? It didn't sound like three.

"Adam," Del called out. "Are you still there?"

Silence.

"Adam?"

Igor stole a glance around the corner. "Nobody there," he said.

She wanted to take the gun from him but decided against it. He seemed able to handle himself. "You go first," she said.

"I think we go back."

"I need to get in there. It's important."

He gave her a look, sighed, and closed his eyes for a second. Nodding, he opened them and crouched, swung his weapon around the corner, and followed it. He got to his feet. Del followed, a step behind and to the side.

A trail of bullet holes had punched through the thin wall beside the door.

Silence. Del put a hand on Igor's shoulder and pulled him back. She peered into the room. Petty remained on the bed with his back against the wall, still cross-legged and looking straight ahead, his head sagging. Staring but not seeing. His eyes were already opaque, his mouth agape.

"God *damn* it," Del muttered.

She checked the corners of the room before stepping inside. Advancing to the bed, she put a hand on Petty's neck. He was cool to the touch. No pulse. Blood had caked at the corners of his mouth. Outside the window, tires squealed against pavement.

Igor walked to the window and pulled back the curtains.

Del went to the desk. Papers were scattered on the floor. She knelt and collected them.

"So, we surprised someone?" Igor said.

"Seems that way."

"Was he a friend of yours?"

"I'm not sure." Del inspected the papers.

"We should not stay. We go back to Kiev? Melitopol? As I said, I have friends—"

"I need to go to the kitchen first." Del stuffed the papers into the briefcase.

"You hungry?"

She held up the sheaf of papers. "Can you get me into the Russian zone?"

35

"Bar-bar-a Waters?"

The big Russian mouthed the unfamiliar words. He stood with his feet apart, straddling the yellow dotted line down the middle of the road. With an AK-47 cradled across his barrel chest, he looked as implacable as the sleeting rain that had begun on the drive out of Tokmak. He had on a tall black Cossack hat, his eyes barely visible under the ledge of it, and head-to-foot digital-print camouflage. Rivulets of water wound their way through a thick gray beard that flowed out and away from his jowls and over the ammunition belt slung across one shoulder.

"Walters," Igor said.

He held his jean jacket over his head in a futile attempt to hold back the rain.

"Nobody knows who Barbara Walters is anymore," Del said. "Who would they know on TV from America? I don't know what they watch." Already soaked, she cowered under the jean jacket with the taxi driver.

Igor's face scrunched up, and he pointed at Del and said, "Oprah."

The big Russian's eyes opened wide, and he turned to his two comrades flanking him. They wore mismatched camouflage under clear plastic ponchos, their automatic weapons slung carelessly from single-point harnesses. Both of them began to laugh. From the pink cheeks and noses and the sour breath even at five feet of distance, three had been drinking.

"Oprah?" The Russian jabbed a meaty finger in Del's direction. "*Tse Oprah?*"

Igor waved his hands back and forth. Words tumbled from his mouth as he gesticulated. The only one Del understood was "Polohy," the name of the town she wanted Igor to bring her to. Twenty minutes and ten miles toward Donetsk, they had slowed to a stop in a line of traffic. Cars turned around, were waved back.

A military checkpoint. Into the new republic of Donbass.

Del grabbed Igor's shoulder. "What are you saying?"

"I am telling them what a famous television celebrity you are." He held out his phone, trying to keep it under the jacket's protection. "Showing them the picture of the Donbass soldier you want to talk to."

The rain began to subside.

Truth and lies. Del knew from experience that it was better to mix in truth when telling lies. Bullshitting was easier than pure fabrication. She wanted to speak to the soldier in the picture. Their cover story was that Del was a reporter for Western media, and she wanted to get the story of the separatists in Donbass as the conflict escalated. She wanted hear the story of the soldier in that picture—that was true.

But she wasn't Oprah.

The laughing soldiers didn't seem to think she was, either.

Igor said, "Do you have the money?"

Del produced the remaining four hundred dollars in a wad. This stopped the laughter. The big Russian inspected the bills and handed them to the man on his right. He barked a command, swung his weapon around on its sling, across his back, and barged past Del and Igor.

He opened the driver's side door to the Lada. One of his men opened the passenger door and began rifling through the glove box. The other soldier pushed Del and Igor toward the side of the road, toward the encampment of a dozen tents lining farmers' fields. It smelled of diesel fuel and sausage and the remains of a campfire.

"This is good," Igor said. "They are searching. If they find nothing suspicious, I think they might—"

The soldier going through the glove box stood up straight. Igor's gun in his hand. Igor began gesticulating again, arguing loudly. The man pocketed the handgun and moved to the backseat.

"*Layno.* Of course I have a gun," Igor complained. "Look where we are." He continued in Ukrainian, but from the look of it, his protest fell on deaf ears.

The man disappeared into backseat and, a second later, appeared with a package of aluminum foil. Del and Igor had found three rolls of it in the hotel kitchen. After the gunshots, the place had emptied out. The soldier pulled out three feet of foil and inspected it, then wrapped it around his head as a hat and mugged for his friends.

They all laughed again.

"At least they're in a good mood," Del said.

She had hidden her Interpol ID under the carpeting of the Lada, and felt a twinge of fear when the soldier returned to the car with the rolls of foil and then shouted out. He reappeared with two blocks of white plastic in his hands. Parts of the 3-D-printed gun Del had made before leaving the hotel in Kiev.

"He's asking what this is," Igor said.

"Tell him it's a toy."

Igor relayed the information. The soldier frowned and took a closer look before throwing the bits of plastic into the back of the car. The big Russian, apparently done in the front seat, slammed the door shut. He swaggered back in front of Del and Igor.

And shook his head.

"What's going on?"

Igor talked to the big Russian, gesticulating wildly again, but finally gave up. "They won't let us through."

"What about the money?"

"They say thank you very much for the contribution to the Donbass republic."

"Wait, just wait a second." Del reached into her jeans and pulled her phone out. Thank God she still had a mobile connection. She logged on to her social media account, realizing that this was a breach of the security protocol she had established with Suweil, but she didn't care.

She found the picture she wanted, and held it up to the soldiers.

***

"Could you drive a little slower?" Del asked. "Try not to hit the potholes?"

She sat in the back of the Lada and focused on aligning the nubs of plastic. Two of them snapped into place. She held out her handiwork and inspected it in the beam of her cell phone light: two of the 3-D-printed guns assembled, one shot each.

The rain had cleared, and the sun had already set over the horizon, lighting up a display of reds and golds in the western sky.

"What is the expression?" Igor craned his neck down to get a better look at the clouds. "Red sky at night, sailors' delight? Does this mean no more rain?"

"I'm no sailor."

"No Oprah, either, but somehow you got us through. What did you show them?"

"It's a secret."

"No secrets."

When Del didn't reply, Igor slowed the car and said, "Miss Devlin, I am risking my life. I'm doing this because I love my country, but I can't—"

Del held her phone up and showed him. "It's a picture of me with the Russian ambassador." The old man in the picture had his arm around Del. They looked like old chums.

Igor put his foot back on the gas. "And that thing in your hands, the plastic toy? This is a gun? It will shoot? Real bullets?"

The soldiers had taken Igor's sidearm but not the five rounds of loose ammunition in the bottom of the glove box.

"I hope so."

"Because you owe me a new one. What were those papers you found in the hotel?"

"It had locations of factories in southern Ukraine."

"Factories?"

"Something called 'print farms.'"

"Farms?"

"That's right."

"Do you know who shot your friend?"

"He wasn't my friend."

"Please, no games."

She wasn't playing. Del didn't have an answer.

Had they stumbled upon Petty's execution—because an execution was what it looked like—at just the wrong moment? It didn't look as if he had struggled. The door hadn't been splintered open. Had Del somehow led someone to him? A fair deduction, because when she got close to someone she was tracking, they often ended up dead.

The list of people who knew where Del was, and what she was up to, was thin.

Maybe only one person.

Her phone pinged. Another message from Suweil.

Del ignored it.

Why hadn't they persisted in attacking Del? She didn't doubt they had the ability, that whoever killed Petty had the upper hand when she got to that hotel. But it felt as though she had surprised them. They had left those papers there in their hurry to get away.

But . . .

Maybe they hadn't killed Del, simply because they knew they could pin it on her. Was she still being led down the garden path? What did this mean for her father?

Strataform had stuck something into his neck.

Del's theory had been that this was a ploy by Petty to get her to back off, but Petty was dead. Did this mean someone else was in charge of Strataform? Or that Strataform had been hacked or compromised?

The big question: What had Adam Petty, a Silicon Valley geek billionaire, been doing by himself in a seedy hotel room on the outskirts of Armageddon? Why hadn't he had any backup with him? Why was he alone? And why did he have this printed-out list of Strataform locations with him? He had to be searching for something.

Something he couldn't let anyone else know about.

Somehow, Del felt safer on the other side of that military checkpoint from whoever had killed Adam Petty. That picture of her with the Russian ambassador was the ace she pulled, and it had worked.

Del held up one of the 3-D-printed guns.

She wasn't deluding herself, though. Their getting through the checkpoint didn't mean that whoever killed Petty wasn't still tracking them. In the gathering twilight, she felt invisible pincers closing, the pressure building on the thin horizon.

***

They pulled into the village of Polohy in oily darkness. All streetlights were extinguished, all the windows blacked out. On the road in, they had seen flashes of bombs in the distance and heard the steady crunch and rolling thunder beyond the Lada's rattling whine.

Igor knocked on doors in the village.

Most residents wouldn't open up to speak to him. One or two yelled at them to go away. He shouted through windows anyway. Around midnight, they pulled up to a four-story brick building on the outskirts, illuminated only by a full moon high in the sky. Slivers of light glimmered between pulled curtains on the third and fourth floors, protruding air conditioners dotted along beneath.

Igor parked next to a playground of yellow metal bars welded together into jungle gyms.

"You sure this is a hospital?" Del asked.

"Pretty sure."

Across the street stood an unfinished structure of metal trusses, angled high into the night sky. It formed an archway bordered by slabs of concrete. A tracked excavator truck was parked in the center, with its shovel-arm claw raised high. Nothing moved.

"You coming?" Igor was already out of his door.

She squeaked hers open. The night air was cool, the scent of a wood fire lingering over the smell of manure from the fields they had driven through out of Tokmak.

Del followed Igor to the door.

He banged twice and yelled. No response. He tried again, then slammed his fist on the door. "I'm telling them that I have someone injured," he said.

A light clicked on beyond the blinds. The lock turned over, and the door opened. An elderly woman in a gray wool cap and a coat covered with a white apron appeared in the gap. She didn't look happy.

At first, she tried to shoo them away, but Igor persisted, and after a few seconds she relented and let them in. After locking the door, she stalked away without another word.

Del said, "You're not making friends."

"You want to take over?"

"I'm not complaining."

"Get the picture on your laptop. We'll ask around."

The interior was dimly lit, with bulbs only at the ends of the hallways. Igor led. They opened doors as gently and quietly as possible. Most of the rooms were darkened wards with rows of beds. They didn't want to wake anyone when they didn't have to.

They found another nurse on the second floor and showed her the picture of the soldier who claimed he was attacked by a giant insect in the social-media post. The woman confirmed that this was the hospital described in the posting, but she didn't recognize the young man.

The next person they found, an orderly with the same gray wool coat as the nurse who let them in, frowned when they showed him the image on the laptop. He began nodding and called over another orderly. The two talked to Igor in Ukrainian and pointed down the hallway.

***

"This is you?"

Del held out the laptop.

The young man grimaced as he got up on one elbow. He looked at the image, then at Del, then at Igor. He said something in Ukrainian.

"I thought you said he spoke English," Del said.

The young man looked at the floor, "I asked him, who is this? Who are you?"

He wore a striped T-shirt with food stains around the chest and was covered by a haphazard collection of floral-print sheets and covers. The hospital bed had wood veneer head- and footboards, and a single bent metal tube overhead in its center, with hooks for holding up bags of blood or plasma for IVs. A series of metal hoops encircled his lower left leg, from which the sheets were pulled back. Metal rods speared into his leg from the hoops, each rod with a bloody bandage taped at the skin.

"I'm an American. My name is Delta Devlin. I work with Interpol."

"Here? You are with Interpol *here*, in all *this?*"

She showed him her ID card. He grimaced again as he leaned over to look. She asked, "Your name is Alexi? That's your post on *Moi Mir?*"

He exhaled and let himself fall back into the pillows. "So, what of it?"

"When did you see these insects?"

"I was mistaken. The doctors tell me—"

Del pulled the phone from her pocket and cued up the video of the bug-bot crawling from the Strataform Replicator in her hotel. She held it up to the young man.

His eyes went wide.

"I've seen them, too," Del said. "Where did you see them? What happened?"

36

Del and Igor retreated to the ground floor of the hospital and found somewhere with privacy, a room that had three exits, including a way outside. They found a large bathroom with doors from two sides, locked themselves inside, and opened the window to the outdoors.

"You think this is Leonardo Bondar doing this?" Igor said.

The young soldier had described a night out on reconnaissance near the villages of Holubyts'ke and Trudove. He described exactly what Del had seen in her video, though he didn't know they were some kind of drone-bots. He thought they were giant spiders or cockroaches. One of them killed his friend after crawling down his throat while he slept. They couldn't recover the body, because they were being shelled by Ukrainian troops.

He wasn't the only one with stories, he said.

Del inspected the open window of the bathroom—a six-foot drop to an empty alleyway beyond. She put a wooden bench in front of the window so they could get out fast.

She said, "So, you know of the Black Army?"

Igor shrugged, yes and no, and lit a cigarette by the window. He sat on the bench. The bathroom was ten by twenty feet, with fresh gray tiles on the far wall, chipped brown ones to each side. A new water heater was affixed over the shiny gray tiles, its pipes connected to a set of porcelain washbasins along the wall, each of them connected to a single drainpipe that ran the length of the room.

Standing beside him, she said, "In the last Ukrainian revolution, a hundred years ago, an organization called the Black Army created its own independent state down here. They called it the Free Territory."

"I am from here, you know," said Igor. "This is my country. My history. I know all this." He took a deep drag from his cigarette. "So you think Leonardo Bondar is starting up his new *Black Army* and trying to build his own country using what? These bugs?"

"Maybe this is only scratching the surface. Manufactured reality. That's what he kept saying when we met."

"When he kidnapped you."

"When President Voloshyn was about to present at the UN meeting in New York, she was going to announce a big strategic deal with Strataform. This would have destroyed Bondar's MakerArmy company—they had invested almost all their resources to win over Eastern Europe. So he went on the offensive. Used his cyber skills to hack Strataform."

Del spread the papers she had filched from Adam Petty's room on the floor. Igor flicked his cigarette out the window and knelt beside her. One of the papers had a list of Strataform facilities in southern Ukraine.

"We should have called the police," he said. "Leaving your friend's dead body there, stealing his papers—I'm not sure this was the right thing to do."

Waiting would have been too dangerous. Del's only advantage was speed and surprise. Her theory was still merely that: a theory. From her backpack, she fished out another piece of paper. It was from the first print farm she had visited. Adam Petty had had one of his people print out a list of facilities for her when she visited with Jacques. Del compared the two lists.

Igor said, "But why would the Adam Petty machines have this capability?"

"Undocumented features. Tech companies do it all the time with new products."

"One holy hell of a feature."

Del scratched out any addresses on the lists that matched. Several didn't. They were on the list from Petty's room only—Strataform facilities that weren't public.

She added, "Bondar weaponized it. Same way he was the first to weaponize regular 3-D printers by distributing plans for guns. Same thing with the flying drones that attacked the Russian embassy. He's created a new type of weapon. Another tech genius gone crazy trying to create his own libertarian state. It's not a new story."

"These little bugs aren't going to stop tanks and real guns."

"Swarms of them might, but he doesn't need to. He's using them to spy, to assassinate. He's creating conflict between the two sides. East and West. Each thinks the other is attacking it, has killed one operative or another. He's creating the conditions to destabilize so he can create this new state. A new Free Territory."

Del picked up her paper. Four addresses weren't crossed out. "This is what Petty was down here trying to figure out: how someone was using his machines."

"Why would he come alone?"

Del said, "The area where those soldiers said they saw these bugs, where they were attacked—are any of these locations nearby?"

Igor lit up another cigarette and inspected the list. "Those two. The top ones."

A staccato burst of automatic gunfire echoed through the open window. Still far in the distance. Crunching thumps of explosions farther off.

"Then that's where we go. At first light."

***

The warehouse was empty. Its corrugated roof was held up by exposed steel trusses, the concrete floor cracked and pitted. Metal electrical conduit was bolted into the cinder-block walls. Circuit breakers had been ripped out of their panels. Igor and Del came in through the loading-dock door. It was unlocked. Early morning sunshine angled through skylights, illuminating the dust in the air.

"I am assuming you have a plan if we find anything," Igor said.

His voice echoed in the open space.

Del had spent the night fighting sleep, one eye always on the door to the bathroom they had locked themselves inside at the hospital. Every ten minutes, she picked up her phone and then put it back down again. She had taken out the SIM card and turned it off.

How was her father? What about that damned thing they'd stuck in his neck? She didn't need to sleep to have nightmares crowding her imagination.

Maddening theories circled around and around. In the heat of the moment, the only option was to move forward. Never let go, and chase the evidence wherever it led. But in the quiet moments, the doubts crept in.

What *was* her plan?

She said to Igor, "We get evidence."

"Don't you have a video?"

"Video can't be trusted anymore. I need something physical."

"That's what the tinfoil is for?"

Del had stuffed the three rolls, minus the three-foot strip the Russian soldier had made a hat of, into her backpack before they came into the warehouse. "Precisely," she said.

"Excuse me for feeling nervous when our greatest weapon is aluminum foil."

"Someone's been in here." Del knelt to the concrete floor and wiped a finger across it. The brown dust had fresh scrapes and skid marks. Someone had been in this factory recently and emptied out its contents. "We need to hurry."

***

The next location was in the center of the village of Bilmak.

The morning skies were clear, but there was a distant rumbling like thunderstorms. Shelling, Igor said. He checked the news on his phone. They had to clear out soon. Regular forces were advancing. Not just freedom fighters and the drunken soldiers at that checkpoint, but the Russian army itself.

Igor parked the Lada next to a brick building in the center of town.

All the stores were closed, but it was still early morning. Everything was quiet. Even the birds had stopped singing. With the fighting this close, she had expected the place to be a ghost town, but as they got out of the car, schoolchildren in uniforms passed by in twos and threes.

She watched them in disbelief, wanted to tell them to get away, to get out of there. But where, exactly, would they go?

A billboard across the street featured a twenty-foot smiling face of President Voloshyn, her hair perfect and blond and braided. The election was three days away, and despite all this they were still going ahead with it. If nothing else, Ukrainians were stoic.

Distant gunfire stuttered, interspersed with heavier detonations. The whistle of artillery rounds ended in hollow thuds. They stopped to listen from time to time, but the noise didn't seem to be getting closer.

"The gate is locked," Igor said from the concrete platform of the loading dock.

Del tested the front door. "This one, too."

She craned her neck up to inspect the four-story structure. The windows at ground level were covered by heavy wire mesh. The same on the second floor. Could she climb to the third floor? Maybe she could use the wire mesh to climb up.

She scouted left. The mesh had broken loose from one of the basement windows. If they could peel it back a little farther and broke the glass, she could probably slip through.

"Come on," Igor said. "You said we were in a hurry."

The trunk of the Lada was open. Igor stood by the basement entrance with a pair of bolt cutters in his hand. "You going to stand there or help?"

He set the cutters over the rusted chain wrapped around the door handles and gritted his teeth. A second later, the chain clattered apart. Del unspooled the chain from the handles and dropped it in the mud. They each took a door and hauled them up and sideways. Concrete stairs led down into darkness.

"I'll go first," Igor said.

"Let me get my backpack."

"What's that smell?" He scrunched his nose up, brandishing the heavy cutters as he descended.

Del followed him. "Diesel?"

"Not that."

The basement was dank. Oily puddles reflected the outside light. What was that stench? It was familiar, but Del couldn't quite place it. She groped along the concrete-block wall until she found a switch. Four bare incandescent bulbs glowed to life down the length of the fifty-by-twenty room, illuminating a jumble of cardboard boxes to one side, and a row of green jerry cans to the other.

"Ryton," Del mumbled.

Igor tiptoed to the wooden staircase leading up. "What?"

"That smell. It's Ryton. A synthetic polymer, high flash point." She turned her phone on, its SIM card still removed, to use the flashlight. "These boxes are Strataform packaging."

"Nobody here." Igor was already up the stairs. "Nobody at the reception."

Hearing a door open, Del froze in place.

"Just me," Igor called out, his voice muffled. "I opened the front door."

She followed him up the stairs. The lobby area was exactly like the one she had visited in Kiev. An automated production factory. That polymer smell in the air meant it was still in use, but the building was silent.

Igor propped open the front door. A fresh breeze blew in. Del jogged back down the stairs to the basement and took a hammer and screwdriver from a workbench. She rejoined Igor in the lobby, and they went to the next floor.

This level was new, freshly painted.

She pushed the second-floor door from the stairwell. The door suctioned open, as if the interior was air sealed. The melted-polymer stink wafted over them. The only noise not their own was the hum of a fan somewhere.

The room was dark and breathless. Del reached inside and found the light switch. Neon tubes flickered on across the ceiling, revealing a rectangular space like the facility she saw in Kiev—about fifty feet wide and a hundred long. No dividers. Floating ceiling tiles. Squat gray Strataform Replicators in ranks of ten, the power cables snaking up into wiring racks at regular intervals. Del counted the rows. Twenty. Two hundred machines.

"What do we do?" Igor whispered.

He pointed at security cameras over their heads, in the corners of the stairwell.

"We hurry," Del replied.

Four floors to this building. Hammer and screwdriver in hand, she led Igor to the next level. Same thing: two hundred idle Strataform machines. She knew they would find the same thing on the next story as well.

"You watch the entrance," Del told Igor. "Start the car and keep it running, I'll—"

A whirring noise interrupted her. A three-wheeled robot, like the ones she had seen in Kiev, came rolling down an aisle between the machines, its arm dangling overhead. Another bot appeared. And another.

"Get the car running," Del said, and shoved Igor toward the stairs.

She walked to the nearest Strataform and pulled the cover off. Putting down the hammer, she used the screwdriver to open the interior compartment, then pried free the main circuit board and memory. She swung off her backpack, unzipped it, and dropped the electronics in. Whatever these machines had been used for, it had to be recorded somewhere in the memory.

Del advanced to the next machine and ripped the top off.

A low thrumming noise filled the air. The concrete beneath her feet vibrated. One by one, the orange Cyclops eye of each Replicator blinked on, first the row in front of Del, then each row in succession. The vibrating thrum built in volume. The machine she had her hand on began to hum. Printing.

"Miss Devlin?" Igor yelled from outside.

"I'm coming!" she shouted back.

Working fast, Del jammed the screwdriver into the Replicator in front of her and pulled out its circuit board. The orange light of its print bay went dark.

She could kill the machines. They weren't magical. Just technology. *Keep telling yourself that.*

The next cover came off, and she worked the screwdriver in and pulled its boards out in less than ten seconds. She dropped both circuit boards into her backpack. This was the closest print farm to where those soldiers were attacked. The place was locked. They couldn't be expecting anyone. The evidence she needed had to be on these circuits.

Del got to the next machine.

Just one more.

The overhead lights winked out, and she waited for her eyes to adjust to the orange-glowing semidarkness. The machine she stood in front of chimed.

A dark sheet of plastic slid from the mouth of its print bay. Del watched in horrified fascination as the sheet quivered to life. She grabbed it and felt the thing squirm in her hand. Del retreated the length of two machines and grabbed the hammer, let the bug-bot drop to the floor, and gave it a whack. The tiny machine shattered.

All around her, the Replicator machines chimed. At first one, then hundreds of rings echoed through the orange twilight like a casino slot machine paying off in Hades.

The floor writhed with dozens of bug-bots wriggling toward her. Hundreds. Her leg pinched. One crawled up her jeans, and she swiped it away and sprinted for the exit. She slammed the doors open and turned and pushed them shut behind her.

Hundreds more chimes echoed. Then more from upstairs.

And down.

"Igor!" Del screamed. "Get that car running!"

A swarm of bug-bots, each the size of a half-grown rat, cascaded down the stairs toward her.

37

Del resisted the urge to run.

She stood her ground, back against the doors to keep them shut. The things crawled closer. Bright sunshine illuminated the stairwell through the windows on each landing. The little bots weren't more than six inches long, and coming down the stairs with their awkward six-legged gait, they fell off each stair and tumbled before taking a second or two to right themselves, like stampeding turtles.

They swarmed toward her, but it was a slow swarm.

The crawling tide advanced at perhaps a foot per second. She could easily outrun them.

Memory cards were good, but actually *having* one of these bug-bots was even better. And that was what she had come to do. It was what the aluminum foil was for, she reminded herself. The metal wrap would act as a poor person's Faraday cage, isolating it from outside communication. These things couldn't be entirely autonomous, could they? She glanced up at the security camera in the corner of the stairwell. Someone was watching her—someone desperate. This was a last-ditch response on the part of whoever controlled the printing machines.

These things weren't magic. They had to have a limited battery life.

Her initial revulsion at the squirming creatures faded.

So far, the only evidence had these things coming out at night. Staying hidden and spying on people or attacking them when they were asleep and defenseless in the darkness. Then the bots slunk away and melted themselves. That hundreds of them had been printed out at once to attack her in daylight, in full view, meant she must have surprised them.

She heard scuffling, scrabbling noises on the other side of the doors she held shut. A fresh wave of the little bastards trying to get out.

The closest bot coming down the stairs was five feet away. Del reached forward and swatted it with her hand. It skittered sideways, rolled over, and fell off the edge of the stair and into open space. A second later, she heard a clatter as it hit a few floors down.

Not exactly terrifying.

Clicking noises came from the stairs below her. She peered over the edge. An advance guard of bots crawled up the stairs toward her. Too small to scale a step by themselves, two or three at a time coordinated their efforts to climb up and over each other.

It was mesmerizing to watch.

Hundreds of pinging chimes rang out from behind the doors and from the floors above and below. Another print cycle finished. Del did a mental calculation. Maybe six hundred machines, maybe a minute per print cycle—that was about ten more of these little critters every second. All she had to do was crush more than ten each second to win.

Her fear subsided.

A wave of the little bots clattered down the last stairs. She let go of the doors, and a clicking, writhing mass of bug-bots slid onto the landing as the door swung open, but Del had already bounded down the first flight of stairs away from them. She kicked the first pile of bots and ran down the stairs in jumping steps, into the lobby. The bug-bots on the stairs she passed turned to follow.

She swung her backpack off and quickly unspooled a yard of tinfoil.

The front doors were ten feet away. She just had to spring that distance, get outside and into the car. She still had a little time to collect some more evidence.

From upstairs, the echoing chimes of another print cycle rang out.

One of the bug-bots climbed onto her sneaker. Del shook her leg but it stuck stubbornly. She reached down with the tinfoil and grabbed it. It clung to her jeans. She had to rip it free as if it were Velcroed to her. One of its insect legs came off and quivered. Del wrapped up the creature in two and then three layers of foil and stuck it into her backpack.

"Ow!" she yelped.

It felt as if she had been stung by a bee. Another of the bug-bots had crawled halfway up her right calf. She grabbed it and wrenched it away, then kicked away a dozen others scurrying toward her. Del held the bot close to her face. A tiny needle protruded from the bottom of its body.

Another sharp jab of pain.

Del threw the bot against the wall and grabbed another that had latched on to her foot. These things could sting. She staggered forward as she threw this bug-bot away. Her left leg felt numb.

Beyond the numbness, a tingling fear and realization: these things had venom.

Dozens of them surrounded her now, circling but keeping their distance. Hunting. A roiling mass tumbled over itself coming down the stairs into the lobby. Del ran for the front doors, kicking away the bug-bots in her way. She grabbed the door handle, turned it, and slammed it with her body weight.

It didn't budge.

Del screamed, "Open the door!"

She looked out the side window. The Lada was there, but no Igor. As she jiggled the door handle, two bug-bots scurried up her leg. She swatted them off. She turned and shucked off her backpack, and with scything motions, she cleared the closest creatures away from her.

Whoever turned these machines on must have sealed the doors. Magnetic locks.

Something fell onto her head.

She screamed and grappled with the twitching machine, pulled the bug-bot from her hair, and threw it over the reception desk. Del looked up. The little bastards were crawling across walls, up the blinds.

Another ringing chime reverberated from up the stairs.

One more print cycle.

How many was that? Five? Six? Multiplied by six hundred machines . . . That meant three-and-a-half thousand of these little inorganic animals. *Time to get the hell out of here.* Another bot fell from the ceiling, missing her, but in an instant it bounced up, scrambled to right itself, and scuttled toward her.

Del kicked away a half-dozen bots near her, and in two jumping strides, she reached the stairs going down, crushing a few of the machines underfoot along the way. The sea of bot-bugs reoriented itself and followed her movement. She slipped on the last leaping step and fell hard.

Her left foot felt like someone else's.

Del's momentum carried her forward, and she tumbled down the concrete stairs, holding her forearms around her head to protect herself. Her knee slammed into a tread, and a shooting pain lanced out. Hitting the landing in a roll, Del ignored the pain and got unsteadily to her feet.

Two of the bug-bots had entangled themselves in her hair, and she tore them away.

One on her right leg.

She slapped it into the ground and stamped.

The things were like cockroaches—hard to kill. The bug-bot underfoot, though damaged, squirmed toward her even after she kicked it again.

A wave of bots had reached the top of the stairs, and they tumbled over each other toward her. Another ringing chime from upstairs—more distant now, but at a shorter interval. Not more than thirty seconds since the last one. Four thousand of these things now? Maybe five?

The exposed incandescent bulbs were still on in the basement. The stench of rotten eggs was stronger here. Del scanned the floor and boxes. Nothing wriggling or moving. *Thank God.* She looked right at the jerry cans of diesel fuel. Nothing moving there.

Grab something from the workbench?

What?

A saw? Another hammer? The little creatures tumbled down another step toward her. Del swung off her backpack and reached into the front pocket. The lighter was still there. She ran past the workbench and grabbed one of the jerry cans. It was full. She unscrewed it and ran to the stairs. The undulating mass of bots was almost into the basement.

Del spilled the diesel over them and splashed it messily up the stairs and ran back a few steps, slopping a trail of fuel behind.

She pulled out her lighter, knelt, and clicked it on, holding it to the edge of the puddle. The spilled fuel didn't ignite. She remembered reading somewhere that diesel was much harder to light than gasoline or even kerosene. Looking frantically around her, she spied an old newspaper. Wadding up a couple of pages, she soaked them in the puddle of diesel. Then she held the lighter to the paper, waiting for the wick effect to spread the flame. When the wad was ablaze, she dropped it on the puddle.

In a couple of seconds, the flame began to spread over the surface of the puddle. A yellow flame licked across the concrete floor. The advancing front wave of bug-bots that she doused in accelerant were catching fire now. No noise. No squealing. They kept coming but slowed and stopped as their burning legs curled up, unable to support them. The flames were mounting the stairs.

That should give her time.

Del ran to the middle of the basement, to the clamshell doors leading up. These were old, wooden, secured by a rusted chain. They couldn't be secured with magnetic locks.

"Igor!" Del screamed. "What the hell are you doing out there?"

She reached the stairs leading to the doors and banged against them.

Dread raced like cold spiders down her spine. The doors didn't budge. she could hear the chain rattle on the other side as she shoved her shoulder against them. She looked back at the stairwell up. Yellow flames had spread across the floor.

Oily smoke rolled across the ceiling.

Del took two steps to the left and scrambled up onto some stacked wooden crates to look out one of the basement windows. Through the wire mesh, she saw that the Lada hadn't moved. Where was Igor? Had *he* locked the basement doors?

Choking clouds of soot wafted past her.

She coughed and gagged before jumping off the boxes to the clear air lower down.

A seething mass of wires and plastic pulsated and grew beyond the flames by the staircase up. The fuel she had dumped was getting depleted; the bug-bots had retreated but were hovering there, waiting out the fire. She didn't have much time.

Del ran back to the workbench and grabbed two more jerry cans of diesel. She waddled to the stairwell, one in each hand. Her left foot felt like a thick stump of wood.

She looked up and tried to comprehend.

Her mind couldn't quite fathom what she was seeing.

On the other side of the flames, the mass of bots undulated and pulsed and coiled into thickening ropes that coalesced together. One of the cords of locked-together bots levitated, becoming a snakelike appendage that rose up to the ceiling and crawled along the exposed electrical conduit, wriggling its way toward her.

"You've got to be kidding me."

She dropped one of the cans, took the other, and sloshed out the fuel. She emptied it, then emptied the next, and kicked two more cans into the middle of the floor as she retreated. The flames roared, the thick soot burning her throat and eyes.

The bot-snake dropped from the ceiling and into the conflagration but came worming up through the flames and shot straight at her. Del grabbed it. The bot-snake wrapped around her arm and tightened like a constrictor. With her other hand, she wrenched it free and held it down on the workbench.

And pounded it with the hammer.

She turned and ran.

Coughing.

Gagging.

The window at the far end of the basement. She had thought of climbing through it when they came in. The wire mesh outside it was pulled away. Del skidded to stop and wiped her eyes, grabbed one of the Strataform boxes, and reached up and swung the hammer. The windowpane shattered, raining shards down on her. She tapped away as much of the glass edge as she could, then jammed the cardboard onto the edge.

Del scrambled against the wall and felt a shard of glass bite into her hand.

Somehow, she wormed her way into the opening.

Wriggled through.

And rolled across hard-packed mud into mercifully clear air. A bright blue sky overhead.

Del lay on her back and coughed, rolled onto her knees, and wiped her eyes. Thick black smoke billowed from the window she had smashed. Flames licked out.

"Igor," she said, getting to her feet. "Where the hell are—"

The taxi driver was on his knees on the other side of the Lada.

Director Dartmouth stood behind him, the gun in her hand pointed at his head.

38

"Katherine?" Del rubbed her eyes again. Tears from the stinging smoke blurred her vision. She stumbled forward, her left foot a club of dead wood. "What . . . are . . . you doing?"

"Thank God you got out," Katherine said. "I was trying to get the front door open . . ." Her eyes went wide. "What the hell is that?"

A thrashing rope of flame undulated from the basement window and slithered across the cracked mud. Ten feet of it came out, the mass of bots crackling and hissing as they burned. It writhed another body length before shuddering to a stop in a molten, dripping mass.

Del turned back to Katherine. "I'll explain later. Igor's with me."

"Igor?"

"The guy you have your gun pointed at."

A hundred feet past the red Lada, at the next intersection, was another car. A black Mercedes. A man in a dark suit and sunglasses crouched in front of its fender. He signaled to Katherine, pointed down the road, and waved his hand forward.

Dark splotches suddenly dotted the bare earth and gravel. Del turned her face up and felt rain against her cheeks.

"We need to get going," Katherine said. "And this guy"—she tapped the back of Igor's head—"is not with you."

"What does that mean?"

"He works for Leonardo Bondar. A Black Army operative."

Del stopped limping forward. "Excuse me?"

"Isn't that right, Igor? Tell her. Go on, tell her."

His hands still clasped behind his head, he lifted his eyes to meet Del's. "I was trying to keep you safe."

"You work for Bondar?"

"You don't understand—"

Katherine slugged him hard across the face with the butt of her pistol. "He's the one that took you to that alleyway where you killed Korshunov."

"I didn't kill him."

"Then they did a good job making it look like you did. You've been set up."

Glass shattered behind Del. Shards fell from the second floor. Flames roared out from the building as the rainstorm intensified. Another window cracked and exploded outward. Overhead, a whistling whine intensified, and a split second later, a shock wave knocked Del sideways. Dirt showered over her.

She staggered to regain her balance. *That wasn't from the building.* "What . . ."

"A mortar round," Katherine said, her voice barely audible through the ringing in Del's ears. "We need to move. Bondar's Black Army faction is on their way in here, fighting the Donbass militia on the edge of town. Help me get this asshole into the car. We need to hurry."

Igor was splayed in the dirt beside the Lada. The guy in the dark suit by the Mercedes was coming toward them, his pistol out.

"How did you find me?" Del said as she reached Katherine.

"Suweil was tracking you. When you went AWOL at the airport, Commissioner Georgiev had a fit. Jacques tried to have them put you on the fugitive Red List, but I knew something else was going on."

"But I took the SIM card out. Turned it off."

Katherine shrugged to say, *as if that made any difference.* "I'm sorry for getting you into this mess."

Gunfire crackled and echoed in the distance. Another whining thump and concussion wave as a mortar round hit the building's roof. Flames roared out the open windows, and soot blackened the structure's sides.

Katherine grabbed Del's shoulder and knelt with her to pick up Igor. "Put him in the front seat. Hurry, we gotta move."

Del grabbed the moaning Igor and manhandled him in, then swung her pack into the backseat.

"That's Ian," Katherine said, pointing at the big man in the dark suit. "He'll ride in the back with you." She rounded the Lada to the driver's side.

Del's mind twisted and seethed like the mass of bug-bots she had just escaped.

"Igor led you into a trap," Katherine explained. "I told you, President Voloshyn was going to give the massive contract to Strataform. Bondar snapped. That's why he killed Adam Petty—"

"You know about Petty?" Del got into the backseat.

The big man in the suit opened the other passenger door.

"We were too late to stop them," Katherine said. She turned in her seat. "We were right behind you."

"I have evidence of these . . . these *things*," Del said.

"We'll look at everything back in Lyon, but for now . . ." Katherine turned the ignition. The Lada's engine whined to life. Igor sat up.

Del's hand felt for the 3-D-printed gun in the backseat. Her brain tried to reassemble what was going on. Why were they in the Lada? Why didn't they get into the bigger, faster, more reliable Mercedes? Her mind flitted back to the Russian embassy. Those rainbow smudges on the power outlets—just like the ones in her room.

Why would Bondar spy on the Russians?

A better question: Why was Petty out here all by himself?

If Voloshyn was about to award him a massive contract, wouldn't he be home celebrating? Especially if Bondar, his nemesis, had taken a dive off the nuts end. Petty was the winner. He should be back home enjoying champagne at his retreat on Lake Tahoe, congratulating himself, surrounded by adoring sycophants—not taking a bullet all alone in a cheap hotel in the back of beyond.

There are no coincidences in life, she heard her father's voice tell her.

Her father. He'd been shot, she was being used as a spy, and her family had been linked to the IRA just as Del was drawn into a conspiracy with another European terrorist group.

The big guy in the suit sat down heavily next to Del.

Katherine hadn't stepped on the gas. She reached down for something. Her face was mottled *ishma*-pink, the periorbital blood vessels bright.

Del looked right. The big guy had a hand in his coat. His face was mottled hot as well.

"Katherine, Ian," she said, looking straight at the man, "thank you so much for rescuing me." She steepled her hands together. "I can't tell you how much . . ."

Del shot her right hand out and chopped the big guy in the windpipe. It didn't matter how big you were if you couldn't breathe. His left hand reached out and pawed at her, but she leaned in and brought her elbow straight down into his crotch with half her body weight. He jerked forward. Anticipating this, she swung her head back hard and caught him square in the face.

She felt and heard the crunch of nose cartilage and bone.

She screamed, "Igor, run!"

39

Rain hammered down on the Lada's roof.

Coughing blood and cursing unintelligibly, Ian grappled blindly. He grabbed a handful of Del's long hair between his fingers. Instead of trying to get away, she felt around his waistband for his weapon.

Katherine said from the front. "Delta, what the hell are you doing!"

Del found Ian's gun and unsnapped the holster. He sensed what she was doing, and let go of her hair. With his right hand, he gripped her hand on the weapon. It was slippery with blood pouring down from his crushed nose.

A hinge squeaked, followed by a rush of wet air as the front passenger door opened. Katherine was half over the divider, pulling Del's T-shirt, trying to get her away from Ian—or trying to get Ian away from her? Katherine cursed. Del still had her face almost in Ian's lap as they struggled over control of his gun. She slammed her head upward and sideways into the man's already wrecked face. He roared in pain.

Del glimpsed Igor sliding in the mud, away from the car.

Katherine let go of her and opened her driver's-side door.

Ian had to be blind from the pain, but he was immensely strong. He wrenched the gun from Del's blood-slick grip. She reached for his crotch to grab and squeeze . . . but felt something else. A hard plastic shell. Del reached under him.

"You goddamn bitch . . ." Ian spat the words along with a mouthful of blood. With his left hand, he wrenched her head back by the hair. He had the pistol in his right.

Del didn't resist. Her left hand had found what it wanted. She pressed the 3-D-printed gun into his groin, prayed, and pulled the trigger.

A muffled crack. Ian's body shot upright as if a thousand volts had just hit him. A split second later came an earsplitting roar and shattering glass. He had fired his gun through the side window, Del realized as her ears rang. She reached past him for his pistol, but he writhed away. She grabbed his arm, but the weapon dropped out the blown window. Both his hands went to his groin as he howled in agony.

Del wound up with her left hand and roundhouse-punched him square in the nose again. His head shot back as he bellowed and spat blood into the Lada's headliner.

She pulled herself away.

Katherine was just visible ten feet in front of the car, her own weapon out. Two loud cracks as she fired at Igor. She glanced back at the car and ran to the passenger door on Del's side.

Del reached over and unlatched it, and as Katherine reached for it, Del leaned back and kicked it open with both feet. The door swung open hard and caught the director in the head. She ricocheted off and slumped backward into the mud, splaying awkwardly sideways.

Del scrambled over the bench. She hesitated but then reached back and found the second 3-D-printed gun under Ian's backside. She stumbled out of the car.

Katherine rolled over in the mud, onto her hands and knees. "What the hell are you *doing!*" she yelled, her face still halfway in the mud.

The spatter of heavy raindrops had progressed to a sheeting downpour. Del ran.

Trust your gut. She heard her father's voice loud in her head.

Through the rain, the building above her gouted orange flames. Del looked back and wiped her hair from her eyes. Katherine was up on her feet now. Was she pointing a gun? Del slipped and fell sideways, skidding into a puddle of gravel and dirt by the edge of an alley.

In two whining roars, mortar rounds hit the ground next to the car and sent up sprays of mud. Katherine ducked for cover. Del scrambled into the alleyway. Her back against the brick wall, she rubbed streaming raindrops from her eyes and, with a shaking hand, brought the white plastic 3-D-printed gun close to her face and inspected it. Did it matter if this thing got wet? Stuttering gunfire from heavy automatic weapons echoed in the distance. From a few blocks away came the crump and hiss of mortar rounds.

Katherine yelled, "Whatever you're doing you need to *stop!*"

She was out of view, her voice muffled by the rain. Del got to her feet and scrambled a dozen strides down the alleyway to an opening in a chain-link fence. Crouching, she squeezed through and felt the wire's rough galvanized coating scrape her back.

"Did Ian attack you?" Katherine yelled out over the rain. "Whatever you're thinking, you're wrong. We need to get out of here."

Was she closer or farther away?

Del couldn't tell whether the director was following her. She was between two buildings, in what was not so much an alley as a garbage-strewn gap a yard wide. Del picked her way over piles of branches and cans. The brick structure was two stories high and maybe a hundred feet long and opened onto the next street—or so it looked in the sleeting downpour.

"Delta, the Black Army is advancing on our position." Katherine's voice was fading as Del gained some distance. "Igor will give us away. He's been tracking you for them the whole time." Her voice was barely audible now. "Delta, please . . ."

Del pulled herself over the last garbage pile and into the next street, her plastic weapon out in front of her. She swept it back and forth, clearing both ends of the street, then leaned into the wall and crept back along it. At the corner, she crouched to peer around and caught a glimpse of Katherine running low.

But not toward Del.

The director was heading in the direction Igor had fled, to the opposite side of the street.

Just visible in the distance was that Black Mercedes. No other cars except the Lada. No sign of Ian, but she guessed he was still in the backseat. Still alive? Probably, but she doubted he was mobile—though he might still be a threat. His gun had dropped to the ground outside, but he could have recovered it, or Katherine may have given it back to him.

Del's chest heaved with each breath. The cold rain soaked deep into her aching bones.

Was this a mistake? She held the plastic gun up to her chest. In the car, something hadn't been right. The hair on her neck had risen like the hackles on a pit bull's backside. Was it Katherine, though? Who was Ian? Was it Igor?

Maybe I made a mistake.

But maybe not.

Del needed to get out of here. That was about the only plan now. The keys might be in the Mercedes, but there was a higher chance they were in Ian's pocket.

"Damn it." She flicked rain-soaked hair from her face.

Del had just braced herself to run forward when a whirring moan reverberated through the drumming rain. She ducked her head and pulled her arms in, anticipating the concussion and roar of another mortar round, but the whine changed pitch to a thrumming beat. Del opened her eyes.

Two eyes peered back at her.

Not eyes.

Two platforms, one beside the other, hovering ten feet up in the driving rain. Each with a cylinder slung beneath and with a black circle at its center, staring back at her. The drones warbled and shivered in the downpour and seemed to consider her. Then they both tipped sideways and accelerated away, tilting as they rounded the corner into the open area beyond.

Del held back for a second, then ran into the street behind them. If they wanted to hurt her, they would have.

She slid to a stop.

Ian was out of the car, slumped against the back window, pointing at her. Gun in his hand.

Del was raising her hands in surrender when a bright stream of fire gushed forth over the Lada, roiling and engulfing Ian. He screamed and fell back into the mud, his arms and legs in flames. The fire seemed to have originated in midair.

Del wiped water from her eyes again.

The gushing fireball hadn't come from the burning building, but from a flamethrower in the belly of one of the drones. Another spurt of flame, this one from the other drone, poured fire into the building's already blazing second floor. A mortar round hit the third floor, showering glass and fragments of brickwork around Del.

She stood transfixed.

Both drones spat fire for another two seconds. Then they wobbled, circled, and sped upward in the air, rising high into the rain until Del couldn't see them. Their whining moan faded, replaced by the groans of Ian thrashing in the mud.

Still with her hands in the air in surrender, Del took one step, then another, and then sprinted the last ten, sliding to a stop beside Ian. His jacket was blackened, the exposed skin on his hands blistered, his face a mass of red. A stench of burnt hair and flesh and gasoline hung between the raindrops.

Dropping to her knees, Del reached into his trouser pockets, first the left, then the right. She found the keys. After turning Ian onto his side so he wouldn't drown in the mud, she glanced in the direction of the Mercedes, then did her best to prop him up against the Lada.

"Did you kill Adam Petty?" she said.

His face was black and red, eyes blistered shut. He groaned in pain. She wasn't going to get anything out of him. She scanned the mud and puddles for his weapon.

Nothing.

Heavy gunfire again. Closer. It sounded right around the corner.

Del felt a pain in her thigh. Was she injured? She felt in her jeans and discovered her phone. It had jammed against her when she fell to the ground. She got up and checked through the smashed window, looking into the backseat. She searched for her backpack with the memory cards and bot-bug inside. It was gone.

God damn it.

She checked the keys in her hand. Mercedes logo on them.

Del began to run at a half crouch for the German-made luxury car, scanning left and right. Two figures appeared in the rain down an alley just ahead and to her right. Soldiers? She didn't stop but accelerated, getting up from halfway bent over to full sprint, running to the left, around them.

"I got him," Katherine called out. She marched Igor ahead of her, a gun pointed at his head. "Igor, you tell Delta everything you told me. Tell her how you told Bondar about Petty's location."

Delta skidded to a stop.

The three of them stood ten feet apart in the driving rain.

Katherine said, "Tell her, you bastard, or I will shoot you in the head."

Igor's hands were up, shaking, the swatch of black hair circling his bald crown matted down, his clothes soaked through. Blood seeped from a wound in his head.

He stuttered, "I . . . I didn't . . . I wasn't . . ."

Katherine raised her gun to his head.

Del lifted up the soiled white plastic 3-D gun in her left hand and pointed it at Katherine. "Don't you dare."

The director's gun held steady for a second. "Do you *ever* give up?" She swiveled her arm around and pointed the gun at Del. "And do you think that toy will work?"

40

Delta and Katherine faced each other in the deluge, Del's hand shaking as she gripped the hard plastic of the single-shot gun and tried to aim. Katherine's arm was as steady as her eyes, her weapon aimed square at Del's chest. Igor crouched between them.

Time stood still.

Del felt the pressure of her finger on the trigger.

A roaring, clanking growl came from her left, and all of them turned to look.

Between two buildings, a massive green snout protruded and grew longer. Wheels and tracks appeared. A hundred feet away, a huge tank rolled into the street and spun in the mud. In its open hatch sat a man with a heavy machine gun pointed forward.

More soldiers sprinted from the alley behind it and started yelling.

On the center of the green tank was a single red star.

***

Del huddled in the darkness.

Her clothes hadn't dried yet. How long had it been? Hard to tell. No windows in this basement two floors belowground. No lights. Pitch black and damp and almost soundless except for the rumble of heavy machinery passing by on the street above.

It had to be Wednesday by now.

Someone had just brought her a mug of water and a hunk of hard bread—the first thing they had given her since they forced her down here. She glimpsed sunshine through the stairwell when they opened the door above. So night had passed. It was sometime the next day.

When the soldiers found her and Katherine and Igor, they had screamed. Del hadn't understood a word of it, but the meaning was unmistakable: put down your weapons or get shot. Katherine had her handgun but was hopelessly outmatched by the tank's .51-caliber machine gun and the soldiers' automatic weapons. Both of them dropped what they had and raised their hands.

Igor had tried to say something to them and got a rifle butt to the midsection for his pains.

The senior officer—Del assumed he was the senior officer by the way he carried himself—tried to question them after they were tied up and sitting in the mud. Katherine told Del to keep quiet, that these were Russians. She said she would handle it, and spoke in halting words, but the commanding officer didn't seem interested. The tank had rolled on through the village, followed by the squad of soldiers, while Del, Katherine, and Igor were frog-marched back the way the army had come from.

Ian was still alive, and two soldiers dragged him from the mud. The last Del saw of him, they were loading him onto an improvised stretcher.

At the edge of the village, Del and Katherine were loaded onto an open truck while Igor was separated from them and put with a ragtag collection of bloodied young men walking on a road away from town. Del tried to get them to bring him with them, but the soldiers shoved her back. Katherine kept telling them that they were Americans, but nobody cared.

They took Del's laptop and phone, searched their pockets, and took their identification and wallets and everything else they could find. She noticed the soldiers pocketing the bills of *hryven*, the Ukrainian currency.

The rain had stopped, the clouds still low and dark, and Del tried to estimate which direction the trucks took them—her best guess was west. After an hour, they had entered a larger village. Katherine and Del were separated and taken to different buildings.

Del didn't need Director Dartmouth to tell her that these were Russians.

That huge red star on the tank, the same red stars on the lapels of the soldiers. Fighter jets had screamed over them at low altitude as they rumbled across the terrain in the truck. The radio in the Lada on the drive in hadn't lied: the Russians had invaded Ukraine, and this time they weren't bothering to hide it.

***

Del flexed her hand.

She had slept in fits and starts on the wooden bench. She was in a basement, in a cage. She guessed it was a police lockup, but this one was older and more decrepit than the earlier one. The cage bars were blistered with rust, and water leaked in rivulets down the slimy walls to the hard-packed earth floor. The sweet-fetid stink of piled garbage by the wall was overpowering, but she was getting used to it. She didn't touch the hard bread they brought, but she gulped down the water. She couldn't remember the last time she'd drank anything.

Wednesday. It had to be Wednesday.

That bright Monday morning when she escaped from the airport was just two days ago, but it felt like a different age in another universe. What had she thought would happen? That she could just drive into a war zone? Traipse through without a care?

She was lucky they hadn't been shot or, even less glamorously, blown to pieces by mortar shrapnel. Was Del the reason Katherine had dragged herself out here?

The darkness allowed her mind too much time to wander.

What had happened to her father? Was he even still alive? Her mind kept circling back around to that. When she was busy, caught up in the action of the moment, she hadn't dwelt, and maybe that was what she had been doing the whole time. Escaping. Trying not to think about it. Hoping that somehow he would be magically fixed and that she could return home the victorious hero.

She could fix it—by solving the crime. Bringing justice.

But she was naive.

As when she grabbed that kid who fell off the roof—she just wouldn't let go. She wouldn't see sense, couldn't see the danger. She had been used; that was the truth of it—had been so blind that she let them use her.

Wednesday.

Two days till the elections, although Del couldn't imagine Voloshyn still holding them.

Her mind circled back.

What did they have? Her cell phone? That was locked, as was her laptop, but no one had come down to ask her to open it for them. She would bet that these soldiers had more pressing worries. And her backpack with that thing in it. No. Katherine said she had flung Del's backpack into the fire, so that was gone.

Del sat upright.

But why? Why would Katherine do that *before* the soldiers arrived?

She rubbed her eyes and stood up from the bench, then went to the corner of the cell closest to the stairwell up. "Anatoly Ushakov!" she yelled.

Two days until the election.

Del yelled again, as loud as she could, "Anatoly Ushakov!"

***

"You want some tea?" The man held a stainless-steel pot suggestively above two chipped porcelain mugs.

Del nodded.

She was still shivering from the cold even under the thick wool blanket they had given her when they ushered her into this closet-size room. The man had on a green greatcoat, and a peaked hat with a metal emblem of an eagle, which he had taken off when they pushed her in. His cheeks were ruddy from the cold outside.

He poured two cups and offered one to Del. She wrapped her fingers around its warmth.

Out the window, the sky looked clear and blue, but this unheated space was cold.

"My name is Golokin—Sergeant Golokin of the FSB." He sat in a wooden chair, across the low worktable from Del. His eyes were blue, and he wore a trimmed salt-and-pepper mustache over a smiling set of well-cared-for teeth. "And you are Detective Delta Devlin, of the Suffolk County Police Department. You are a long way from home, Miss Devlin."

"Where, exactly, am I?" She took a sip of the tea.

He picked up a file from the table. Del's phone and laptop were beside it. "So it says here you were charged with killing one of my comrades, Yuri Korshunov."

"I didn't kill him."

"Who, it seems, shot your father." He looked up from the file. "This is quite a story. Almost unbelievable. Why were you yelling Anatoly Ushakov's name downstairs? You are meaning our ambassador to Ukraine, yes?"

"I need to speak with him."

"Why would you want to do that?"

"We're friends."

"I find that hard to believe."

She leaned forward, letting go of the blanket, but held her hands out, palms up in surrender, to let him know she didn't mean to do anything stupid. "Can I take my phone? Show you something?"

"By all means. We have already copied the contents of both devices; I'm sure you understand."

Del turned it on and brought up the image of her with Anatoly—the image from when she was in the ambassador's office. "I need to speak with him right now."

"Speaking of friends, yours are already here." Golokin pointed out the window. "It seems they very much want you back, judging from the noise at very high levels. You're either a very lucky woman"—he shrugged—"or a *very* unlucky one."

Out the window, Del saw two figures walking between the khaki army trucks, flanked by soldiers on both sides. She would recognize that gleaming brown head anywhere. It was Jacques, and he had Suweil beside him. Suweil saw Del through the window and waved enthusiastically.

But were they the cavalry, or her tormentors here to finish the job?

Del turned back to Golokin. "Then we have to hurry."

41

Del traded one prison cell for another. This one smelled better, at least. Three walls of polished metal, one of steel bars that looked as if they had been installed yesterday. It had that new-prison smell. Three other cells in the small block, but Del was the only occupant.

Friday morning, as best she could tell.

Four days locked up.

After Del's meeting with Golokin of the FSB, Jacques had insisted that he see her—to make sure she was unhurt, he said. He descended into the room like a mother bird scooping its hatchling back into the nest. Suweil followed, babbling about tracking her signal and how he hadn't been out of the office in so many years.

She wasn't sure what to think.

They didn't bring her back with them, though. She was bundled into another Russian truck, then transferred into a Ukrainian vehicle at a checkpoint. Wednesday night she slept on a cot in an army barrack somewhere outside Kiev, and Thursday morning, she was escorted onto an almost empty Ukrainian military transport. It was just her and two soldiers tasked with guarding her in the back of a voluminous Antonov An-24, holding the green webbing, wrapped up in a parka and gloves and boots.

Del kept asking to use a phone, begging them to let her contact her father.

Thursday midafternoon, the plane landed in Lyon. Del recognized the city as they opened the transport on the runway. The soldiers handed her over to dark-suited men who put her in the back of a van, handcuffed to the seat, like a common criminal. When they opened the back doors again, she saw the familiar lines of the Interpol headquarters, but she wasn't released.

They took her into the basement. Why were lockups always in the basement?

Del demanded a lawyer. They gave her a change of clothes.

No one said a word to her.

***

The main door of the cell block opened, and a familiar face appeared.

"Jacques," Del said, "what's going on?"

Without a word, he advanced to her door and unlocked it. She stood up from the metal cot as he opened the door, and held out her cuffed hands. He shook his head and stood back and pointed at the cell door, motioning for her to go ahead of him.

"What about my father?" she said.

He lowered his head. "We cannot speak. Please. This way."

Del walked ahead of him and up a flight of stairs. A uniformed guard opened another set of steel-grated doors and pressed an elevator button. She stepped inside when the doors slid open. Jacques pressed "8," the top level. The elevator accelerated upward.

"Jacques, please," she said, "I'm begging you. I need to speak to my family. Don't I have the right to a lawyer?"

"We are not in America," he said. "And right now you might not even be in Europe."

"What does that mean?"

The elevator doors opened. Del recognized the octagonal interior of the Interpol building. Green spider plants hung over the balconies.

Jacques gestured for her to walk ahead of him. She had no choice. His face was dark, splotches of red heat across his cheeks. The man was trying very hard to hold something in.

He stopped at a door, opened it.

"Go inside," Jacques said. "I've done everything I can."

In the center of the room, at a stainless-steel table covered with files, sat Director Katherine Dartmouth, in a crisp business suit. In the corner, a camera perched on a stand.

"Come in," she said.

Jacques closed the door behind Del.

"There's no need for those," Katherine said. She stood and walked to Del, took her hands, and unlocked the cuffs. "Please, sit." She nodded at the chair across the steel table.

"I need to speak to my father," Del said.

"I understand." Katherine walked around the table and sat down. "But we need to speak to you first." She pointed at the chair. "Please."

Del rubbed her wrists and grudgingly sat. "Who was Ian?"

"You mean the man in the car you attacked?"

"Who else would I mean?"

"A special agent."

"With Interpol?"

"There are no Interpol agents."

"With who, then?"

"This was a very delicate situation, Detective Devlin. It wasn't just anyone who could get behind enemy lines in a developing war. We are very lucky."

Del rubbed her wrists, put her hands flat on the table, and fixed Katherine with a direct look. "Who, exactly, is the enemy?"

"The Russians, of course."

"And yet, here you are. Showered and rested, dressed up and smelling of perfume."

"You have no idea what our government had to do to get us out of there."

"Please enlighten me."

Del stared straight at Katherine, watched the heat bloom at the edges of her eyes, yet her expression didn't change.

Getting up from her chair, the director took two steps to the back of the room and clicked a button on the recording device. The green light switched off.

Del said, "You were going to shoot me, weren't you?"

"I think you, in fact, were about to shoot me. What the hell were you thinking?" The heat around the director's eyes shot into her forehead and cheeks.

"I was trying to stay alive."

"Then you should think about making it out of this room."

"Is that a threat?"

Katherine returned to the table and picked up a file. "You were already under reprimand, under escort by French authorities out of Kiev—"

"French?"

"Jacques. You escaped from his custody at the airport and went straight to the Russian zone. Do you know how this looks? And you are still the prime murder suspect in Yuri Korshunov's death. Your DNA is on the shell casing retrieved at the scene."

"As is yours from the scene of my father's shooting."

Katherine's anger seemed to evaporate, replaced with a blank-faced stare. "I picked up that shell casing. Korshunov's DNA was on it."

"Those videos were faked. You know that. Interpol internal security guidelines were breached. It was never tested. The UN Building is extraterritorial to the United States, which gave you complete jurisdiction—"

"You've got to be kidding me." Katherine slammed the files onto the table. "Do you know how far I had to hang my ass over the line to save yours?"

Del looked out the window and blinked in the sunshine. She watched a tree branch floating down the Rhone, turning lazily in the current. How easy it was to be swept up.

"You threw my backpack into the fire," Del said after a pause. "In Bilmak. You were getting rid of evidence even before those Russian soldiers arrived."

"Just being careful."

"Of what, exactly?"

Katherine exhaled, shaking her head, and rummaged in the files and papers on the desk. She fished out a newspaper front page, looked at it, and put it down on the table.

"Russian Troops Withdraw," read the *Guardian* headline.

Del scanned the article. The Russian government had reached a last-second agreement with Voloshyn's government and agreed to pull back. The elections had already started, with Voloshyn leading in the early exit polls.

"We know what you did," Katherine said quietly.

"I just want to go home. I need to speak to my family. Can you at least let me do that?"

"We need to establish some ground rules first."

"For what?"

"For letting you get back to your family."

The knives were finally coming out. "What did you do to my father? What did Strataform put into his neck?" When Katherine didn't respond, Del said, "What happened? Why wouldn't you let me get back to my family?"

The director's face hardened. The friendly mask slid away. "Because you're a traitor, that's why."

"You killed Adam Petty, didn't you?" Del said it in a measured voice. She scanned the room for anything she could use as a weapon. The recording device was off, the cuffs removed. Katherine could say that anything happened in this room. That Del attacked her. That she had no choice but to defend herself. "You're the one who left me those papers. The list of 'hidden' facilities? You wanted me to find that print factory. You wanted to pin all this on me. You were the one controlling those . . . *things*."

"Petty died in the expanding Ukrainian conflict. And those devices you discovered—you were the one who uncovered them. It was Leonardo Bondar who hacked the Strataform Replicators and unleashed them."

Del stared at her in silence.

The blood flow around Katherine's eyes didn't flicker even a bit when she said what both of them knew was a lie. What did it mean? It meant that Katherine was a true believer, that the lies had become her truths, that she believed she was doing this not for herself, but for a greater good, for another purpose higher than she.

The director was a fanatic, ready to kill for her cause.

Del couldn't risk her father's life again. Finally, quietly, she said, "So, that's the price for getting my family back?"

"We need to establish the truth. About what happened out there." Katherine picked up another folder. "This background report about Jonathan Murphy, the IRA terrorist, doesn't need to become public knowledge. And I'm sure you want the Korshunov murder to be resolved. Everything goes back to the way it was before."

Del sat back in her chair.

Petty had been working for Katherine; that much, she could piece together. Using his technology as some kind of spy tool—and ultimately as a weapon to kill with. Things must have gotten out of control. That had to be why Petty was down there by himself, trying to figure it out. Trying to subvert Katherine's control. He died for it.

"You still have a country," Katherine said. "You are American. Voloshyn canceled the naval operations center in Ochakiv, but perhaps not all is lost—"

"So, that's what this was all about?" A light flickered in the back of Del's brain. "You didn't want Voloshyn to win that election. You wanted to start a war."

"Not a war. Just a conflict."

Del exhaled and took a deep breath. *Return to the breath; always return to the breath.* "You murdered American citizens."

Down by the river, Del watched a young birch swayed in the breeze. Sometimes it was better to bend with the wind than to break fighting it.

"Fine," Del said.

"Excuse me?"

"I'll toe your line. I just want to get out of here."

"It's not a line; it's the truth. You remember that." Katherine collected her files. "You're a very lucky woman, you know that?"

That was the same thing Golokin, the FSB officer, had said two days ago. "Lucky?" Del sure didn't feel it. "How so?"

"You've awakened the interest of very powerful people. Way above my pay grade." She handed a phone to Del. It was her old one, the one she had left in the Kiev airport.

"What kind of people would those be?" Del took the phone.

"The kind that build artificial islands in the Pacific." The director took her things and opened the door, paused for a second, then let it close behind her.

Del immediately dialed her father's number. It picked up on the second ring.

"Dad, are you okay?"

"Delta, hunny, is that you?" It was her mother's voice. She burst into crying, but between the sobs she said, "My God, sweetheart, you need to come home."

42

Del tapped the roof of the cab and leaned down to thank the driver.

The young Pakistani man smiled and said that she was very welcome and asked whether he she had all her bags. Del thanked him again before he drove off down East Sixty-First Street.

She took a deep lungful of air. It was the middle of May.

There was nothing like New York in spring. The new leaves on trees lining the street were bright green in the early morning sun. She watched the taxi pull around the corner and thought of another cabbie.

Igor had made it out.

She had called him before she left Lyon. Thanked him for risking his life for her. He had apologized, said he hadn't been truthful, that he had been working for Bondar—but that his goal had been to keep her safe while at the same time helping her uncover the truth.

He had succeeded in both, she told him.

By the entrance to Presbyterian Hospital, an American flag flapped in the breeze. Del stopped a moment to watch it. What did she feel? Proud? Of course she was proud of her country, proud to serve and protect, but something had changed. Some switch had flipped in her mind.

Del grabbed the handle of her bag and walked to the entrance, past three people in wheelchairs, smoking cigarettes in the middle of the parking circle. She pushed open the double doors in the lobby and scanned the direction board. The morgue was in the basement.

Why were morgues always in the basement?

She imagined that this one was the same lime green as the one in Kiev.

Del walked to the elevator and pressed the eighth floor. Her father was in the ICU, on the eighth. He was getting out in a few days.

***

As quietly as she could, Del slid open the door to room twenty-five. The interior beyond the curtains was darkened. Machines beeped. It had the familiar scent of antiseptic cleaner she had come to dread. She expected to see her father asleep but instead was greeted by her niece and nephew, who pulled back the curtains.

"Auntie Del is here," they both chirped.

Del's mother was bent over her father, in the middle of giving him a kiss, and her sister, Missy, sat on the daybed at the other end of the ICU room.

"Oh, my God," Missy said. She covered the twenty feet at a run and embraced her sister. "We were so worried."

Her niece and nephew hugged Del's legs at the same time.

"I'm fine," Del said. "You're here early? Not even eight yet."

"We have been here early *every* morning," Missy said.

Not even ten seconds past thanking God she was okay, and already her sister was digging in to make her feel guilty. It was nice to know that things hadn't changed. Del kissed her sister's cheek, thanked her for taking care of Mom and Dad, and whispered that she loved her.

"You have a hug for your mama?" Del's mother held her arms wide.

"And can someone please open the blinds and let some sunshine in, for God's sake?" her father said from his bed. "This isn't a funeral yet." His voice was scratchy and weak but still had that lovable sarcastic lilt.

Del squeezed her mother and wiped away her tears while Missy opened the curtains.

"So, how is he?" Del said.

Her father quipped, "You know I'm right here, right?"

"The radiation and chemo worked," her mother said. "The tumors are in complete remission."

"Your friend Adam Petty saved my life," her father said. "That 3-D-printed plastic stent they made for my throat was a bloody miracle. I wouldn't be speaking without it. Might not even be alive."

"We are very sorry to hear what happened to him," her mother said in a hushed voice.

"He was killed in the fighting in Ukraine?" Del's father said. "It's been in all the news. He's being hailed as a hero. His company just got a huge new government contract. Poor bastard."

"We're getting a Replicator for our house," Missy said. "Just as soon as we get back."

"Maybe you should hold off on that," Del said.

"Why?"

"Just . . . wait a bit."

"But they're amazing. Have you seen what they can do?"

"Oh, yeah. I've seen what they can do."

Only her father seemed to catch the irony in her voice. He frowned.

"What happened?" Missy asked. "Why did you miss your flight last Monday?"

Today was Sunday. Less than a week since Del decided to head into Melitopol, but it seemed like a different lifetime already.

"Just a mix-up."

"The Russians have completely withdrawn from Ukraine," Missy said. "Voloshyn won the election. They're saying the American ambassador was instrumental in helping negotiate a new peace deal. They're saying that Lenny Bondar's Black Army tried to take a piece of the south, but they stopped him. Did you meet him? What happened?"

Del went to her father's bed and met his eyes. "It's complicated, what happened. Freedom fighters. Terrorists. The truth isn't always obvious."

Her father met her gaze. "Sometimes it is complicated." He turned to Missy. "Why don't you take the kids down for some breakfast? Take your mother with you. Maybe give me and my Delta a little time alone?"

***

Del waited for them to leave before saying to her father, "Did you tell her?"

"About my brother Johnny?"

"About changing your name. About everything."

"Do you think she needs to know?"

"*I* needed to know."

"I'm sorry. I should have told you."

Del pulled up a chair. "It doesn't matter. Not anymore. I'm just glad you're okay. And no, I don't think Missy needs to know. Not if you don't want to tell her."

"Don't lie for me. I'm an old man. Maybe it's time."

Del said, "They promised to keep it a secret, at least for now."

"Who is *they*?"

"Director Katherine Dartmouth of Interpol. Or *ex*-director. She's been removed from Interpol." Del tried to keep her voice even and calm as she said this.

"Sounds like you didn't like this Katherine,"

"Do you want to see him?" Del changed topics. "Your brother. He's out of jail. What about your father?"

"He sided with my brother in what happened. That's a big reason I did what I did. And anyway, my father is dead now."

"From the fighting?"

"Drinking." Her father pushed a button on his bed controller, and the headrest angled higher. He brought himself almost to sitting upright, so he could look his daughter in the eye. "So, what really happened out there, my love?"

Del closed her eyes and exhaled, let it all out. "They used me. As a kind of human lie detector. They couldn't get their artificial-intelligence lie detectors into the Russian embassy, because no cameras were allowed, no digital devices. So they used me."

"Used your talents, is more like it."

"That was just a cover. A reason to justify getting me there. They used our family, your secret past, to make it look like I was connected to a terrorist group in Ukraine. Make it look like I killed someone in revenge for what happened to you."

"You mean Korshunov?"

She nodded. "But these terrorists—freedom fighters or whatever—weren't even real. Not really. From what I can tell, they were harmless, just a fringe hacker group, but someone manipulated the media, created stories, and amplified the lies to make it look like they were dangerous criminals."

"Leonardo Bondar and the Black Army—that's who you're talking about?"

"He knew he was being targeted," Del said. "That's why he ran, tried to escape to Ukraine, back to his family there."

"I'm going out on a teeny limb here, but did this have something to do with your boss, Katherine Dartmouth? From the way you said her name . . ."

She was her father's daughter. She couldn't hide anything from him. "I think she worked for the CIA. That's who everyone at Interpol kept thinking I was really working for, and eventually I figured it was because I was working for Katherine. They were field-testing a new kind of weapon that used Adam Petty's Replicators to assassinate targets and make it look like it was the Russians or the Ukrainians. A new cyber weapon that turns digital into physical, that can get by almost anything."

"So, that's what happened to Mr. Petty? He got caught up with the wrong people?"

"I think so. His company was in financial trouble, I think. He started working with them, but I think he got cold feet. I think they killed him for it."

"Thank God you got out."

"I thought this whole thing was about money," Del said. "About a power struggle between Bondar and Petty for control of the future, about a Fourth Industrial Revolution—but they were just pawns in a bigger game."

Del paused, but she needed to confess.

"I told the Russians. I'm a traitor."

"You're no traitor," her father whispered. He took her hand.

"Katherine took my evidence, but she didn't know I had a video on my phone. I showed it to the FSB, got on a call with the Russian ambassador and then with someone on the Politburo. I told them everything: how I thought that it was Americans who had targeted their operatives, assassinated them, that they had done the same to the Ukrainians. That the two countries were being manipulated into starting the conflict."

Her father whistled. He did that only when he was really impressed. "That's why they withdrew? You might have stopped a war."

"But I failed."

"How?"

"Katherine. She's the one that shot you. Not Korshunov. She planted that 3-D gun, picked up the bullet. She arranged so that Korshunov would be there. He knew about the CIA's new weapon with Strataform. She knew he was trying to get to Voloshyn to tell her. She planned the whole thing to drag me—us—into this. To use our family as a scapegoat. I solved it. I figured it out, but she's gone free. I can't get to her."

"You didn't fail. You saved lives. What about Georgiev? The Kiev police commissioner?"

"He didn't know," Del said. "Katherine was using him, too. Trying to set me up for the Korshunov murder. Using your connection to the IRA to paint me into that picture."

"I didn't read about anything of this in the news," her father said.

"The Russians are keeping it quiet. That's their way."

Her father exhaled long and slow. "So, what are you going to do now?"

"I don't know."

43

Dark eyes stared back through time. Were they sad? Regretful? Or proud? A bloodied and severed right ear was covered by a wrapped white bandage that itself was held in place by a thick Russian fur cap. Smoke curled from a wooden pipe clamped between the solemn man's teeth.

Del sat on a wooden bench ten feet in front of the Van Gogh self-portrait and searched her own feelings. Was she sad? Regretful?

Or was she proud?

A week back in New York, and the events of Ukraine seemed like scenes from someone else's life. Like a fever dream in which she had almost cut her own ear off. She had just walked all the way up from Greenwich Village to the Guggenheim on East Eighty-Eighth Street—an hour and a half to contemplate and think. She had entered the Guggenheim and walked up its dizzying spiral walkway to the special Van Gogh exhibit, wondering whether her life was spiraling out of control. Or maybe it was really spiraling into its own true orbit.

She looked back up at Van Gogh. Why had he cut off his ear?

The official explanation was a fit of mania after a fight with fellow artist Paul Gauguin, after which he gave the severed lobe to a prostitute named Rachel, as a token of his affection. Another theory, though, was that he cut off his ear in a fit of rage when he heard about his brother's marriage—because his brother was his only source of financial support, and his brother getting married meant he would lose his income.

So, was it about money? Or about art? Or just insanity in either case?

No one would ever really know the truth.

US Marshal Boston Justice had called her said that he had replaced Katherine as the Director of Interpol's Washington Bureau. He apologized for her hardships but came short of admitting what happened. He said that she was still detailed to his office, that she could take as much time as she needed with her family, and that they would talk. He realized that his predecessor had abused her position, he said, but they all needed to work together for the good of the country.

Officially, Korshunov was still pegged as the man who shot her father. His own murder was still listed as unsolved, joining the hundreds of other solved-but-unsolved assassinations in the Ukraine.

But behind the scenes, behind the curtain, the whispers began.

The French Interpol Bureau director had called Del on Wednesday morning—unofficially, of course—to apologize for the way it had treated her. The director had assumed that she was working with Katherine's organization, he said, but they had found out what Del did. That she had almost single-handedly stopped the conflict from escalating. Jacques called as well, said he had filed a request with the Washington Bureau and Interpol headquarters to bring Delta back to Lyon. In Europe, she was a hero.

At home, a traitor.

Del could almost feel the target on her back.

Some of the truth was already coming out.

The *Guardian* had run a story yesterday detailing the way Lenny Bondar's Black Army hacking group had been conflated with its historical namesake. That the media stories about it becoming a paramilitary organization were untrue. It listed bot webs used to propagate social-media posts and influence operations to shape the world's view. A technique called "fish wrapping" had been used, reposting old media stories with new URLs, amplifying the disinformation campaign.

Strataform had even released a new specification for its Replicator, detailing how fully formed bots could be produced by some new models that were already released. Already, hacker sites were figuring out that you could remotely create a bot that could crawl out of someone else's Replicator, and the Black Hat conference was talking about patches to make sure it could be stopped.

***

Del walked back down the spiral staircase. A giant chandelier a hundred feet high, in a glittering fantastical crystal menagerie, hung over the center. Another 3-D-printed masterpiece. The technology was here to stay. Even without Petty and Bondar to lead it, the Fourth Industrial Revolution was already well under way.

No way to stop progress.

She had thought more about it. What Bondar had said about manufacturing reality wasn't really true. Reality included ideas, and it included anything that humans could manufacture. Rearranging atoms didn't mean manufacturing reality. It was still natural. To say otherwise was the same idea as saying that a machine gun or skyscraper wasn't natural.

They were just as natural as a termite mound. Del had read that the largest geoengineering project on planet Earth wasn't carried out by humans, but by termites in the dry forests of northern Brazil, where they had excavated hundreds of cubic kilometers of earth and formed into mounds dozens of feet high, spaced out across hundreds of square kilometers, like a vast city of pyramids.

Everything humans could do was natural. The problem was our own perception of ourselves.

The kid who fell off the roof, the one Del tried to save, had woken up. He admitted that someone had paid him money to retrieve something from the 3-D printer room at the police precinct. That was why he knew Del's name. Why he offered her the circuit board before he fell. Del suspected it was Katherine, already testing out her new weapon, already targeting her.

When she was gazing at the Van Gogh portrait upstairs, she realized that this man had really cut off his own ear because he was suffering—suffering as a result of his genius, his talent. From now on, she would keep her talent hidden. Van Gogh never sold but one painting in his life. Del decided she would use her gift to get what she could.

She hadn't found justice, but she had uncovered a web of deception that almost destroyed her family. She would never let anyone use her again like that. That was what had shattered: her innocence.

Del had someone she needed to find. Her uncle Johnathon. Even if her father didn't want to meet him, she did. Even though her father had put him in the past, the man was somewhere out there. A threat she didn't understand.

What did she want to do now?

One thing was certain: she couldn't go back to being a Long Island detective. She couldn't get into the FBI, and what other branches of law enforcement were there? Even though her background report wasn't public, it was still out there.

She took her phone out and called a Washington number.

Boston Justice answered on the second ring. "Detective Devlin, how are you?"

"Recovering."

"Are you still interested in working with Interpol? We've got a lot of people in Lyon who are asking for you back."

"I might be."

"I'm glad to hear that."

"On one condition, if you want to keep me quiet."

"I'm listening."

"I'd like you to deputize me as a US marshal."

MEET YOUR MAKER IN REAL LIFE

First off, thanks so much for reading. I sincerely appreciate your support and your interest in my work. Feel free to email me if you want to chat about anything in the book. My contact information is at the end of this section and also on my website. This is the first full-fledged Detective Delta Devlin novel. *The Dreaming Tree* was more of a prequel, where she came to life as a secondary character, and I'm looking forward to watching her grow and develop for many more years.

There is a lot to unpack from this book. First off, if you've read any of my other work, you'll know how much I love mixing reality into the fiction. Much of this book is based on real-world events and technologies: the blurring line between physical and digital, the (already underway) Fourth Industrial Revolution, 3-D printers used to make guns and other weapons, "deepfake" video manipulation, autonomous robots that mimic biological organisms, and, of course, tetrachromats—real humans, like our hero Delta Devlin, who have a recessive gene giving them superhuman vision.

To kick off the discussion, as you may have noticed, parts of *Meet Your Maker* were inspired by Edgar Allan Poe—in particular "The Murders in the Rue Morgue," in which detectives find the body of a man stuffed into a chimney, with no way that anyone could have come in or out. The discovery of Timothy Hutchins's body, wedged into the ventilation duct in a room that no one could get into, was inspired by this.

Many consider "The Murders in the Rue Morgue" the first modern detective story ever published, and I thought that a nod to it would make a great start to my own new detective series. Throughout *Meet Your Maker* are other nods to Poe, including being buried alive and trapped in a crypt underground. In case you were wondering, Poe is one of my favorite writers.

One thread running through all the Delta Devlin novels is the idea of truth versus fiction, or telling the truth versus lying, information versus misinformation or pure disinformation. With the advent of the internet's free and open dissemination of information, there was a great hope that truth would win out. Unfortunately, as we all have seen, the opposite seems to have happened—the deluge of content bombarding us is riddled with misinformation, making it increasingly difficult to distinguish fact from fiction. A central plot point concerns a "deepfake" video that had been altered. When I wrote the book, this technology was bleeding-edge stuff. By the time the book came out, it was a common app available on any cell phone or desktop. That's how fast technology and society are moving.

Yesterday's science fiction is today's old news.

Another central theme of *Meet Your Maker* is the blurring line between the physical and digital worlds—something I've written a lot about in other books. This story was inspired by the idea of digital things somehow making that transition to real, physical things—effectively, biological things—almost by themselves. In this story, humans use the technology to create physical bugs from digital ones, to the point that they become semiautonomous creatures when they escape the digital world.

For me, this is an endlessly fascinating topic and one I'll continue to explore.

Using 3-D printers to make guns isn't new. The first plans for a 3-D-printable gun, the Liberator, were made widely available online in 2013 by the open-source firm Defense Distributed, after which the US Department of State demanded that they be retracted. A federal judge recently blocked the release of blueprints of the Liberator, but by now a second wave of 3-D-printed guns has become available online—this time, through a decentralized community of hundreds of people. There is now a wave of underground 3-D-printing gunsmiths around the world, creating totally untraceable weapons. There are plans online for polymer Glocks, AR-15s, and more. I invite you to do an online search for "3D printed guns are back" and see what you find.

But it doesn't just stop there. Several attacks have occurred using drones, some of them made entirely with 3-D printing, others modified from commercial versions. The most recent and eye-opening was an attack on Saudi refineries in 2019, carried out by a small group using ten inexpensive drones that knocked out half the country's oil production. The fear now is that 3-D-printer technology makes it possible to produce weapons of mass destruction that are chemical, biological, or even nuclear.

In the mid-1990s, Boy Scout David Hahn used household objects and scientific knowledge he gleaned from the web to start building a nuclear reactor in his backyard. Government officials intervened before he could finish, but today, with 3-D printers and the proliferation of online plans, it may be possible for almost anyone to manage such a feat. The government contractor Raytheon uses 3-D printers to create entire missiles, and the Los Alamos National Laboratory is using the machines to create high explosives.

Even more frighteningly, one of the great potentials of 3-D printers is to create living tissue, perhaps even the ability to lay down materials molecule by molecule. But imagine the potential for bioprinting viruses, whose plans can be distributed via the web.

Which brings us to the main topic of *Meet Your Maker*: the Fourth Industrial Revolution. The First Industrial Revolution brought human society from agrarian and mostly handmade production into the age of mechanical production, with the advent of the steam engine in the 1760s. The Second Industrial Revolution came with the start of mass production in the early twentieth century, Henry Ford's auto assembly line being the most famous example. The digital revolution is the third. It began in the 1960s with the advent of computing, then microprocessors, and eventually information technology, which reshaped global supply chains.

So, what is the Fourth Industrial Revolution?

The term was coined only in 2015, by Klaus Schwab, chair of the World

Economic Forum, but the concept encompasses sweeping changes that stem from 3-D printing, manufacturing on demand, artificial intelligence, bioengineering, and other fast-evolving fields. And the confluence of all these things is creating new technologies that we cannot yet imagine. One thing we can't discount is the breathtaking speed of change we all are experiencing in our lives as this Fourth Industrial Revolution gains traction.

For all the frightening possibilities I described above, there is a list twice as long of exciting possibilities the future will bring, such as new medical devices and technologies to extend and improve human life, and ways to improve the environment and provide clean energy.

I tend to be an optimist, albeit with a grain of realism, so I look forward to the future and all that it brings. Of course, we do need to be wise about what we wish for.

Thanks again for reading.
Matthew Mather
September 19, 2019